The Island

of Cats

Patricia Lee

Published by Duck Farm Press
East Kangaloon
NSW, Australia
www.duckfarmpress.com.au

First Edition
Book design by Patricia Lee
Printed and bound in Australia
ISBN: 978-0-6456524-0-6

Books by Patricia Lee
Fiction:
History at My Fingertips

Kingdom series:
The Island of Cats

Poetry:
Speak to the Moon
How to Smoke the Soul-Poetry for the Heart and
Mind

Non-Fiction:
Land of the Rippling Gold by Una Clarke Activity
Sheets-Blackline Masters

The Life and Times of Charles Frank Field 1850-1950

In memory of our cat, Foxy 2006-2020

Chapter One

'As you wish, Sire!'

His brother bowed low concealing the scowl William knew would be etched on his face. Gerard backed away from the throne through the murmurs of the courtiers lining the dark-walled reception room. William motioned to his Chancellor, enough.

Leaving the throne, William sought the sanctuary of his sitting chamber flinging the door closed behind him. Today's Audience was longer than usual. Insufficient grain, emaciated animals and villagers, polluted water – the list went on and on. Did they think he could control the weather? He'd already depleted half of the Treasury's reserves in supporting his countrymen and women. Mortally tired of the ashen faces presented to him, he would find out for himself what was really going on tomorrow.

Mounted on his second-best cream charger and liveried as a castle guard, the King had donned a black wig and had his valet dye his ginger beard black. He also wore a large felt hat pulled down over his face. Passing by men he knew, he was pleased to see they failed to recognise him. Accompanied by only two other mounted soldiers, they left through the North Portcullis on to the well-worn cobbles of the Drummoyne Road. His valet had packed both victuals and drink so they could wander all day, if need be.

From where they rode, the late summer fields of golden stubble stretched out before them. Upwards of fifty gleaners were busy combing the rows for stray grains tossing them into the sacks secured to their backs. They appeared to be finding quite a lot.

Suddenly William turned to one of his men, 'Where are the granaries?'

'Sire they are a few leagues north of here.'

As they continued, the road turned to dust as carts trundled along it, their owners ragged and thin and the beasts that drew them looking almost skeletal. There was a serious discrepancy here, thought William who was determined to discover the reasons behind an apparent healthy harvest and a near-starving population.

By mid-morning, they reached the first granary, a low-slung mossy stone barn, thatched with wheaten straw now grey with age.

1

There were two half asleep peasants 'guarding' the entrance who jumped up on seeing the distinctive blue and yellow livery of the soldiers.

'Hey, you peasant, do you think it wise to be asleep guarding this granary!' shouted Rufus, one of William's soldiers.

'No, mi'Lord, sorry mi'Lord', gushed one of them while the other hung his head in shame.

'Look lively, then' said Paxton, William's other companion. 'Get water for our horses and set them grazing on that grass over there'. He indicated the grass at the side of the granary.

They all dismounted and stretching their legs walked around the granary to observe its general condition. There were gaps in the walls and the thatch looked almost rotten. Paxton reached down. He could almost fit his fist into one of the holes in the granary wall.

William shook his head. This did not bode well for what was in the interior. They tracked back to the entrance and bowing down, for the door was low, entered the building. For a few moments they couldn't see much for there were few tiny windows up high under the thatch letting in little light.

'The wheat is moving,' gasped Rufus. Indeed, hundreds of tiny creatures were fleeing from their approach scattering all over the heaps of grain. A foul stench of urine and faeces assaulted their nostrils as the animals moved. Almost gagging, the men peered closer to take in fully the scene before them.

'I've seen enough,' exclaimed William in disgust. They rapidly exited and stood coughing in the sunlight. 'Who is responsible for this!' demanded William of one of the granary guards.

'For what, mi'Lord?' William struck the man across the face, 'For the vermin, imbecile! Why is nothing being done?'

'Excuse me, mi'Lord, but what is to be done?' offered the other, bracing himself for a similar blow.

The soldiers stared at him. How could it be that nothing was being done?

'Are there no cats,' asked William, 'to catch the rats and mice?'

'Cats, mi'Lord?' asked the bolder guard.

'Cats? Have you no cats?'

'I never seen a cat here,' offered the other, a bruise now blossoming on his face.

'Dogs, then?' asked Paxton.

'We never seen any, mi'Lords, never here. I never seen a cat ever. Have you, Ploughman?'

Ploughman furrowed his brow, 'Nope, heard of 'em but never seen 'em.'

William, exasperated, ordered the granary guards to fetch them stools which were set well away from the rodent stench of the barn.

In the little glade nearby, William and his companions drank and ate a little food. When they were fully satisfied, Paxton asked his Sire, 'I knew that cats and dogs were expelled from the City, Sire, but I never believed there were none in the countryside as well.'

'It seems that We are not aware of much that has befallen the crops and their storage. Cats must be obtained but that may take some time. What is to be done meanwhile to save what is left of this harvest?'

They sat in silence tossing ideas around in their heads when finally, William expounded an idea. 'Rats and mice drown, do they not?'

'Yes, mi'Lord,' answered Rufus, careful not to call William, 'Sire'.

'Well then, we must have made a barrier of water they cannot cross around the granary. We shall organise a group of men to destroy what animals are residing in the barn and then construct a small moat around each granary to prevent them returning. This will take some time, but it will be worth it if we can preserve the grain. However, as sure as the sun rises and drops each day, the vermin will return and we need a more permanent solution for them. We must obtain cats.'

'Agreed,' said Rufus and Paxton, impressed at their King's practical abilities.

'First, we will visit the other granaries and see if the same thing is happening.'

'Aye, mi'Lord, let's continue,' said Paxton.

Ploughman and his fellow guard were given written instructions to seconder farmers to destroy the rodents, meanwhile masons and engineers were to be sent out from the City to construct the small but hopefully effective moats and devise how to keep them filled but not overflowing.

William and his men found throughout the day that similar laxities besieged the other granaries. William was very angry. 'Who is in charge of overseeing the granaries?'

Paxton was hesitant to answer. 'Well?' demanded William.

'That would be your brother, Gerard, mi'Lord.'

William seethed all the long way home. They reached the North City Gate just on dusk. The guards refused them entry because they didn't have the day's password and reluctant to reveal who he was, William and the men retreated to a Way Inn to spend the night. Once the horses were stabled, they entered the Inn and ordered Porter, bread and a soup laden with meat chunks.

Tucking into their repast, they listened carefully to the talk in the Inn of trade with their neighbouring lands, of the price of beef and lamb, difficult to obtain and very, very lean, of this one's daughter who had an ague and this one's son who was proving to be a poor blacksmith. William was fascinated because conversation within his earshot in the Palace was always circumscribed and stilted. Here he was getting people's real opinions.

William listened to the conversations in the end interspersed by the calls for victuals and the clanking of lead tankards brought by barmaids to thirsty patrons. Paxton and Rufus seemed relaxed as this was their natural environment honed by many evening's diversions after hot and sweaty guard duties. Still, there was no reason he shouldn't use the opportunity to gain information about his Kingdom particularly the mysterious Island of Cats.

He called out to a barmaid to have his tankard filled and when she returned with the jug, he asked her if she had ever heard of the Island of Cats.

'No mi'Lord,' she curtsied overawed by his livery. 'Perhaps Suzanne might know.' She bid Suzanne to come who after serving some patrons arrived wiping her wet hands on her ample muslin apron. 'Yes, mi'Lord? Are the victuals to your liking?

'Ample and hearty,' replied William, 'I thank you. However, it is of another matter I would like to inquire. Your girl here says you may be able to tell us information about the Island of Cats?'

'Aye, my Lord. I have heard of it but not much. All I know is that many years ago, a wild woman, crazy some said, was deeply affected when the burgermeisters began killing cats in the City. She wailed and screamed at them, but they ignored her and pushed her out of the way. She so annoyed them that they devised to fill a boatload of cats with her in it and cast them out to sea. They figured to solve two problems at once. No one knew what became of the harridan and her unwanted companions. However, two years later a sailor came here and told us of an island some leagues off the coast where he'd seen a windswept figure around whom moved great numbers of furred creatures. The rocks prevented the sailors getting any closer but ever since the place has been known as the Island of Cats.'

'And has anyone landed to find out if this sighting was true?'

'Not as far as I know, my Lord.'

'Thank you, Suzanne. Now we would like accommodations for the night. Do you have anything available?

Soon they were lying on straw palliasses in a modest oak lined room, the exertions of the day having taken their toll.

'Will you not be missed, mi'Lord?' asked Paxton.

'Fear not, I told my Chamberlain I was going early to my country estate by myself and was not to be disturbed for a week. This hiatus gives us leave to pursue this legend and find its truth. Can you procure a ship tomorrow?'

'Aye, mi'Lord, it's possible. I will go to the dock at daybreak and see what I can secure.'

'Excellent! Then good night men. Tomorrow may prove as fatiguing as today.'

Not long after dawn they embarked on a modest sailing vessel with a handful of crew whose captain was glad of the gold sovereigns he'd earn from the trip. However, he warned his passengers, 'Mi'Lords, there are many islands off this coast which match your description. It may take some time to find.'

'Very well, do your best Captain,' said William whose pleasure at being away from Court for longer was more appealing than not.

By day's end they had visited or inspected five or more islands none of which had cats or even human inhabitants. After dinner they anchored and each spent the night sleeping in gently swaying hammocks. It was on the third day they came to an island surrounded by rocks. It was impossible from the ship to tell if it had inhabitants so accompanied by some sailors they sailed the ship's skiff around protruding rocks and landed ashore. The island had a small grey sandy beach, no trees only a low growing scrubby heath covered in tiny purple blossoms leading to rocky outcrops in the centre of the island.

Finding narrow paths through the heath they struck forward towards the rocks. The soldiers carried loaded muskets, William and his men only their swords. They heard loud mewing and hissing within a few yards of a deep fissure in the rocks. Alert the party paused, waiting for whatever creature was within to emerge. As seconds ticked by, tension built and William expected a large wildcat to launch itself at them. Unable to contain himself any longer, he called gently into the caves entrance, 'Hello there! Show yourself. We mean no harm.'

Not a lithe cream wildcat but a young, lean woman dressed in skins ducked her head out from the shadows. 'Go away!' she hissed. 'There is no gold here. Leave me alone or it will go badly for you!'

William was amused but the humour left his face when he saw she had an arrow drawn and ready to fire into his chest. 'Please we don't want to hurt you.' He made the men lower their weapons. 'We are searching for an island of cats but perhaps we were wrong.'

'Nay, there are many cats here,' explained the girl, lowering her bow.

'We were expecting an old woman,' said William, as the raven-haired girl emerged from the shadows. He held his breath for though ragged and dirty, she had a grace and loveliness which struck him greatly.

'I am William, Commander of these men. Let me explain myself. We have a land many leagues from here besieged by rodents who are destroying our grain. We come in search of cats to deal with the infestation. We will pay you well for them!'

The girl stood boldly before them, hands on her hips. 'They are my friends,' she explained, 'for I have no others.'

'Do you live here alone?' asked William, astonished.

The girl stepped back and raised her bow again, 'You will not steal them,' she shouted, defiant.

'Please,' begged William holding his hands palm outwards towards her. 'We will pay a fair price, however if you are alone as you say would it not be better to accompany us back to civilisation, among your own kind?'

'My own kind sent my mother to her death, or so they thought,' she replied.

William understood now. The old harridan sent seaward with her cats must have been with child and this girl was her issue.

'Aye, she was badly done by,' added Paxton, 'and for this we all apologise and wish to make amends to you and your animals. But we really do need your cats now, that is if you still have any?' The girl seemed reluctant and twisted her face into a grimace. She was torn with emotion both attracted by the men, whom she had only heard of spoken of by her mother, and afraid of them.

'And where am I to go in this place of towns and villages, where I know no one? Tell me this?'

William tried to reassure her. 'We will pay one gold sovereign per cat for your trouble. With this money you could buy a small farm or house. We would leave you a male and female cat to breed and earn money. You could be self-sufficient and until you are settled you're welcome to live in my house. It has many rooms.'

'Oh,' said a girl, deeply conflicted. To go with them she must leave her island, the only home she knew and where her mother was buried, a life of complete freedom and self-reliance to go to a place where crowds of people would frighten her. However, she knew to be alone was a terrible sorrow which in the last year since her mother died had worn her down with torments.

'How many cats do you have?' asked Rufus, ever practicable.

The girl thought for a moment, 'About twenty dozen at least.'

William grinned. The boat would be awash with them. 'Very well young maid, what is your decision and if I might ask, what is your name?'

'My name is Klyesha.'

'Good day to you, Klyesha,' replied William, waiting expectantly.

She looked at the men, heard the mewing of her cats who are always hungry despite the mice she bred for them and quickly made up her mind. 'It will take some time to catch them all.'

'Very well, let us begin,' replied William, 'by having something to eat.'

They opened the satchel Rufus was carrying and spread its contents on a cloth. The men had not long had their breakfast and they could see how interested was the girl and how entranced by every new food she tasted so they let her eat the lion's share. Perhaps it was the food or their friendly banter, but Klyesha's mind was made up after the feast. 'You must let me coax them,' she declared, rising from the food.

It took many hours to catch and crate the cats and store them below decks. Brindle, white pawed, ginger, glossy black, tortoiseshell, patchwork cats of all colours and ages stowed in the crates. The men couldn't go near them for they would hiss and spit and bar their teeth and claws. Klyesha's tiny bundle of belongings touched William as he helped her up from the skiff onto their ship. The Captain was already alarmed at his loud and hissing cargo but William reassured him he would be well rewarded for the assault on his ears.

By next day's break they had reached home port where Paxton and Rufus organised carts to transport the cats to the various granaries where they were to be stationed. Klyesha truly agonised over which of her precious companions to keep and finally settled on a handsome marmalade Tom and a quiet, silky black female. She carried them in a small wicker basket along the gangplank to the Wharf where her eyes widened at the buildings and numbers of humans who crowded the docks. Awestruck, she remained transfixed quietly staring at all before her. Indeed, many stared at her too clad only in her cat furs.

William realised how overwhelmed she must be and gently persuaded her onto a cart which he himself drove away flinging commands over his shoulders to his men as they left.

At the castle gate, he flung off his black wig and the castle guards stared as they hurriedly waved him through. Klyesha was amused at their obvious deference to him and wondered what it meant and also why he had been wearing a wig. For some reason she was greatly delighted by his flaming orange hair. Quickly, he manoeuvred the cart into the mews of his own apartments shouting to servants who hurried to greet them.

The building's solid stone walls comforted Klyesha reminding her of her now abandoned cave home. William escorted her himself to a chambermaid he could trust who was instructed to bathe her and find her suitable fresh garments. He took the cats gently from her and placed them in a guest bed chamber awaiting their mistress. He fetched a dish of cream for them from the kitchens and leaving hurried to his own ablutions neglected for the past few days while on the high seas.

Refreshed and able to eat a substantial lunch, his brother Gerard broke in on his repast, 'Sire, we were worried. Reports came you didn't reach your estate. We feared you captured by bandits.' The look on Gerard's face did not match the concern in his voice.

'Brother, I am here, as you see, quite well before you. Even a King needs a holiday.'

'Yes, Sire, as you wish. Only please inform us next time you go roving, so we can provide you suitable escort.'

'Of course, I will. My venture required a somewhat clandestine approach, dear Brother, please excuse my indulgence. As you are here, I do require you to justify the neglect of our granaries which I believe you are solely responsible for?' Gerard coughed and turned away embarrassed struggling to find a suitable response. William continued, 'You might have made me aware of their state in time to allay the worst of the grains' destruction. May I assure you, I will attend to the granary's proper husbandry myself in future. The sufferers of this neglect have traipsed too many times before me during Court receptions.'

'Of course, Sire, as you wish,' blurted Gerard, still red in the face. 'May I inquire as to the outcome of your recent excursion?'

'You may. I have obtained cats, long excluded from the Kingdom to our great loss, to replace those culled in previous years. They are a part of my plan to halt destruction of the grain supplies. Also, there is a young woman, Klyesha, whose husbandry of the cats has given us this opportunity. You will soon meet her. Her presence here is not to be questioned and she is to be afforded all due courtesy as she is under my protection.'

Gerard's eyebrows raised, 'Good Sire, but is that...'

'Wise?', William interrupted. 'It's certainly not up to you to judge. She may not be with us long, anyhow. Is there anything else you want?'

'No, Sire, except to say the household, indeed the country is gladdened by your safe return.' He bowed low and left. William returned to his meal uneasy at the vibes of insincerity his brother gave out.

He was almost finished his meal when a chambermaid entered the dining room and requested if the young woman was to join him or be given her meal in the kitchens.

'No bring her in. She can dine with me.' answered William. The young woman who entered the dining room was almost unrecognisable! Clean, her face shone with a healthy suntan, her green eyes made bright by the pale green gown she wore so closely laced over her chest but flowing river-like from her waist.

Klyesha stood awkwardly, unsettled by the tightness of the gown's bodice and totally unsure about how to behave in the presence of who she now knew was the King.

'Come,' said William, gently aware he had stared at her too long, 'Sit beside me and eat.' He called servants to bring her a platter of bread, cheese and roasted meats and a glass of wine.

'Thank you, Sir, I mean Sire,' she said, quietly astonished at the pewter candle sticks on the table and the fine silver cutlery none of which she knew how to use.

'I placed your cats in your bedchamber,' he explained, 'and they finished a dish of cream in seconds!' he laughed.

She smiled at that. 'I do not even know what cream is, Sire,' she whispered.

'It seems you do have much to understand about our foods, customs and ways. I do not envy your learning journey but permit me to say, I intend to assist you in any way I can.'

Now she was embarrassed and did not know where to look or put her hands, folding and refolding them on her lap. The food appeared and thankfully for Klyesha there was no need to talk.

William sat sipping his wine trying not to watch her too much. Silence filled their repast. Unsure whether his presence upset her, William stood and bid her finish her lunch, he would see her later and asked she rest until then.

He left and went to the balcony of his room looking out over the City to the now yellowing agricultural fields beyond and asked himself whether he was most to blame for the poverty of his people. How could he have been so blind and so lax as to leave critical decisions to the brother he knew hated him? Now he had wrenched a young woman from her world and made her enter his. Had she ever really had a choice to give up her island and her cats? He was determined to reward her, to show her how much this sacrifice would help his people and most of all to nurture her and win her approval.

At dinner that evening he invited his brother and sister-in-law and several members of his court to allow Klyesha to see more people and perhaps to help her adapt. They sat in their finery on the dais a yard above the floor of the Great Hall, the heavy tapestries of the realm hung on the walls behind them surrounded by swords, shields and other weapons. He bid a small minstrel group play from the balcony opposite. Their lutes and mandolins adding a delightful calm to the atmosphere. He purposefully set Klyesha between two other young maids, neither loud nor too quiet, to help her feel at ease. However, every time he observed her between courses, she appeared startled and nervous.

Klyesha was deeply alarmed by the sound of people talking, by them sitting near her and even by the music. It was all so totally unfamiliar. She smiled at the girls who tried to speak to her but was unable to answer them with anything more than a yes or no. When the King's brother, Gerard, welcomed her to their Kingdom with a toast, she went a bright red and was unable to look up at anyone. She did not know how to courtesy before the King or use a spoon or even what she was eating. Everything and everyone was strange. Even though in her mind's eye, she saw the gentle, heaving sea of her island, the vast sky and felt the gentle breezes on her face, she became even more panic stricken at her present surroundings. She begged the friend on her right to escort her to her room.

William only saw her leave with a pale drawn face and clumsy movements. He feared her ill but could not forsake his guests to follow her. Sometime later, he flung down his napkin and excused himself from the gathering, wishing them all good e'ven.

Making his way to her suite, he wondered if it was unreasonable to disturb her but he could not stop himself. He knocked gently on her door and whispered, 'Mistress Klyesha, are you a'right?' He leant on the door but heard nothing so he knocked and called again. Still no answer. He hurried to fetch the chambermaid who had a key to the door and bid her open it and accompany him inside.

The drapes were closed and the room was cold and in darkness. He flung open one to let in some moonlight to discover she was hidden under the bedclothes sobbing. 'Fetch a light, quickly!' he commanded the maid, 'Some warm mead and bring a manservant to light the fire'. As the maid hurried off, he slowly pulled back the covers. The girl was curled around her cats, shaking, tearful and anxious.

'Nay, gentle creature, do not fret,' he soothed. 'It is my oafish nature to force society on you who has known none. Everything is strange to you. What was I thinking!'

She looked up at him through ruffled, black hair and tried to say she was sorry but only a sob escaped her. He petted the velvet head of the Tomcat only to have him swipe at his hand causing him to jump back, the blood already dewing along a deep scratch.

Klyesha reached for his hand and wiped the blood away with her gown. It was an innocent gesture but it stirred feelings in him he thought best to deny so he withdrew his hand. 'It is I who should say sorry to you. It was thoughtless of me to make you attend the dinner, it is all too soon.'

She attempted to calm herself and reply but was shaking so much from the cold she could not get the words out. He fetched an ermine coat from the wardrobe and placed it around her shoulders. Soon the maid entered with warming mead and the manservant who made up the fire. The maid got Klyesha to drink, all the while the cats were purring as if to comfort her themselves.

After he left her, he slept poorly, getting up more than once in the night to set wood on his own fire. How he wished his mother was still alive to advise him on how to approach this young woman or even his father who had always been ready with kindly words of wisdom. He vowed on the morrow to remove her from the Palace to his country estate with its orchards, meadows and streams, the sheer beauty of its nature must surely be restorative for her.

However, when he inquired after the girl in the morning when she didn't appear for breakfast, he was dismayed to hear she was sick and feverish. He sent immediately for his apothecary and a physic to diagnose her and waited impatiently whilst they attended

12

her. It was not good news. The girl had contracted both a rash and a fever and was becoming increasingly delirious.

'You say she has known no humans apart from her mother?' asked the Physic. 'Well then, it is not unreasonable to assume she has no natural resistance to any of our common diseases. Such that any of them might affect her in diverse and serious ways. I think we should remove the cats.'

Holding his head in his hands, William looked the physic in the face, 'Prescribe what potions she needs and my apothecary shall make them up. Leave a message with the dosage which I myself will administer. Do not touch her cats!'

'Sire, I feel it may be unwise to...'

'I shall do as I wish. The maid and I will nurse her. No one else is to go near her. Do you understand?'

'Yes Sire, of course. I will also leave a tincture for you to strengthen your blood in case.' The Physic snapped the clasp of his doctor's bag shut and hurried away.

William was so ashamed he could barely speak or think. If this young woman died, he was to blame. The killer of all the cats in the Kingdom twenty years ago was also to blame as was his superfluous brother who had mismanaged the granaries. But chiefly it was himself. Maybe it was better he had left her on the island with a few cats for company.

The next few days were slow, the disease loathsome and the patient's suffering great. Each night he lay in fear of them coming to tell him she was dead. He only left his room to sleep or eat. He was sharp with everyone apart from the maid and her patient and he only smiled at his brother when he protested that the King was putting himself in danger. The only change was that the tom and his little companion hissed at him less.

On the 4th day, as he let fresh air and sunshine into the room, he heard the girl sigh deeply as she placed her arms on the counterpane. He bathed her face himself and was pleased to see her skin a little less hot and her lips a little more red. The maid fed her broth and more of it seemed to be swallowed. The cats had stopped purring. He didn't know if this was good or not. Unable to look at her any longer with hope that might be vain, he left for a turn in the garden needing fresh air himself and to gather his thoughts.

Klyesha opened her eyes after he left and asked the girl for water. Then she asked to be held up to use the cistern in the corner of the room. Quite weak still, the maid supported her there and back also helping her with warm wet cloths to bathe and into some fresh linen.

'Where is the King?' asked Klyesha.

'He was here. He has been here every day you were ill.'

That a King would attend a lowly person as herself, dangerously sick with no thought to himself. Why would he do that? She patted her cats as she sat on the edge of the bed wondering what the future held.

Delighted, William greeted her soon after the maid brought him news. 'You look different,' she said.

He laughed, 'The beard is gone. A black beard on a redheaded man? What can I say?'

He gave her a dish of dried figs and fresh apples from his estate. 'When you are well enough, I will show you the garden.' He left her in peace and called for Paxton.

When Paxton arrived, William asked him how it went with the cats. 'Sire, it took some effort at first to extract them from the crates.' He showed them many scratches on his arms. 'But once in the granaries, they were crazed with desire for the pests. My men have reported many very well-fed cats sleeping off their indulgences.'

'And the rodents?'

'They are much reduced but still some remain.'

'So, when the pests are all cleared, I want the cats housed properly and fed meat regularly. Every week or so we will let them back into the granaries to clear any lingering pests. You may bring several back here to the Palace, as I hear Cook is in need of them.'

'Of course, Sire. But where are we to house the cats?'

'In suitable barns which can be set out with fresh hay. I will have special catteries built for them where my citizens can come and borrow a cat as long as they leave a sovereign deposit. Anyone harming a cat, I shall throw into the dungeons. Let it be known.'

'As you wish, Sire.'

William was very pleased his scheme had succeeded and the cats had proved their usefulness. However, Klyesha had been the one to suffer for its success and he was determined that she should suffer no more.

The next day, he arrived to find her dressed and waiting for him in her bedchamber. She wore the same pale green gown which so set off her dark hair and eyes. 'I wonder if I may take the cats outside?' she asked.

'Of course, they can join us in the garden.' She handed him the Tom, who struggled at first but settled when she petted him and murmured sweet phrases of love to him. William was astonished to find he was jealous of a cat.

The garden was set out in a knot design with trimmed hedges of lavender, shrubs with the lingering orange and pink leaves of autumn and flowers yellowing and setting seed. A high stone wall enclosed it, mossy with age so they could let the cats free knowing they couldn't escape. Both immediately darted into bushes searching for birds or other food. 'They like it here,' said the girl.

'Do you?' asked William, smiling.

She looked at him unable to compose her face into the grateful expression she wanted. 'I don't know,' she said quietly.

'It is to be expected. Illness has followed strangeness. It is no wonder you are disturbed.'

'Might I ask you a question?

'Of course.'

'Why do you, a King, give someone like me, a person of no status at all, why do you...'

'Attend on you?'

'Yes.'

Now he had trouble arranging his face and had to look away. 'Well, we are grateful to you. Your cats have saved our harvest and many more to come. You are more valuable than you think.'

'Valuable?'

'Valued,' he replied looking again at her. Now she could read his eyes and what she read there unsettled her further.

'I see,' she murmured.

'I have a proposal for you.'

'Oh?'

'Would you like to go to my country estate far from the crowds and retainers here? We would take the maid you know and your cats. It is a beautiful place and peaceful.'

'I would be honoured,' she replied.

The carriage took a half day to arrive at the two-storey thatched stone residence which sat among extensive wooded grounds and pastures. William had ridden his horse to give her space in the carriage with her maid.

He helped her down. 'This is lovely, she said, his strong hand holding hers for the first time.

'Yes, it is,' he said, looking at her. Espaliered apples lined the walls beside the door and stone urns held water lilies. The housekeeper, a stout middle-aged rosey-cheeked woman called Ruth greeted them at the door. 'Sire, Madam,' she curtsied.

Klyesha was enchanted with the homeliness of the rooms- wooden panelled, with tapestries on the walls and on couches, sideboards bursting with baskets of fruit. 'I hope you will enjoy it here,' said William. She nodded. Ruth took her to her suite while William caught up with the staff. He warned them to afford Klyesha all she desired and to allow her cats free range of the house. Leaving the house, he checked on his horse in the stables who was being rubbed down by a stable hand and fed her an apple.

'How goes it, Ranald?'

The boy bowed and explained they had had a new foal a few weeks old. A little white mare. William was delighted and visited the foal and her devoted mother pastured behind the stables. He coaxed the young foal towards him and stroked her flank. 'She is a fine young beast!'

'Yes, very like her mother,' replied the stable hand.

'Anything else to report, Ranald?'

'Sire, we have had provisions stolen from our stores. Some apples in the far orchard have been stripped of their fruit. Vines also have been uprooted and removed. Nothing major but still...'

'I see. Any thoughts on who might be responsible?'

'Probably some of the villagers. Many of their crops failed this year due to late rains. We have not seen any of the culprits.'

'Thank you, Ronald, I will look into it.'

He returned to the house to find Klyesha finishing a small meal set out in the kitchen by the Cook. He might have scolded the Cook for placing her in such a lowly position to eat but he did not wish to start off on the wrong foot with her. 'Do you wish to eat, Sire?' the Cook asked him.

'No, not now thank you. Though I am expecting a hearty dinner.' The Cook curtsied.

He asked Klyesha when she stood if she would like to see the grounds. She followed him out the back entrance into the kitchen garden filled with beds of cabbage, spinach, cauliflowers, potatoes and onions all tended well and healthy. A high wooden fence excluded any marauding animals or humans for that matter.

She picked some onion flowers and crushed them to look at the seeds. They lay, tiny and black, in her hand. She blew them back into the garden, 'Such abundance.'

'Yes, we have excellent soil enriched by the stable sweepings. The vegetables here are the sweetest you can find.'

They left through a gate and entered rows of orchards, apples, pears, walnuts and plums some last of the fruit still on the trees. He picked a yellow apple for her. 'These are quite crisp and a little tart. We use them to make cider.'

She took a bite. 'Yes, quite tart,' she laughed. He contained the wave of happiness that swept over him on hearing her laugh. The sky was blue but beginning to lighten as the day drew to a close.

'I will show you more tomorrow. Let us inside as the evening grows colder.'

She sat near a large sandstone fireplace which now blazed with luxurious warmth while he warmed the backs of his legs in front of it. Klyesha was again overwhelmed at the richness of his properties but most at the growing warmth with which he treated her. Where was it to end? Should she not be establishing herself in her own domain with the gold he promised? Why did the King not already have a wife? Unable to put it off any longer she asked him.

'Yes, it seems unusual but it is simply because I have not yet found a woman to suit me. Many have tried,' he laughed. 'My brother has brought numbers of highly suitable potential brides before me and I have rejected every one of them. They all seem to lack something.'

'And what is that, Sire?'

'They all lacked mettle, resilience. They seemed hollow creatures who expected me to be everything for them. They lacked substance.'

The young raven-haired woman, still a little weak from her recent illness wondered if she had these qualities. She certainly felt weak and overwhelmed. She was hardly a match for the important, decent man before her.

'How did you live on the island? How did you survive?' he asked.

She sat thoughtful for a while. 'My mother taught me everything. She was a country girl so used to nature but it was also very hard for her. She always lamented having no chickens or cows for milk and butter. The island, she told me, when she arrived had many small animals who lived in the heathland- small rodents, also seabirds who nested amongst the rocks and on cliffs. Her cats, only a dozen in number at first, fed themselves. She collected bird eggs and seaweed and eventually speared fish she trapped in small dams of rocks she'd made at the sea's edge. Driftwood and sticks she used to make fire for warmth and eventually the dried guano of the seabirds. I was born about six months after she came to the island. She both loved and feared for me but I grew strong in the fresh air and took my first steps among the sea sprayed rocks.'

'We did what we could to make the cave comfortable. She built up the walls with rocks to make it more secure. She wove mats from grasses for bedding and fashioned furniture from rocks, cushions from layers of heather. In the small boat she'd been set adrift on, there'd been rope, some barrels, sailcloth, some few tools. We gathered water first from the natural basins in rocks, then used the barrels to collect rainwater. From the sailcloth she made me clothes. We ate well on fish, eggs, roasted seabirds and shellfish. When cats died, we cured their skins with salt and sewed them into clothes.'

He listened with pity and wonder. There are many who would perish in the situation Klyesha's mother had found herself. But she had not only survived, she'd also raised a daughter teaching her to speak, to read words scratched into the sand, to sing all the songs she remembered from her childhood. He was greatly saddened to think of her alone on the island after her mother died, to be in fact alone forever if he and his men had not found her.

'What did you think when me and my men arrived?'

She looked directly at him. 'I was both amazed and afraid. My mother had described men but usually in terms of hate but when I saw you, when I saw men for the first time I was... I was...'

'I understand,' he said, 'both a joy and a terror. But you were also so brave. Ready to shoot us with an arrow.' He smiled.

'Ships sometimes passed in sight of our island. My mother acted strangely- both drawn to them and worried for me. She prepared me to defend myself if any should land who were hostile.' She wondered why she lied to him. Why she felt she needed to be so careful?

'Here in this land, I know you feel strange and foreign but you are strong. You simply need to find your strength again.'

They went to dinner after their conversation and dined well, as he'd hoped, on mutton and vegetables with a sweet apple and plum pie for dessert. The estates' cider complemented the meal. Klyesha had never tasted such a delicious drink before which both warmed her insides and also made her lightheaded.

Yet, he left her alone in the night. A man, her mother had told her, would always find a way to gain his pleasure. She also remembered the many tomcats on the island who had shown her the rudiments of sex but her mother had never told her how women felt, that they too were drawn into the sex bond with men so that she wondered over her own feelings for William. She wondered if wanting him close was normal.

They petted the young foal the next day and then set off with fishing lines for a trout stream. After a small picnic, he cast his line but she eschewed this slow process and asked for his knife. All men carried small knives and he passed his to her. She found a willow and began stripping bark from one of its branches and then sharpening one end until the tip was a fine point. Walking upstream to where the sunlight lit the water and revealed the true depth of the river down to the pebbles and rocks, she waited silently knee deep in the stream. William watched her from his position on the bank, amused.

After about fifteen minutes, a brown speckled trout glided by, a sliver of copper in the sunlight. Quickly, she thrust the spear which compensated both for the speed of the fish and the distorted angle of the spear as it entered the water. She expertly caught the fish and flung it spear and all onto the bank. William jumped up from his spot on the bank very surprised at her skill. 'He's huge!' he grabbed the fish, stopping it from flopping back into the water. Klyesha climbed back onto the bank.

'You wanted to see my strength. This is one of them,' she grinned.

'Most impressive!' William put the now still trout into their catch basket where it nestled on fresh ferns. 'It seems we will have a change from mutton for dinner tonight.' They replaced their shoes and spent the rest of the walk searching for hazel and walnuts on the ground under the estate's trees.

'None of the women who've dined here have ever caught their own supper,' he admitted to her while they sat at the dinner table. 'Have you ever speared running prey?'

'Sometimes,' she replied enigmatically.

'Oh?' he asked but she refused to be drawn.

'I do have something I should discuss with you. You mentioned when the cats and I arrived that I'd be rewarded? That I might set up an establishment of my own?'

William flushed, 'Of course, forgive me, I'd forgotten.' Too busy enjoying her company, he had completely forgotten she was more than a guest in his home. He had made a business deal with her. Perhaps she had been chafing the whole time she spent with him, waiting for her payment. Perhaps it had all been under sufferance? More formally he added, 'Tomorrow I will instruct the Estate Secretary to draw up a draught for you for the amount.'

'A draught?' she asked.

'Pardon, it's a promissory note for 250 gold sovereigns. It's actually a small fortune.'

'I am much obliged, Your Majesty.' Klyesha bowed her head. She should be impressed, she thought, but wealth was something she'd never needed, only heard about. However, it would give her freedom. Even the freedom to return to her island with proper supplies. With a skiff to row, furniture, fishing nets, lobster pots -all the supplies she and her mother had dreamed of in the nights they talked around the fire. The possibilities were endless.

William tried to lighten his mood, but he was disgruntled. This young woman seemingly pliant in his hands had a mind and spirit of her own. How many times he'd wished for this in the women he met never realising what it actually meant was that they didn't need him! Those women who'd been startled by the jewels he gave them or the extent of his lands and properties, he'd spurned eventually on the notion that he lifted them up the social ladder to dizzying heights but they did nothing for him. But what could Klyesha do for him? What could she possibly do for him?

Chapter Two

The cottage was stone built with a roof of wooden shingles and a walled garden around the whole house. There was a covered well and a separate kitchen. There was even a bathing area inside the house with a copper heater to supply warm water for the bath. For Klyesha, this was a superlative luxury, she who had only ever bathed on the island in a shallow depression which accumulated rainwater. The bedrooms were furnished with beds and robes, dressing tables and chairs and paintings. To her paintings were an extraordinary delight. She always paused before a painting to drink in their secrets.

The Estate Secretary, Phillip, was more than the bearer of the promissory note. He had organised for her the viewing of properties, had personally recommended some to her, had hired a cook and a maid for her who would share the cottage and give her companionship. He arranged the village's provenders to deliver meat, vegetables, milk and firewood regularly to her cottage. He visited her once a fortnight to fulfil any of her wishes not provided for by the visiting hawkers. She was very grateful. She was very comfortable. She was very busy with the laying out of the kitchen garden and the planting of fruit trees. A driver and carriage arrived once a week to take her and her maid to any destination she pleased. They visited the granaries and the catteries. They visited shops to buy clothes, linen and supplies for the house. They visited the wharf and the harbour but when she smelt the sea, waves of longing overcame her. She had everything she needed and more. Yet why was she so bereft?

The King, meanwhile, impressed his courtiers with his sudden and increased diligence in all of the Public Assemblies. His notaries now recorded all disputes and questions and he methodically combed through them every night writing his verdicts and suggestions. He regularly sent his guards led by Paxton and Rufus to all the villages of the Kingdom, recording harvest totals, local problems and disputes which were all transferred to his records. He set up a whole room of accountants to tally taxes, distribute alms for the needy and oversee public works and repairs. To his brother Gerard, he gave 'Roads' chiefly to give him something to do. A portfolio whose neglect was also very obvious and easily reported by the guard sorties who ventured into all the areas of his Kingdom. The true management of the Kingdom lay on his shoulders alone, as it should do but had not for far too long a period. He felt proud of what he had achieved for his subjects, but he was not happy. He had not been happy these last two months.

Some days after their excursion to the Wharf, Klyesha noticed her pretty black cat, the little female called Roxy was missing. She asked both the Cook and Rachel, her maid, had they seen her as well as the gardener who had dropped in for a days' work. 'No, Mistress, he said, doffing his cap, 'But I will look out for her'. Her ginger Tom, Henry, was beside himself too. Very unsettled, he kept close to her day and night. The women walked about their neighbourhood for many hours calling for Roxy but she didn't appear again. Klyesha believed she'd been stolen but hoped whoever had her would give her a good home.

The next day a parcel arrived at the cottage. Rachel brought the package into the sitting room where Klyesha was drawing near the fire.

'Who is it from?' she asked.

'I don't know,' replied Rachel, handing her the package.

Using scissors to cut the string, Klyesha unwrapped the parcel. In it laid two rectangular objects the likes of which she had never seen before. 'Oh, some books,' observed Rachel.

'What are books?' asked Klyesha. Rachel felt a pang of anguish for her employer. It was at this moment she realised the effect of the total isolation which was Klyesha's upbringing. So much of their society she knew nothing of.

'Books can teach you a lot,' offered Rachel, 'But can you read?'

'Yes, a little but perhaps you can read one to me?'

Rachel sat beside her and they opened the first book, a handsome volume of world voyages bound in green leather and tooled in gold. Inside on the title page was an inscription which simply said 'From William.' Klyesha felt a rush of blood to her face. So, he had not totally forgotten her. Did he want a reply? 'What is the other one?' she asked instead. It was smaller and red and contained poetry idylls of the countryside. The volume fitted entirely into her hand and would make pleasant bedside reading.

'Which one should we read first?' asked Rachel.

'Let's read about the sea.'

Rachel took up the first green volume and began to read. It was an account of 15th century exploratory voyages and the brave captains who commanded the vessels which sailed into the unknown. It was these men who first made the maps of the whole world based on experience rather than mere speculation. The first story was about Vasco Da Gama, a Portuguese nobleman born sometime in the 1460's. The extract from his manuscript began:

'In the name of God. Amen.

In the year 1497 King Dom Manuel, the first of that name in Portugal, dispatched 4 vessels to make discoveries and go in search of spices. Vasco Da Gama was the captain major of these vessels, Paulo Da Gama, his brother, commanded one of them and Nicolau Coelho another.' (The last was captained by Bartholomew Diaz.)

Klyesha was particularly taken by the passage describing Da Gama's landing at Saint Helena, which he named and his encounter with the *'tawny coloured natives'* who dressed in skins and ate seals, whales, gazelles and the roots of herbs and she wondered how, like herself clad in skins, they reacted to the Portuguese in their doublets, hose and helmets.

'Have you ever eaten whale?' asked Klyesha.

'No, can't say I have,' replied Rachel.

'Once a piece of whale much savaged and half eaten was washed ashore on our island. My mother and I struggled to bring it ashore. We had never seen so much meat before. We rendered down the fat and found it useful for many things as well as cooking. Mother made tiny lights from the oil with pieces of wick made from twisted grasses. With the meat, we cut into strips and dried in the fierce winds of the island. Our cats and ourselves fed very well for a week on the fresh meat until we were so satiated, we couldn't look at another piece. The cats grew fat and their coats glossy. So did we and the oil made our hair lustrous and sleek. But it was the small lights that made us most cheerful for to hunt the dark from long nights in winter is really a most precious gift.'

Rachel was astonished. Never had Klyesha been so wordy. Of course, it was the topic, the world she had known.

'What about seals?'

'Seals? Yes, we had seals but they are large and dangerous when aroused, especially the bulls. We might have taken a pup if careful but they have the sweetest faces so we never could bring ourselves to club any. Besides we had fish enough, dried whale meat and young seabirds which were much easier to obtain. Their flesh is very succulent roasted.'

'So, you can kill a bird, take out the entrails and pluck out the feathers?'

'Yes, it is not difficult.'

Klyesha really is like no other young lady I have ever met, thought Rachel. 'Then perhaps we can keep some chickens in the garden for eggs and meat?'

'Yes, of course! We would have some more activities then to do as well.'

She returned to the manuscript and Klyesha was dismayed to hear the natives of Saint Helena had attacked four or five of Da Gama's shore party so they had to set sail again for the Cape of Good Hope. 'Why would they do that?' asked Rachel, 'After the Portuguese had given them gifts and fed them and they had all shared a meal of the native victuals as well?'

'Perhaps hospitality can be misinterpreted,' answered Klyesha. 'Perhaps they fed the voyagers so they would return to sea and when they did not, the universal language of violence could not be misunderstood.'

'Perhaps you are right,' said Rachel, 'Shall we continue?'

'First, is this Saint Helena and Cape of Good Hope, are they far?'

'Yes, they are on a different continent entirely.'

'What is a continent?'

'It's like a very large island but let's see if there's a map in the book, shall we?'

Sure enough, in the middle of the book was a foldout centrepiece, a map of the world. Rachel showed her the continent of Africa where they located the Cape of Good Hope. As Klyesha had never seen a map before, they spent quite a while pouring over it with Rachel pointing out the Kingdom and its surrounding countries and the main continents of the world. The map included the route of all the explorer voyages mentioned in the book and they eagerly followed Da Gama's route across the globe. Then Klyesha wanted to find her own island but Rachel pointed out that it was too small to be shown on such a large scale map. 'Are there maps of the Kingdom we could look at?'

'Not in this house. We would have to go to the Map Guild's Rooms in the City to find them.'

Klyesha wanted very much to see where her island was in relation to the Kingdom, out of both interest and future endeavour, so they planned for a trip to the City in the next few days. Klyesha asked Rachel to help her write a thank you note to William which she planned to deliver to him herself.

Leaving Rachel at the Map Guild's rooms she instructed their driver to take her to the Palace. The streets were cobbled with cross-cut stumps of wood in the poorer areas but as they got closer to the Palace the cobbles used were stone. Klyesha was grateful for the protection of the carriage which allowed her to see out of the windows but remain largely unobserved herself. She was surprised to observe the condition of the people in general appeared less ragged than when she had first arrived. Children laughed and played on the streets and hawkers shouted out their wares. Soldiers in the livery of the King lounged at street corners keeping an eye on everything while occasionally, a wealthier person was seen, the women with wooden platforms under their shoes to lift their hems out of the dirt and muck, their servants sheltering them with elaborate parasols. Smells of manure, urine and sewerage assaulted her nose in the poorer areas but even then, she observed street cleaners sweeping up muck and tossing it into carts while others used buckets of water to wash down the streets or thrown hay to dampen the mud. The buildings were old and wooden for the most part, but even now and then in a recently cleared area she could see stone buildings rising up, their sandstones a sharp contrast to the older wooden edifices.

Closer to the Palace, more stone buildings appeared and the roads became steeper leading up to the high stone walls of the Castle itself which protected the Palace buildings. When they were stopped by the guards at the Castle Gates, she was glad she'd remembered the Pass William had given her in case she ever needed to visit him. She beckoned the guard to her window and he examined the Pass. Seemingly bemused, he waved the carriage through.

Once inside the Castle, the sheer numbers of humanity began to thin out and an orderly calmness filled the air. Klyesha had noticed none of this when she first arrived at the Palace no doubt still traumatised from being taken off the island and being separated from her cats. Her own very spoilt Tom was at home luxuriating in front of Cook's kitchen stove. She was very nervous thinking about seeing William again and she wondered how she would be received. Soon the carriage stopped moving and her driver helped her down. She asked him where the Royal Apartments were and he indicated the door to head for while reminding her he would be waiting in the same place to take her home.

Gathering her skirts, she made her way up to the large metal studded red door over which William's arms were displayed. She was used to seeing his crest in the many places he'd shown her in the Palace, so she recognised it instantly. She knocked on the door and had to wait several nervous minutes for someone to open it.

'In the King's name, Madam, what is your business?' the imperious flunkey at the door eventually asked her.

Somewhat confused she hesitated at first then stumbled out with, 'I am here to see King William!'

'No doubt,' replied the man, 'So is everyone else. Please state your business!'

She thought for a moment, 'Please to tell his Majesty that his faithful servant, Klyesha, is here to see him.' She hoped that would be enough. It wasn't. The man kept insisting on a reason for her admittance and she could hardly say 'We are friends'. She turned away in frustration then remembered she had the thank you letter Rachel had helped her compose. She handed the man her letter, 'Please to deliver this to the King as soon as possible'. He looked down his nose at her but took the letter and promptly slammed shut the door.

Bitterly disappointed, Klyesha returned to the carriage and awaited her driver who had taken himself off for refreshment all the while ashamed she had come, acutely aware of her inexperience and naivety of Royal Protocols and how easy it had been when

William himself was in her presence. She waited a full hour for her driver to return and just as he did, she heard a knock on her carriage door. Expecting it to be the driver asking instructions, she was surprised to see William's pleasant face looking at her. She smiled broadly at him and he helped her down from the carriage.

'I sincerely hope you have not been waiting too long for me, Mistress Klyesha?' he asked, still holding onto her hand.

'No, not long,' she lied, grateful her journey had not been in vain. 'I hope Your Majesty is well?'

'Yes, and you?' She nodded. William could see she was a little plumper and fresher compared to her post illness self when she had convalesced at his Estate. They walked up to a different door where William produced a key and they followed corridors until in the Apartments to which she was familiar. William shouted orders and refreshments were soon before them on a small table between chairs in his own sitting room.

'This is indeed unexpected and of course, a pleasure. I was hoping to call on you soon but after our initial close contacts I thought perhaps you needed a rest from ... Royal matters'. She read uncertainty in his voice as if he was unsure his presence would be a pleasure to her.

'First of all, thank you so much for the books. They are a delight!'

'My pleasure and which one did you like the best?'

'My Maid, Rachel and I have been reading the 'World Voyages' one together and it has sparked my interest in geography and maps. Rachel is at this moment in the Map Makers Guild searching for a map which shows my island.'

William wasn't sure how to take this comment. Why did she want the map? Was it to find and return to the Island of Cats? 'Of, course, you must be interested in where it is. It took my men and me some days to find as well and we had no map. It is south-west of the coast about three day's sailing if going direct.'

'Oh,' said Klyesha, forgetting that William already knew how to find it. 'Still, it is not only my island I am interested in. I never knew a whole world existed beyond these places.'

'Yes, there are many worlds and I have visited a few but alas, I am unable to do so currently due to my commitments.'

It was a rebuff of sorts, he was letting her know if she set off on voyages that he wouldn't be accompanying her. 'You must tell me of your adventures, one day.'

'Assuredly, I will. However, not today. Today we will visit my library.'

Klyesha soon found out what a library was. It was a square room entirely lined with dark oak bookshelves and from every shelf pushed out fat volumes, thin volumes and ancient volumes of books. The room had a distinctive smell of aged leather and dry parchment. 'Goodness!' Klyesha was overwhelmed. 'I believe books are expensive.'

'Yes, quite,' said William. 'I am fortunate to have had ancestors who were bibliophiles that is, book lovers, and each has added to this collection. The ones I sent you are from here.'

'Oh, do you wish them returned?'

'No, of course not. You are also welcome to any volume from here you wish.'

Klyesha began stroking the books' spines until a thick, fat volume caught her eye. Made from orange leather with thick uncut pages, the book was a history of the Kingdom. 'You have never read this one!' She was surprised.

'No, but it's not the only volume I have of our history. Do you wish to borrow it?'

'Yes, if I may, I am very interested in history as well as geography.'

William called for a servant and ordered that the pages be cut for her. This meeting was difficult for him. Today she was so beautiful and having her so close was almost a torment. He had pressing matters that needed him, but he could not prise himself away. He showed her a large beautifully illustrated book. 'This is one of my favourite books from childhood' He handed it to her but it was large and she almost dropped it. He grabbed the book and their hands brushed. The touch unsettled them both. 'Please,' he added. 'Let me set you up with the book on a table where you can peruse it at your leisure.'

'Oh, it's a book of plants!' she said on settling into her seat.

'Yes, the illustrations are all hand painted and I delighted in their beauty as a child. The plants are endemic to my country.'

She was entranced. The flower pictures of delicate blossoms and strong, colourful broad-leaved bushes and trees were exquisitely rendered in great detail with separate parts showing the nuts and flowers each plant produced. She could become lost in such a work.

'My d...' He'd almost said 'darling'. 'My dear Klyesha, please forgive me but I must leave you for a short time. Does it please you to stay here with the books?'

She could not think of anything she'd rather do but she couldn't leave Rachel waiting outside the Guild House as the day was nearing dusk. She stood. 'Forgive me, Majesty, but my maid is awaiting me and the day draws in. We must go and collect her and return to my cottage.'

He was greatly disappointed. He who was the King and could have anything he wanted could easily have Rachel picked up and keep them both at the Palace for a meal and overnight but he was aware of the delicate thread of their re-established relationship and thought it best not to push too hard so early. 'Of course, I am disappointed your stay is to be so brief. Perhaps you might permit me to call on you later in the week?'

'Yes,' was all Klyesha could say. She too was somewhat overwhelmed by seeing him again and was glad of a chance to renew their companionship. He escorted her to the outside door where a guard led her to the carriage. They were soon off and had collected Rachel with her bundle of maps and by dark were again at home in their chosen comforts. She realised then she had forgotten to tell him about Roxy.

William was in a turmoil. This latest visit with its all too brief and tantalising closeness was driving him insane. He must secure her and have her for his own. He would not do this in an underhand way and make her his mistress. She must be his Queen but the prospect of this and convincing all who mattered that this was the correct course for the Kingdom was such a daunting task, he didn't know where to begin.

The next day, a man was brought before him. An evil, snivelling thief who bowed too low and who wouldn't meet his eyes. The man had been caught mistreating a 'Royal' cat thinking he might enjoy it's pain and then sell it for a fat gold sovereign. He was not the first who had been caught trying to make money from the cats but he was the first who had been cruel to them.

William ordered the cat be brought before him and it was young ginger tabby whose eyes were unnaturally wide and whose tail was broken which the cat painfully whished in the air.

'Who is the witness?' asked William, almost hoarse with anger. Another man stepped forward. 'I am Jaggery,' he said, 'One of the cattery keepers. I noticed the ginger missing last night and made some enquiries which led me to this man's hovel where he had secreted the cat. I could hear it howling with pain as I approached his hut. He claimed when I caught him that he'd found the cat and was going to return it the next day.'

'Well, imbecile! Speak!' William shouted to the culprit. The man began cowering on the floor. 'Drag him up!' The guards did so.

'I was... I WAS going to return it,' he gasped.

'Injured? And how do you account for its injury?' William seethed.

'Caught in a trap it was. I got it out,' the man explained, clearly terrified.

'Jaggery is this a trap injury?' Jaggery examined the cat, 'No, Your Majesty, there is no blood. The tail had been broken a different way.'

William looked at the thief. 'You inflict pain, but can you take it?' He asked the man who increasingly struggled between the guards. He turned to Paxton who sat beside him on a lower chair. 'Take him and break his leg. Throw him in the dungeon. He shall see no Physic for a week otherwise feed him as normal. When he has recovered, he will work for Jaggery for a year with no wages only sustenance. Take the filth away!' William stood. 'Let it be known by Proclamation what sentence this man has been given. And add the warning, if any mistreat the Royal Cats and it is proven, they will hang by degree of William the third.'

Gerard, the King's younger brother, watched the whole scene in astonishment. This would win William no friends- to put a cat's life above a man's was the height of foolishness. All to the good. Let him make more of these mistakes and the day edges closer to that glorious day when he loses the Crown. That girl has been here again just when I thought he'd forgotten her as well. Time to do a little digging into that young lady's past and then we shall see what a suitable bride she will make him, one hopefully that all will detest! He left the Public Audience and set about putting some plans in place for the day he would be King in William's stead.

The next day found Klyesha and Rachel unrolling and pouring over the maps Rachel had borrowed from the Mapmakers Guild. Klyesha found the Kingdom had a coastline but on three sides was bounded by foreign countries. 'Who are these people?' she asked.

Rachel pointed to the mountain range shaped like a horseshoe which followed the Kingdom's land boundaries: 'This is dense forest and high, rocky mountains. The passes I believe are difficult to travel and few people live here. We don't travel to these countries and they don't travel here.'

'What about by sea?'

'Perhaps. At the Wharf did you recall seeing strangers with unusual clothes or features?'

'No.'

'Then the answer is generally they don't. We keep to ourselves. We don't need strangers here.'

I wonder if they need us, thought Klyesha. Do people in those countries suffer famine as we have here? Could they one day come to take away what is ours? She mused on the fears often contemplated by those who are comfortable who see poverty around them and fear that one day they too might be poor. Shaking her head, she got up and inquired about lunch which Cook had already prepared. They ate a simple soup and homemade bread.

'Did you find out about chickens?' asked Klyesha.

'I believe we can buy some at the Farmers Market in the Square on Wednesdays. However, they are not laying at the moment. When we pass the shortest day, they will start to lay again.'

'Therefore, we must prepare for them by making a hen house.'

'I have no experience with tools neither do we have any. Phillip may know of a carpenter we can employ,' suggested Rachel.

'We shall ask him when he comes tomorrow.' After lunch, they returned to their maps which were laid out on the dining table with small rocks to hold down the edges.

Klyesha found a more detailed map of the coastline than the previous one they had looked at. In this she hoped they would find her island. They did find islands scattered off the coastline but of course most were unnamed and none had the name 'The island of cats' for this was the name she and her mother had given their island themselves. She realised the only person, apart from the captain on whose boat she first sailed to the Kingdom who could help her, was William. He did say he would call on her soon. She would have to wait until then. Meanwhile, as the maps were too costly to purchase and they would have to return them soon, she was determined to make copies for herself.

They obtained inks, chalk, rulers, pens and parchment from a local supplier and so began some very busy days copying the maps. Rachel was given the large map showing surrounding countries to copy while Klyesha worked on the coastline map with all the islands. They used the chalk to draw guidelines and the rulers to position all the map features before beginning the painstaking transference of details to ink. They needed to be very careful as a mistake could not be erased. Several false starts required them to start over again until they got the hang of just enough ink in the pen and a careful, steady hand.

They had been working on the maps for several days, totally absorbed in their projects when sometime before dinner, a knock came at the door. They put down their work and leaving the dining room closed the door. Klyesha sat quite excited on a chair in the sitting room while Rachel answered the door.

Before her was a very well-dressed man with blond hair and beard in his late 20's whom she knew to be the King's brother, Gerard. That he should call on them caused her to be dumb struck at first.

'May I see Mistress, Klyesha?' asked Gerard again.

'I beg pardon, Sire,' answered Rachel bowing and allowing him to pass into the house. She led him down the hallway to the sitting room where Klyesha stood staring at this unexpected visitor.

'Sire,' she curtsied.

'Em, please, not on my account, 'mi'Lord' will do when addressing me' bowed Gerard, 'I realise I am disappointingly not the King. May I sit?'

Klyesha gestured him to a seat while Rachel closed the door to give them privacy.

'I did not expect you,' said Klyesha quietly, her face a mask of emotions.

'Yes, and might I say at the beginning, I mean you no harm. Actually, I'm here to do you a service.' Klyesha waited. 'As you are aware, my countrymen in the past did your mother a great disservice and I am motivated to address any wrongs you may have suffered on their account and to bring to justice any of them still living.'

'I see,' said Klyesha.

'However, to begin to make this redress my inquiries need certain information I hope you may furnish.'

'I will do what I can.'

'First of all,' he said, taking a roll of parchment out of his jerkin and a stump of charcoal, 'I need to know her name.'

'My mother's name was Diana.'

'And her last name?'

'I believe it was Culaine but I'm unsure of the spelling. She never wrote it for me.'

He noted the names, 'No matter, this is a good start. Permit me to ask, if it is not too painful, did she ever mention the names or circumstances of her abandonment on the sea?'

'No, I'm not able to recall. She was very frightened of men in general even ships that did pass occasionally. Then she demanded we both remain unseen until they passed. She feared what sailors may do to us.'

'Understandable,' said Gerard, his face seemingly sympathetic, 'considering what she had already suffered. The rowing boat she arrived on, did it have a name?'

'Yes, it was called 'The Swallow'. The name was painted on the bow.'

'Superb!'

They were interrupted by a knock with Rachel asking if she might bring in refreshments. Klyesha opened the door and took the tray, 'Thank you, Rachel.' She brought the tray in, set it down and poured Gerard a tankard of ale and offered him a dish of nuts and figs.

'If we may continue?' he asked, putting down the tankard.

Klyesha nodded.

'Do you know the name of your father?'

To this Klyesha paled and her hands gripped the arms of the chair. She shook her head again and looked away.

'Please forgive me, I know this is difficult. So, you never knew who your father was?'

She shook her head again and looked away. When would this horrible man leave? She wondered how she could make him? However, she did not have to wait long. Gerard rose and bowed again, all agreeable as he'd gotten what he came for. 'Please, I beg your forgiveness if my questioning has upset you. I only hope to set things a'right for you.'

Klyesha rose too, 'You are very welcome. Please give my compliments to your wife.'

Gerard nodded and turned, taking out a small parcel from his satchel, he presented it to her. 'Actually, she sent you this, a small token of her esteem.' He handed her the gift.

She bowed and thanked him and walked him to the door. Rachel gave him his hat and cloak and he left as quickly as he came.

Her heart beating hard, Klyesha returned to the sitting room and collapsed on the chair. How dare he? How dare he drag personal details from her in such a way! When she recovered she poured herself some ale and drank it quickly. Its mildness settled her stomach but her mind was still racing. Curious, she took up the parcel and unwrapped it carefully. For some reason poison came to mind but it was a horror of a different ilk. Inside was a very small coin purse made with a jewelled silver clasp. It was pretty and she touched it gingerly. The purse was made of fur, jet black fur, soft and velvety to the touch. When Klyesha realised what it was she flung it across the room and began to sob until it seemed her heart would break.

Rachel brought hot tea and tried to calm Klyesha.

'What is it? What has he said or done?' Klyesha was incoherent for minutes. Finally, she pointed to a corner of the room. Rachel went to the corner but could see nothing, 'What is it?'

'It's a purse.' Rachel looked harder and managed to retrieve the purse where it had landed on a shelf. On seeing the fur, she immediately knew its significance. She put the purse in her apron pocket, thinking what was its purpose? A warning? Were they themselves to be threatened?

'I have made a decision,' said Klyesha, 'We're going to the island.'

'The Island of Cats?'

'Yes,' said Klyesha, 'Of course you don't have to come,' she added.

'Will this be...'

'A permanent arrangement? I don't know yet. We will begin preparations tomorrow.'

As it turned out, their preparations were delayed. The same evening, not long before dinner another knock came at the door. Rachel opened it to a servant carrying a large wicker basket. 'With the compliments of His Majesty,' the man said. Rachel got him to set it down in the kitchen.

'Why, there is a whole feast in here!' said Cook, unpacking tureens of soup, casseroles of meat, fruit and wines, all packed in straw. It was very lavish, better than many people's Christmas dinners. Rachel told Klyesha but she did not even rise to go and look.

Minutes later another knock came at the door and this time it was the King himself. Rachel recovering from shock, curtsied and let him into the sitting room.

'My compliments, mistress,' he said bowing to Klyesha, the grin fading from his face when he saw how upset she was. 'Whatever is the matter?'

Klyesha sat with her hands tightly folded in her lap but forced herself up to curtsy. 'Please,' he said, holding her arm and making her sit down again. 'What is it that troubles you?

She looked at him knowing she couldn't tell him. She couldn't set brother against brother. 'It is nothing,' she said looking down, 'I am just missing my island.'

'I see,' said William, brutally disappointed. He was hoping she was missing him and this meeting would be joyful. 'Forgive me for neglecting you. I have been very heavily involved in the affairs of the Kingdom.' Did she even care? What was going on in her mind?

'Of course. I do not expect to see you often.'

'Are things so bad? You seemed much happier when you came to the Palace a week ago.'

'I miss the sea, that is all,' she answered. Gerard had put her in a bad position. If what he uncovered about her past was as shameful as her mother becoming pregnant due to rape, how could she even look William in the face again? What if her background was entirely debased? He was better to look elsewhere for love. None of this could she tell him. So, she asked him a question instead 'What affairs are you arranging? What is happening in the Kingdom?'

'Much is happening both good and bad. The cats have happily done their job in the granaries which are now practically rodent free. What grain which remained unsullied has been ground into flour. More winter crops of wheat have been sown. We expect a better harvest this summer. Lawlessness, however is increasing and more men are in my dungeons than ever before. Poverty has made people desperate and outlying farms are now under siege. I have sent soldiers out to help where I can but there aren't enough.'

'I see,' Klyesha realised how worried he was. 'Winter months are hungry months.' She knew this only too well. Howling icy winds, no bird eggs, few birds only seaweed, molluscs and fish. It was always a time of hunger for them on the island.

'Well, your hungry months are behind you,' he offered, brightening, 'Do you know what my manservant brought for you tonight? Let's go and see.' He ushered her to the kitchen where Cook nearly collapsed when she saw the King. On the table was hot food, sides of lamb and hams, vegetables, oil and wine. She'd been wiping the straw off a bottle and placed it down just in time not to drop it.

'We shall have a feast tonight!', he grinned.

Rachel began to set the dining table while Cook transferred the hot food to serving vessels. Some late Autumn foliage in vases gave the table a colourful atmosphere.

While they waited in the sitting room, the knot in Klyesha's stomach started to unravel. William had more good news to tell, 'Your cats really were a good investment, Klyesha. The people who hired them to rid their houses of rodents became quite attached to them. My men report many tearful farewells at the catteries when temporary owners return their charges. So much so, we started a special breeding section producing weaned kittens to sell. They are so cute and fluffy, people actually fight over who is to buy them so we've instituted a lottery to pick owners for the first litters. In the future, we hope to supply enough to meet demand and tickets won't be necessary'. He really hoped this story might raise her spirits but she still looked downcast.

'My Roxy has gone missing,' she explained. 'We haven't seen her for a week.'

'I understand your sadness now. This is indeed a blow. Has she been sought?"

'As much as possible. Both neighbours and our gardener have searched for her without success.'

'She may still return,' offered William hopefully, totally unaware of what Klyesha knew. Roxy would not be returning. 'I shall find you another kitten to replace her meanwhile. Do you want another black kitten?'

'It doesn't matter, any colour will do as long as it's a little female. Our Tom misses her.'

'Of course, he does.' William was feeling himself in the Tom's place more than Klyesha knew.

With the feast laid out, they sat at table. William insisting Rachel join them. Rachel was surprised but more used to dining with the nobility than Klyesha, so she didn't feel awkward. The meal carried on apace, the hearty dishes helping to lift Klyesha's mood and William regaling them with humorous anecdotes.

After dinner, Rachel retired and left Klyesha showing William the almost completed maps they'd been working on during the last weeks. He was most impressed with the women's skills. 'Would you undertake a longer project making maps?'

'I suppose so, what do you have in mind?'

'There are several very ancient maps in my library which need copying before they disintegrate. They are quite fragile, too fragile to move. You would need to come to the Palace to work on them and of course, you could stay. Is this possible?'

It was a simple yet ingenious scheme. William feared for the women's safety alone in a cottage without a live-in manservant. He could easily have arranged protection for them but this seemed a much better solution to have her under his roof again.

Klyesha blushed. So, this was it. He could wait no longer. She didn't know what to say.

'This desire of yours to visit your island. You could arrange a vessel and supply it and go alone with your maid but you don't know how ruthless men are. You may never reach the island in safety. Better I go with you and take a detachment of soldiers.' She knew he was right. In this society, a woman alone was vulnerable. On her island it was a different matter. She had proved it in the past but just getting to the island safely was an issue. She knew she would have to acquiesce and allow herself to be controlled. Why did this feel so wrong?

William was all propriety and did not stay the night instead sending for them and their boxes in the morning. He even sent a travelling basket for the Tom. The cook and the gardener would eat well on the victuals left behind.

Chapter Three

'Diana Culaine was the daughter of a journeyman clockmaker. They lived in a terrace house in the clockmaking district. His repairs were good and the clocks he made kept excellent time. He made a reasonable living until one of the bigger concerns, a clock making firm called Heysens, employed more apprentices both carpenters and metal casters and they were able to make clocks faster and cheaper. The Heysens' clocks began to undercut all the other clock makers in the district until Culaine was able only to do repairs. Apparently, this was not enough to live on and he was declared a bankrupt, his stock and home seized and he himself thrown into prison. The daughter, Diana, was taken in by her aunt, an eccentric old woman who kept a lot of cats. Diana apparently helped her with the cats and kept the cottage clean. The father died in prison, her mother had died when Diana was only a child. A few years later when Diana was about 16, her aunt also died leaving her the property.'

'About 20 years ago began the period called 'The Cleansing of the Cats.' The Apothecary Guild met one day and declared cats carried disease, their best explanation for a mysterious outbreak of measles during which dozens of children in the City died. This set parents in a panic and hundreds of cats were given up to be killed by special detachments of soldiers. Of course, there were owners unwilling to give up their cats and they were threatened with prison until they agreed. Diana was a headstrong young woman who having virtually brought up herself was independent and rebellious. She outfoxed the detachment of soldiers on many occasions by hiding her cats in the cellars but eventually they were seen by neighbours who had children and feared the cats Diana hid would bring disease to their own doorsteps. They informed on her and she was arrested.'

'She put up such a fight, kicking and screaming, biting and scratching that the soldiers wanted to make an example of her. They gathered about a half dozen of her cats and put them in crates, the rest they killed in front of her. By this time, she was so crazy to be almost insane so she was bound and dragged to the wharf. Some wanted her tied to a rock and drowned but because of her age, only 18, the more reasonable soldiers among them suggested she be cast out to sea with her cats to let fate choose her destiny. This was agreed and she was put aboard a ship whose captain agreed to drag the skiff out to sea and let it loose into the currents to drift where it would. This was done and Diana was never heard of again, though occasionally reports of an 'Island of Cats' have been heard in conversations among sailors in taverns.'

'This will not do!' Gerard was irritated, 'Lindquist, I do not doubt your meticulous search for the details of this story but it lacks, shall we say, zest. How was this Diana made pregnant? For we know Klyesha is her daughter. No, we must find a suitable father for this scheming young woman who seeks to make herself Queen. Go search out some base fellow who is willing to concoct a story. If he is a former soldier, so much the better. Diana can have been raped by the soldiers before being towed out by the galley and set adrift. No, go!'

Gerard was unhappy. The daughter of a clockmaker was altogether too respectable. It even gave Klyesha rights to her Great Aunt's property. No, this was too nice a story by half. They needed to find a much juicer one. One that stained Diana's daughter for ever.

Rachel and Klyesha sat at large deal table surrounded by rolls of parchment, inks, pens, chalk and rulers. They were studying the first of several very old maps of the City and the Kingdom. Paper weights from the King's own collection sat on the edges holding the maps, for the women dared not touch them lest they fall apart in front of them.

'Five gold sovereigns each, we will earn from this,' encouraged Klyesha, for the task was indeed daunting. 'Which one do you want to copy?'

'I'd prefer the larger scale one of the Kingdom as it is similar to the other map I already copied,' said Rachel.

'Very well, I shall attempt the City map. Can you believe how crooked the streets are? I'm tempted to straighten them out so the map looks better,' she laughed. Rachel was happy to see her mood improved.

'Perhaps we will study them until lunchtime and then this afternoon begin to trace some outlines?

'Agreed,' answered Klyesha.

They set to carefully observing the keys used, the tone of colours, how rivers were depicted or important buildings. 'Have you noticed, Rachel, how the districts of the City are named for their products?' She pointed to the sections: 'Here are the wine merchants, here bakers and pastry chefs, here are carpenters, builders and metal casters, here are potteries and clockmakers.'

'Did you know my family are bakers?' asked Rachel.

'So, they live here do they still in the Baker's district?'

'Yes, they do. In fact, these districts are little changed today. We now have a cloth district and within it a Silk Emporium to display imported silks and brocades. Not much has changed from a century and a half ago!'

'And this knowledge is useful to us too. If we need pottery we no longer have to go to a shop in the Market, we can buy direct from the potters themselves and cheaper too.'

'Also, when we need new fabrics, we can choose bolts from the Silk Emporium and have seamstresses make them up for us. We shall get better quality dresses that way.'

'And thinking about the clockmakers,' said Klyesha, 'We have need of a reliable clock. The one we have currently is very old and I'm sure keeps poor time!'

'We shall have the five sovereigns each spent before we even earn them,' laughed Rachel. Klyesha giggled with her.

'Perhaps we'd better start on the maps straight away. We can always negotiate a better price if we can finish them faster and so copy more!' added Klyesha.

'You underestimate the ease of your negotiating skills with the King,' commented Rachel. Klyesha looked embarrassed but she knew it to be true.

In the evening, they dined in the King's private quarters without other guests. They ate soup followed by oysters with salt and lemon. The main dish was baked ham. Dessert was fresh fruit and local cheeses. William smiled when Klyesha specifically asked for the Estate Cider.

'You have developed a taste for it,' he commented.

'Yes, I find it more refreshing than wine. Fortified wine quite slows the digestive system.'

'I do believe it does,' he laughed, 'though there are many who are not put off by this fact. How goes the mapmaking?'

'We have studied them well and made a beginning this afternoon. Pray forgive us,' she looked at Rachel, 'but accuracy requires that progress is slow.'

This doesn't bother me at all, thought William, all the longer to have her near me. 'Accuracy is paramount. Please convey if you are in need of any more supplies?' he asked.

'We will. All is at hand momentarily,' Klyesha replied. 'Rachel has a question for you.' Rachel placed down her napkin and looked at the King, 'I was wondering why we don't trade with the surrounding countries? We might have exchanged goods for more wheat?'

'An interesting observation,' replied William, 'It's an idea I have considered myself. However, we currently have no diplomatic channels through which to negotiate. Relations between our countries ended decades ago.'

'Then perhaps it is time to send an emissary. Do you have anyone whom you could trust?' asked Klyesha.

William was slightly taken aback by their comments on diplomacy. They were, of course, correct. Relations could be restarted even after this long interval. 'I will think about it,' he said simply. He paused to sip wine. 'I thought perhaps tomorrow after you have spent the morning in copying, you might like an excursion?'

Klyesha was excited, 'Yes. A diversion would be most refreshing. Where did you have in mind?'

'Perhaps you have some shopping you need to do? I need to order some new doublets and coats and intend choosing the fabric myself.'

'I need a new clock,' said Klyesha, 'To replace the old one we have at home.'

'Excellent! It is decided. If you can be ready after luncheon, we should set off then. Now please excuse me, I have matters of state to arrange. Shall I send in my minstrel with his lute?'

'Yes, it would be a soothing end to the evening. Thank you,' said Klyesha rising. 'Until tomorrow?' She held out her hand to the King who took it and kissed the back of her hand.

'Tomorrow,' he sighed. His paperwork really was very tedious but necessary.

The minstrel played sweet melodies for the two women for three-quarters of an hour when they thanked him and made their way to their bed chambers which sat side-by-side. Klyesha said goodnight to her friend and returned to her room and locked the door. Ever since Gerard had visited her and presented the horrific purse, she had been nervous at night and restless for many hours trying to sleep. She believed being under the King's roof would not allay those feelings especially as Gerard resided in the Palace as well.

In her nightgown with the tom, whose name was Henry, curled up in her bed, she took up the little red volume of verse and read a number of poems both romantic and sweet. How wonderful would the world be if the sentiments in those poems were always true. Lovers never separated, beauty adored, handsome men getting their heart's desire. She was both alarmed and relieved William never visited her bedchamber. Did he not desire her? Was she too lowly to spark his interest? And yet if he did come and take her, what prospect would the future hold but to become his mistress? Klyesha knew she'd rather be alone on her island than become a mistress who would envy a Queen. A Queen who would have William's true heart while she just supplied his needs. And then if she had children, they would all be bastards with no status, ever second-class citizens whose existence would be feared by William's legitimate sons and daughters. No, she might be chaste and lonely now, but it was better than having her future ruined.

The next day after luncheon, William came to fetch them from the library. They gathered their cloaks, put up their hoods against the cold and stepped out into the mews where a plain carriage awaited them. William didn't want his excursion being obvious, Klyesha surmised.

As they drove through the streets, William indicated the function of the buildings: The Guild Hall, the Wool Exchange, the State Treasury- all classical buildings with columns and pediments

44

built in the local bluestone. They passed by the vegetable market, the meat market and as they neared the wharves, the fish market.

'They are not so crowded,' observed Klyesha.

'No, there are reduced supplies being offered now as it is Winter.'

She noticed one lone line of ragged, grey-looking people near a stable block and asked what they were lining up for.

'They are receiving their portion of flour milled in our own flour mills,' answered William. 'It is one way to help alleviate poverty.'

Klyesha was surprised by how long the line was and wondered what would happen when the flour ran out. At least her cats had made some contribution to preserving what wheat the Kingdom still had. Would these people starve? She guessed at the pressure and strain William was carrying at the moment, as if the whole world was sitting on his shoulders. He seemed to act as if none of this mattered but the state of the Kingdom must surely torment him. And here they were ignoring all the misery to go shopping.

Passing by the wharves, the roads began to narrow and they entered the older district of the City where all the buildings were ancient half-timbered dwellings occasionally standing out with freshly applied whitewashed stucco walls contrasting with dark timbers. The shingles which hung out announced each shop's goods whether it be in the street of fabric or clothes, raw wool or gold and silver smiths. Turning, they entered the Clockmakers Street. The firm of Heysons had a handsome set of buildings that dominated the street, but Klyesha shook her head when William suggested stopping as she wanted to support a small retailer where their custom would make a difference. She pointed out a small shop with a dusty window but whose clocks looked reliable and solid. The carriage came to a halt and they all stepped out onto the pavement. The King's great woollen overcoat was mud splattered and slightly worn and he didn't look like a King. The women looked more elegant. However, there were few people about so they might not have worried about being noticed.

Whether it was instinct or something else that made Klyesha choose this shop but entering it would change her life forever. First, she looked into the small shop's window observing the clocks there and seemingly having made up her mind, she entered the shop. The others followed. The shop smelt ancient of old timbers and machine oil overlaid by a fragrant lavender candle burning in the counter to cast a little light. A young man of about 30 was behind the counter and Klyesha was surprised to find he looked familiar though she did not know why.

'Good afternoon, Sir' she began, 'I am desirous of a carriage clock for my sitting room and I see you have one in the window. Would you care to show it to me?'

The young man moved quickly, shocked out of his revery as the day had so far proved exceedingly slow. He unlocked the window's interior cabinet and procuring the clock set it upon the counter. The clock's case was made of mahogany with a gold leaf decoration. The handle was made of brass and the workings too. The dial was of a delicate light blue enamel with black numbers and royal blue hands. The young man proceeded to show Klyesha the clock's workings, its use of a pendulum to keep time and how to wind it each evening.

'What do you think, William?' asked Klyesha.

'It is a solid clock, quite serviceable though not particularly ornate. Perhaps you would prefer a gold-plated casement?'

The young man turned and entering the room behind brought out a very handsome clock, not really believing his luck as few customers came into the shop in these difficult times especially not to ask for an expensive clock. Placing the clock next to the carriage clock made the former look like a threadbare cousin.

'Now, this is a clock!' announced William. Rachel dragged herself away from looking at pocket watches to admire it also.

The young man proudly showed how the clock worked and demonstrated its shrill, clear chimes for the hour and half hour. 'This clock was made by the former owner of this shop, a clockmaker by the name of Alfredo Culaine. Do you see his signature inscribed on the workings at the back?' Klyesha peered intently at the signature her heart racing. For this clock was made by her mother's father. Alfredo Culaine was her grandfather. She knew nothing more, until now, than his name. Her mother had never spoken of him.

'Tell me about him,' asked Klyesha, trying not to sound anxious.

'He was my father's elder brother and he established this business- it must have been, say forty years ago now. He was very skilled and taught my father, Leo well who also taught me. Alfredo's clocks were famous because he was so meticulous, but they took a long time to make. Exquisite though they were, he couldn't charge

46

as much for them as they deserved as the company whose shops you have recently passed, 'Heysons and Co' produced solid, good clocks quite rapidly and more cheaply and Alfredo could not compete. Despite having his brother as an apprentice, unfortunately Alfredo's business was declared bankrupt and he was sent to a debtor's prison. There he died.'

Klyesha gasped. How harsh a life her grandfather had experienced!

'My father,' he continued,' worked for Heysons for a time long enough to rent this shop and carry on the family business which you see before you today.'

Klyesha was staggered to discover a cousin and all this information about her family while shopping for a clock. It was so unexpected. 'Thank you. I am so glad you've been able to continue the family tradition. What is your name?'

'My name is Lucca. Lucca Culaine,' he bowed, 'Pleased to be of service, Mistress…?'

'I am Mistress Klyesha and these are my friends, William and Rachel.' The young man bowed solemnly to them all. 'This clock interests me a great deal' added Klyesha, touching delicately the piece made by her Grandfather. 'If I purchased it, would you be so kind as to set it up, adjust it or whatever is needed, when you deliver it?'

'Indeed, Mistress Klyesha, 'It would be my pleasure.'

'It is settled then.' She wrote her address on a parchment for the purpose sitting on the countertop. 'How much is the clock?'

'It is 10 gold sovereigns, Mistress.'

It was a great deal and Klyesha blushed. She did not think it would cost so much.

'I can assure you, mistress, it is worth every penny. It is a one-off, irreplaceable. An impeccable choice, if I might add.'

William turned her aside and whispered, 'I will advance you the map money. It won't be a problem.' She gritted her teeth but nodded gracefully as William took out his purse and handed over the money. Lucca took the gold and wrote a receipt.

'Will tomorrow be a good time to deliver the clock?' he asked.

Klyesha looked at William who said, 'A week from tomorrow would suffice. Can it be done?'

'Of course, and thank you again, mistresses and mi'Lord. I shall polish it myself before delivery. Until then,' he bowed again.

They left the shop but not before Rachel purchased a fob watch from money she'd saved herself. They examined it as the carriage drove on. 'What an exquisite little face,' admired Klyesha.

'Yes, small but useful. We can use it to tell the time until you get delivery of your clock.'

'Yes indeed,' said Klyesha nursing her information, not sure whether to share it before she turned it all over in her own mind.

As it happened, they were too busy at a drapers and the Silk Emporium to discuss her news. William insisted on buying them scarves for winter and buying bolts of cloth for his own clothes. Klyesha was very taken with a rose and blue damask and before she knew it, William had purchased it for her. Laughing and not feeling very guilty about their expensive purchases in the midst of poverty, the three stopped for mead and soup at an alehouse before returning to the Palace where they all rested before dinner in their separate chambers.

Klyesha made up her mind. She would tell them her news over dinner.

William's Cook roasted a turkey for them with sweet sauces and gravies. They ate vegetable soup and had a fruit pudding for dessert. Klyesha asked William what he was going to do with the bolts of cloth and he explained the clothes he would have made. The King had his own tailor and a room of seamstresses. He offered them to Klyesha for her gowns. 'Do you have any serviceable cloth suitable for breeches,' she asked.

'I can ask my tailor, I'm sure he will find something. Who are the breeches for?'

'For me,' she replied, 'Gowns are too cumbersome for gardening and even for walking. Both Rachel and I want pairs.'

William was surprised, 'It is unusual. I'm not sure what people would think of a pair of young ladies wearing breeches.'

'I have learned not to care what people think, William. The breeches will be very serviceable when we visit my island.'

'Your island, yes, I hadn't forgotten. Perhaps after you finish the maps?'

'Yes, indeed,' replied Klyesha. Her impatience to visit her only true home would have to wait. 'On another more significant matter,

I have news from today I have been debating about whether to share with you both. My origins, apart from the island and my unfortunate mother, are unknown to you both, indeed were unknown to me also until today when we entered the clock makers' store.'

'How so?' asked William, intrigued.

'The shop was my grandfather's. My Grandfather was Alfredo Culaine and until today his name was the only thing I knew about him.'

'So Lucca is your cousin?' asked Rachel.

'Yes, he is. It is why I wanted him to deliver and service the clock so I could talk to him further about the family.'

William inwardly breathed a sigh of relief. Klyesha's origins were very pertinent in Court society. A clockmaker's granddaughter, though humble, was quite respectable. Members of the business classes were accepted at Court, underneath members of the nobility of course, but acceptable nonetheless. Her origins might well be a barrier to any union as much as he didn't want to admit it. If her birth was too lowly, the people of the Kingdom would never accept her as Queen. However, Alfredo Culaine died in prison. This was a strain, yet bankruptcy was not in the same class as murder, rape or thievery. It was unfortunate no one had helped Culaine out of his bankruptcy. Perhaps he was a proud man who refused to take charity even if this refusal eventually killed him. William's heart went out to Klyesha today. She had gained a grandfather but one whose life had been so full of tragedy.

'How do you think your mother was cared for if her father was in prison?' asked Rachel.

'I do not know. My mother never talked of her past. Lucca must be able to tell me something to fill in the gaps in my knowledge.

'Let us hope he can,' sympathised William. And now due to the map copying she would have to wait another week to find out. William could feel her frustration. He looked at Klyesha. Today's news seemed more of a relief to her than a burden. To be almost totally ignorant of your heritage, your parentage, must be like swimming through murky water. The visit to the clockmaker had turned murky water to clear. Still, she needed to swim which meant maintaining the courage to hear the full story whatever that turned out to be.

Chapter Four

It was during the Royal Assembly several days later attended by Klyesha and Rachel, that Gerard made his move. The assembly was crowded with all manner of Court retainers, businessmen and petitioners all eager to see and hear the King. Gerard knew of the information for some time but for its effect to be maximised, Klyesha needed to be in attendance to hear. Now was his chance. After the usual sorry tales of woe by impoverished farmers, his man stepped forward. The creature couldn't have played a better part or looked as decrepit or imbecilic if Gerard had plucked him out of his own imagination. He was of medium height, bald with sunken in cheeks and thin, spindly legs. He walked with a limp and fingered his cap nervously. He was as hollow as a man could be.

'I wish to petition the King for assistance,' he began, his voice trembling. 'There is a person here in this Chamber who is a relative of mine but she does not know it. If I had approached her on the street, I know she would spurn me. But I am her own flesh and blood, though she has never seen me before or me her. Until some months ago, I never knew she existed but as I have no family, I seek her out to acknowledge me.'

'And who is this person of whom you speak?' asked the King.

'She is Mistress Klyesha,' said the odious man, 'and she be my own true daughter.'

Klyesha stared at the man and had to clasp her chair harder in order not to faint. How could this disease-ridden man be her father! He looked nothing like her!

'This is an extraordinary claim,' said William, deeply sceptical, 'and what evidence do you have to back this petition?'

'I have the word of these three former soldiers,' said the man, calling his equally loathsome friends to step forward. 'These men and I loaded Klyesha's mother, Diana, onto a ship as we were told to do so by our commanding officer. We loaded half a dozen of her cats on the ship with her.'

'And...' demanded the King.

'Well, I'm not proud of it but I had me way with her before that. Afterwards we dragged her from her house. And this girl before you,' he said pointing to Klyesha, 'was born on the island so I'm her father and I want her to acknowledge me.'

William was speechless with rage, 'How dare you!' He stood up going to the man. 'If what you say is true you are nothing more than a rapist. As for you, what you have to say!' he demanded of the men.

'We say what he says is true,' each one repeated as if they'd been schooled to answer all the same.

'Huh! You say this is true! Well quite frankly, I don't believe any of you. Mistress Klyesha looks nothing like this imbecile… what is your name?'

The man was taken aback and muttering under his breath, his nervousness increasing, 'My name is Mutton, Joseph Mutton and I'm no fool, Sire!'

'Well, we shall see about that! Guards throw them all into the dungeon. A few lashes will loosen the lies from their tongues! Take them out of my sight!'

There was considerable murmuring amongst the crowd and looks towards Klyesha. She had never seen William so angry and she had never before felt so sick. A child of rape? The daughter of a diseased, decrepit soldier who had degraded her mother in the worst possible way. Surely this wasn't real? The Court continued to be abuzz with gossip. She felt everyone was staring at her and was sick to her stomach that her past had been dragged through the gutter before all these people. Taking Rachel by the hand, the women fled from the chamber.

Gerard couldn't contain his glee. The men and their story, even if later proven untrue, had thrown so much mud some of it would surely stick. William was almost apoplectic. He closed the Assembly and dismissed everyone. Gerard thought all his scheming was worth it just to see the rage on William's face. See Big Brother, see the type of woman on whom you bestow all your attentions he thought. See the base piece of shit from whom she emanates. Look upon her degradation and despair brother, but know this is only the beginning! Gerard left triumphantly to share a congratulatory glass of expensive wine with his wife.

Klyesha and Rachel returned home after finishing the maps, laden with new clothes including two sets of breeches each. Cook was pleased to see them. Fixing meals for herself and occasionally the gardener left her little to do. 'Welcome home,' she said opening the door for the women and helping them with their parcels. 'At last, some voices! It has been too quiet here with no Tom to pet either.'

'He is as pleased to get home as we are,' said Klyesha, letting him out into the sitting room. He immediately set to cleaning himself followed by curling up into a ball to sleep on his favourite chair.

'Today, we are to expect the clock, yes?' asked Rachel, checking her own fob watch.

'Yes, I believe so.' replied Klyesha, still distracted and still shaken by Mutton's 'confession'. Court was the last place she wanted to be even if it meant she wouldn't be seeing William for a while.

It was sometime after noon when the expected knock came at the door. Rachel opened the door to Lucca, who true to his word, was delivering Klyesha's handsome new carriage clock. He doffed his hat and appeared quite nervous for the home was elegant and expensively furnished. 'Please sit down,' asked Klyesha as Rachel ushered him into the sitting room. 'Can I offer you some refreshment? Some cider or wine?'

'Just water, thank you.' Rachel went to fetch it and he began to unpack his package. 'Is there any particular place you'd like me to set up the clock?'

'Yes, just there on the round table near the settee where I can easily see it from my favourite chair.' Lucca lifted the glass dome from the clock and began to wind it, checking the mechanisms and adjusting the time.

'You will need to wind it each night with the key. Can I show you how?'

Klyesha rose and stood beside him as he explained the process. 'It really is quite simple. Would you like to try?'

Klyesha carefully wound the clock with Lucca's encouragement. 'Do you think you will be able to manage?' he asked.

'Certainly,' replied Klyesha, 'I will just have to remember to do it.'

'I find it helps to wind my clocks all at the same time each day to establish a routine. Of course, I have so many to wind the process takes me some time.'

Rachel brought in the water and a dish of oranges, smiling at Lucca as she set them down.

When they both returned to their seats, Klyesha began, 'There is another reason for me asking you here. Can you guess it?'

'Why mistress, I cannot, though there is something about you I cannot quite fathom,' he said embarrassed.

'My name is Klyesha Culaine.'

Lucca's brow furrowed, 'Culaine, you say. Are you a relative?'

'Yes, one you didn't know of at all. My mother was Diana.'

'What Alfredo's daughter! You are Alfredo's granddaughter?'

'Yes, I am, which makes us cousins. Permit me to ask for there is no one else, can you tell me what happened to Diana?'

Lucca looked shamefaced, 'Yes, I can tell you some things although I was only 11 at the time. She was dragged away by soldiers many years ago. My father Leo tried to come to her aid but was beaten back by those men. He took many months to recover. We all assume she had drowned at sea.'

'I am sorry to hear of your father's injuries. Is he still alive?'

'Alas, no, he too died some five years ago of a debilitating illness which crept over him after the beating.'

Klyesha expressed her regret to hear of the further ripples of tragedy engulfing their family. 'As you are my cousin, Lucca, do you not think we look alike?'

Lucca looked at her honestly, 'We both have the family's black hair yet we have different eye colours. Yours green and mine are blue. Strangely when I saw you for the first time, I did feel some kind of connexion between us.'

'As did I,' Klyesha confessed. 'I am so delighted to find a relative here in this Kingdom where I know so few people. But let me tell you my story first.' Klyesha related the tale of her mother's banishment from the Kingdom, of her finding the island and giving birth to a daughter there.

Shaking his head, Lucca said, 'What a story! Such resilience and good fortune both but also what a lonely life for the two of you. Is your mother still alive?'

'No, she died this last year some months before my rescue by the King.'

'The King!'

'Yes. You met him in your shop.'

Lucca blanched, 'He was the King!'

'Yes, he is my friend. He needed my cats to rid the Kingdom of the rodent plague and we became friends.'

Lucca was stunned to think the King entered his shop and he didn't know it. 'Could I say we have Royal Patronage now?' he chuckled.

'Perhaps not.' Klyesha laughed, 'Seeing it was I who bought the clock!'

True, he thought as they sat quietly for a few moments each taking in all the possibilities of their newly revealed connexion.

'So, tell me about yourself, Lucca.'

'I have the shop and complete repairs in between customers. I am an only child, so I inherited the shop when my father died. I manage to make a living but only just, however as there is only me to support it is sufficient.'

'What are your aspirations? Do you also make clocks?'

'Yes, in my spare time. Clockmaking is a very slow process. I have to cast my own metal pieces in order to repair clocks. As you could imagine, to cast enough for an entire clock takes time.'

'I see, yes it must be very involved. So, you are not married?'

'No,' he answered, 'and you?'

'Definitely no!', laughed Klyesha. 'Rachel, my maid and I lead a quiet life here. Where do you live?'

'Actually, I live where your mother once lived in our Aunt Clarice's house a few blocks away from the shop. My father and I took it over when our Aunt died to prevent it falling into disrepair, but I suppose...'

'Suppose...?'

'I suppose the house is actually yours as Aunt Clarice left it to Diana when she died.'

'Oh, I see,' said Klyesha, 'Please don't despair. I'm quite happy here in my own home. I shall not remove you from yours.'

Not being the legal owner of his house was a worry to him, this was good news.

'There is something else I wish to ask you, Lucca. Maybe you're too young to remember, however, certain reports surrounding the circumstances of my mother's arrest have come to light recently with very disturbing allegations. It is of a delicate nature but concerns my parentage. I do not know who my father is and I was

54

wondering if you knew anyone who was seeing my mother before her arrest? Did she have a man friend?

'Permit me to ask, if I may, what were the allegations first?'

Klyesha reddened. 'There was made the most distasteful report during one of the King's recent Assemblies. A man called Joseph Mutton, a former soldier, claimed to have raped my mother before she was cast out to sea.'

Breathing deeply, Lucas said, 'I may have been only 11 yet my memory of that time is very clear. I will tell you what I saw. My father received a message and rushed out of the house. I followed him. It was quite early in the morning, foggy and cold. We ran to Aunt Clarice's house, all the while my father begging me to go home but intent on adventure, I only pretended to drop back whereas I actually kept following him. I was worried for his safety too. I arrived at the house to see my father arguing with a small detachment of rough-looking soldiers. They had my cousin, Diana, between them and she was pulling and screaming and trying to bite them. My father attacked one of them and got a musket butt to the skull for his trouble. He staggered away and I ran to him. They tied Diana to an open cart and tossed several crates in beside her. Off they went down the laneway, my Aunt Clarice's Housekeeper, who was elderly, hobbled out to our aid and called an apothecary for my father. He was able to speak enough to tell me to follow the cart, which I did. Clarice's Housekeeper, a woman called Margaret, assured me she would look after my father.'

'I caught up with the cart quite quickly having young strong legs. They went to the Wharf where the soldiers argued with and threatened a Galley Captain until he agreed to take Diana onto his ship. She was by now seemingly still and insensible and was carried quite limp up into the Galley.'

'I didn't know what to do. To try to rescue her and jump onto the ship but I also feared for my own safety and wanted to see my father to make sure his injuries were cared for. So, I noted the name of the Galley – 'The White Swan' and rushed back to my father. He was already fetched into my Aunt's house where a physic bandaged his head and recommended quiet rest.'

'I was so busy those next few weeks going between my father and the shop which I could only open for a few hours a day and our own house with hens and roosters to care for, I could do nothing for

Diana. When my father recovered his senses, we sent for the Sheriff to investigate this captain from '*The White Swan*' but we were told the man denied my whole story, denied ever having seen Diana with the soldiers. So, who would believe an 11 year old boy over a sea captain? To our regret there was nothing we could do and we feared Diana lost forever.'

This guilt still affected him, thought Klyesha. 'Such a burden for a young boy. I am so sorry my mother's affairs involved you and your father and to such cost. However, your story contradicts this Joseph Mutton absolutely and may be vital to expose his lies. Would you be willing to tell this story to the King?'

'Yes, of course if it would help you. To my regret I could do nothing to help your mother but perhaps I can help you.'

'Can you remember anything about my mother before her arrest. Did you or your father visit her?'

'Occasionally, yes. My father wanted her to live with us for her own protection but she insisted she was an independent woman and could mind her own affairs.'

'Yes, she certainly was and in her later years had total independence apart from the responsibility of me. Did you notice if she had any male friends?'

'I cannot recall presently,' said Lucca, 'but I will think upon it. When do you want to see the King?'

'Would tomorrow be too soon?'

'After I close the shop at two o'clock, I could come here and we could go together.'

'Excellent. Now tell me if my Aunt's housekeeper who became my mother's housekeeper is still alive?'

'Indeed she is, as she is my housekeeper now but it is only a token role. She is too old to do much and her daughter does all the hard work. Shall I bring her?'

'Yes, please, if she is able to travel.'

'She would travel a long way to see Diana's daughter. I won't need to persuade her.'

Joseph Mutton and the soldiers were brought up from the dungeon to stand before William in his rooms. They were a pathetic group, chastened further by a water and bread diet and twenty lashes each administered by the King's gaoler. 'You presented a story, Joseph Mutton, to my Assembly we both know was all lies. What do you say for yourself, now?

John, the most pathetic of the group stood weakly on his thin legs, 'Your Majesty, I was paid for my story. The only truth is we was all soldiers in the past, but injuries cast us out of them ranks. We was desperate for food for our families, Sire!'

'So, you admit you lied about Klyesha being your daughter. In fact, the rape never happened?'

'Yes, mi'Lord, I mean, Sire.' Mutton hung his head.

'Then you will tell me who made you repeat these lies? Who put you up to it?'

'That I cannot say, Sire, or I am a dead man and these men too.' He pointed to them. Fear crossed their faces.

'I see. We could try more whipping to loosen your tongues but I have a better use for them. You will publicly deny your story to the whole Court. Otherwise, you will spend the next three years in my gaol. What do you say?'

Mutton's struggles were palpable. His face twisted in agony.

'You have made a very public false confession which has harmed a young woman of my acquaintance,' said the King. 'A person who has my protection. You'll make good of this or rot in gaol!'

The men began whispering amongst themselves.

'If you fear reprisal, as you say, I will have you transported to a remote mountain area where you can hide. Your families can join you at a suitable time. But try my patience more and this offer will cease to exist. What do you say?'

The man conferred for a few minutes. They knew it was the best they could hope for. Mutton spoke for them, 'Sire, we will do as you say on condition we are all guarded until we reach the mountains.'

'As you wish. Tomorrow you will confess. Speak nothing of our arrangement for your own safety.' He called the guards back in. 'Take them all back to the dungeon. They are to be fed full rations.'

It had been easier than he thought to convince them, thought William, too easy. This worried him but the confession would help Klyesha and by proximity, also himself.

The Court was unusually crowded for the Assembly. Guards had to exclude people who simply couldn't fit into the space. Fortunately, Klyesha, Rachel and Lucca with Lucca's housekeeper all arrived early where they apprised the King of their evidence. He instructed Lucca that if things went awry today, he may be called upon to retell his story of Diana's arrest.

As was usual, the King dealt with minor issues first, his clerks recording details for his later consideration. William rarely made judgments in the Assembly, preferring now to consider them quietly at his leisure and relate the news directly to the petitioners. With these matters out of the way, William whispered to a guard to bring in Mutton and his fellow soldiers.

They were little changed from their first appearance. A less reputable group could hardly be imagined. Gerard sat somewhat apart from William on the royal dais, his hand cupped around his chin. He did not seem disturbed by the appearance of the soldiers.

Once the men were assembled in the space before the King, William addressed them, 'You were here before the Assembly two weeks ago in which you, Joseph Mutton, confessed to the rape of Diana Culaine, mother of Klyesha. Are you here to recant?'

Mutton shuffled on his feet. He knew he was between a rock and a hard place but loyalty to his wife and his children was uppermost in his mind.

'Aye, Sire,' he said.

'Go on,' directed William.

'I recant that I have no family. I do. A wife and two children. But that is all I recant, Sire. Everything else is true- the rape and that she's my daughter. I've been forced to stand here again. My family's being threatened,' he yelled. Everyone looked at the King.

William was momentarily stunned. This slippery fish had a backbone or more importantly, someone else's threats had been more dire. He was beginning to realise who that person must be. This time, William constrained his anger as he'd suspected this creature might turn against him.

'Someone has paid you to bring this falsehood to Court and now your failure to recant as well. That someone who has threatened your family, the Court will note, is not me. But I shall make it my duty to expose that person whomever they may be. As it stands, there are other witnesses to the arrest of Diana Culaine here in Court today. I call upon Lucca Culaine to relate his story.'

Nervously, Lucca stepped out from Klyesha's side into the space in front of the Assembly which Mutton and his men had vacated. He doffed his three-cornered hat and bowed before the King.

'Good morning, Your Majesty, he said, 'I am Lucca Culaine, clockmaker. What do you wish to know?'

'Master Culaine, I wish you to report to the Court your recollection of Diana Culaine's arrest.'

'As you wish, Sire,' Lucca explained in intimate detail the story he told to Klyesha of his involvement, his father's beating and of him following Diana in the cart to the galley at the Wharf.

'Thank you, Master Culaine. You may sit down.'

Gerard heard the story. He wasn't particularly troubled. How well could an 11 year old remember the facts?

'I now call on Margaret Leeman, housekeeper to Diana Culaine. Mistress Leeman was helped to the space by Lucca who stood beside her until a chair was brought for her.

'Mistress Leeman, how did you know Diana Culaine? Do you recall the morning of her arrest?'

'Your Majesty, I am Margaret Leeman, housekeeper to Clarice Culaine, Diana Culaine and now, Lucca Culaine. I knew Diana for four years since she came to her Aunt Clarice when her father, Alfredo, died. Though I am old, I recall her arrest very clearly. It was a most traumatic time. One does not forget such times even with the passing of years.'

'Indeed, your mind seems quite clear, Mistress. I have several questions to ask you. Before Mistress Diana Culaine was arrested in the hours of that morning, was she ever out of your sight? Did men enter the house and ravish Diana prior to Master Lucca Culaine seeing her in the street?

'No, Sire. No one entered the house. Diana was called out by the soldiers into the street. She dressed warmly and I believe she knew something was amiss for she hugged me and said goodbye then she left through the front door.'

Tears welled up in Klyesha's eyes as she heard the old housekeeper's story.

'Did she re-enter the house when the man went in to get her cats?

59

'No, she did not. She was very afraid. Anyway, one of the soldiers restrained her on the street.'

'Were there any other witnesses?'

'Many neighbours began coming out of their houses. There are many others who witnessed her arrest but the soldiers who remained outside had their muskets at the ready and prevented anyone interfering. They hit Lucca's father, Leo, on the head because he tried to pull Diana away from them. I went out to help him.'

'Thank you, Mistress Leeman, I have one more question for you. Did Diana have a man friend?'

'I couldn't be sure though there was talk she was meeting a young clockmaker of the Firm of Heysons. She did not speak of it openly, as the Firm were rivals of the Culaines. The Heyson business caused the bankruptcy of her father, Alfredo.'

'Most interesting,' said William, 'You may return to your place, Mistress Leeman.'

Shifting in his seat, Gerard became increasingly uncomfortable. These were respectable witnesses and each had chipped away at the credibility of Mutton and his decrepit soldiers. After the Assembly, he would begin arrangements made months ago. He must be away when William sought to question him.

'I have one final witness,' announced William, 'Diana was taken aboard a galley which sailed out to sea where she and her cats were loaded into a skiff and set adrift. I call on Captain Stevens who was captain of the galley 'The White Swan'.

An old man stepped forward dressed in a faded navy overcoat and half-length leather boots. He doffed his cap and bowed unsteadily to the King.

'I am Captain Stevens, Your Majesty, at Your Service!

'Captain Stevens,' asked William,' Were you the captain of 'The White Swan' which took Diana Culaine aboard after the arrest by soldiers?'

'Yes, Sire, to my regret.'

'Tell us what happened, please.'

'We was docked at the port, Sire. My ship 'The White Swan' was due to off load fabrics from the Silk Coast when a detachment of soldiers appeared at the wharf with a cart. They all carried muskets and they looked like trouble so I warned me men. The main man, a captain, came up the gang plank and demanded to see me. I got down from the bridge to meet him. Nasty fellow. He was full of threats. He showed me his orders which was to arrest a young woman who I could see was lying in the back of the cart. The orders said to 'Arrest' that's all. He explained she was a public nuisance who'd refused to have her cats destroyed and must be made an example of. Oh, says I. He said she was in defiance of a Public Health Order and refused to have her cats culled. They was sick of her resistance and wanted to solve the problem permanently. So, you would not shoot her then, I asked. No, he said, he had a better idea than murder. He said he wanted her placed in our skiff with her cats and set adrift. Oh, says I, that ain't in the orders. He got nasty then and aimed his musket at my chest. You do not refuse an officer, he says, following orders of the King. I didn't like the look of him nor his men and to be honest I wanted no trouble. The King could revoke me licence to trade at any time and me livelihood was sunk. Much as it went against me better judgement, I couldn't refuse him. I hope you will understand?'

'Perhaps,' said William, 'Go on.'

'So, we took charge of the young woman who was completely out cold and her crates of cats. We set sail out of the harbour as instructed until we reached the southern currents where we loaded her and her cats onto the skiff. I insisted she be given some supplies as well in case. It weren't me finest moment to be sure, but we was due back in Harbour to unload and we didn't have time to fetch her up onto an island, besides I was hoping the currents would eventually wash her up on the coast where people would find her and help. Is that what happened?'

'No, it isn't. She fetched up on a remoter island where she remained alone with her daughter for the next 18 years,' said the King.

The Captain looked very shame-faced and pale, 'Oh, she had a child too!' He shook his head. 'I do regret the whole incident, Your Majesty, I do.'

'Captain Stevens, did any sailor or yourself, assault this young women or ravish her while she was aboard your ship'?

'On me honour, Sire, I made sure no one touched her. I watched over her meself.'

'Was she awake when she was set adrift?'

'No, Sire. She was not. Our doctor gave her a sleeping draught lest she fight us or throw herself out of the skiff. We tied her, the crates of cats and her oars into the skiff so none could fall out in case of bad weather. I am sorry for me part in this, indeed I am,' confessed the Captain.

'I believe you, Captain. The officer who persuaded you gave you little choice. He is more to blame. May your public confession go some ways to assuage your guilt.'

'Yes, Sire, thank you, Sire.'

'You may sit down,' said William.

By this time, Klyesha was openly sobbing at the full story of her mother's treatment. Cast off never to see a friendly face again, excepting her own. It was truly an inhuman punishment.

William stood, 'Let the Assembly be apprised, the father of this young Klyesha Culaine is a man unknown and he is certainly not this Joseph Mutton, who despite his denials has been proven a liar by all these witnesses. The whole episode is a shameful one, a stain on justice and also on my Father, who was King at the time, for without his instructions Diana Culaine would never have been set adrift to meet her fate, a banishment that is as cruel as it is abhorrent. Today is not about revenge. The people who gave their testimony truthfully and openly have nothing to fear. As to those who come here and lie to my face, justice will seek them out. As compensation to Klyesha Culaine for the treatment of her mother, Diana, I award 300 gold sovereigns. If she is to seek out her true father, that is her own business, no one else's. I will make an example of anyone who approaches her to harass her in any way. She is entirely blameless in this matter, a victim of unjust laws, the panic which follows on from the terrible tragedy of childhood disease. We now know cats never gave children measles as the disease broke out many times after all the cats of the Kingdom had disappeared. All the cleansing of the cats did was encourage rodent pests to multiply. The return of cats, thanks to Klyesha, has saved our harvests now and into the future. This is the legacy of Klyesha Culaine. She is the saviour of our harvests, let it be known. This Assembly is closed!'

Gerard hurried into his apartments calling for his wife, Sophia, 'Make haste and assemble your boxes. We are leaving now for the mountains!'

'The mountains!' wailed Sophia, 'At this time of the year!'

'Do not gainsay me, woman! We have little time, do you wish me in prison?'

'No, never. Has it come to this!' she wept, 'What are we to do?'

'We flee, that is what we do. No time for tears,' he said, shoving her. 'Get moving!' She hurried to the cupboard in her bedchamber where her boxes sat packed and ready for such a day. They contained spare clothes, shoes, her jewels and money. She grabbed furs from her bed.

Gerard called frantically for his footmen to ready their carriage. They were to strap fresh horses to the back of the carriage who could easily be swapped when the front ones became exhausted. 'Hurry!' he shouted at them.

Servants gathered up the boxes while Sophia glanced uneasily around her room. What would she regret leaving behind? She noticed her diary on the bedside and grabbing it and some quills and ink shoved them in a silk draw string bag. Gathering her cloak and pulling on stout boots, she was ready just in time for Gerard to push her out the door, 'Go,' he said, 'To the stables. I will meet you there.'

He raced to the Royal Strongrooms and ordered them be opened. The guard was reluctant and received a stinging backhander to the face for his delay, 'By order of the King, open it,' screamed Gerard. The guard complied. Gerard rushed into the lead-lined room grabbed muskets and shot and powder and a small sack of gold, 'Get out of my way,' he yelled at the guard. Gerard ran down the main corridor of the Palace only to hear the King and his retinue coming out of the Assembly. Hiding in a maid's cupboard, he waited until they passed. His chest heaving, he whipped out only to trip a servant who was carrying a tray, 'Get out of my way, imbecile!' he yelled. The man lay spreadeagled on the tiles, the remains of an afternoon tea scattered around him. He was the last man to see Gerard flee.

Almost out of breath, Gerard finally reached the carriage and screamed at the footmen to leave. He was relieved to see Sophia, red-faced, already installed in the carriages' interior. If she had not made it on time, he would have left her. Nothing would stop him now. 'I hope you have a good reason for this.' She hissed at him. Unable to speak, all he could do was scowl.

Chapter Five

William left the Assembly and escorted Klyesha, Rachel and Lucca to his apartments. He felt drained and guilty. This had been such a public humiliation for Klyesha, rubbing her face in her mother's agonising treatment, stamping illegitimate on her birth forever and then his own Father's involvement as King! Was he so cruel? Did he even know the effect of those orders on Diana? How could he have sanctioned this? His own soldiers? His own men? His father was dead from five years ago when he'd had a stroke, suddenly and awfully. William had been bereft but how would his father have answered those questions if he were still alive? William knew the compensation money for Klyesha was a mere token, a public show of guilt by the Crown. He knew Klyesha didn't care about the money. But what could he possibly do to help her overcome the events of this day? When they all reached his sitting room, guilt sat heavy on his shoulders. All he could do was say he was sorry.

Klyesha wouldn't even look at him. She stared into her lap, tears still sliding down her cheeks with Rachel's arm around her. How William wished it was him comforting her. He called for refreshments, including cider. He thanked Lucca for his testimony and asked about his father. Mistress Leeman looked at the King but Lucca answered him, 'My father, Leo is dead these ten years back,' replied Lucca. 'He never really recovered from the beating he got that day.'

'How very unfortunate, Lucca, please accept my condolences,' said William, more waves of guilt washing over him. How much harm his father and his father's men had done to this family! He didn't know what else to say except, 'If there is anything I can do for you, please let me know!'

'It is not your guilt to bear,' answered Lucca, wise beyond his years, 'You are not your father. While today was very painful for Klyesha, at least today we heard the truth of Diana's story. What was done to my dear cousin will not be easily forgotten now. Why is it the innocent suffer when people panic? Why do they blame those who have nothing to do with their troubles?'

'It is human nature, unfortunately, to lash out at anyone or anything when tragedies occur. However, this reaction only compounds the evil rather than lessoning it.'

'Is this why no one stepped in to save her?' asked Klyesha. 'Did they blame her for their children's deaths?'

'They blamed her cats,' answered William, 'and her because she defended them. It was a witch hunt, pure and simple. They almost drowned her too, a common punishment for witches. My father, though his reputation has been besmirched today, outlawed cruelty to those women named witches during his reign. He banned any witch hunts, gaoled witch hunters and released from gaol any accused of witchery.'

'In name, at least, but not always in fact,' commented Klyesha, lifting her red face to look at him. William turned away and sighed. When the servants brought more food and drink, he excused himself, coward perhaps that he was, but it was also to allow Klyesha to go home and recover in peace away from crowds. He stood and bowed to them and addressing Klyesha said, 'I will be in touch.' To Lucca and Mistress Leeman he said, 'Thank you for your testimony today. Please ensure Klyesha returns home safely. My carriage will be ready to take you home when you have need of it,'. He bowed again, 'I wish you adieu.'

Lucca left Klyesha and Rachel at their door with instructions to call on him whenever they had need of him.

Inside her room Klyesha flung herself on her bed and cried her heart out until no more tears came. William thought he was doing well for her, then why did she feel so bad, violated even, so alone, so abandoned and so far from him as never before? A gulf had opened up between them which might never be spanned. Indeed, did she even want it spanned? Did she want closeness to a man whose father had banished and humiliated her mother? To the man who thought money might compensate for the 18 years her mother spent cast out of society to survive on a remote uninhabited island? No, no, no, no, no, she kept repeating to herself until exhausted she slept.

William's guilt rapidly morphed to anger. He went straight to the apartments where Gerard and his wife, Sophia, resided throwing open the doors and yelling for his brother. 'Where is he?' he

65

accosted the first servant he could find, the one Gerard had already knocked to the ground. The man answered in a dignified tone, straightening his doublet, 'Sire?'

'Where is my brother?'

'Sire,' answered the man, 'I believe your brother and his wife have left.'

'Where? Where has he gone?' William's voice was raised.

'Perhaps the stables?'

William raced out of the building to the stables and grabbed the first groom he saw, 'Where is the Prince?'

The groom looked afraid for the King had never spoke to him before, 'I saw them,' he offered.

'Where?'

'Their carriage was hitched up to a set of horses, Sire. They left not half an hour ago.'

'What direction?'

'I do not know, Sire.'

'Then find out and come tell me when you do.'

'Yes, Sire.' William ran to fetch Paxton in the barracks, one of only two soldiers he really trusted. In the barracks the soldiers were lounging around, their kits half on or off, some polishing muskets others washing their clothes in tubs of soapy water. 'Where is Captain Paxton?' he asked the assembled men.

'In his room, Sire' replied a sergeant.

'Show me,' asked William.

Paxton was writing up a report about Joseph Mutton and his men whom he'd just finished questioning. He jumped up from his desk and saluted, 'Sire.'

'Sit, sit,' insisted William, 'Listen. Gerard has fled. You know what that means.'

'Yes, Sir, I had my suspicions in his involvement with Joseph Mutton.'

'I need him brought back now. He sought to discredit Klyesha and by association, me. He wants my Crown, Paxton. We must stop him.'

'Yes, Sire. I will arrange a detachment of troops to follow him and bring him back.'

'Bring him back unharmed, I wish to speak to him.'

'As you wish, Sire.'

'Now, go, immediately!' William strode out of the barracks, his orders causing a flurry behind him. Paxton would bring him back if anyone could.

By morning Klyesha was over grief and trawling deeply through disgust. Disgusted at this Kingdom's treatment of her mother, the Assembly's avid hanging onto all the minute and embarrassing details of her life and William's approach, his solution involving compensation. At the bottom of it all deep, deep, down in the recess of her heart was her bitter disappointment. The slurs and stains flung against her had stuck and created an impenetrable barrier to her ever becoming William's Queen. The sheer magnitude of such an idea, of her, a cat fur wearing ignorant savage, even sitting as an equal next to William was the height of stupidity. This was very clear to her now. She would not seek out her father, even if he was still alive. She wanted only to leave all this grief in the past.

She called to Rachel and while they ate breakfast outlined her plan. As soon as the 300 gold sovereigns arrived, she would leave some for the house's upkeep and the rest would be used to buy a carriage and horses, supplies, clothes, even muskets. She would hire a driver and she would need one other man to join them. 'Would Lucca come do you think?'

'Perhaps,' said Rachel, intrigued, 'Where are we going?'

'We're going to explore this country,' said Klyesha, more determined than she'd ever been before. 'We shall take our maps and explore all the places far away from here. One thing may alarm you, however.'

'Oh?'

'We will have to appear as men.'

'Men?'

'Yes. We will have to wear breeches and dress and act as men. Two women like us would be too easily set upon. We shall have muskets and two men to accompany us.'

'And what is our purpose?' asked Rachel.

'We go to explore and see our purpose as we find it. All being well, we enjoy the scenery, however, I don't envisage all being well and then we may find out our purpose.'

'Oh!' said Rachel. She wasn't following. Was Klyesha mad? Lost her senses due to yesterday's trauma? What was she thinking? However, Rachel could see her determination and one so determined was not easily dissuaded. She could not let her go on this adventure alone in her still distraught state. She was a danger to herself. No, she and Lucca would go with her and keep her from harm. 'I suppose I had better pack,' answered Rachel.

Klyesha wasn't surprised she'd been so easy to convince, then Rachel had a rebellious streak too. One which chafed at the docile, female role. In her, she'd found a fellow soulmate, a woman who didn't want to be controlled. In honour of her mother, Klyesha vowed men would never control her, forestall her or circumscribe her life. Eighteen years in the confines of the island was enough for one lifetime. Now she was determined to be free.

Phillip, the Estate manager, arrived the next day with a purse of sovereigns. 'With the compliments of His Majesty,' he said placing the purse in Klyesha's hands. 'Is there anything you wish me to procure for you, Mistress?'

'Not at all, Phillip. We intend to be circumspect and save this money, for eked out slowly, it will keep us comfortable for many years.' Phillip was offered refreshments but he refused and left.

'So, we aren't getting Phillip's help?' asked Rachel.

'No, for then the King will know what we are doing.' And he will prevent us, she thought. 'We will procure what we need ourselves.'

Rachel nodded. It was the start to independence. She went out to the road to hire a carriage. Together they would go to convince Lucca to come, a task she didn't expect would be easy.

It had been days and still no news. Gerard's rapid departure was sure evidence of his guilt. Not being found proved he planned this escape and was holed up somewhere while Paxton and his men searched in vain for him. William was beside himself with frustration, so he went to the barracks and insisted on sword practice with some of the soldiers. He sweated in his gambeson dodging blow after blow. A blow to his helmet sent him reeling. Recovering, he continued fighting but proved too slow and was forced to surrender with a wooden sword pointed to his throat. 'Thank you, soldier,' he told the man. 'Too many fine dinners,' he said, smiling and patting his stomach. He threw the sword away and placed the gambeson on a pole. After drinking and resting, he ordered his horse saddled and food and spare clothes in his saddlebag. He had to take someone with him and he chose Rufus, his lieutenant.

Passing through the town gates, he received the day's password and tomorrow's in case of being longer away than expected. His heart told him to ride to see Klyesha but his brain said no it was too soon after the traumatic Assembly. She needed more time to recover and he was afraid his compensation payment was not well received by her. How did money compensate for what was done to her mother? How did it compensate for her own humiliation in front of the crowded Assembly? She may well hate him. Dragging her family name through the mud earnt no favours, but what else could he have done in response to Mutton's lies?

The more he thought Gerard was behind Klyesha's humiliation, the angrier he got. Spurring his horse, they cantered through the countryside, down hedge-lined lanes, through pine forests and past the fine sheen of green which showed winter crops breaking through the soil. The men's and the horses' breaths puffed out white in the icy air but soon the horses needed a rest. To run them too hard in the cold was not fair to them.

They were surrounded by countryside, no way stations or inns anywhere. Fortunately, they'd brought provisions, so they camped beneath some oak trees and while the horses nuzzled for grass, they ate.

'What news of Paxton, Sire?' asked Rufus.

'No news. No news at all. Do you have any clues where Gerard and his wife may have fled?

'We soldiers don't usually mingle with servants. I suspect some of them may know. Certainly, they could say where Gerard has gone in the past. Have you asked them?'

William blanched, 'I have not. I assumed Paxton would have tracked him down by now. I will do so as soon as we return.' They continued to eat their bread, dried figs, nuts and drank watered wine from their flasks.

'It's peaceful here,' observed William, breathing out and watching the horses graze.

'Yes, the City and the Castle are not places for quiet contemplation.'

'No, they're not,' agreed William. 'Quite frankly, I'm sick of seeing petitioners, Court hangers on, everyone out to get something done or given to them by me. I'm beginning to see the benefits of the island life Klyesha lived. No souls to disturb them. Only the solid wind, mighty sea and the cats for company,' he sighed.

'I don't envy you,' said Rufus frankly. Your life really isn't your own he thought. It's obvious he loves this woman, Klyesha. Why defend her in front of all the Court? Yet how can he have such an unsuitable woman as his Consort? For once Rufus was grateful he was an ordinary soldier.

'Out of interest...' interrupted Rufus.

William was tossing over in his mind how his life was controlled. He was King but not King of his life. 'Yes?'

'After Gerard, who is next in line for the throne?'

William could see Rufus's reasoning. If Gerard was banished or punished and passed over for the throne and if William wasn't around who was next? 'Gerard and his wife have no children so it would be my cousin, Henry, who was next in line.'

'And how old is he?'

'He's 28, two years younger than me. He runs his own estate in the Western Province. I don't know what he produces. Sheep or goats, probably. He hates the Court, the Castle and the City and told me so last time I saw him that he'd never appear in any of them again.'

'Oh,' asked Rufus.

'He said,' and here William laughed, 'At least sheep are honest. If they're hungry they run to you for oats or hay. If they have decent grass, you never see them. I think he was referring to the burden of looking after people. These spoilt harvests have taken a toll on everyone and I'm ultimately responsible.'

'It's also about other people doing their job.'

William knew to whom he was referring, Gerard. 'True, I can't do everything yet I also need to know if someone isn't doing their job.'

They sat in silence and time until Rufus asked, 'So what is your plan for today?'

William didn't really have one. He knew it was pointless trying to find Gerard himself, he just needed some space to allow his thoughts to wander. 'Let us finish this meal and take a different road. We shall find some inn or even a barn to rest in overnight.'

Rufus nodded. He'd thought as much. There was no plan. William may be King but he was not always certain of his direction.

As it would soon happen, they would have action thrust upon them.

Klyesha and Rachel were laughing fit to burst. They'd constructed padded cummerbunds to disguise their waists and give them a straight torso like a man's yet wearing these padded accessories under their shirts made them both look too fat. The result was hilarious.

'Would it be easier to bind our breasts,' asked Rachel.

'Mine are too big!' explained Klyesha, 'Silly as these are they will have to do. We haven't got time to change them.'

Not sure why they didn't have time, Rachel had to agree. What was the haste, she thought? Was it to try to get away before William might visit them? Would that be so bad anyway? However, this new adventure gave Klyesha red cheeks and smiling eyes after the unhappiness of Court.

Lucca surprisingly had given in to their suggestion to accompany them quite quickly. Little did they know how bored he was in the shop and how in need of adventure. The money from Klyesha and Rachels' purchases in his shop would keep his household afloat for months. Now would be a good time to adventure, his delighted face told them. He'd shaken hands with the women and agreed to meet them the next day. He apologised as he hurried them off, explaining he had a lot to organise.

Wearing breeches, shirts and doublets was not enough. 'Now for the big leap,' warned Klyesha, taking up some sewing scissors and handing them to Rachel, 'You can do my hair first.'

They stood in the laundry while Rachel snipped off Klyesha's beautiful black hair. Cook was horrified when she came with a basket of folded washing.

'My goodness no, Mistress Klyesha, what are you thinking?'

'Do I look like a man yet?' she asked.

Cook tut-tuttered, 'Never! You're too pretty but if you let me cut your hair you might pass for a boy.' Rachel gratefully handed over the scissors. Soon Klyesha sported a short haircut of the like men had who wore no wigs. 'There, that's better,' said Cook, admiring her work. 'Now you, mistress,' she said to Rachel.

Protesting, Rachel reluctantly submitted to being shorn. Soon her red gold hair lay in heaps on the laundry floor like pieces of sun. 'I never knew I had so much hair!' she exclaimed. Klyesha handed her a mirror and Rachel screamed, 'How could you!' She was almost in tears.

'Think of how much time you'll save in the mornings and at night not having to pin up your hair or put it up in rags? Sacrifices must be made Rachel, if we are to have an adventure.'

Rachel nodded, still distraught. All my lovely hair she kept thinking. Cook gathered up the hair and put it in the fire where it created an awful smell. 'Sorry,' she apologised, 'I forgot it was unpleasant.'

'No matter,' said Klyesha, fully aware when she explained to Cook what they were doing more unpleasantries would follow.

After dinner she told Cook who burst into tears. 'I'm to be left on my own again,' she sobbed aware as a servant she had no say in the matter.

'I will leave you Tom,' soothed Klyesha, 'he can't come with us and you may ask your niece to stay here with you for company.'

'Thank you, mistress,' Cook bowed. It was a little better, she thought, at least her mistress was thinking of her.

'We leave tomorrow after Lucca arrives. Can you please pack us food for a few weeks? Baskets of apples, oranges, boxes of figs and nuts, a ham and some water in large bottles. Also a Flint. Do you have one?

'Yes, I have spares. And blankets, bedding?'

'Blankets, yes and cushions and an oilcloth in case it rains and we need to sleep outside.'

'Outside?' Cook was alarmed.

'We will have two men with us, Cook, as well as muskets. We shall be perfectly fine,' assured Klyesha.

'I hope so, Mistress and I hope you won't be long either.'

'No weeks rather than months, I believe,' replied Klyesha, 'I shall leave you sovereigns for provisions. Allow no one into the house apart from your niece and the gardener and don't let Tom out till we are gone a half day at least.'

'Of course, Mistress. I'll get to with them supplies.'

'Excellent!' Klyesha gave her a hug, 'and don't worry. Worry helps no one.'

'Yes, Mistress.' Cook bowed again and the women retired to their bed chambers to finish packing.

Chapter Six

After leaving the City, the roads deteriorated the further they travelled from the Capitol. Bands of ragged impoverished paupers were camped in stands of trees near rivers. On hearing the carriage, they ran to the side of the road with their hands outstretched. Lucca warned the women not to stop or throw anything to them. 'They will attack us,' he said. 'Good intentions won't count with them. They are starving and desperate.' Klyesha and Rachel reluctantly agreed and the carriage sped on.

'So many!' commented Klyesha when the carriage passed three more such groups during the day. 'It appears they stay near rivers for fish and water,' observed Lucca.

It was the scale of the problem which troubled them all. What would happen when these ragged groups reached the City? Would mobs tear the City apart? Would they accost innocent citizens and pillage their homes? The lack of flour was having far reaching effects and Klyesha wondered how it would all end.

The cultivated fields and stands of fruit trees began to make way for gently wooded hills and broader rivers as they travelled further north. Deer and hares darted away from them at the side of the road, hawks and falcons began circling in the grey sky above, drifting on updrafts of warm air seemingly resting but ever ready to plummet to the ground when they saw prey. Fat pigeons cooed from oak branches and red squirrels ran up trees startled by the carriage wheels. Every now and then a white farmhouse peeped out from the woodlands, their red roofs contrasting with the green lushness of the trees' canopies.

Evening was not long off when Lucca asked where the women wanted to spend the night. 'You could sleep in the carriage while Jack and I can sleep on the ground near it,' he suggested.

'Are there no way stations near or perhaps a farmer's barn?' asked Klyesha.

'We have about an hour before dark,' replied Lucca, consulting his fob watch. 'We must find one soon.'

The sky gradually lightened and to their left a mesmerising colour show of pink and orange layers like shaved skins of fruit heralded the sunset. The woods darkened too and owls began to sweep through the trees in search of mice. A huge grey owl, its face a white dish with massive black eyes, almost collided with the carriage but swerved at the last minute.

Rachel knew owls were associated with death in their Kingdom and crossed herself in case. Klyesha noticed but didn't ask. The adrenaline of escaping the Castle and the City was still strong in her veins. She wanted nothing to spoil the joy of freedom this journey brought her.

'There in that woodland ahead, is that a farmhouse?' she asked pointing.

As the carriage neared the spot, the farmhouse was revealed: a heavy timber building with a thatched roof, small glazed windows and a solid metal studded door.

'We can only ask,' suggested Lucca.

Arriving, they alighted from the carriage, their horses' backs steaming in the cool air.

Klyesha took the initiative and knocked on the door. No one answered yet a faint glow from a fireplace showed someone was in residence. So, she called out in her lowest voice possible, 'Hello! We are travellers seeking to spend the night in your barn, hello!'

They saw a face round the edge of a curtain and heard the door unbolt, 'What is it you want?' asked an elderly woman. She had a long piece of wood like a club in her hand.

'We wish you no harm,' said Klyesha quickly, 'Only to spend the night in your barn if you have one. We can pay.' She held out a few silver shillings.

The woman grunted, ''Tis always bandits about now, young master, you'd be better off inside here with me and my husband behind a strong door.'

'As you wish, mistress. Thank you kindly.' Klyesha asked Jack to get their boxes. Lucca went to help him. 'Can we water our horses? Do you have a trough?'

'Yes, in the field next to this house there on the left near the barn,' said the old woman.

Soon they were established in front of the fire, bowls of soup in their hands. The farmer's wife introduced her husband, a frail old man who sat in a rocking chair near the fire. 'He's John and I'm Millicent.'

Klyesha and Rachel introduced themselves as 'Carl', 'Robert' and Lucca, indicating it was Jack who was outside tending to the horses. The couple's four wolfhounds were curled contentedly by the fire.

'You from the City?' asked Millicent.

'Yes,' said 'Robert', 'We are on a journey to the mountains.'

'Oh,' said Millicent, 'Good luck with that.'

'Oh?' asked 'Carl', 'Is there something the matter?'

'All is lawless,' muttered John, 'Nowadays it ain't safe venturing from your house no more.'

Millicent added, 'Is them gangs. Some of 'em on horseback, some just walking but all with weapons mostly swords or pikes. They came last week and set our haystack on fire in the middle of winter too when we need it to feed our cows. It was criminal. The dogs were barking mad, only thing what kept them away from the house.'

'They didn't bark at us,' said Lucca patting one of the huge wolfhounds.

'No, they got a sixth sense. They know a friend when they smells him,' said John.

Jack came in rubbing hands and Millicent passed him a bowl of soup. He found a stool near the fire, thanked Millicent and gratefully started on his soup. He was wary of the dogs but they left him alone after sniffing him.

'Aren't you afraid to stay here?' asked 'Robert'.

'Where else do we go?' asked Millicent, 'We have no house in the City.'

'I do,' said 'Carl' 'and you're welcome to my house anytime if you find you can't stay here.'

'My that is polite of you, young master,' said John, 'One day when I'm gone, Millicent might take you up on that offer.'

'My pleasure,' grinned 'Carl', 'Now do tell us more about the bandits.'

They spent another hour discussing the problem. The cause was easy to discern: poverty; lack of food and shelter; spoiled harvests. The solution, however, was much harder.   Millicent wanted to know why the King's troops weren't restoring order and patrolling the highways as it was his responsibility. 'Carl' felt embarrassed for William explaining that perhaps he didn't know about them. The discussion disturbed all the travellers each wondering if they might be attacked at any time on their journey. Perhaps it would become more of an ordeal than a pleasure.

In the warm double bed in a simple wood-lined room provided to them for the night, 'Robert' and 'Carl' discussed their trepidations. 'Robert' was more cautious while 'Carl' refused to have her plans curtailed. She wanted to reach the mountains, even to enter another country, at least to have knowledge of their own. Why this was important to her, she didn't say but she had an instinct about it. She was determined to have the measure of the Kingdom.

Jack and Lucca lay on rugs near the fire, hand knitted blankets over them. Their main fear was for the women. They spoke quietly so as not to be heard by the old couple in their adjoining bedroom. They might look like boys and it seemed the old couple had been fooled but the women's real identity would soon be found out if they were captured and manhandled. They parried back and forth with ideas until they both agreed Klyesha, that is 'Carl', would be convinced to return to the City in the morning. They would gainsay no variation to this return. Rachel or 'Robert' would do anything her friend told her to do.

Yet in the morning, their resolution of the night before could not be set in motion. After dawn, when the old couple were already awake and Millicent was refreshing the fire to brew warm water for porridge and their visitors were still abed, a ruckus was heard outside of the house. Forty or more men were marching down the highway, carrying oak staffs, axes, pikes and a few swords. They did not march in step, rather they shuffled along journey-worn, their faces pinched and their legs unsteady. Jack had fortuitously hidden their carriage and horses in the couple's barn and bolted and locked the door with the key provided by Millicent, otherwise the men might have seized both their carriage and their horses to ease their own journey. Their leader, slightly taller than the others with black curly hair, seeing the farmstead went up to the door and knocked hard demanding entry. Millicent put her finger to her lips to prevent John calling out. The door was too sturdy to move even with axes as it was studded with heavy nails alongside metal strips. At dusk, John had shuttered the windows from the inside and though the glass might be broken no one could break in through them.

The wolfhounds began baying deep, throaty bass sounds which woke their visitors and set the hairs up on the mob leader's neck. Millicent motioned to the visitors all to be quiet.

'We just seek a bit of bread' pleaded the man from the other side of the door. 'Jus' a wee bite of bread,' he continued. Millicent shook her head as all six in the house waited nervously for what would happen next. Millicent again shook her head vigorously when 'Carl' gestured towards the kitchen.

Again, the man called for food and again the hounds began baying long, low sounds fit to raise the dead. A tense silence grew as they heard the man swear and move away from the door. More men yelled curses at them from the road. Everyone in the house was astonished to hear so many more outside. For minutes they stood frozen in silence listening for other sounds of attack however it seemed the men had given up and were moving away from them along the road in the direction 'Carl' and her party had come.

John went to a piece of wood in the sidewall and carefully slid it back to reveal a peep hole disguised on the outside of their house by a clump of Ivy growing up the wall. He looked carefully for a minute, slid back the wood and returned to whisper, 'They're going down the road towards the City. Looks like there was about forty of them, there was.'

Millicent motioned them all to sit and hush while she began their breakfast getting Jack to stoke the fire with more wood. After about half an hour, John checked the peephole again and reported they'd disappeared.

'You really do have a fortress here,' said 'Carl' admiringly.

'Yes,' agreed Millicent, 'It's how we've survived this long.'

Everyone admired the old couple after this encounter and wondered at their resilience. 'Carl' and his friends were determined to help them out before they all left, so Jack and Lucca set to chopping wood while 'Carl' and 'Robert' fetched it inside and stacked all by the fireplace. They helped feed the animals and the women stopped themselves helping Millicent in the kitchen to maintain the disguise of being boys.

'Carl' spoke with her men outside, 'Well, it seems we cannot return to the City even if you felt this would be the safest course as if we go back the same way, we might run into that mob. Even our muskets would not deal with so many. We would soon be overrun.'

Lucca looked at Jack and reluctantly nodded but he remained terribly worried as finding another farmstead to shelter in on their journey, similar to the old couple's fortress was not likely.

'Carl' arranged to buy more food from Millicent: excess apples; dried prunes and oranges and some pots of preserves. Millicent was delighted with her two sovereigns.

They thanked their guests, shook hands and farewelled them at the door.

'We should have bought a wolfhound,' said Lucca from his seat next to Jack on the carriage. 'Carl' shook her head and said, 'Apart from good locks, they were the old couple's only defence. However, if we see any I might be tempted.'

'I thought you only loved cats,' commented 'Robert'.

'Now I see the advantage of dogs,' said 'Carl' laughing, 'Nothing is scarier than those big baying hounds!' They both laughed. The tension in the morning had been intense and they were happy to be on their way again.

William and Rufus had been riding all afternoon. They followed a road still on the plains but could see the faint purple of steep hills and mountains in the distance. Fields remained cultivated, the forests were creeping closer and farmsteads now very scattered. They slowed to a trot scanning the horizon and seeing the sun sinking like a stone in the west. Up ahead on the road was a faint puff of pink dust. William assumed it was perhaps some farmer herding his sheep. They both continued now at a walking pace to give the horses a break. Rufus's sensors picked up first that the dust was not sheep. 'I believe a group of men are ahead on the road, Sire.'

William's hackles raised. Would they be friend or foe? he thought. 'What should we do?' he asked.

'If they're on foot we can outride them,' explained Rufus, 'However, as a precaution have your sword ready.'

William unbuckled his sword and lay it still in its sheath across his lap. As they got closer, they could see indeed it was a large group of men. 'What the devil are they doing out here in such a mob?' cursed William.

'Bandits,' explained Rufus, 'Desperate, hungry with nothing to lose therefore dangerous. We should leave the road and get back into the forest.' However, the road was now lined by stone walls too high and wide for the horses to jump.

'Should we retreat?' asked William, but as he asked the mob began running towards them. Retreat would not be so easy.

'I say we run at them,' said Rufus, 'The horses will frighten them. They'll get out of the way.' It was a good theory but as many theories go, it was untested. Rufus and William spurred their horses on and tired though they were the horses responded. The noise from the men ahead suddenly broke through the dust cloud and William was horrified to see pikes and clubs raised. Their horses shied and the men had to fight to keep them straight. 'Fast as you can,' shouted Rufus, more confident than he was.

William braced himself for the attack, raising his sword in his right arm. The mob was taken unawares, sure the horses would slow in the now narrow road. They screamed and threw themselves aside as no one was commanding them it was every man for himself.

William felt the crunch of bone as his horse hit men and scattered their bodies. He slashed with his sword at the vicious pikes aimed at him and his horse, the blows jarring his arm. Rufus slashed expertly with his sword aiming at anyone who approached his horse. The mob parted before them, the screams of those at the front deterring those behind from getting close enough to attack. Rufus was through but cantered on wanting to distance himself from any thrown pikes or stones the men might simply pluck from the walls. William was parrying well but his horse was tiring. A pike had slashed her chest, not deeply but enough to frighten the horse and she began to panic. William fought with her for the safety of distance. Just as he was through the mob, a man aimed a pike at his leg stabbing him in the thigh. William cried out to Rufus but managed to pull the pike from his leg and throw it back at the attackers. Blood was coursing from his leg as he exited the mob spurring his horse on.

Rufus turned to see William unsteady in his saddle, white-faced with shock. He slowed to grab William's horse's rains and yelled at him to hang onto the saddle. Thus, they cantered along the road until a break in the wall where they made for a wood. The wood sloped gently to a stream which they crossed and headed up the other side. Only then did Rufus dismount and rush to William who was swaying in his saddle. He pulled him down and checking his thigh, got rags from his saddlebag to bind it. William winced in pain, afraid the mob would follow them.

'I can't see them.' gasped Rufus, 'Here on this slope we can see all the way to the road.' William looked up and was relieved to see he was right. The road lay in the distance and though obscured by the stone walls none of their attackers had followed them through the gap in the wall.

'We injured quite a few,' said William, his hand putting pressure on his wound, 'Perhaps they thought better of pursuing us,' as the pain began to peak.

'What we do next for shelter is of most import,' observed Rufus, his brow furrowed looking at William. If the King died on his watch... He gave William some watered wine, 'Drink as much of this as you can. We can refill from the stream. You need to replace the blood you've lost.'

'I shall be fine, thank you Rufus,' said William, 'Find us some shelter.'

'Yes, Sire.' Rufus took his horse and William's horse to water them at the stream. He washed the blood from William's mare. She was freaked and nervous but the wound was superficial. He thought she'd recover without care but shouldn't be ridden hard for a while. He brought the horses back and tethered William's to some low hung branches on an oak. 'Will you be alright if I go and search out some shelter?'

'Yes go,' said William. Really, he just wanted quiet to rest and recover. 'But give me some food then go,' he called out. Rufus did so and left moving through the trees leading his horse and keeping to the slope beside the stream to survey more of the landscape and not get lost.

William cursed himself for his decision to leave the City with only one soldier and now this injury which might be the death of him. Gerard would win and in his hands the Kingdom would suffer even more than under him. He was ashamed to think of the lawlessness of the countryside and him hardly aware of it existing. After a period of negative self-reflection, his thoughts went to Klyesha who he was pleased to think remained safe in the City. He so much missed her company and the thought of never seeing her again made him heartsick. He drank more water and ate more food but on trying to stand he fell over and cursed his vulnerability and his situation afresh.

Rufus wandered some few miles before he found an unoccupied woodsman's hut providing a fireplace and sleeping platforms, some kitchen pots and utensils. Plain but practical. He called a few times to see if anyone was about but heard no replies, so he left his horse tethered there and set back alone to fetch William.

He thought William was dead propped up against the tree but he was merely exhausted and asleep. Rufus gently roused him and with difficulty put his good leg into the stirrup on his horse causing him great pain. He strapped him on with rope to the saddle and urged him to lean forward to rest while he led William's mare gently along the slope to the woodsman's hut.

Inside, he put William on a sleeping platform under blankets while he set a fire in the fireplace, got water to boil and set to cooking the dried meat they carried while William slept. The hut had a lantern which Rufus lit and placed on the crude table. He also put a pot of boiled water there to cool so they could drink in the night and he could bathe William's wound. He bolted the door with a heavy piece of wood which simply slid across the door frame secured by iron straps. William was woken and urged to eat hot food. The warmth of the food pushed some of the shock and injury from his muscles. Rufus checked his wound which no longer bled as profusely letting him loosen the binding after bathing it well. He elevated William's leg with some staves of wood and asked if he was comfortable. 'You are quite the nurse, Rufus,' smiled William weakly, 'Now you need to rest too.'

'Indeed, I'm truly grateful to find this hut,' said Rufus, stoking the fire. 'To be out amongst the cold all night would not have gone well for you.' William only smiled and let a disturbed sleep wash over him.

Having taken their leave of Millicent and John that morning, they spent the next few hours travelling on roads which became gradually steeper, farmlands decreased and woodland spread out on either side of them.

Klyesha decided she needed a history lesson. 'Rachel,' she asked, 'Why is so little known of the foreign lands which surround us? Why don't we trade with them?'

Rachel considered the question, 'There's no one answer. Previous Kings have made sure we produce what we need here. We've learned lessons from other's mistakes, I believe.'

'Which mistakes?'

'The countries near us have traded, do trade amongst themselves but not without conflict. Each tries to gain advantage over the others, to get higher prices for say, their grain, and to disadvantage the other countries which grow grain.'

'But if they co-operated, they could fix the price of grain to each's advantage. They'd be more powerful operating as a bloc.'

'I suppose so,' agreed Rachel, 'However they don't look at things that way. They blockade ports or sink supply ships to get an advantage.'

'Wouldn't that cause wars?'

'There have been wars, some for many years. In the long run everyone suffers, so we here in the Kingdom have kept out of it, kept to ourselves. We may be accused of being backward or too conservative and so on but up until the last year it played to our strengths.'

'And in the last year?'

'Well as you know, we had good harvests but pests spoilt our grain.'

'And if we traded, we might have smoothed over this dip, hiccup or slump whatever you might call it, with imported grain therefore we may not have this situation of armed lawless men in gangs wandering about the countryside.'

'Yes, it's true not trading in a famine is a great disadvantage, yet this is only one year. We've avoided many years of conflict and trading wars previously.'

'So, what does the future hold? This increasing lawlessness is a serious problem for William. Where might it lead?'

'I hate to think. We do have an army, the King's Army, yet I'm not sure if it's big enough to stem a widespread rebellion. Do you think it's coming?'

'A rebellion? Yes, it's possible.'

'So, if it does come where are we safer? In the City or in the country?' asked Rachel.

'Perhaps not anywhere in the Kingdom. Perhaps we'd be better off on my island.'

Rachel thought for a while. After hearing Klyesha's tales about her island, they'd be giving up a civilised life in exchange for a primitive subsistence lifestyle. It was not a lifestyle Rachel wanted to live.

'Well, what do you want to do now?' asked Rufus the next morning as William lay resting after they'd had food. 'We're nearly out of supplies.'

'And there's nothing here?' asked William.

'Nothing. I could go hunting for rabbits or an elk but that would take hours, possibly without success.'

'Our only alternative is to leave and find a farmhouse where we might rest until I can travel more,' said William.

This decided, Rufus packed up their belongings after checking William's bandages and helping him up onto his mare, they carefully set off. The day was bright and clear though distant orange-grey clouds indicated poor weather was approaching. They needed to find a suitable shelter and food within the next few hours to avoid being caught out as temperatures plummeted.

William's leg hurt abominably but he contained himself so as not to worry Rufus. He didn't know how he'd last ten minutes let alone hours on the road as the horse's movements jarred his leg. He was soon hot and sweating with the effort of holding on as they cantered down the road.

After about half an hour, William's body had had enough and he slumped forward over his horse's neck causing her to shy and whinny with the added weight. William felt himself falling towards the road. Rufus noticed and rushed towards him but was unable to prevent him falling. He caught the mare's reigns and pulled her to a stop. Tying the horses to a tree, he rushed back to William's aid. He was groaning on the road, his hand pressed to his leg and fresh blood leaking around his fingers.

'Nay, this was not a good idea, Sire! You should have told me how sick you were!'

William shook his head in pain his mind too distraught to answer.

What were they to do? thought Rufus. He scanned the countryside for any sign of a dwelling. There were none. Perhaps they should go back to the hut, yet William's wound would take no more movement. He needed a warm dry bed to rest but where was one to be found?

In the distance they heard a sound coming from behind them on the road they'd already travelled. Who was it? Had the mob of bandits returned to seek revenge? Rufus looked frantically around for shelter. They must leave immediately. Rufus began dragging William off the road to some trees he could see a few yards away. If only they might hide for a while, allowing their pursuers to pass them by unseen. In moments he had William propped up under a tree and the horses tethered behind out of sight. Keenly he scanned the road warning William to be quiet.

Coming into sight, Rufus saw a fully enclosed carriage drawn by four horses. It seemed incongruous out here in the country, a City carriage. He saw two men at the front, one dark and one fair. The dark one had a musket laying across his lap and in the carriage he saw two people. Were they friend or foe? Could he risk being shot at? William groaned loudly. Rufus knew he didn't have much choice. He would have to risk it. Jumping onto his horse, he rode after the carriage yelling 'Ho! Help!' Finally, the driver heard him and the carriage slowed to a halt. Soon Rufus found himself looking into the barrel of a musket.

'Who are you?' called the dark-haired man, 'What do you want?'

'My companion is injured and in need of help.' Rufus held his hands held out in surrender, 'Please, can you help us'?

'How many are in your party?'

'Just the two of us and our horses. Please, my companion is bleeding. We were attacked by a group of lawless bandits yesterday.'

'About 40 men with pikes and clubs?'

'Yes, I believe so,' agreed Rufus, 'Can you help us?"

The dark-haired man got down off the carriage still aiming his musket at Rufus. 'Show me your companion.' Rufus got down off his horse and they walked over to the trees where William sat looking pale and sickly.

'Sire!' gasped Lucca, the dark-haired man.

William looked at him, 'Rufus stop worrying. This man is a friend.'

'What are you doing out here, Lucca?' asked William.

'I could ask you the same thing, Sire,' replied Lucca.

Between them, the men walked William to the carriage. Jack got down to help secure their horses to the back of the carriage. William was supported by Lucca and helped up into the carriage. As he helped him in, Lucca winked at 'Carl' who also squeezed Rachel's hand in warning. 'Carl' held her breath as William looked at them both without recognition. It may have helped that both she and 'Robert' were wearing three-cornered hats.

'Carl' said, 'What has befallen you, kind Sir?'

'Arrrh!' groaned William, adjusting his leg to rest in the space on the seat opposite. He looked at the two young men seated across from him. 'We were attacked by bandits as we rode through their group. They were walking so we risked it but myself and my horse were slashed with pikes. It was a mistake. We should have avoided them. I fear my payment may be great for that error.'

'Carl's' heart beat hard. Here was her William possibly mortally wounded in front of her, yet for some reason she decided not to reveal who she was saying instead, 'We have bandages, liniment. Do you wish me to look at the wound?'

William shook his head, 'It appears to stop bleeding when elevated. Perhaps when we rest for the night?'

'As you wish, Sir. What brings you to these parts anyway?'

'Lucca knows me so I may as well be honest. I am your King, William.

'Sire!' said the young men bowing from their seats.

'We are at your service,' said 'Robert'.

'Good, good. No need to be alarmed. The more friends I have the better. When we have secured accommodation, we can make plans for the 'morrow.'

'Indeed,' replied 'Carl'. 'Your bandits I believe, we have already seen this morning. They approached the farmstead where we were staying and begged for food. The homesteaders, an old couple cautioned us to ignore them. Bandits had fired their hay this last week. They could not be trusted.'

'A sensible response, said William, wincing at the pain, 'For they showed us no mercy. Did they not try to break into the farmhouse?'

'No, for it is well secured. That is why the old couple have survived this long,' replied 'Robert.'

'I see. Then it is to be hoped they are not caught outside next time,' William offered. The young men nodded, worried for their friends. 'Robert' poked 'Carl' in the ribs.

'What brings you to these parts?' asked 'Carl'.

William winced, 'Simply to clear my head. A day or two away from the Castle however it has turned into something else. Have you heard or seen any other carriages on this road?' He was hoping for information about Gerard.

'No, Sire,' answered 'Carl', 'Apart from the bandits and the farming couple and yourselves we have seen no one.'

No soldiers either thought William. Where were Paxton and his men?

'And what brings you onto this road at this time?' asked William.

'Carl' looked at 'Robert'. 'We're on a journey of discovery to see the Kingdom. We are headed first to the mountains.'

'Why there might I ask?'

'To get the lay of the land. Perhaps to visit another country,' replied 'Carl'.

'I see,' said William, who was too busy to visit other countries.

Their conversation lapsed allowing each sometime to examine their own thoughts. 'Carl' was beside herself with worry for William. With no physic or apothecary, how was he to be treated? Should they take him back urgently to the City where he needed to be? William was too polite to ask them to turn back.

'Robert' couldn't understand why they needed to deceive William as to their true identity. What was Klyesha playing at?

William was in pain and despair. His injury had forcefully given him a first-hand experience of the lawlessness of his kingdom's hinterland. How long had innocent citizens been suffering under these conditions too frightened to leave their homes, turning their homes into fortresses? What was he doing about it? He who was responsible. Instead, he sent his best man to trace his brother. Surely in these new circumstances that expedition was mere indulgence. He really did need to get his Kingdom under better control and quickly.

They journeyed for several hours during which William slept. 'Carl' and 'Robert' discussed in whispers their situation. 'Let it not be added to his already heavy burden fear for our safety,' counselled 'Carl'. 'Robert' reluctantly agreed but what would William think when he found out who they really were?

At the back of 'Carl's' mind as well as worry for William's welfare was this unparalleled opportunity to quiz him about herself. Never had either of them disclosed their true feelings for each other, she believed. So here was a chance to find out before she committed herself to a relationship. If he was really determined, perhaps they could overcome society's prejudice towards her. However, without a solid commitment from the King, Klyesha could never take her place beside him at Court.

Chapter Seven

Gerard screamed at his men, 'There must be a way! I can promise them anything- land, wealth, horses. Without them we remain stuck here with no way forward.' It seemed like a week but was only days since he and Sophia arrived at his secret estate tucked away among hills in the countryside to the north of the Capitol. Here for years, he'd stashed away coin, supplies, horses, weapons, even men for this very eventuality. Years of planning had set up the place where he might even establish a rival Capitol if need be from which to conduct his rebellion. Since the accident of birth leaving him second in line to the throne, he'd waited for this day when he could begin to wipe that smug smile off his useless brother's face. Wait till he is thrown into a stinking dungeon with slime crawling down the walls and piss and dung under his feet. Only then might he realise the extent of Gerard's hatred for him and his determination to replace him on the throne.

The spoiling of the grain was quite deliberate on Gerard's watch. He knew, he'd hoped, the famine would foster hatred amongst the people and drive them to rebellion. William thought he had things under control. Cats! Gerard laughed aloud until tears run down his face. Cats! He thought cats might solve the problem. Phaw! Poppycock! The discontent was far more endemic, far more widespread than William imagined, or Gerard hoped. The motely, foul, ragged assemblage of men sprawled in his horse yard was evidence enough. Starving, angry men would make a very motivated and determined army. They just needed direction and leadership. So, he would have to step up. Everything depended upon it.

He walked out into the horse yard flanked by his heavily armed guards stepping up onto a half barrel, Gerard faced the rabble. Sweat broke out on his brow despite the cold and his throat suddenly felt dry but he was determined.

'Men,' he called to them. Some turned to him, others didn't. He had one of his guards fire a musket into the air. That got their attention. Fear was smeared across many faces and anger too. 'Men,' he called again. The ragged ranks were all looking at him now. 'I am Prince Gerard, the King's brother. You may already know me. I am not here to listen to your troubles and send you away with a few pretty words as my brother is wont to do. (Here were heard cheers) No, I am here to change your lives. When did you last have a good solid meal of meat? When did you last have wood for your fires or milk or medicants for your children? When did you last have a clean doublet or new breeches? (They started to murmur) For too long have you suffered hunger, cold, abandonment by my brother, the King. He has ignored you, thrown you out of your homes, taken bread from your children. He has taken away your hope. (More cheers) Today that will change, my friends. Today you will be fed. Today you will find hope for the future again. Today things are going to change.' (Loud cheers)

'Please, I ask only two things of you- your patience and your help. Today my men will distribute food and if you have none, weapons. I need your help to oust William as King. To remove the man who has taken everything away from you. He does not deserve to be King. He deserves prison. (More cheers) Please friends, come with me to the Capitol. Let us gather all our ragged friends together and we can take the Capitol. We can throw William out. I, Prince Gerard, will rule in his stead. I will bring you better times with full bellies, warm homes and a purpose for the future. Together we can win!' (Loud excited cheering)

Gerard stepped down from the barrel and gave instructions to his guards. Finally, today the world would change.

Paxton and his men sat mounted in the corral next to the stables of a country inn. Their horses' breaths puffed white in the cold air as they moved nervously more than ready to set off again. He and his men were well provisioned, their bellies full and a good night's sleep behind them. The last few days had been frustratingly unproductive as they searched countless valleys, hamlets, small villages and farmsteads for Gerard to no avail. They went east from the City to the extent of civilised occupation crossed over to the West and followed the coastline. Apart from understanding there was a groundswell of discontent in the taverns, in the towns and even remote villages towards them as the King's representatives, they gained no significant information. Some had openly cursed them while others allowed their displeasure to sit in foul looks on their countenances. However, under all was a seething reaction to everything Royal. The King needed to fix what was wrong in the Kingdom. Paxton knew William had no idea how widespread the resentment was. He could smell rebellion in the air and the King had to be apprised of the situation as soon as possible.

'Men, we return to the City today,' ordered Paxton. 'We can do it in a day if we ride hard and change horses.' His men, some twenty liveried soldiers nodded, happy to return home to their families. They all turned for the gates and began cantering on the road back to the City.

William was moaning aloud by the time a suitable barn was found adjoining an abandoned and falling down farmstead. Lucca and Jack on either side helped him into the barn where 'Carl' and 'Robert' had fashioned a platform out of old crates overlaid with blankets. 'Carl' tucked further blankets over him, while 'Robert' got a fire going in an old stove. The barn was large enough to accommodate all the horses and they were led into stalls and given hay. Their big heaving bodies would help warm the space. Rufus closed and bolted the big barn doors. Everyone wanted to be close to the fire.

In a satchel packed by Cook, 'Carl' found liniments and bandages and a draught to help with pain. 'You need to drop your breeches so I can see the wound,' explained 'Carl'. William nodded. He was beyond remonstrance. She helped him with the belt buckle and eased the breeches down. A loin cloth covered his private parts noticed 'Carl', gratefully. The bandages were stiff with blood and she had to wet them down to remove them by carefully cutting them off. 'Carl' was not unfamiliar with dressing a wound, many of which needed to be attended to on their island where they used moss and seaweeds. William's wound looked clean though it bled anew when the filthy bandages were removed. 'Carl' washed the wound and applied liniment to muslin which was pressed against the cut. Then she carefully bandaged his thigh, a strong manly thigh, with fresh bandages. As her hand touched his flesh a spark ran along her arm, an electricity of attraction. 'Carl' jolted but William had his eyes shut, too much in pain to notice, she thought. She finished the job carefully and got him to ease the breeches up again and she re-buckled his belt. Only then did he look at her, startled.

William felt embarrassed at the feeling which washed over him in the presence of this young man. His face flushed and his loins stirred. He'd never reacted to a young man like this before and he quickly pushed the thoughts from his mind. 'Carl' gave him the draught of crushed poppy seed which he swallowed with water.

'Why have I never seen you at Court?' he asked.

'Carl' stood up, 'Oh, we have been there, Sire, many times. Perhaps you never saw us because it is always crowded.'

'Perhaps,' murmured William, puzzled. 'And what do you think of Court?' he asked.

'I believe it must be very disagreeable for you, Sire, to deal with so much... need'

'They're all my subjects and I need to help them.'

'Of course, Sire. Still, it is a burden for one man alone.'

Alone, yes! This did sum up his duty. It was very much alone. He had few friends and his brother hated him. There had only been for a time, Klyesha.

'Carl' sat on a crate beside the King. The only light was from the stove now where 'Robert' and Lucca were cooking dinner. Jack was rubbing down the horses and Rufus was already snoozing. 'Carl's' face was in shadow, the King's back half turned to her. 'Is the pain easing?' she asked.

'Yes, gradually. Being able to rest without the jolting of the carriage certainly helps.'

'Indeed,' replied 'Carl', realising how painful the journey must be for him. She debated in her mind what she planned to say next. Should she just leave him alone? However, at any moment he might realise who she really was and the opportunity would be lost.

'I remember Court last month quite well,' began 'Carl' hesitatingly, 'The sad tale of Diana Culaine.'

'Yes, a terrible injustice,' agreed William.

'The daughter, what was her name? ... Clarice? She did very well out of it though.'

'Klyesha is her name,' answered William, annoyed. 'How did she do well?'

'300 gold sovereigns is nothing to sneeze at,' observed 'Carl'.

'What was done to her was an abomination!' William's face clouded at the memory.

92

'True, I suppose,' said 'Carl' 'but even with money how could such a woman find a respectable place in society? I believe she was wearing the skins of cats when she was found.'

William almost growled, 'And if she was? What of that? They were abandoned on the island. It was all they had to clothe themselves.'

'But can she even speak, a woman like that? Untutored with only sea creatures from which to learn of the world.'

William's tone rose, 'She had her mother to educate her.'

'And what kind of woman was she? Already pregnant when she arrived on the island and no father for her child.'

William turned to 'him', 'And what do you know of hardship, young man, with your privileged background? Who are you to cast blame on anyone?'

'I am merely voicing some of the concerns of the Court, Sire, I apologise if I have upset you.'

'You know nothing of the courage of Klyesha, her endurance, her qualities. You don't know her as I do.'

'There have been rumours of... please forgive me for being frank, Sire... of your involvement with her?'

'What I do and whom I choose is of no concern of yours!'

'Indeed, Sire, but if she is to be Queen, we as your subjects will all be involved.'

'Of all the women who have aspired to be my Queen she with her humble origins and tragic life, she alone has the integrity, the grace, the foresight and the courage to be my Queen.' Everyone turned to look at the King when he said this.

'Carl' coughed in embarrassment at extracting this confession from the King in such a deceptive way, yet deep down her self-esteem rose higher. He really did have feelings for her!

'As she is so worthy...' uttered 'Carl'.

'Speak no more of her!' warned the King. 'When I return to the City I will see her. Let this be an end to the topic.'

'As you wish, Sire' offered Carl subdued, 'I believe our supper is ready.' 'Robert' brought them bowls of hot meat and potatoes in a salted broth. The food was good and satisfying on a cold night and for some time no one spoke as they enjoyed their sustenance.

Lucca sat near the stove next to 'Robert' and whispered, 'How long are we to deceive the King as to who you are?'

'Robert' whispered back, 'Please leave it up to 'Carl' to decide. He has his reasons.'

'I don't like lying to my King,' replied Lucca, 'He's already suffering. Do you think it's wise?'

'It's not up to me,' replied 'Robert' 'But don't you think he will be more worried when he finds Klyesha is not safe in the City that she's here instead among bandits with little protection?'

'As you put it that way, however I still don't like it.'

'Please don't give us away, not yet?' pleaded 'Robert'.

'I will keep your counsel, but the bigger question is how sick is the King? We need to get him seen by a physic soon!'

'I agree we must find a physic. Do you have the lay of the land? Are there any villages nearby?'

'I believe there is a village on the northern border. A trading town. I sent clocks there years ago. They once traded across the border but it's much smaller now. They may have some learned person we can consult. And it is closer now than returning to the City. Should we suggest this to 'Carl'?

'Yes, by all means. We need somewhere much more comfortable for the King to rest. I'll ask them.'

'Robert' having finished her food went to inquire after the King, 'How goes it, Sire?' she bowed.

'I am more at ease, thank you, 'Robert.' Your friend 'Carl' has ministered to me well.'

'Sire, 'Carl', Lucca has knowledge of a town on the northern border. He has not visited it but believes you will be more comfortable there and we may find a physic. Do you agree?' asked 'Robert'.

William called Rufus over, 'Rufus, do you know of a border town to the north?'

'Hamleyvale, I believe it is called,' yawned Rufus. 'It is not large but has a beautiful river through the town. What do you want to know?'

'Perhaps I could rest there? I prefer no one know that the King is visiting. Can it be done?'

'We could travel there tomorrow. I could go ahead and secure accommodation to allow you to enter the village unseen.'

'Excellent.'

'Carl' recalled her maps, 'So I have...' She stopped, remembering also the map would be a giveaway as to their identity. 'Um... nothing. It's a good plan, I agree.'

William looked at her, 'Then we shall go. I beg use of your carriage a little longer.'

'Indeed, Sire, the carriage is yours for as long as you need it.'

'Thank you, then we should all rest so as to journey early and reach the town before night,' advised William.

They bunkered down as best they could closest to the stove as possible. 'Carl' had time to whisper to 'Robert' that her plan went well.

'How so?'

'He admires me.'

Robert squeezed her friend's arm, 'And what else?'

'I believe he wants me for his Queen.'

'Robert' let out a sigh, 'How exciting! You were wrong to downplay your role.'

'Perhaps I was.'

'Should we tell him? Should we reveal ourselves?'

'Not yet. Something tells me it is too soon.'

'As you wish, now we need to sleep. If you can!' They were like a pair of schoolgirls.

'Indeed, my mind and heart are abuzz. Yet I will try to sleep, good night.'

'Good night, 'Carl' said 'Robert' grinning. She too was happy for her friend. To win the King's affections- this would truly change their lives.

They slept to the crackling of the fire, the gnashing of the horses as they chewed their hay and their movements in the stalls. Mice crept out in search of crumbs but no one noticed as all were exhausted and slept too soundly.

'I am Captain Paxton, chief of the King's Guards, open in the name of the King!' demanded Paxton at the West Palace Gate.

His livery proudly displayed, the guards had little hesitation in opening the portcullis to Paxton and his weary men. They made their way to the barracks where grooms took their horses and the kitchens provided food. It was already nightfall and the other soldiers had finished their evening repast. Paxton sat with his stew and bread calling for Rufus. 'Rufus is not here,' answered one of the soldiers.

'Where is he?' demanded Paxton, both weary and impatient. The soldier shrugged his shoulders. No one else knew where he was either.

I'll speak to the King, thought Paxton finishing the last morsel and pushing back his stool. One of the barrack's cooks took his platter and spoon. Throwing on his cloak, Paxton walked to the Palace where he asked leave to report to the King. He was led in not to the King's rooms but to see Albert Strong, the Chancellor. 'Well, what news Paxton? Have you located Gerard?' asked Albert who sat at his own table. He passed Paxton a goblet of wine and Paxton sat down next to him.

'We went east and then west along the coast. No one has seen or heard of him but this was news for the King.'

'The King is not here,' explained Albert, who was an elderly but well-muscled man who no one could fail to admire when they met him.

'How so?' asked Paxton.

'The King has been gone for a week. He left soon after you. Guards at the Portcullis Gate reported he got the password for two days. So, I suspect he only meant to be away for two days.'

'Has no one had word of him?'

'No, no one has heard. I was hoping you might have seen him in your travels.'

Paxton shook his head. 'We did not see the King, however we did see a number of armed ruffians headed towards the Capitol. I would have engaged them but that wasn't our mission.'

'Indeed, together with your report there are many more. Bandits, ruffians, a rabble of the destitute, call them what you will, but more have been seen. I was reluctant to send out a large search party for the King in case we needed all the troops here.'

'And Rufus is with him?'

'Yes.'

'Only Rufus?'

'I believe so.'

Paxton let out his breath, 'This is unfortunate, Albert. What if he was waylaid by these ruffians?'

'I have sent out scouts to find him. They have returned with no information about the King.'

'This may be a good thing.'

'Yes, it's possible but why would he negate his responsibilities like this and just leave?'

Paxton shook his head. Why indeed. It was not like the King. 'He was awaiting news of the Prince, yet he left before he received any news.' It didn't make sense. 'What do you want me to do, Albert?'

The old man took another sip from his goblet. 'I know you have just returned and must be tired but I want you to find him. I trust you and Rufus. I do not trust the Prince. I do not know what plot he maybe hatching but it cannot be good for the King.'

'You believe he is in danger?' Paxton's eyebrows rose.

'It is possible as only William stands between the throne and Gerard and we know Gerard hates him.'

'Then we must act. Give me tonight. I will assemble fresh men in the morning to find the King. How many can I take?'

'Twenty, no more. In the absence of the King, I am taking charge of the defences. We may need all our available men, if and it's hopefully not likely, the random groups of rebels organise themselves into a ragged army and attack the Castle.'

'What will happen to the City?'

'The City cannot be defended, as you know.'

Paxton blanched. All those people just left to defend themselves! 'Shouldn't we get them into the Castle?' he asked.

Albert grimaced, 'And feed them for how long? Our supplies here are much down due to the famine.'

Paxon's soldier brain was calculating the risks. Citizens of the City might join the rebels or they might secure themselves in their homes and hope for the best. Paxton then remembered Klyesha and Rachel, two women alone in their house. What hope would they have? He must warn them before he headed out to look for the King. But what he would tell them he didn't know. With his dark locks, dark eyes and pockmarked skin he had no wife of his own to worry over.

'Is there any report as to the direction the King and Rufus took?' he asked at last.

'We believe they headed north, it's all we know.'

'Thank you, Albert. I will ready the troops in the morning and start them on six hourly watches along the fortifications. You can trust Captain Johnson. I'll send him over to you when I get back to the barracks.'

'Thank you, Paxton and god speed in finding the King. We desperately need him back here.'

'I will find him, be assured,' confirmed Paxton, taking his leave of the Chancellor.

The Kingdom was effectively without a Monarch at present and the Chancellor was an old man. Really his place was here, organising their troops rather than on a wild goose chase looking for the King, damn him! But Paxton also knew if the King was in grave danger, so was the Kingdom. If God forbid, Gerard tried to stage a coup they were all done for. For Gerard was a flawed man, full of hatred and venom. A man who would put his own interests above his own countrymen. A man who could not be trusted to rule a Kingdom.

Cook returned all in a flurry, 'Flora,' she said to her niece, 'There's no flour! The bakers have no bread. I asked Laurentio, Rachel's father, whether the millers were out of wheat? He said unfortunately, yes. They'd run out a week ago. He had some sacks of rice which he'd sent to be milled but he didn't know how to make bread from rice flour and didn't know if it would work.'

Flora looked aghast, 'No bread! How are we to feed everyone?' Everyone included Flora's younger brother, 17 year old James, the Gardener Walter and his wife and their three daughters.

The week before, a few days after Klyesha and Rachel had left on their journey, Cook had gone to the marketplace. There were rumours everywhere at all the stalls of a high degree of restlessness and dissatisfaction in the countryside.

'My sister said...'

'My aunt reports...'

'Joe, my uncle...'

All the rumours were the same. Men were angry and starving. There was talk of a march on the Capitol. Country people were locking themselves in their farmsteads out of fear.

When Cook walked back home she gave the outside of the house a critical appraisal. A solid brick wall ran around the whole house apart from the front where it was a little lower and separated by two heavy iron gates. There was no lock on the gates, only a small bar which could be pushed through from the house side to secure the gates together.

She'd dumped her groceries in the kitchen and found the gardener. Walter was raking the old vines and sticks out of the garden in preparation for burning. 'What is it, Mistress?

'Walter, there is trouble brewing,' she began and explained the situation to him. 'We need to make this house and yard more secure.'

'What would you have me do?'

'Can you buy a lock and chain for the front gates? A big one.'

'Anything else?'

'We'll need the cellar cleaned out and some beds set up.'

'The cellar!' Walter looked alarmed.

'It's only a precaution but we will be safer in there if the house is attacked. We need supplies down there and a privy set up.'

'Yes, mistress, but if you believe things are going to get out of hand, what is my wife and the children to do? We live on the verge of a canal in a simple wooden hut.'

'I see. Well, if your wife agrees to help me with the housework, they can all come here too. Mind they bring all they need. If this rebellion starts who knows when it will end?'

So, it was their household of three grew to eight overnight. Flora's brother, James, an apprentice blacksmith, made a chain for the front gates as every chain in the City seemed to have suddenly become unavailable and he helped Walter set up the cellar.

'Thank goodness we have our own well and don't have to trudge half a mile to draw water,' said Flora.

'Indeed, my cherub, this house is a solid one, well set up. Mistress Klyesha bought soundly. I only hope she and Rachel are somewhere away from this awful business for they have only Lucca and Jack and a few muskets between them.'

It so happened the next week with all the new residents already installed, James was fixing the front gates when Captain Paxton arrived to speak to Cook and found out Klyesha and Rachel were away.

Gerard looked at the men before him: Lewis, St Alban and Cottersloe. Men he had known for many years. Men who had been waiting for this opportunity. They were all in their 40s, tough, country men who could build stone walls, lead a plough horse and thatch a roof. But could they also lead an army?

'I want you three to organise the rebels we have camped here. Fill sacks with hay and set them up for practise with the pikes. Get some wooden planks and fashion them into swords for the men to practise sword fights. I've set the two blacksmiths, Jones and Salter, to making swords and pike ends but I know they can't make many. We'll need wooden clubs too.'

The men nodded. They'd all woken to the day Prince Gerard arrived knowing their lives would never be as quiet and peaceful as they once were. Ploughing fields, threshing, stacking sacks of grain had hardened their muscles and given them a cast of endurance. Hard work, hard bodies. It was a life without luxury. No wine or cream for them. No soft beds or cake. Now a whole new world of luxury was opening up before them. As the Prince's lieutenants, they stood to have enviable positions in a new government, a new monarchy. They would have their own stone houses, their own horses, carriages and women. Gerard promised them everything if only they could create an army out of a rabble. Not just this rabble but the other desperate groups lurching hungrily towards the Capitol. Had not Gerard already shown them the gold he promised to share with them, the *largesse* of the Palace? Only one thing was in their way, one man, King William. How easy to eliminate him and place Gerard on the throne. A King they had helped make would never forget them. His promises were glorious, intoxicating, mesmerising and it was all possible.

St Alban, a tall solid brown-haired man, decided he'd be the first Lieutenant. To do so, he'd have to take the initiative and organise the others. Cottesloe with his wide big-eyed face and Lewis with his pinched rat-like features would look to him for leadership. He'd be the right-hand man to the Prince in the new Court. And as such, he'd all the more *largesse* behoven to him.

'Cottesloe, I want you to do an inventory of the weapons. Can you write?' Cottesloe nodded. 'Good, then I expect you to begin at once. I want it done in an hour. And Lewis, you can get the men to start setting up the practice areas. Get them whittling wooden swords. Bind the handles in rope to grip. Get others to fill sacks. You've got the afternoon, understand?'

Lewis' eyes glinted, 'Yes, Captain,' he said his chest puffing out at his new responsibility, 'It shall be done!' Even he sounded a bit formal to himself but St Alban grinned and told him, 'Good man!'

St Alban felt satisfied, he enjoyed giving orders. He turned to report back to his Sire, Gerard or soon-to-be Sire, anyway.

Chapter Eight

The small village of Hamleyvale was in a valley tucked up high in the Vespasian Mountains. It was reached by a mountain pass which zigzagged to reduce the incline. There was just enough room for the carriage to pass, so everyone was thankful no down traffic appeared. The horses soon became tired, however, so everyone who could walked. At the start they had taken the precaution to swap to the fresher horses. Jack unbuckled the spare four and 'Carl' and 'Robert', Lucca and Rufus were tasked with leading them up the slope. It was a slow and difficult journey, so it was thankful they had begun early with hopefully time enough to reach the top before dark.

Jack felt privileged to be driving at the front of the carriage and little guilty, yet he was the best driver of the team and a less experienced person could not be risked here. Thankfully, though cold, the weather was clear as slippage may have been a problem on a wet muddy road. 'Carl' enjoyed the fresher mountain air and pointed out to 'Robert' the changes in the verdant tree canopy as they ascended. The green sea of leaves reminded her of clumps of seaweed and this made her miss the sea. Worry about William also nagged at her and she was looking forward to the time when she might reveal her true identity to him.

William himself was enjoying the views having never travelled this high before. The vastness of the landscape was breathtaking to him. The pains in his leg had settled to a bearable level, yet he missed the company of 'Carl' and 'Robert' in the carriage. He was annoyed also at the aspersions 'Carl' had cast Klyesha's way and wanted to extol more of her virtues to him.

Lucca was still puzzled by the women's stance. 'Why do we keep deceiving him?' he asked 'Carl' again careful not to let Rufus hear who was walking behind with 'Robert'.

'I'm waiting for the right moment,' confessed 'Carl'. 'He will be upset with me. He thinks Klyesha is safe in the City. He won't be happy I'm here so when he's feeling better maybe then...'

'What if he doesn't get better?' ask Lucca.

This was Carl's greatest fear but she would not voice it, 'Give him time to rest, more herbs and liniments. He'll soon be well.'

Lucca wished he was as optimistic. He was also concerned over what was happening back in the City. William's officials must be frantic as to his whereabouts especially as there were the indications of insurrection in the countryside. What would happen to his shop, to his home and to his housekeeper and her mother? What had begun as a joyful excursion was now a dire distraction from where events must be escalating.

'Rufus,' asked Lucca, 'surely the Palace is worried as to the King's whereabouts?'

'The King and I have discussed this. Once you are all settled in the village, I am to return to the Palace with the news King William is well.'

'I see,' nodded Luca, somewhat relieved. 'I think,' he said quietly to 'Carl', 'that we should all return home at the earliest possible juncture.'

'You are probably right,' replied 'Carl', 'however it must be done with the King's safety uppermost in any decisions.'

Lucca breathed out. At least 'Carl' appeared to see reason. The King's presence in their party made any fanciful excursion into the Kingdom a much more serious endeavour.

By the tenth sharp zigzag on the Pass, the village's roofs became discernible over the treetops. They were red tiled as houses in the area typically were and their walls were painted white with floral and leaf designs.

Now they were looking down over all the village which had a pretty stream running through its centre which earlier inhabitants had lined with stone. No muddy banks were apparent. A water wheel was turning slowly in the middle of the river with an attached mill. Villagers could be seen carrying firewood or food piled in baskets on their backs. No one appeared to be riding horses.

'Stay here,' called Rufus to Jack, indicating a level area near the Pass but quite wooded to shield them from sight. 'I will venture into the village alone,' he told the others. The previous night he'd stowed the King's livery he wore into his saddlebag instead wearing a calico smock as farmers wore to keep William's identity a secret. He made his way down the sloping road alone, leaving his horse behind. After some time, Rufus returned, 'There is a comfortable Tavern with accommodation and the tavern owner also has a vacant cottage with a walled garden and a barn for rent,' he told the King.

'Secure us the cottage, it will be more private,' commanded William, handing Rufus sovereigns.

So, it was near dusk, they entered the village. As few people were about, they managed to stow the carriage and horses in the barn without being noticed. William was settled in the quaint sitting room simply furnished with couches and an open fire which 'Robert' set to starting. 'Carl' unpacked their food in the small kitchen excited to find the cottage also had a bathroom as her bathing was long overdue.

She sent Lucca and Rufus with coin to fetch a pot of hot stew from the Tavern and freshly baked bread which repast they all enjoyed at the long wooden table in the kitchen. William's leg was set up on a stool to ease his discomfort. There was visible relief and merriment among the party to be thus again in a civilised setting. Even William was able to laugh at Lucca's description of the broad country accents in the Tavern which he imitated to humorous effect.

When it came to bedtime, 'Carl' offered to dress William's wound but he insisted on doing it himself, somewhat gruffly. 'Carl' wondered how she'd offended the King but allowed him space. He of course, was given the grandest bedroom if grand was a description which might attach to simple wooden furniture and a canopied bed. 'Carl' and 'Robert' shared one room and Jack and Lucca the other. Rufus bedded down in the sitting room nearer the fire. The house smelt musty, and the linen sheets were a little damp but this was soon repaired with a good airing in the morning.

'Carl' was up first to heat water for her ablutions. She didn't want the King or Rufus to surprise her and her bath, so was pleased the door latched. She peeled off the hated cummerbund which concealed her breasts and her smelly attire, grateful for the change of shirts and underwear Cook had packed for her. She was tempted but refrained from sprinkling dried lavender flowers in her bath because such a sweet-smelling youth would surely arouse suspicion. The warm water was unbelievably luxurious after long days on the road and a few hurried washes from bowls when she'd been able. The dirt and tiredness sloughed off and she felt happier than she'd been for a long time. She heard the sweet sounds of birds coming from the garden and amongst them the unexpected but longed for sound of purring. A black cat had jumped up onto the bathroom windowsill and was purring and rubbing herself against it, the steam from the bath obscured her a little but she was a beauty with deep yellow eyes. 'Carl' laughed with joy and had to stop herself from leaping out of the water. She luxuriated a little longer using plenty of soap until her skin shone and her hair was squeaky clean.

Drying herself, she replaced the hated cummerbund and dressed to become 'Carl' again leaving the water for 'Robert' to enjoy. She dragged 'Robert' out of bed lest the water become too cold and set to frying fresh eggs from the Tavern for breakfast and buttering chunks of bread. The delicious smells soon roused the other men apart from William. She knocked politely at his door, 'Sire, we have breakfast ready. Would you like some?' There was no answer. Carefully she opened the door.

William stood with his back to her naked, 'Pass me my shirt,' he ordered. She found his shirt and passed it to him. He turned to her buttoning his shirt and she couldn't stop the redness creeping over her face to see him naked before her. 'I need help with the loincloth,' he asked. She picked the cloth from the chair but had no idea how to fasten it.

'I'm not used to such a garment,' she muttered looking away.

'Why not?' demanded William, 'Just give it here.' He seemed angry.

She bowed, 'I...um...don't wear one.'

'I see,' he said looking at her. 'You look very clean.'

'I just had a bath,' she explained.

He groaned, 'If only I could immerse my leg, it would be delightful.' His red locks dishevelled, he really did need a bath.

'Carl' nodded. She didn't know what she'd do if he asked her to help him bathe.

'Jerkin,' he called then, 'Breeches.' He put them on, 'Now to breakfast.'

This is not good, thought 'Carl', her face pink and shining. I do not want to be his valet, it is torture. She smirked despite her embarrassment.

At breakfast, 'Robert' unkindly commented on her red face. The bath she explained. 'Robert' shook her head teasingly.

'It was a rare luxury,' 'Robert' explained, 'but I'm afraid the water will need to be refreshed for anyone else'. Lucca laughed at her.

Rufus was filling his face with bread heavily spread with butter. 'Well, friends,' he announced, 'As you are all so nicely set up, I will take my leave. Lucca, may I take two of your horses and leave ours here to rest?'

'As you wish, Rufus. The King's mare needs more time to heal.'

'Carl' was a little annoyed seeing it was her expedition and her right to decide when and how things were done, however, as 'Carl' she needed to be subordinate.

'Godspeed, Rufus,' said the King, 'Have you my letter?'

'Yes Sire,' he replied, patting his jerkin. 'Into Chancellor Strong's hands alone.'

William nodded. Rufus rose from the table. 'It has been my very great pleasure to know you all. Your assistance to the King and I, has been incalculable. Adieu!'

'Adieu, Rufus! Safe journey,' said 'Carl' bowing.

When he had gone, 'Carl' asked the King if he was expecting to leave soon to return to the Palace.

'When I have found a physic, yes. My Kingdom needs me.'

Indeed, thought 'Carl' and I need you too. Was she to journey on without him? The thought was unbearable. Trying to shift her mood, she remembered, 'A cat was purring outside the bathroom window this morning, so we shall have no trouble with mice!'

'How interesting,' replied William, 'that in this remote place cats have survived.'

'Perhaps they also never had measles here,' offered Lucca.

'Remoteness has its advantages.' commented 'Robert, 'Let us hope that they also welcome strangers.'

But it was the cat which was to be 'Carl's undoing.

After breakfast, Lucca and Jack went into the town to find a physic and crutches for the King. 'Robert' set about in the kitchen chopping vegetables and meat for a soup. 'Carl' had found some onions in the garden, chives and parsley to add to the dish. William was helped to a seat in the walled garden as some bright morning sunshine reflected off the flagstones and created a little warmth. 'Carl' went to sit with him bringing mulled wine. 'It is a small yet delightful garden,' said the King. 'Can you see there are still apples and pomegranates on those trees?'

'Carl' looked at the small orchard, 'Let me get a basket to pick some for you.'

'No, drink your wine and rest. Tell me more about yourself.'

'There is not much to tell,' began 'Carl', who had been dreading this question. 'My father is a cloth merchant. He wants new supplies and markets. That is part of why I'm here.'

'To get new cloth or markets?'

'Both. He wants to expand the business. I am his oldest son and I too want our business to prosper.'

'Aye, a good son must obey his father. Will you go into other countries?'

'If there is a road from here and the mountains not too steep.'

'Why did you not go via ship?' asked the King.

'Carl' was not happy with the idea of ships after her mother's experience but instead she said, 'My father prefers land transport as it is cheaper.'

'I see,' said William. They sat in silence for a while. 'Carl' was conscious of the King's gaze on her. Embarrassed she desired to flee and not keep up the pretence but she didn't want to appear impolite. Just then the little black cat wandered out slowly from a bush and presented herself to them.

'What a pretty cat!' said William, 'She reminds me of another cat.'

'Carl' almost answered this comment but stopped herself in time. Before she was aware, she held her hand out to the cat who came to her and she stroked her flanks while the cat rubbed against her legs. Soon she was up on 'Carl's' lap and was being petted. William looked at her strangely then and reached over to stroke the cat too. Their hands brushed together and then their eyes met. 'Carl' could not look away and guilt crept all over her face.

'Klyesha!' William called out, 'Can it be?'

'Carl' turned away, tears in her eyes. 'Forgive me, Sire!' She could not look at him.

'What the devil!' William was astonished. 'It was only when you petted the cat the same way... but why, why have you deceived me? Am I your fool?'

107

'Carl' was openly weeping now, 'I am so sorry, I only thought to…'

'What, to talk about you freely, to get information by deception!' He was really angry now, 'And I thought you were safe in the Capitol! And don't tell me, is 'Robert' really Rachel?'

'Yes, Sire.' 'Carl' was so embarrassed she hid her face in her hands.

William could say nothing for minutes.

'I wondered how I could be attracted to a boy! When you dressed my wound I was so ashamed. But to find out it was you all along…'

'Can you forgive me, Sire?'

'No. Not until you tell me why you and all the others are engaged in this charade.'

Klyesha swallowed hard, 'For one, I didn't want you upset like you are now seeing me somewhat unprotected on this journey. But I am not like other women. I won't be stopped from following my dreams and trouble beckons me irresistibly. More importantly, I wanted to see how you would defend Klyesha if she was attacked. I did not know how you felt about me. We have terrible obstacles to overcome if we are to be…'

'Together? No, we have none except your cruel lies to me. How can I ever trust you again?'

Klyesha was quite distraught, 'Oh Sire, I did not make myself a boy to be cruel to you! We decided, Rachel and I, we would be safer on this journey disguised as youths. Lucca agreed and it worked, we deceived even you.'

William was speechless for minutes. Klyesha continued to cry, dreading what her deception had done to her hopes.

'Yes, your disguise worked but my feelings for you cut through that disguise. And did they for you?' He had calmed somewhat but his heart was still beating hard.

Klyesha wiped her face, 'I was so embarrassed to see you naked this morning. The redness would not go from my cheeks.'

'I noticed but chose to believe it was the heat of your bath.'

'Oh, Klyesha!' He grabbed her hand and pulled her towards him kissing her face, her lips, her neck. She kissed him back as hard so relieved he didn't hate her. So happy the gulf between them was now closed. The cat continued to purr amongst their legs until they noticed it and laughed.

'I want a bath,' said William suddenly. 'Call 'Robert'.

'Carl' went to fetch 'Robert' and between them helped the King to the bathroom. 'I am so in need of a bathe' explained the King. 'Robert' left to return to her kitchen tasks. 'Carl' do you mind bringing the water?'

'No, Sire,' grinned 'Carl'.

When she returned to fill the boiler and build up the fire, William expressed his guilt at being unable to help. 'Carl' put the last of the buckets into the boiler and turned on the bath faucet, 'It's warm enough' she said.

'Help me undress.' 'Carl' went to the King and unlaced his jerkin and pulled his shirt over his head.

'I'll leave the loincloth to you,' she laughed.

'No need, I'll take it off in the water and wash it then you can hang it to dry on the boiler pipes.'

'Yes Sire.'

'Yes, William,' he said, rising and hobbling over to the bath.

'The bandages!'

'Can be washed too. Pass me the soap,' said William easing carefully down into the warm water. 'This is so good,' he grinned.

'Isn't it! Should I leave you now?'

'No, please stay. Alone together, you are my Klyesha again. However, you can also be useful. Can you wash my hair?'

Klyesha soaped and lathered bubbles through William's long, dark red locks, massaging his scalp and ordering him to keep his eyes shut.

Much as the heat of the bath hurt his wound, Klyesha washing his hair was an unexpectedly sensual and luxurious experience. He couldn't help groaning with pleasure.

Klyesha laughed, 'If only I knew how easy it was to make you happy.'

'*You* make me happy, my love,' he murmured.

'Now for the rinse.'

'So soon!' he protested. The water was tipped over him in torrents from a jug. He laughed and shook his wet hair spraying her with drops.

'Child!' she scolded, wiping her face with the linen. He grabbed her hand and drew her close and kissed her dry face with his wet one.

He murmured, 'Now you can wash my back.'

Klyesha consented but only if he got out soon as she feared him catching a chill.

As she soaped his strong back with her hands feeling the contours of his muscled shoulders, his neck, the expanse of his spine, the golden hairs of his chest, a wave of sensuality washed over her. Washing off the soap, she kissed his neck. William pulled her around and kissed her mouth. 'Linen,' she protested and he let her go to fetch some.

Pushing himself out of the bath with his strong arms she helped him out but refused to rub him down. 'No?' he asked shoving the linen at her.

'No!' she demanded and turned her back while he dried himself.

'The loincloth and bandages aren't dry yet,' she reported, feeling the muslin.

'Leave them,' he said, wrapping the linen around his waist.

'Fetch 'Robert' to help me to the bedchamber. 'Carl' did so and he was soon relaxing under the bedclothes. Thank you, both. 'Robert' I shall nap now. 'Carl' can you bring me water?'

'Aye, Sire,' she said.

When 'Carl' brought water, the King was lying under the bedclothes. 'Put it on the table,' he said indicating the bedside table.

'Now I have one question for you.'

'Yes, Sire'

'Do you want to remain as 'Carl'?'

'No, Sire,'

'Call me William.'

'No William, I am your Klyesha.'

'Then come here, Klyesha, I want you!'

'But your wound?'

'My wound can go hang. Come here!' he said in a low tone. Klyesha removed her jerkin, her shirt and the hated cummerbund.

'I wondered why you are so fat!' laughed William.

'I hate it,' said Klyesha, tossing it aside.

'And have you missed me?' asked William.

110

'So much!'

As they clung together in the intimacy of connexion so desired by lovers, both realised emotions not missed because never known, pinnacles of love they couldn't believe existed and joy which seemed to have no boundaries as they found each other.

As William slept, Klyesha realised her life would now be forever changed if William's love proved steadfast. She could not believe after their lovemaking that their bond was a shallow one. However, she still feared what would happen if she became pregnant and remained without status. She did not know how to approach the topic with William. She need not have worried.

When William woke, his Klyesha was still beside him, her warm body warming his under the blankets. She lay staring at the canopy above them. 'What are you thinking?' he asked stroking the line of her chin with his thumb.'

'I am so happy, I'm scared,' she said at last.

'Why frightened, my Petal, I am here?'

'How can we make this last?'

'What do you even need to ask? You know how,' he answered.

'How?' she said nervously.

'I will never let you go, is how,' he said. She did not answer.

'We will be married,' he assured her after silent moments where her fears grew.

'Are you sure? Should we?' She sounded wary.

'I am the King. I can do as I please. We love each other. Today is proof enough of that. I think we have loved each other ever since we met.'

Klyesha laughed, 'I think we have. I wondered why you gave me such attention, defended me. I thought perhaps he is just feeling sorry for me.'

'Never,' he said turning her head to him and kissing her. 'I admire you, your strength, your individuality. I felt sorry for your treatment by my Kingdom but you are too strong to be pitied.'

'Thank you,' she replied, genuinely grateful for his admiration.

'So, when should we marry? Is it not a sin to enjoy each other before marriage? Having spent months wanting you, not a day will go by without pleasure.'

'I agree,' Klyesha giggled. 'What a strange place to talk about marriage!'

'Do you think I may not last?' he asked, indicating his leg.

'Never! Your wound is healing but I have the feeling troubles may soon rain down upon us. Can we marry in secret?'

'Why not? You can remain as 'Carl' by day for safety. Only at night will you be my Klyesha, my wife. 'When the time is right, we can announce our news. All we need is a priest and witnesses. I could see a church Spire as we entered the village.'

'What will your brother say?'

'In my heart I no longer have a brother. I never think of him.'

'Did you know he visited me?'

'What! When?'

'Before Mutton made his ridiculous claims in Court, Gerard visited me and asked about my family.'

'Did he, the scoundrel! So, he fished up that creature to discredit you, twisting his story with what he found out about yours.'

'Yes, there is one other thing, but I fear to tell you as it will make you angry.'

'What?' called William rising up in bed, 'What did he do?'

'If he was to be believed it was what his wife did.'

'And?'

'She sent me a present. A purse.'

'A purse?'

'Yes, but what it was made of!' Klyesha began to cry again.

'What, my sweet, what was it made of?'

'Of a black cat's fur,' cried Klyesha.

William was too angry to move, 'Not your own cat, Roxy's fur?'

'I fear so. She went missing in the previous week and we never saw her again.'

'I threatened death to anyone who harmed a cat,' he fumed. 'That man is pure evil. I shall throw him in the dungeon if ever again his deceitful countenance comes in front of mine. I am so sorry my love!' He hugged her and she turned to him.

'Perhaps we can take the little garden cat with us when we go?'

'Of course, if she will come but she might be as independent a creature as you!'

112

Chapter Nine

Rufus had overnighted in the same abandoned woodsman's hut near the section of road where William and he were attacked. 'Carl' had made sure his satchel was well-provisioned and he chewed on dried meat as he rejoined the road very wary now where to flee if he was again approached by a menacing crowd of wastrels. The road sloped down towards the coastal plain and as farmsteads grew in numbers, fields looked more cultivated. He stopped at a stream to water his horses and himself and for a few miles walked both of them to give them a rest.

It was thus unprepared and unmounted, he saw a group of horse riders in the distance. These were no unruly mob for none of them had horses, yet he quickly remounted his freshest horse and drew his sword, scanning the countryside for possible cover. Too soon they were upon him and he spurred on his horse preparing to enter a wood for cover. Yet instead of the shouts of desperate man, he heard his own name called 'Rufus, you devil! Where is the King?' He looked up to see Paxton cantering towards him with twenty of his fellow soldiers.

Laughing with relief, Rufus jumped down from his horse and the men embraced. 'What are you doing here?' asked Rufus.

'You first,' insisted Paxton, 'Tell me our King is safe!'

Rufus sighed, 'He is in the village of Hamleyvale on the border. We were attacked.'

'Attacked by whom? Is he injured?'

'Let me finish, man!' insisted Rufus, 'Yes, King William was wounded in the thigh with a pike. We tried to ride through a bandit group unaware they were armed. However, he is recovering and his leg appears to be healing. He is with friends.'

Paxton raised his eyebrows, 'Who are they?'

'Lucca a clockmaker, his driver, Jack and two of Lucca's young friends, Carl and Robert.'

'Can they be trusted?'

'Yes, they saved us. William couldn't walk so they put him in their carriage, they fed us and cared for his wound.'

'Come, we will sit awhile. Men!' he called to the soldiers. 'Dismount and tether the horses and make a meal.'

Paxton sat with his back against an oak and passed Rufus his flask of watered whiskey. Rufus gratefully drank, 'You have no idea how glad I am to see a friendly face,' he explained.

'The mob you mean?'

'Yes, but tell me, how is it in the Capitol?'

'We are preparing for battle. I only left because the safety of the King is paramount. Rebellion is afoot I am afraid.'

'Who are they and what do they want?'

'They are everyone and no one. No one leads them but they have ugly designs and are prepared to commit crimes. They are fuelled by their empty bellies. We passed several groups headed to the Capitol, but a few musket shots told them in which direction to go, meaning away from us.'

'I bring news of the King to Albert Strong the Chancellor, he needs to know.'

'And no one else. Do you have a letter?'

'Yes.' said Rufus.

'Guard it with your life. No one is to know the King is not in his Palace. It will spur on the rebellion.'

Rufus drank again and took some cheese and bread.

'Look this is how it will go,' said Paxton. 'I will split my men. Ten can ride back with you to the Capitol. Lord knows we need them there. Now I know where the King is, bringing fewer men with me will bring less notice to him. It's imperative his whereabouts remains unknown. If he is captured, the rebels will hold the centrepiece of the chess board. They can ask for anything.'

'What of Gerard? He may see this as an opportunity.'

'We couldn't find him, though we searched everywhere. I only returned yesterday. He is definitely a loose cannon. If he could somehow take hold of this disaffection and mould it, we will have trouble indeed.'

Rufus nodded. 'Shouldn't we go together and bring the King back before any trouble really starts?'

'That will be up to the King when I see him. No, it's important you get back to Strong with the news of the King then he can focus on strengthening the Castle.'

'How could a rabble take the Castle?'

'Unlikely I know, but still they are a danger especially if they start attacking citizens in the City.'

'Then my friend, I shall leave it up to you to convince the King to return where he's needed,' said Rufus. 'If things go badly in the Capitol, I will send word. In fact, I will send word anyway about what is developing.'

'Agreed.'

Paxton rose and explained the situation to his men. He chose the soldiers with families to return to the City with Rufus and instructed them to take their families with them into the barracks when they arrived as they would not be safe in the City. The men looked worried and were keen to leave.

'You have a day and a half ride before you,' said Paxton to Rufus.

'You have a similar journey but remember the road into Hamleyvale is very steep. Exhausted horses and men should not attempt it.'

'Noted,' replied Paxton as he mounted his horse, 'Godspeed'.

'And Godspeed you too! May you keep the King safe,' called Rufus looking at the mounted men who would accompany him. Paxton sped off.

'We have a way to go, so we had best begin,' he ordered the men. A very relieved Rufus returned to the road giving his spare horse to another soldier to lead. He was worried what he'd find when he reached the Capitol and to do so alone was to dally with misfortune. Now at least he had armed men to help him get William's letter to the Palace.

Paxton and his reduced group of ten men resumed their journey northwards. Of one thing he was dismayed. He would have to tell the King that Klyesha and Rachel were not in their home. They are travelling their Cook had said. When he inquired where they were she didn't know. He wanted to know if they took anyone with them. The Cook told him they had taken two young men with them. Paxton was surprised at this and the King would be even more disappointed. He was not relishing telling him the news.

'I don't want these filthy men in my house!' screeched Sophia, going quite red in in the face, her black curls shaking. 'You must send them away!'

115

'These filthy men as you call them, will make me King,' said Gerard.

'Oh, how?' asked Sophia. She was unconvinced due to the food they were consuming and her cooks were run off their feet. 'And for how long will they be eating everything we have in the larder?' she asked.

'We can refill the larder, silly,' coaxed Gerard, uncharacteristically upbeat. He chucked his wife under the chin. 'In a week you may be Queen. How will you like that?'

Sophia calmed down and a look of greed crept across her face as she thought about the royal jewels a queen would inherit. She had seen them in the strongroom. 'I want the diamond tiara with the emeralds for my coronation,' she declared, 'they suit my eye colour.

'That's my sweet,' said Gerard kissing her. 'Now run off and do an inventory of our food. I must know if we're running out.' Sophia who hardly ever troubled herself with work sprang up and went to look for her quill and notepad.

'You shall have it before lunch,' she announced happily.'

Gerard was glad to see his wife occupied. Little did she know, putting her on the throne beside him would be a difficult and bloody process. The most important first step of which was to eliminate the King. His spies in the Palace could simply poison him. A quick and blameless exercise seeing Gerard need not even be there at the time. He would send a secret message with Lachlan his Courier today. Promotions and gold would be promised. Gerard laughed at how easy it was to manipulate people. However, his simple plan would soon be altered when one of his spies arrived at the estate later that afternoon.

Gerard was at table, drinking wine and discussing strategies with St Alban when the young, sweaty man knocked at his door. He came in taking down his satchel and handing Gerard a rolled parchment. It was sealed with his friend Mullion's seal. Mullion was a secretary to Albert Strong the Chancellor. It read in code:

'The Canary has left the cage.
Where he has flown is not known.
The cage is empty and its door is open.
Many, many little mice are hurrying to eat up crumbs

under the floor of the cage.'

Gerard stood and laughed aloud, 'The King is not in the Palace,' he shouted to Saint Alban. 'He has flown the coop and not only that more of our hungry friends are gathering near the Palace. Tell me about the City?' he demanded of the courier.

'Mi'Lord, the City is preparing for a siege. Lawless rogues are already attacking vulnerable houses. Citizens are arming themselves with anything they can find. Cobbles are being lifted up from the sides of roads but once thrown are simply thrown back by the mobs. Fires have also broken out and a part of the market is already demolished.'

'What of the people? Where are they going?'

'They are in a panic, mi'Lord. Some are took to their carriages, some are trying to get on ships. The Chancellor won't let them into the Castle.'

'Won't he indeed!' he turned to St Alban, 'You see what an opportunity this is for us don't you?'

'Yes, mi'Lord'

'We must move at once. Ready the men. We march at dawn to the Capitol. There we win the leaders of the gangs to our cause. This will not be easy but my presence may sway them. I have plans for entering the Castle despite its defending troops. My God, that it should come so soon!' Gerard was almost delirious with excitement. He ran to tell his wife.

'You asked me to marry you just to do your laundry.'

William groaned, 'I brought no change of clothes apart from a shirt. Seeing you clean this morning I was very envious.'

'Carl' frowned at him, 'We never did laundry on the Island of Cats.'

'One of its advantages then.'

She took his shirt, 'You'll have to stay a'bed till it's done.'

'What a shame,' murmured William, grinning.

Soon Lucca and 'Robert' returned with a packet and an old pair of wooden crutches. 'They have no physic,' explained Lucca to William in his bedchamber, 'But they do have an apothecary. We have brought fresh bandages, moss, liniment and tincture of poppy seed.'

117

'Excellent, Lucca and 'Robert'. Give them to me. I'm getting quite expert at dressing my own wound. More water though please for the tincture. How many drops?'

'No more than six, four times a day.'

'Understood, now while I do this, tell me about the village.'

Lucca sat on a chair, 'Well as you saw, it is small. Known for its sweet red onions which everyone seems to grow. They are traded for wool and meat as sheep don't thrive here. There is a village church, a tavern, the apothecaries, one or two shops selling general goods with the market on a Saturday. What do you know about Svartlund, the neighbouring country?'

'Not much. My father went there, very mountainous and cold. Few villages as they favour cities. A thriving maritime trade. We had a falling out with them, I'm less clear on why but father stopped trading with them.'

'Well, it seems Hamleyvale has some attraction for them. Svartlunders are known to holiday here.'

'Indeed, how fascinating. Any here now?'

'I do not know but we can make inquiries.' Lucca said nothing for a while. 'Beg pardon, Sire, but don't you think you are needed back at the Palace?'

William grimaced, 'I know I'm needed but I'm not much use at the moment. When Rufus returns with his report I will go back.'

'Rufus, Jack and I had been talking about the possibility of a rebellion coming.'

'Have you indeed! Based on what? On one lawless group?'

'There are more, Sire, according to the old couple...'

'Who are hardly aware of what's happening, Lucca.'

'True, however...'

'We shall stay here. I shall stay here until I have better intelligence as to the state of the Kingdom. You and the others are free citizens. You do as you please.'

'Sire, I beg you to allow us to assist you in anyway. I know I am only a humble clockmaker...'

'Thank you, Lucca, your help has already been invaluable and will not be forgotten. If you wish to help further, take these coins, buy more supplies and find out if any Svartlunders are staying here. I wish to speak to one of them.' William threw him a purse.

'My pleasure, Sire.' Lucca took the purse and left.

William did not want to show how worried he was. Last night, he hardly slept with scenarios going through his mind. If the rabble might conjoin into a full-scale rebellion? If Gerard found out he was absent from the Palace, might he return? Strong would not entertain him or any of his suggestions he was sure of that. Gerard alone could do nothing but Gerard with help? 'What ifs' flooded his brain again as he bandaged his leg. The biggest 'what if' stood up and begged for attention: what if the Palace was overrun and Gerard stepped into the breach he'd left? What if he lost his Kingdom? Sweat broke out on his brow as he began to shiver uncontrollably. He'd noticed the wound was inflamed but didn't want to worry Klyesha. He lay back on the bed hoping the tincture would work soon. Thoughts tore through his mind, marching like warriors. He gritted his teeth. He couldn't die and leave Klyesha alone. He couldn't abandon his Kingdom to Gerard. Then in the midst of despair he remembered the militias.

From the outskirts of the City they could see plumes of black smoke. It was nearing dusk and they were all tired. They slowed their horses to a walking pace to negotiate the carriages and streams of burdened citizens hauling their precious possessions out of the City. Children had dirty streaked faces, women looked haggard and men grim as they trudged along.

Rufus leant down from his horse and spoke to one man, 'What is happening?'

'Nothing and everything,' said the man.

'What do you mean?'

'We were being attacked in our homes and the King's troops are nowhere to be seen. Where is he?'

'Who is attacking you?' asked Rufus.

'Bandits, crazy men with pikes, hungry and dangerous. I had to get out.'

'Thank you, good luck,' he said to the man.

Rufus and his men rode on towards the wharves where crowds of men stood jeering at ships laden with frightened citizens. All of a sudden, a cannon blasted into the mob, mortally wounding men and flinging their bodies like bundles of rags into the air. Rufus and his men covered their faces as debris rained down around them. 'Quick get away before the next one' yelled Rufus as he swung his horse away from the docks towards the narrow alleyways between warehouses. The screams came first as a fog came down with the night. Ahead of them in a lane, a group of men were manhandling a woman who had a small child clasped to her chest.

'Leave her alone,' yelled Rufus, drawing his sword. The rabble ignored him so he rode into them slashing at arms and torsos in his way until he reached the woman. His men followed dispatching bandits who tried to run away.

'Here! Take my hand!' yelled Rufus to the woman who was cowering on the cobbles. Quick now!' She raised her weary head and realising he was a rescuer reached up to him. With an extraordinary effort, he pulled her up swinging her behind him. 'Hang on now. You'll be safe,' he called. Another band of men were gathering before them and not wishing a repeat of his encounter on the road with the King, Rufus turned and retreated with his men.

The City was in chaos. Lawlessness was supreme and every citizen was desperate. Now Rufus' intimate knowledge of the City he had grown up in came to the fore. 'Follow me, men!' he called. They gave a wide berth to the docks and headed South to the Castle to a far gate edged by open land. Through narrow lanes and back alleys, they rode. The horses were exhausted and rattled by the smoke and noise. They followed a canal and found the bridge. All the while the woman behind him was sobbing. Finally in an open field, he could speak to his men, 'Go to your families and prepare them to stay in the Castle. Approach the gates only in darkness. I'll inform the guards. Go, now!' The men dashed away many fearful for their families.

Under a copse of trees and through an orchard, past pigsties and chickens and back onto a cobbled road, they went. The moon shone weakly now through the fog and they had to go slowly in case his horse stumbled. Finally, he could see the gate. He called to the guards, 'Captain Rufus of the King's Guards. Open in the name of the King!' A lantern was lowered from the battlement to where they were. He repeated his demand and then remembered he still wore the countryman's smock so he turned and pulled his livery from the satchel and held it up. Moments passed and finally the gate crept open and they were through.

'You took your time,' he criticised the men.

'The City is in chaos and you might have been a saboteur, Captain,' explained the Guard.

'Very well, help get this woman down. Take her and her child to the barracks. My horse, feed her and rub her down. Where is the Chancellor?'

'I believe he is in his chambers, Captain,' said one of the guards.

He turned to the woman, 'You are safe now. Go with these men. I will see you later.' She thanked him gratefully and made her way off with one of the guards. Rufus tore off his country shirt and replaced it with his livery. At a trough, he quickly stopped to wash his face and hands and smooth back his hair. Straightening his jerkin, he knocked at the Chancellor's door.

'Captain Rufus!' Strong rose from his chair knocking it over.

'Where is the King?

'He is safe. I have his letter for you.' Rufus pulled out the sealed parchment and handed it over.

Strong read the King's letter, 'He is injured?'

'Yes, but not mortally. He will need crutches to walk. He can't ride.'

'Where is he?'

'The letter did not say?'

'No.'

'Then I cannot tell you. He made me swear to tell no one where he is. However, you will be pleased to know Paxton and ten of his men are travelling to the King. I have brought ten men back with me who are gathering their families as we speak. Paxton and his men should be with him by now.'

'A blessing that he is not alone.'

'Yes. There were more in our party as well. People we met on the way, one of whom the King already knew.'

'I see.'

'The situation is out of hand in the City.'

'Yes, you have seen. Lawless groups are everywhere pillaging, burning. What else did you see?'

'Refugees on the roads out of the City. Ships full of people with sailors lined up firing their cannons into the mobs and anyone who comes too close. Fires, gangs of armed leaderless men. It is absolute chaos.'

'We believed it so. As to the troops, they are all guarding the Castle. We have too few to assist anyone in the City.'

Rufus shook his head, 'How could this happen so fast? All was peaceful when I left?'

'Believe me I want an answer to that question myself. But back to the King. Should I risk sending more men to bring him back?'

'No, I believe such a journey, which would have to be in a carriage is too dangerous for him. He is safer where he is.'

'Then those of us left shall have to step up and defend his Kingdom for him.'

'Yes, mi'Lord, yes, we will. Give me a night and I may have the energy to do so.'

'Indeed, thank you Rufus for your efforts so far in protecting the King. We will speak again in the morning. Go eat and rest, you look exhausted.'

'Thank you, mi'Lord.' Rufus saluted.

Back at the barracks he stopped to strip off his livery and put on a fresh linen shirt after washing his chest and face. He asked a soldier about the woman and her child.

'She is in the kitchen near the fire, Captain.'

Rufus went to the kitchen. She was on a stool, her shawl folded tightly around her shaking with fear. Her head was bowed over her child. 'How is she?' he asked one of the cooks.

'We gave her a warm broth, Captain and bread but she is fully afeared and full nervous. What are we to do with her?'

'Give her milk warmed for the baby and let her sleep on a palliasse near the fire here tonight. Now where is my food?'

Chapter Ten

Gerard, his men and his ragtag army were camped outside of the City in a meadow protected by a forest from sight of the road. They could see people trudging along the road headed away from the City, though the numbers had dropped as dusk began to fall. They had eaten and were now in full conference with a select few members of the army. A large boned man called Ironsmith had taken a quasi-leadership role amongst the disaffected men.

St Alban was questioning the man, 'What made you gather together with your weapons and set off from your homes?'

Ironsmith swore, 'It was that or die in a ditch. At least if I left the little food we had could go to my wife and babes.'

'But what made you join together?'

'We talk. We might live on farms but we do see each other at church or the inn. Everyone was in the same boat and we was jack of seeing our family slowly starve when the King and his men must be feasting aplenty in the Capitol.'

'But don't you have vegetables and fruits in the country?'

'But no meat nor flour. No grains for animals and none for us. Most of us have sold or eaten our animals when we couldn't feed them. Then we ate the grains for next year's harvest, our preserves, the last of our vegetables. We only have apples and a few eggs to live on at home and my wife's a milking our goat for the babes.'

Gerard broke in, 'But what did you hope to achieve by marching on the Capitol?'

Another man with a grizzled beard spoke up, 'We was going to demand food from the King. We are his subjects and he can't ignore us.'

'He has and he will,' warned Gerard, stroking his beard. 'His mismanagement of the Kingdom has brought starvation upon you all. He will not give you anything but as you know I am different. We just have one problem.'

'Oh?' asked Lewis. The others waited expectantly.

'If, as you say, others have done as you have and marched on the Capitol, we need to rally them to our cause. Which is of course, to oust the King.'

'It won't be easy,' offered Cottesloe.

'We might be walking into the middle of riots,' commented St Alban.

'Indeed, we may but the rioting will cease or pause. Men can't fight all day and all night. They must rest at some stage and that is when we will win their hearts. Show them the fabric, Cottesloe.'

Cottesloe threw open a bundle of fabric containing hundreds of strips of red cloth. Gerard took up several of them, 'I can't give you uniforms but I can give you a symbol of rebellion- The Red Armband. He tied one on his forearm. Everyone who takes one of these agrees to join us and will be rewarded by me when we take the Castle.'

Cottesloe spoke up, 'But how are we, however many we recruit, to breach the Castle's defences?'

Gerard looked at the man angrily, 'That is for me to know. Do you not trust me? If not go now. I won't have gainsayers amongst us!'

'Mi'lord...' said Cottesloe.

'Enough! I have a plan. Do you think I'm stupid?' Gerard stood. 'You, Ironsmith, St Albans, Lewis have to recruit more men. When we get to the City find them when they are exhausted or resting. Promise anything. My City Villa will be our base.'

'What am I to my to do, mi'Lord?' asked Cottesloe, sheepishly.

'You are going to guard our rear. Hurry any stragglers along and leave any sick behind.'

'Mi'Lord?'

'You heard me! Don't ask again?'

'Is everyone fed?'

'Yes, mi'Lord,' answered St Alban.

'Then we march. Rouse the men, St Alban. Get me my horse, Lewis. Today will be a day no one in the Kingdom will ever forget!'

'Carl' found him shivering and unwell when it was time for dinner. She scolded him and demanded to see his wound which she discovered was an ugly red, oozing pus. He shook his head and closed his eyes. 'You won't give up on me now, William, now we have truly found each other.'

Back at the dining table, 'Carl' explained the situation and sought advice. Keep the area cool suggested Jack with wet cloths.

You must draw out the poison counselled 'Robert' with a poultice which she would make. She thanked everyone explaining William seemed to rely on her as his nursemaid. Learning about cloth making from her father had not prepared her for this role yet she must attend him. She said she would stay in his room through the night and told them it was in case he needed medicines or assistance. She pleaded that there must be someone with medical knowledge in the village. Lucca suggested they search again tomorrow. Jack warned them all they could not let the King die and that everything must be sacrificed for his welfare. Lucca held 'Carls' gaze but now was not the time to reveal who she really was as she and the King had agreed.

Sometime after midnight, Rufus' men began to reach the Castle with their families. He had warned all the guards at the Castle gates to let them in on sight of the King's livery. Crying babes, confused toddlers and fearful youths were ushered in with their resilient but exhausted mothers given new courage by the unbelievably welcome sight of their husbands and fathers. The barracks were a scene of chaos until Rufus woke and bid them all bed down in the mess hall as best they could, waiting for more suitable accommodation on the 'morrow.

In the morning, Albert Strong made the executive decision to house the ranking officers in Gerard's suites in the Palace freeing up their dorms for the 10 new families. The King would not mind accommodating them in the Palace he explained to half a dozen captains and lieutenants who appeared with their satchels and bedding. As for Gerard, he almost told them to use everything of his for he deserved none of it. Rufus, he promoted to Commander in Paxton's absence. They were hold up for most of the morning and some of the afternoon reviewing the Castle's defences. Every battlement was furnished with cannon and cannon balls. Every soldier had a musket and supply of powder, musket balls and a flint.

After inquiries made at the Tavern, Paxton and his men found the cottage where the King was staying. He rapped on the door which was opened by an unknown youth. 'Is the King here?' he asked.

'And who are you?' demanded the youth.

125

'I am Paxton, Commander of the Kings Guard. Tell him I'm here.'

'As you wish,' The youth closed the door but soon returned and let Paxton in where he was taken to the King's bedchamber.

'Sire!' he exclaimed for William was a'bed and seemingly delirious. He approached the bed. 'Sire, it is Paxton!'

The King opened his eyes and recognition flickered in them, 'Pax...' he murmured.

Paxton took the liberty of touching his forehead. He was burning up! Alarmed he left the room and looked for the youth. 'The King is very unwell,' he said, 'Where is the physic?'

'Carl' looked hollow eyed from lack of sleep. 'There is none in the village,' she said wearily.

'But something must be done!'

Just then their group entered the house initially wary of Paxton until he introduced himself.

'I am glad to see you, Commander,' said Lucca. 'The King will be pleased to see you too.'

'Indeed, though he is too unwell at the moment.'

'May I introduce Thorsbard Strum,' said Lucca of the man who stood beside him. Strum was a very tall blond-haired man of middle age with piercing blue eyes.

'He has some medical knowledge,' added 'Robert'.

'Who are you?' demanded Paxton.

'And greetings to you too, Commander,' said Thorsbard, smiling. 'I am of Svartlund over the border. Some of us journey here, like myself, for a milder clime. Lucca here found me and mentioned you had a patient.' He held a jar. 'This is what he needs.' The jar he held up had some thick black worms squirming inside.

'Leeches,' said Paxton.

'The same but our own variety. They are good at sucking out bad blood.'

'Carl' raised her head and looked hopeful. This tall imposing stranger seemed very confident.

'If I may be permitted to see the patient,' asked Thorsbard.

'Carl' led the way followed by the others. Thorsbard felt the King's forehead. 'Damp cloths now,' he commanded, 'and some clean linens.' He withdrew William's bed sheets and carefully unbandaging his leg inspected the wound. 'The bandage was too tight but that may be a good thing. I also need a knife held for a time in fire. 'Robert' and 'Carl' went to fetch his requirements. 'How did this happen?' he asked Lucca.

'A wound from a pike six days ago.' Thorsbard touched the wound causing William to groan in pain.

'I need some spirits as well. Do you have any?'

'No,' replied Lucca, 'Only ale.'

'One of my men will get some from the tavern,' said Paxton leaving.

'He is highborn?' asked Thorsbard. Lucca nodded. 'I could tell from his good physical condition. Too many of your countrymen are starving.'

'Carl' and 'Robert' returned with the supplies.

'Now we just wait for the spirit,' said Thorsbard.

'What is it like in Svartlund?' asked 'Carl'.

'It is very much colder than here,' he laughed, 'but you people live in a mild clime compared to ours. It is six months of the year under snow. It is a tough life but we do well and eat lots of fish and fatty whales to stay warm.'

'Are there many people there?'

'Probably several millions but no one has ever counted us.' Thorsbard dipped some cloths in water and bathed William's forehead. Paxton returned with a bottle of whisky and Thorsbard washed around William's wound with it neat. He took the knife and washed it too in spirit. 'Now everyone must hold him down!' They arranged themselves around the bed and each took hold of one of William's limbs. Using the knife, he made an incision in the wound. William cried out and struggled but the wound oozed out thick yellow pus. 'Hold him!' commanded the doctor. He pressed on the edges of the wound and more pus streamed out. When it had turned to a clear red fluid he stopped and bathed the area with more watered spirit. Using the linen, he cleaned the whole area and taking the leeches put them into the wound. 'There my little friends do your best. We must wait until they feed and drop off,' he explained to the others. They let William go and he stirred but didn't speak.

'We shall wash with salty water only after this, no more moss, understand?' 'Carl' nodded thinking perhaps the moss had made his wound worse. They'd used moss on the island for wounds but it had always been rinsed in salty water first.

The leeches were soon fat and bloated so Thorsbard used his tweezers to pick them off replacing them in the jar. He washed William's leg with the salty water, dried it and bandaged it firmly. 'See not too tight. Who will dress him each day?'

'I will, mi'Lord,' said 'Carl'.

'Good, then do the same. Come get me in two days to check him again. The fever will break tonight. Thorsbard took a silver amulet in the shape of a boar surrounded by inset amber stones from his own wrist and placed it on William's wrist. 'For good luck and protection. An old Svartlund tradition,' he said explained.

'Thank you, Thorsbard,' expressed Paxton, 'I've never met a Svartlunder before and if everyone is like you, you must be a fine race, Sir.'

'Haha! We are a nation of grumblers, drunkards and scoundrels. I just happen to be the best.'

They all laughed. 'Carl' had been sick with worry over William but felt now he may indeed improve. They left William to rest as all assembled in the kitchen around the dining table.

'I've sent my men to stay at the Tavern but their horses are here. Is that OK?' asked Paxton.

'Yes, absolutely,' said Lucca, 'Anything we can do for your men or the King, please let us know. How is it in the City?'

Paxton looked sombre, 'Do you have family there?'

'Only my housekeeper and her mother,' said Lucca, blanching.

'In my house are my cook and her niece,' replied 'Carl'.

Jack shook his head.

'The situation is not good,' continued Paxton, 'Insurrection, fires, bands of lawless men. People are fleeing by road or are holdup on ships.'

'What if they don't flee?' asked 'Carl'.

'Stay indoors I expect,' he replied.

'And what are the King's troops doing?' asked Lucca.

Paxton was shamefaced, 'Protecting the Castle. We don't have enough troops to protect the City.'

'Isn't there something else to be done?' asked 'Carl' imagining Cook and her niece being terrified by mobs outside the house. They all looked at each other. Nothing of this sort had occurred for decades in the Kingdom. No one was quite prepared for this level of lawlessness.

Thorsbard drained his ale, 'We'd be getting the gibbets ready. Hang a few and the rest might start behaving.'

'Easier said than done,' said Paxton. 'There's too many. The gibbets and executioners would be overrun. Perhaps that was a solution for before things got out of hand.'

'What about the militias?' asked Lucca.

'Yes, now you are onto a possible course of action. For those of you who don't know every nobleman's estate and every village has a militia. They are supposed to practise their areas' defences and be prepared to take up arms if called. The thing is we don't know if any of the villages or estates still have their militias. Have they run off and joined these lawless gangs? We just don't know.'

'I may be a guest to your land but you need to find out quickly,' said Thorsbard.

Paxton nodded, 'I will see how the King is tomorrow but if he is unable to discuss strategy then I will take command. The men I have brought with me some could be sent to find and vexillate the militias.'

Thorsbard filled his pewter mug from the ale jug, 'If you would like help from Svartlunders, I have the ear of our King.'

'Who is he?' asked Paxton.

'King Gunnar of the Svarts. He resides in the Capitol, Yalsbad, which is about 100 of your miles from here. It's actually where I have a townhouse. I also have an estate over the border some twenty of your miles from here. I have quite a few Kralls to work it there, all at your disposal.'

'Kralls?'

'Serfs, servants, farmworkers. They owe allegiance to me for the right to work my land. I know you have left this master/servant relationship in the past but we are an old, conservative Kingdom, set in our ways. Christianised true, but also Pagan still in many ways.' He took a deep draught.

'Carl' became excited. Here was a friend, someone who had influence and might be able to provide what the Kingdom needed. What they all needed apart from a way of keeping the peace, was obviously food. But what did Svartland produce? Did they have a surplus?

'If dear Thorsbard, I may ask a question,' said 'Carl' twisting her mug around on the table, 'What food do you produce in Svartlund?'

'We have two seasons- summer and winter. Winter is for keeping our animals alive and living on the stores put up in summer. Summer always seems too short and too wet. If we get to eat strawberries, it's a very good year. If it's a bad one, lingonberries must suffice. We produce milk, cheese, yoghurt, beef and pork. Our shipping fleet is one of the Continent's best. The fishing grounds off northern Svartlund are known for their herrings. Yet other fish are also caught and occasionally whale. In the warmest areas we grow wheat, barley and oats as well as rye.'

'And how have the harvests been for those?' asked 'Carl'.

'Excellent. We have full silos on nearly every farm.'

Lucca and 'Carl' looked at each other. Both were racking their brains for what the Kingdom could exchange for some of this food. Paxton's eyes lit up too. So much food when everywhere in the Kingdom there were shortages.

'How are you off for clocks, fabrics, jewellery, gold and metal goods?' asked Lucca.

'We are always lovers of luxuries, anything foreign. We have our own excellent silversmiths as you could see from the amulet but of gold we have little.'

Both Lucca and 'Carl' were excited. Perhaps they had a role to play in these troubles without being soldiers.

'When the King is well we have much to discuss with you, Thorsbard. Will you be in Hamleyvale for long?'

'Some weeks yet, I hope,' he answered.

'Then please return tomorrow and eat with us,' offered 'Carl'.

'My pleasure,' he answered rising and looking for his coat. 'Robert' gave it to him. 'Until tomorrow,' he said bowing and leaving them through the front door.

'Carl' and Lucca exploded with delight as soon as he left. 'Did you hear that every silo on every farm is full!' said 'Carl'.

'Paxton, you have to convince the King to seek help from Svartlund,' said Lucca.

Paxton was less enthusiastic. 'That will be easier said than done. We don't trade in the Kingdom. We haven't traded for decades. We haven't needed to.'

'Well, we need to now,' offered 'Robert', 'for many of us face death by famine.'

'Carl' left them to their excitement and went to attend William. She locked the bedroom door and slipped in beside him under the bedcovers. William was muttering in his sleep, still feverish. 'Carl' clung to him, stroking his chest and his forehead, willing the fever to break, willing him to return to her healthy and happy now they had finally found each other. The gentle rise of his chest was intoxicating to her but also soothing so that she too was soon asleep dreaming of carts laden with wheat sacks, crates of dried fish and barrels of cheese. She dreamt of a deep, blue silk gown with sapphire tiara on her head as she walked with flowers strewn around her down the aisle to William at their wedding. She dreamt of happy, pink, healthy faces in the congregation which slowly became pinched and grey, their clothes dropping into shabby rags. She dreamt of Cook and her niece in the cellar screaming as wild men beat on the cellar door. She dreamt of blood running in the streets of the City, broken bodies everywhere, muck and smashed furniture. She dreamt of a tiny boat rocking in a wild sea and her screaming as she left William behind on the shore, his arms outstretched.

She woke with a start. Night had fallen and her heart was beating hard but the terrible images soon faded from her mind. William was speaking, calling 'Klyesha! Klyesha!'

'I am here, my love hush! I am here!'

He reached out to her in the dark and pressed his face to hers.

His face was wet with sweat, runnels cascaded down his chest, pooling in the pit of his stomach. She rose and pulled back a curtain, and in the moonlight found some cloths and bathed his face and chest. She put water to his lips and he drank thirstily once and then again. He breathed deeply and sighed as if his illness was a bad vapour which could simply be breathed out and away.

'Sleep my love,' she urged him, 'sleep and dream.'

William did dream, first of honey-soaked cakes and abundant fruit piled on his table. He smashed the fruit into his mouth, their juices ran down his chin soaking his jerkin. He drank goblet after goblet of thick red wine. All the while, faces were looking at him through windows pawing at the glass, starving people who moaned at the sight of all the food. But he ate on and on and on and laughed at them throwing them pieces of ham and legs of chicken they couldn't reach, tormenting them. And he just laughed and laughed and danced under showers of gold coin and threw bolts of silk cloth around the room stomping them into the food, ripping fabulous paintings out of their easels and frames, shredding them into tiny pieces he tossed in the air. Now his stomach began to expand and fatten and so he could hardly walk and his face in the mirror was bloated and grotesque. He found the meat on his plate had turned into pieces of human arms and hands and eyes and tongues and he kept eating it all until he had to vomit.

He sat up in bed and grabbed the chamber pot beside him and vomited into it until he could vomit no more. Klyesha gave him a slice of lemon to suck which settled his stomach and he slept again.

This time he dreamed he was on a hill in a park in the City and people everywhere were coming from over the City and he smiled at them and laughed. They threw flowers to him and purses of gold and they joined hands and in great, long lines danced around him never tiring and his face positively glowed with the love they sent towards him. But as the sun was dropping, they began to sink to the ground with seeming tiredness and one by one they fell into the grass and stopped moving until their bodies were bones with no flesh which began to pile higher and higher and higher around him until he was on top of the hill full of bodies.

Then a hand reached out from the bodies and pulled him up to where a gibbet was standing black and stark against the sky. From the gibbet hung a noose and the person leading him turned into Klyesha. She smiled at him and led him under the gibbet and put the noose around his neck, all the while smiling at him and holding her finger to her lips to keep him quiet. He felt the noose tighten around his neck choking him, gagging him, his own huge body pulling the rope so tight he had no breath and he wondered how long his breath would last as the hill of bodies fell away.

He woke coughing and gasping for breath and almost pushed Klyesha away until he remembered where he was, the moonlight outlying objects in the room. He pulled himself out of bed to use the chamber pot which must be full of vomit but she had cleansed it and he could relieve himself.

She was sound asleep beside him. He wondered how she'd gotten there from the City then he remembered she was 'Carl' with her beautiful hair all cut off and they had rescued him in their carriage. He wondered if Rufus had reached the Palace and if his dream was any indication, what horrors might he find in the City there. He drank more water and suddenly felt hungry. Seeing the crutches, he tried them on for size, realising he could hop about with them now and not rely on two women like an old man to get about.

He unlocked the door and went to the kitchen where from the light of the stove he found figs and apples and ate them remembering the gluttony of his dream. Was this his life? Was he just a rich glutton who ignored his starving people? He found bread and butter and ate them. He was looking for wine and wondering if he should drink it when Paxton came into the kitchen.

'Sire!'

'Paxton! What are you doing here?'

Paxton poured him some well-watered wine. 'Not too much too soon,' he advised. William nodded.

'I'm here from the Palace. I arrived yesterday. You don't remember?'

'No, I don't. What is happening in the City?'

Paxton explained in so much detail, William felt sick again. He held his head in his hands, 'What have I done, Paxton?' he moaned.

'Sire you did all you could. No one foresaw this coming!'

'I should have! My people starving, mad with hunger. How could I not see this happening?'

'You did what you could with the granaries, but we had no reserve grain.'

'Indeed, but this is all on my watch.'

'Technically, yes, but the Prince was in charge. He betrayed your trust.'

'Do you think he fermented this rebellion deliberately?'

'I suspect so, Sire, creating famine would discredit you. I do not know what his next move will be, but I believe we may need to oppose him with arms.'

'As you say he can't be trusted. Oh, damn this leg!' William pulled it up onto a stool and groaned with the pain. He drank some more watered wine. 'The militias,' he gasped.

'We have already been talking about the militias just this evening. An emergency measure never used before so untried. We

133

do not know if any militias still exist or how many of these men have already joined the rebellion.'

'Surely some of my subjects are still loyal to me!'

'I believe they are, Sire but we must find them. Let me send five of my men to seek them out in the major estates and villages. If we do find them, where are they to assemble and more importantly, how are we going to feed them?'

William was beginning to feel light-headed again. 'Forgive me, Paxton. I believe my fever has broken by I'm still unwell. We will speak on this again in the morning.'

'As you wish, Sire. Let me help you to your chamber.'

'No need,' said William hurriedly. He did not want Klyesha discovered there. 'I can use these crutches. Let me not disturb your slumber further. Until the morning.'

'Yes, Sire.' William went back to his room and Paxton returned to the couch in the sitting room. There he slept without dreams, his heart the lighter for seeing his King's health improved.

Chapter Eleven

A heavy cold rain poured over the Capitol, running off roofs, bursting in torrents from downpipes and overflowing streets. The cobbled roads were soon full of water gathering sticks and rags, paper and rubble as it went flooding towards the canals which interspersed the City. Muddy water flooded into the canals, narrow boats rocked on their moorings and some smaller skiffs, filled with rainwater, started to sink. Everywhere people huddled where they could: under porticos; verandas; under the vast roof of the market; anywhere to avoid a drenching.

The lawless cowered as any of the City's homeless inhabitants. Without thick coats or strong boots, they shivered and stamped their feet and cursed their hunger and their separation from their families. Their eyes were dark with fear and hatred but the rain calmed their resolve to act and the terrible rioting of the last week was abruptly brought to a halt.

Gerard predicted that tiredness or exhaustion would slow the rebellion, he hadn't counted on the weather. His men and himself were equally miserable as they entered the Capitol at dusk. It was not the triumph he envisaged, instead they all wanted shelter and a hot meal. Gerard had a City residence, spectacular as a Prince's should be, made from local white stone with a grey slate roof. It was joined by a large courtyard with stables and an exercise yard for horses. To this villa they trudged, Gerard on horse and the rest of the men walking mechanically due to tiredness and the discomfort of being wet.

He was sharp with the servants who had little foreknowledge of his arrival and they scurried like mice to light fires, provide blankets and hot broth, stable the Prince's horse and prepare a larger meal. His ragged army were dispatched with a few servants to the servant's wing of the building where they gathered, sodden, to partake of food and peel off their drenched outerwear.

Ironsmith, the big, large boned man who had never been to a City, was himself as awestruck as his men who'd gazed in wonder at the scale of the Prince's villa and its furnishings.

'Is this how the rich live?' blurted out one of them as he drank his ale and dipped bread into his broth.

'Is this what we is always working for?' asked another, 'For them that has everything to have even more?'

'Now men,' scolded Ironsmith, 'don't be ungrateful. The Prince has brought you here to improve your lot not make you feel worse. Have we not a purpose now and a leader who has promised a better life?'

'Aye, but we'll never have this!' scoffed another.

'Maybe,' said Ironsmith, 'but is there enough in the Kingdom for all of us to have such a villa? A good house, a warm fire, no worries is all we need. What would we even do with such space?'

'I'd get me a harem like they has in Arabia,' said one man. They all laughed.

'I'd eat and never stop,' said another.

'And your stomach would burst and splatter the ceiling,' laughed Ironsmith, 'No, men, we need to be content with a better situation from what we have had and no more. Greed is a sin as you know.'

'I just want dry clothes,' complained another, holding his shirt and jerkin out to the fire, while standing in a loincloth and undershirt, his breeches draped over a stool.

'That we all want,' said another, 'so leave us some room near the fire!'

'Aye, come if you want,' answered the man without breeches.

'We are all tired and cold. I'll ask the servants for more clothes and some bedding. But I suppose Jackson over there wants a feather pillow!' The men laughed again. Ironsmith spoke to one of the servants who rushed away to do his bidding.

So, it was some hours after dark when the men were quiet, a lot warmer with full bellies and arranged on paillasses or bundles of blankets on the floor, Ironsmith left them and asking a servant was shown the way to the Prince.

The apartments increased in grandeur the further he left the servants quarters behind, tapestries, paintings, sculptures, China in cabinets, clocks, each object astonishing him more as he advanced. Perhaps he might take a small souvenir before he left? Would the Prince even notice? Finally, they arrived at a green painted door with gilded framing and big brass and ceramic door handle. He was led in.

'Ironsmith!' called St Alban, 'How have the men settled?' The Prince and the other men looked at him from the table where they were seated.

'To be honest, mi'Lord they is all a bit awestruck by this Palace.'

Gerard grinned, 'It's a villa, Ironsmith. The Palace is much larger. Please sit down. Wine?'

'Nay, mi'Lord. But I'll have ale if you have it.' Gerard clicked his fingers at a servant who went to fetch some.

'We were just saying, Ironsmith, that the weather has presented us with an opportunity,' commented the Prince.

'How so, mi'Lord?'

'The rioting seems to be quietened down for the present. It allows us tomorrow to make our way among our disaffected friends and convince them to join us.' Ironsmith nodded.

'How should we do that, mi'Lord?' St Alban asked.

Gerard gave a sigh, 'Do I have to spell everything out! Ironsmith and his men will be led in equal groups by you, St Alban, Lewis and I suppose you too, Cottesloe, and you will seek out these bandit groups and recruit them to our cause.'

'But mi'Lord,' interrupted Cottesloe, 'what will we say to them?'

Gerard slammed his goblet on the onto the table, 'Damn you Cottesloe, can't you use your imagination? What do they all want? Huh, what do they want?'

Cottesloe look desperately at St Alban for guidance. He came to the rescue, 'Mi'Lord, I believe they will be won over with a quart of bread.'

Gerard jumped up, 'Absolutely and the promise of more. My cooks are hard at work baking the bread as we speak.'

'But how have you flour?' blurted Lewis, wide eyed.

'Don't worry about that. Just know we do and plenty for more bread.'

'So...' said St Alban cautiously, 'those of them who take the bread also get a red armband and promise to serve us?'

'In order to get more bread,' added Ironsmith.

'Yes, yes!' said Gerard, leaping around the table. 'Bread equals loyalty. They think with their bellies these people.' Forgetting these people also sat before him. 'Arh... these desperate people. They can't see past their next meal therefore we use that.'

The men nodded, sipped their wine or drank deeply of their ale. They desperately wanted answers from Gerard regarding less optimistic scenarios but each was afraid of being ridiculed. Ironsmith, due to his stature, was afraid of few men so he ventured with his first question to the Prince. 'Beg pardon mi'Lord, but what if they won't cooperate? What if instead of taking bread calmly they attack us and steal the bread or threaten to break our heads?'

'Ironsmith, I might be young compared to you men in your 40s but of human nature I am assured of one thing and one thing alone. Every man has his price. Those short-sighted hooligans who think they can simply attack us will be beaten into mincemeat. That is why you are going in groups and that is why you will explain to them that without loyalty there is no more bread. Even the wealthy of this City are feeling the pinch at the moment, so how do you think the poor are going? Now, I don't know how you feel but my bed calls me. It's been a long day. We will rise early, plan a little and act on our plans. Nothing or no one is stopping me from becoming King.'

He left them and Ironsmith returned to his bundle of blankets near the fire, 'Everything is in hand,' he told the men who were still awake, 'Tomorrow we act.'

A solid night's sleep followed by a hearty breakfast saw William much improved by luncheon of the next day. He remained deeply troubled by the uncertainty of affairs in the Capitol but in his heart, in his core, he felt much more solid with Klyesha. He felt with her by his side he could face anything. Loss of blood made him weak still and his usually pale complexion was starkly white. Everyone who saw him counselled rest. He listened to them though his mind was competing in a marathon of worry as there was so much to organise.

He widened his war committee to include 'Carl', 'Robert', Lucca and now Thorsbard as well as Paxton. Jack remained busy seeing to the horses and going on errands as required.

'Let's say,' argued William, 'the Castle is already taken, can we secure the port?'

'I don't see why not,' answered Paxton. 'It's too far from the Castle to be strafed by cannon.'

'So, we make the port and its warehouses our base.'

'Agreed, we need a meeting place,' said Paxton.

'But how can the Castle be taken, Sire, with your troops inside?' asked 'Carl'.

'We're talking worst case scenario. Rufus is in command in the Castle. I know him well enough that he won't listen to Gerard and if he does succeed in keeping him out then all to the good. However, we must plan for the worst eventuality,' argued William.

'The ports strategic,' commented Thorsbard, 'for I can land my kralls and the supplies there safely with you in control. It also gives us the advantage to land some Svartlunders if need be.'

William had taken some convincing on this suggestion. Never had citizens of the Kingdom relied on foreign troops before. Their entry into the country was strictly forbidden. Interactions with foreigners were unknown and the Kingdom was a very insular and inward gazing nation, beholden to no one but themselves. It had been Klyesha as 'Carl 'who convinced the King otherwise.

Earlier in the meeting, she and Lucca explained their plan to trade manufactured goods such as clocks, cloth and gold in exchange for grain and the specific food products for which Svartlund was known. Thorsbard agreed this was possible and vowed to negotiate the exchange. The manufactured goods to be exchanged when the Capitol and the Castle were secured by King William and peace again reigned in the Kingdom. William and Thorsbard had shook hands on it.

William explained to everyone and to Paxton in particular, how the militias worked. Every village and estate had an official, be they the Estate manager or a nobleman such as a Duke or in the case of a village, the mayor, who was in charge of summoning the tenants of the land to a special meeting. This was called the ceremony of the Wardstaff. The Wardstaff was a wooden staff cut from a willow in a special way. It had to be 27 inches in length and 8 inches in circumference. It was revered and had its own linen cloth and was laid on a special cushion.

During the ceremony, the official took the staff to a place where all the tenants of the land or the village had been summoned. Each man would present themselves as a loyal servant and for each man a notch would be cut on the wardstaff. Thus, the wardstaff became a record of the 'fencible' men of the area who could be called upon to keep the peace from murderers or robbers. The staff became a symbol of the Law in that district.

'Therefore,' said William to Paxton, 'Your soldiers need simply to ask to see the wardstaff to count how many tenants are available to upkeep the Law. In this case, to support my troops. I will furnish them with a written decree to the effect they must within one day set out to travel to the Capitol and assemble at the docks there to await further orders.'

'You really should not travel so soon, Your Majesty,' counselled Thorsbard.

'I am expecting the process of vexillation to take about a week,' said William, 'So in a week we will travel back to the Capitol and establish ourselves at the docks. Can you bring the food supplies to the docks in that time, Thorsbard?'

Thorsbard nodded, 'I will try my best, Your majesty.'

Paxton interrupted, 'There's a big problem, Sire, which is you will only have me and five other soldiers to accompany you to the City.'

'Oh, we will come as well,' offered 'Carl' looking at her friends for reassurance.

Internally William bristled, he did not want Klyesha or Rachel to be put at risk however he thanked them all. 'You might remember, Paxton that Hamleyvale itself should be able to contribute some men.'

'I'll check that out,' said Paxton. William asked for paper and quills.

Thorsbard rose and added, 'Well, I should leave by and by, though I will see how the King progresses over the next few days. The time frame is tight but I will see what I can do in Svartlund for your cause.'

'Any contribution from you or your countrymen will be most welcome,' said Lucca. Thorsbard smiled.

'How will they communicate with us?' asked Paxton.

'Oh, I will be leading them so not to worry. I haven't had an adventure for a while. Quite looking forward to this one,' he grinned.

The rain was torrential. For the fourth night in a row, Cook, Flora, James, Walter and his family slept in the shelter of the cellar. By day they were in the house but at night Cook believed the risk was too great to be caught in the house unawares. Rocks thrown had smashed their windows but they'd reinforced inside the windows with wood and so far no bandit or robber had successfully broken open the gate.

On the first night they'd suffered badly from the cold and the little ones whimpered that their fingers and toes were freezing. Flora was all for setting up a Brazier in the cellar but Cook was horrified, 'We'd die from the smoke,' she said, 'and do the job them ruffians want to do on ourselves.'

'I never thought on that,' admitted Flora, so they opted for hot water in flat ceramic flasks instead. Even with these and extra bedding it was a miserable night and Cook rose from her bed stiff with rheumatism and aching bones. 'Oh, how I could do with a warm bath,' she complained in the morning but didn't dare to stay undressed for long enough to have one in case a gang of hooligans broke in and found her so completely undefended. A hot wash from a basin was all she could muster to take the chill from her bones.

'Lord, hurry up with that stove,' she cussed Flora as the poor girl scurried to warm up the kitchen crowded with the wood and kindling Cook had made Walter and James collect together and stack. Mrs Walter was too busy fussing with her babes to help much. Lucy was two, Rose was four and Emily, six years old. Emily was useful to peel potatoes and stir a stew and even Rose's chubby fingers wanted to help with the suet pudding. Lucy played happily with a wooden spoon and a few darning mushrooms which Emily had found and fashioned into dolls for her. Barrels of water stood about filled by the men from the well in the garden. Mrs Walter did Cook's bidding without a word spoken. Indeed, Cook thought she was a mute until a saucepan dropped on her foot the second morning and she emitted a loud yell.

Flora tried to include her in conversation by asking her questions, yet Mrs Walter only nodded in answer or smiled. 'Ain't she a quiet one!' Flora complained to Cook when Mrs Walter was out of earshot.

'Oh, leave her alone,' said Cook, 'your prattling 23 hours out of 24 more than makes up for it.' Flora blanched. She only wanted to be helpful and was quiet for a full 15 minutes afterwards until she decided to teach the babes their numbers from 1 to 20.

James was most at a loss missing the Smithy, wondering how his workmates were faring. 'We had so many orders for axe heads and Pike ends too,' he complained to Walter, 'who'd be doing them now?'

'Why didn't they hold up in the Smithy? They wouldn't be short of metal there to make bolts and chains.'

'They could have. They wanted me and the other single men to stay because the married ones all went home to protect their families. Then my sister needed me here and the other single men left too so they shut up the shop. I dare say no one'd get in there unless they burn the whole place down.'

'Good thing too. Wouldn't want no ruffians rifling the place for weapons to kill innocent folk.'

They spent the day feeding the chickens, patrolling the boundaries and digging over and weeding garden beds in preparation for the spring planting. Walter had a few cabbages, silver beet, beetroots and onions under glass cloches and these were carefully watered and fertilised and the grass kept low to allow what feeble sun there was to warm them.

The next day everything was sodden by the rain and the men were out in oilskins digging ditches is to stop the garden flooding, clearing downpipes or guttering to keep water out of the house. 'At least we won't suffer for lack of water,' grimaced Walter as he and James stood dripping just inside the kitchen door.

'Be off with ye,' roused Cook, and drip somewhere off me floors!' So they left and dried themselves in the laundry but were soon back near the kitchen fire to get warm.

'Suet pudding, eh?' said James grinning. Flora tweaked his ear. 'And there'll be none for you till supper mind! You'll be getting a bite of bread is all.' His forlorn face turned Cook's heart and he was sent on his way with a piece of yesterday's fruitcake. 'Mind you check them shutters,' she ordered the men so they took their mugs of ale and food elsewhere.

On the second and third nights they listened, terrified, as hooligans raged against the splendour of the house by throwing cobbles at the windows, exhilarated when they all smashed and pieces fell into the garden. The rabble's curses and screams went on for a solid half hour which Cook thought would never end. 'If only I had me old washing club,' wished cook exasperated, 'to flail their hides till they was as flat as pancakes.' The others made no comment due to Cook's status in the household and her kindness. Mrs Walter had tears in her eyes when Cook let the little family inside for the first time. Words weren't needed to show how grateful they all were.

Late at night in his bedchamber, Prince Gerard met with one of his closest allies, Lindquist the Deputy Chancellor. 'How many troops?' he asked.

'About 400, mi'Lord.'

'All on watch in the castle?'

'Yes mi'Lord.'

'Are there anymore?'

'I believe Paxton has taken twenty men to search for the King.'

'Where?'

'No one knows. Not even the Chancellor.'

'He must be found.'

'Agreed but to do so you will need to send someone.'

'I have a few servants who are good horsemen. I'll provide them with gold they can use to bribe others for information.'

'But will they find him?'

'I have a plan,' conceded Gerard. He laid out his plan. Lindquist believed it was his best one yet and if successful would assure Gerard the crown.

Chapter Twelve

'I've met with the Village Mayor. They eventually found the wardstaff but unfortunately it was last used 100 years ago.'

William swore. It was yet another problem he would have to deal with in the future. This could slow things down if the same situation had occurred in other parts of the country.

'Be that as it may, Sire,' said Paxton, 'the officials have to make good for their laxity. They will have to summon the tenants and call on them to uphold the law.'

'Meanwhile things are deteriorating in the City and Gerard's scheming has more time to come to fruition. We should go tomorrow.'

'No Sire, beg pardon, but that would be foolhardy. I could not guarantee your safety. You would be at risk of abduction or even murder with so little protection.'

William looked out of the window and down to his bandaged leg, 'I feel like a hostage here unable to do anything.'

'You are doing something, Sire. You are planning and organising. Please be patient. Hopefully the news from my soldiers about fencible men in other parts of the country might be more promising.'

'How many might Hamleyvale itself contribute?'

'The Mayor said up to 40 men.'

William nodded. 'There's nothing to do but wait, then.' Paxton agreed. He felt for the King who was like a hound chafing at his leash or a man whose whole world was crumbling around him.

William argued with Klyesha in the night, 'You won't be safe! You have to stay here!'

Klyesha shook her head, 'I will be by your side. Nothing is going to separate us again.'

'No, I won't risk you. You are too important to me, my darling!' He held her close and kissed her again. 'Let us not argue. All our time is precious. I will soon be leaving.'

Klyesha started to cry and he stroked her hair away from her face. 'You know a disguise is good,' she said, 'It worked for me and it can work for you. Rachel said you can use walnut skins or pomegranate skins to dye your hair black and you can shave off your beard.'

'But the people need me as a rallying point.'

'Do they or will they see you as the enemy? The King who has brought famine upon them.'

'Yes, I am that aren't I?'

'You and I know Gerard is more to blame. The people see only their circumstances and not the reasons behind them. I believe you are more in danger as the King. Please listen to me, we can't make any mistakes now.'

'Maybe you're right. We can make a start tomorrow. But on your safety, I won't be moved. It is a command- you are staying here!'

The day after their arrival the rain eased. Loading up wicker baskets of bread and carrying bundles of red arm bands, Lewis, St Alban, Cottesloe and Ironsmith set out into the City. Those not carrying bread, carried arms. Muskets were carried by the few men who knew how to use them and each group had at least one. If the mobs got too close, the muskets were to be fired as a warning.

Lewis's group went to the Central City Markets, a covered area with temporary stalls which set up every Wednesday. As it wasn't market day, they expected fewer people. They were wrong. The markets were crowded with the destitute and the hungry. Mostly men, they'd spent a miserable night with no food in their bellies and sodden clothes. In winter this could mean death and there were a number of pathetic bundles on the ground representing men whose spirits had departed in the night.

As soon as Lewis's group were seen carrying bread, the starving lame, sick and troubled men surged towards and around them. A number of Lewis's men were knocked off their feet in the mad scramble for bread. His men fought back, pikes, clubs and axes inflicted terrible injuries on the desperate creatures reaching for food. The musket bearer finally fired which sent a number of the desperados scurrying for cover while the braver amongst them used the distraction to pluck bread from the already blood-soaked cobbles. Lewis' pleas to stop and listen to him went completely unheeded. No one heard why the bread was being distributed. No one heard about the red arm bands. No one heard how the arm bands could guarantee more bread. It was complete mayhem.

Lewis decided a strategic retreat was needed in order to protect the lives of his men. He ordered them to cast away the bread baskets and follow him back to the villa. They did so, though a few became enmeshed in the basket straps and stumbled. It was the last thing they did as they were trampled by desperate bread seekers. Lewis ordered the musket bearers to turn and fire into the mob which added to the chaos and carnage.

Running now, Lewis's men were pursued by a small group of desperados who had to be deterred with pikes and axes swung about until they too retreated howling in pain and anger like a dispirited pack of starving wolves.

Lewis's group, some four or five men down, ran for their lives through lanes and backstreets splashing through some minor flooding, startled at every turn by other menacing groups until they finally reached the safety of the Prince's villa and desperately knocked on the solid wooden gate. They were let in breathless, their lungs heaving and the muscles of their legs cramping with pain.

Lewis shook his head with disbelief. He praised his men when he could breathe enough to speak again. Some of them had lost their weapons and all the baskets for bread too were lost. He didn't know how he would tell the Prince the bad news. As for the other groups, how they had fared he could only guess.

As it turned out, their stories were very similar. The desperation and sheer numbers of the mobs made negotiation with them impossible. Each group had had to make retreats for better or worse, trying to preserve their men as they did so. Cottesloe's group fared worst as they'd ventured near the docks where empty warehouses had been taken over by homeless mobs who believed food might be found there. They were attacked viciously with anything the mob could obtain: planks of wood, coils of rope or cobbles. Cottesloe called desperately to a ship's crew to let down a gangplank to save his men but they refused, afraid the mobs would also use the bridge to get onto their ship.

Caught between the docks and the harbour, Cottesloe and his men fought hard but they were heavily outnumbered. All they could do to save themselves was to jump into the harbour. Some few sailors feeling sorry for them threw them wooden buoys to cling onto, for nearly all were country men who'd never learned to swim. Cottesloe jumped and hit his head on a wooden plank jutting out from the wharf. He was unconscious as he hit the water and his men tried to save him but were unable to swim towards him so he drowned. Five only of his group of 20 survived. Those few paddled themselves further around from the wharves and clung to wood until they heard the mobs disperse. Unfamiliar with the City, it took them all night to find the villa again and report their disastrous expedition.

St Alban did not return to the Villa that night. He had been injured badly in a melee and sought refuge in an Inn. The innkeeper was loyal to the King. When St Alban asked for assistance, the innkeeper sent to the Castle for help, pretending to assist him. During the night, guards from the Castle were let into the Inn. When they went to drag him from one of the Inn's rooms, St Alban was already dead from his injuries.

So, instead of recruiting men, Gerard had lost more than 30. Of those remaining some were injured but all were traumatised. Lewis and Ironsmith survived but were appalled by the insidious nature of the mobs and their complete lawlessness. No one knew what had happened to St Alban. His men too were either dead or scattered. They did not return to the Villa.

As Gerard heard their stories, he went puce with anger. Screaming and shouting, he railed at them with their broken arms and scratched faces. He won no friends. The men saw him for the spineless tyrant he was. They only stayed for the shelter and food he provided. Lewis and Ironsmith were stunned by Cottesloe's drowning and the loss of St Alban, even Gerard's foul invective could not increase the shame they felt at failure or the enormity of the task he'd set them. He didn't know what it was really like out there. Ironsmith, who feared no one told him so. Gerard screamed at him and turned tail and disappeared into his own lavish apartments before he did something he'd regret.

The rest of the men collapsed in the servants' quarters which overnight had become a military hospital where the servants helped them as much as they could, distributing ale and food, linens and bandages, liniments and tincture of opium. Men groaned and moaned from their injuries throughout the night. Too exhausted and dispirited to converse, even Lewis and Ironsmith were quiet as they contemplated their own individual futures and whether the Prince would play a part in them.

He may have been resistant but his passengers, unwelcome as they were, became his responsibility when they came onto his ship. Most of them were the families of his sailors who he vowed he would not neglect. Others were neighbours or the desperate who thought of his ship as a way to escape the predations of the mobs. Below deck was a shambles to say the least. Every inch was covered with bedding, personal possessions, boxes of food, kitchen utensils and on top of it was crammed human beings of all sizes, strengths and ages. It did not smell good. He commanded the hatchways open and a bellows brought to push in fresh air.

He'd anchored his ship far enough from the docks to prevent missiles, usually bricks or cobbles, from reaching the deck or rigging. This had allowed many passengers free range on the deck though the occasional spear made its way between them scaring everyone.

Today he'd made up his mind. They were nearly out of food. Water was sufficient due to using barrels to catch rainwater but food was not to be had anywhere. They lifted the anchor and set sail for the high seas. No local island was suitable for landing being inhabited mainly by seabirds. Even the Island of Cats where he'd taken the King and rescued the young woman was not suitable to sustain his 150 passengers. The only course was to set sail for another country. Svartlund seemed the obvious destination though he was unsure how a shipload of refugees from the Kingdom might be received. He really had no choice when some of his passengers became so weak from hunger, they could not leave their beds. He could not allow them all to die, not in his ship and under his jurisdiction. Svartlund would have to be risked for they were all dead if they remained docked in the Capitol's port any longer.

William wasn't happy, 'Why not here?' he asked.

'Carl' shook her head. 'I can do nothing here. In Svartlund I can help organise supplies and Lucca will help me draw up trading contracts, but we'll need another written decree from you authorising them.'

William groaned partly from his leg and partly from frustration. Svartlund was almost totally unknown to them and while Thorsbard seemed a genuine man perhaps he would change when he returned home? It was true they were running out of options for food and as everyone knew, an army marched on its stomach. Food represented as well as gave weight to any negotiations to quell the riots. Food was essential, however if he, Paxton and the fencible army arrived in the Capitol too soon before the food supplies had arrived by ship from Svartlund, they risked defeat pure and simple. Klyesha as 'Carl' could ensure the success of the expedition to Svartlund. She was determined and smart, while Lucca was practical. Was it worth the risk? At least she'd be out of the volatile situation in the Kingdom.

William reluctantly agreed. He knew the gold reserves in the Palace would be sufficient to pay for the food. Future supplies could be exchanged for their manufactured goods as a harvest was still six months away. He didn't quite realise the gravity of the situation though until she was arrayed before him kitted out ready to leave. As he could not kiss 'Carl' goodbye he remembered instead their previous night's lovemaking when with their emotions heightened, they again pledged eternal love for each other. Today was business. He handed her the decree rolled up and sealed to be delivered to King Gunnar in Yalsbad. He couldn't even give her money as what little he had was needed to be spent on supplies for his trip back to the port. Klyesha had assured him in the night she still had the money she'd brought with her.

He stood on his crutches at the cottage door. 'Godspeed Thorsbard, Lucca, Robert and Carl! What a great adventure is ahead of you,' he said. Jack stayed with him.

'Thank you, Sire.'

'Godspeed to you.'

'Good luck with your army.'

'We will see each other soon,' were the parting wishes they gave him.

He watched them as they mounted their horses for the journey over the mountain pass. 'Carl' stared back at him for as long as she could, tears in her eyes.

Tears welled in the King's eyes too. He'd never felt so helpless, so lacking in Kingly command. He could not even keep his loved ones safe.

He and Paxton sat in silence for a while at the kitchen table, the kitchen suddenly very silent and large with four less humans crowded into it. William sipped his watered wine staring at the door. Paxton cleared his throat. 'Sire, there is a piece of news I have kept from you not wanting to speak of it in front of your guests.'

'Oh?' asked William.

When I was in the Capitol, I called on Klyesha and Rachel concerned for their safety due to the lawlessness in the City increasing. And I'm sorry to report, Sire, they weren't there. Their Cook said they were on a journey with two young men.'

William looked at him startled, 'Two young men!'

'Yes, Sire,' confirmed Paxton reddening.

William composed himself, 'Paxton, thank you for your thoughtfulness. If Mistress Klyesha and her friend Rachel embarked on a journey, then I am sure they chose the young men wisely and planned the excursion very thoroughly.'

'But are you not concerned for their safety, Sire?'

'No Paxton. I believe the character of Klyesha and Rachel is such that they can look after themselves very well. I am sure they will both surprise us.'

Indeed, thought Paxton, perplexed. Perhaps the young lady was no longer an object of the King's affection? Or perhaps, the King knew her better than he did and she was more than the polite but tragic figure she presented at Court. The life of a recluse on a remote island may have furnished her with more life lessons than the average young woman. As he pondered these thoughts, a knock came at the door. He stood up and went and opened it.

'I have a message for the King,' said a young man.

Paxton stared at him sternly, 'I do not know where the King is. I am the Commander of the King's Guard. What is the message and who is it from?'

'It is for the King's eyes only,' reiterated the messenger.

'Then, as I have already told you the King is not here. Either leave me the message to pass on to him when I see him or leave.'

Paxton motioned to his men stationed near the door. They came up and stood right next to the messenger. The young man became visibly agitated.

'My message is for the King,' he repeated.

Paxton made a hand gesture and the messenger was seized and dragged into the reception room. He was placed on a chair while Paxton's men hovered at his elbows.

'Excuse my manners. I will fetch you a tankard of ale seeing you have come on a journey.' Paxton left and the messenger continued to complain which the soldiers ignored. In the kitchen, Paxton motioned for the King to be quiet and when he left with the ale, he closed the kitchen door. He placed the tankard before the messenger and out of politeness the young man drank.

'Who sent you?'

'The Chancellor, Albert Strong.'

'I see and that's his letter is it?'

'Yes, but it's only for the King not you,' said the youth. Paxton grimaced at the youth but restrained himself from slapping his face.

'All correspondence for the King comes through me. I decide if it is worth him reading it or not.'

The youth was very nervous and began to sweat. Paxton wondered why a messenger would be so agitated. After all, he was just delivering a message. He hadn't written it.

A simple slide of his eyes and one of his men held the youth while the other took the parchment and handed it to Paxton. The youth made to protest what was held firmly by the guards.

'Now, I shall examine this message while you wait here and enjoy your ale. Alright?'

The youth nodded sheepishly. Paxton went to the kitchen and again motioned to the King to be quiet as they retreated to his bedchamber well out of earshot of the messenger.

Paxton handed the King the parchment. He examined the seal and unrolled it. It read:

'King William,

If this is to find you safe, I am a happy man. The whole Palace is distraught with lack of knowledge as to your wellbeing.

The situation in the Capitol is out of hand. I have instructed the Kings Guard to remain in the Castle to secure it from the many lawless mobs roaming in the Capitol. It is my unfortunate belief that 400 men would soon be outnumbered by them and overrun. I cannot commit any troops to such an ill-advised cost. Captain Rufus agrees with me. Nor can I commit a large detachment of troops to come to your aid.

My esteemed advice, forgive me if I give it, is for you to remain where you are hopefully in safety.

I will send word when the mobs disperse or otherwise decrease in number and your safe return can be assured,
Yours sincerely,
Albert Strong, Chancellor'

William looked at Paxton and handed him the letter. Paxton read it and shook his head, 'Things have indeed deteriorated in the Capitol, if this is to be believed.'

'I believe there is some truth in it,' observed William, 'however I don't believe it was sent by Strong. I know his handwriting and this is a fair attempt at reproducing his hand but it is not his work. Also, the seal is wrong. A similar seal has been used and the wax carved and then perhaps a candle has been passed over it to conceal the handiwork.'

'If it is a form of treachery then what is its object?'

'Quite simple,' said William tossing the parchment aside, 'To find out where I am.'

'I told the messenger you weren't here,' said Paxton.

'Good man. We must keep it that way. My gut feeling is this is Gerard's doing. Perhaps the messenger would simply alert assassins once he knew I was here.'

'Then what shall we do with him?'

'We cannot know if he has come alone or not. Nothing he says will I believe and we don't have the manpower to follow him.'

'We kill him.'

'Yes, we might but if he has companions and he disappears our presence, my presence here will be assumed.'

'So, what do we do?'

'You write a note for Strong and reseal it in the parchment. We know it won't reach Strong but it will reach Gerard. Simply say you are still searching for the King and will send word when he is found. But it means we have to leave ourselves today. Luckily my hair is dyed black and one of your men can give me his livery to further disguise my appearance. When we leave if anyone is watching we will look like a detachment of the King's Guard.'

'But where shall we go?'

'To the nearest estate to gather troops. Are any of your men back yet?'

'Most, Sire.'

'Then question them. We go to the Estate which is closest and can provide the greatest number of men. Hurry now and write the reply. Quills, parchment and an ink well are on the kitchen dresser.'

'Immediately,' said Paxton who rushed off to write.

William gritted his teeth. How duplicitous was his brother! Still, he knew how many troops were in the Castle and maybe it was a good guess Rufus was one of them, then maybe not. Gerard's spies were almost certainly in the Palace. They couldn't get Strong's ring which was his seal because he never took it off, but they could copy other seals from documents. Perhaps the long hours he'd spent reading Strong's letters to petitioners had finally been useful. He knew his handwriting intimately and this latest forgery was easily recognised. Were assassins really waiting for him somewhere in the village? If so, they had to outsmart and outride them.

For the first time that day, William was glad Klyesha had left for Svartlund. Maybe she really was better off away from him.

Chapter Thirteen

The mountain pass was steep and just wide enough for a cart though few if any ventured here according to Thorsbard. They all wore cloaks and hoods against the cold and the occasional flurries of white, sparkling snow which fell around them. 'Carl' had never ridden a horse before and made no secret of the fact so hers was led by Lucca while she clung desperately to the saddle and tried not to look down the dangerous precipice only feet away. 'Robert' was more confident yet she too skirted close to the mountainside away from any drop. Thorsbard patiently plodded ahead on his white steed both having made this journey many times before.

It was with great relief they reached the mountain peak after an hour's ride and there stopped to catch their breath and take in the vista. Before them, when the clouds parted long enough to see, were valleys surrounded by steeper snow-laden mountains. Immediately below them were white dusted beech forests divided by brown trails and on the cleared slopes, tiny log houses emitting pale threads of smoke. The scene was breathtakingly beautiful and 'Carl' congratulated herself for this was the type of experience she longed for when shut up in a house in the City. Nature made her blood run faster and her brain filled with possibilities. Nature was where she belonged.

Thorsbard pointed out a cluster of tiny buildings in the distance, his estate. They could see a frozen river nearby and many buildings of various sizes. 'We should be there by mid-afternoon,' he announced, 'if you can wait upon your meal until then I can promise you a very hearty one.'

'Thank you, Thorsbard.' said 'Carl'. 'Can we see Yalsbad from here?'

Thorsbard turned his horse and pointed east to where they could see the blue of the sea meeting the land. 'It's quite hard to make out buildings from this far away, but Yalsbad sits near the indent in the coastline where is a port and much flat low-lying land nearby which is easier to build on than the sloping hills you can see before you.'

'Carl' longed to get down and stretch her legs and back, but she gritted her teeth and put her face again into the bitter wind as they began the downward ascent. The road here was wider and better maintained.

'Are we in Svartlund now?' asked Lucca.

'Yes,' smiled Thorsbard, 'you've noticed the better roads?'

'Carl' frowned. So much of the Kingdom required attention she thought. They stopped briefly at the bottom of the winding mountain pass to drink and stretch their legs. The horses scraped at the snow to find roots to eat. Thorsbard passed around his flask of watered spirit and they all felt the warmth of it flow through their bodies. Unused to alcohol 'Carl' and 'Robert' partook of only a few sips.

On horseback again they made good progress and after another break with a further hour of riding, they arrived at the stone fence surrounding Thorsbard's estate. It was 'Carl' noted, completely different to William's country estate. Here all the buildings were made of logs with wooden shingle or turf roofs. All except the main building were single story. Many people clad in furs and woollen breeches or skirts came out of their huts to greet Thorsbard and the unusual sight of foreign guests. For people of the Kingdom never came here. Thorsbard called out to them all and the warning gave his kralls in the main homestead time to build up the fires and set cauldrons of meat to heat over them. Tall, blond-bearded men took their horses to be rubbed down and fed in the largest barn.

'Welcome,' said Thorsbard, encouraging his guests to enter his home. The floor was stone covered with woven carpets but the walls were all lined with pine planks. Numerous elk horns and deer skulls were mounted on the plank walls. He led them to a room off to the right of the main entrance hall where benches covered with furs sat around a central fire pit. They were soon all luxuriating in the warmth and toasting their hands and feet at the fire. Mugs of mulled mead were soon brought to them on wooden salvers by rosy-cheeked plump women who looked as blonde as their men. They all soon removed their cloaks and were relaxing and chatting comfortably while their host left to arrange an early evening meal.

155

The meal was served in a large hall with long wooden tables and benches all orientated towards a huge stone fireplace blazing with a massive log fire. Wooden bowls held a hearty meat and potato stew while trenchers were stacked high with warm, brown rye loaves not like the light and fluffy bread in the Capitol but solid and hearty so that only a little smothered in butter was needed to become quite full. Their utensils were all wooden except for the knives which were of iron mounted in a wooden handle, small and sharp, excellent for paring the apples which followed the stew.

'My apologies for no sweets,' said Thorsbard. 'We usually have a pie made with apples, sugar and nutmeg but they require time. Perhaps tomorrow,' he looked happy and relaxed in his own home and they soon met his wife, Liza, and his son, Roman, a youth of about 16. They were both shy of the foreigners as neither had been over the Pass to the Kingdom. Liza was obviously happy to have her husband home early and she kept kissing him and he squeezed her tight.

'Well, my friends as you are warm and full perhaps showing you to your rooms is best to do now rather than see more of my estate?' They all heartily agreed and were shown into small separate cubicles each with a warm bed made of wood, a washstand with warmed water in a dish and fresh linen. 'Carl' removed her outerwear, the stupid cummerbund and jumped into bed wearing her long shirt and warm socks. Much as her mind grieved departing from William, her body took over and she was soon in a deep dreamless slumber.

By morning the area lay under a new layer of crisp, white snow. Only the tracks of foxes and the occasional wolf could be seen in the snow outside the corral. Birds tweeted in the birch trees hearkening to the pale warmth of the sun. After a big bowl of barley porridge and milk, Thorsbard led his guests around his estate. Krall families wearing furs and skin caps bowed and smiled at them insisting they enter their huts for refreshment. Not wishing to disturb the workers, they only entered one. While they sat on fur-covered benches they were presented with dried plums and freshly made yoghurt. 'Carl' thought it delicious having never had yoghurt before. The krall couple's three children, all under five, smiled shyly at them and the boldest, a girl of five, stood near 'Carl' touching her clothes. She was scolded by her mother, but 'Carl' smiled and shook her head.

Reaching into her Cape, pocket she drew out a string of glass beads and handed it to the little girl who beamed with excitement.

'How many kralls live here?' asked 'Carl'.

'About 90 including their families. This is their slower time when they spin wool or make small wooden objects in the warmth of their homes. The men hunt animals for winter furs which you can see are of high quality. 'Robert' stroked the fur of a wolf she was sitting on. It was luxuriously thick and warm. As they stood to leave, the mother insisted 'Robert' and 'Carl' take the furs they'd sat on, although they tried to refuse.

'Hospitality is sacred here,' commented Thorsbard, 'so they will be very happy if you take the furs.' So, it was decided. 'Robert's thick black wolf fur contrasted with her red hair and 'Carl's red fox fur complemented her black hair. Lucca was presented with a cow horn used for drinking. He bowed and gave the father a small pocket watch. It was the first timepiece of any kind a krall had possessed and he was deeply grateful. 'Robert' gave the mother a thin gold necklace she took from around her neck. She too was overwhelmed by the gift.

'Well enough of gift exchanging, let's look at the barns,' said their host. They followed him out into the crisp snow which men were clearing from the pathways and roads with wooden spades. They all bowed to them and stared as they went past.

The first barn was of double storey height. Huge oak beams held up the roof in a crosshatched pattern. Massive mud brick silos held wheat, barley or rye which Thorsbard showed them by opening tiny chutes at their bases. The grains were fat and glossy. 'This is what we spend all summer harvesting,' he said, 'there is enough grain here for our estate needs for two or more years. We sell the excess to millers in Yalsbad and other Svartlund towns. What we will be doing here over the next few days is to gather barrels of grain for trade to the Kingdom. I have carpenters building new barrels as we speak. Would you like to see?'

The men, called coopers, were hammering metal straps for the barrels or cutting the planks which were thin but strong. One man heated them in a steam furnace while another fitted them into bases and pushed the ready-made iron straps around them. Another caulked the barrels with a pitch like substance. The Smithy was deliciously warm on a cold winter's morning but also noisy and smoky. Already ten or more barrels stood stacked and ready to be filled. The guests were all impressed by the efficiency of Thorsbard's workers.

In another area of the same barn, men were building solid sleighs to take the barrels horses would drag on the road to Yalsbad. Lucca was amazed at how quickly Thorsbard had organised this work.

'We don't really stop doing it,' he explained, 'barrels are needed all year round and if we're not making drays, we're making sleighs. Unfortunately, these workers don't get much of a rest in winter. I give them time off in summer before the grain harvest when they go fishing or swimming in the river. Some take their families to Yalsbad to buy goods we can't make here, trading furs or wooden utensils. We don't use money much in Svartlund. It's still very much a barter economy.'

Our gold might really change their society, thought 'Carl' which would be a pity. Everyone seemed so industrious and skilled. Other barns held milking cows, young animals which were fattened for meat, pigs, chickens and geese. Women were plucking chickens, while others were making sausages from minced pig meat. A special lined room held hundreds of curing hams, sausages, salamis and sides of bacon.

This was why everyone looked so well and healthy, thought Lucca enviously. If only their own farmers were as efficient, however in the Kingdom the model was individual farmers with fewer estates. As theirs was a money economy, the paying of wages to tenants had become increasingly difficult for estate owners and managers especially if income was low in times of poor harvests. This had helped encourage the spread of individual farmers on smaller allotments.

'Robert' wanted to know how yoghurt was made, thinking she'd try her hand at it when they returned home. She was taken to the dairy where dairymaids churned butter while others made cheese using rennet from cows to separate the milk. Yoghurt was made by starting with a spoon of yoghurt which was added to warmed milk and kept in large ceramic jars with lids. Fresh yoghurt was made every day. Pats of butter were piled high to go to the huts and the main house. 'Carl' couldn't resist tasting some on a knife left nearby. It was amazingly smooth and rich.

In the afternoon they were invited to go hunting with Thorsbard's men. 'Carl' and 'Robert' declined not wanting their lack of prowess with the muskets revealed. Lucca went and was extremely proud to have helped net a white wolf, a huge male with a magnificent coat, which one of the kralls promised to skin and cure for him.

They feasted on salmon, ham, pickled vegetables and the awaited apple pie at dinner that night. The wolf, too gamey to eat, was divided for the estate's hounds who'd help flush him out on the hunt.

After dinner they played draughts and chess by the light of oil lamps. Drums and flutes played some traditional tunes and some of the women danced. 'Carl' was shocked to see one of the younger women looking intently at her and she was sure if she was indeed a young man that more than blankets might have warmed 'him' in bed that night. 'Robert' reported similar glances which they giggled over in the isolation of 'Carl's room that night. 'Do you think Lucca might succumb?' asked Carl. 'Robert' frowned and looked pained so it was the first inkling of 'Carl's which indicated 'Robert's feelings for Lucca. So caught up was she in the King's affections, she hadn't noticed what was happening between 'Robert' and Lucca. Out of embarrassment for her friend, she refrained from teasing her about it but vowed to observe their interactions more closely in the following days.

Paxton left a man at the cottage in Hamleyvale, together with Jack, as two soldiers had yet to return their reports of fencible men from the districts to which they had been sent. Jack was to return the key to the Tavern keeper and together with the others meet himself and the King at 'Rosethorn Estate' which laid due west from Hamleyvale in the foothills of the mountains which divided the Kingdom from Svartlund.

To 'Rosethorn Estate' the King, Paxton and seven soldiers travelled all bedecked in the King's livery of blue and yellow together with 20 of Hamleyvale's tenants, the 'fencible' men who volunteered to help restore order in the Capitol. The other twenty had instructions to march for the Capitol in one week there to meet at the docks. Jack would go with them.

The journey took two days. The roads were mere paths and the settlements few, though they found a woodsman's hut to shelter in which he kindly shared with them on the first night. William's leg still needed dressing but it was healing well now with no sign of reinfection. As his health improved, so did William's resolve to maintain order in his Kingdom at whatever cost.

The principal of 'Rosethorn' Estate was a nobleman by the name of Antonio Declerq. He was an old man still sound of mind yet infirm of body. He could barely walk and William immediately sympathised with his condition. The old man suffered from gout, a product of too much rich meat and whisky. His estate was a cold one fully surrounded by pine forest and the Castle was dank and chill despite the huge fires always blazing.

Duke Declerq greeted William with a reverence which was quite overwhelming for the young King, as no one of any rank of royalty had ever previously visited. The Duke plied William, Paxton and the senior of their soldiers with butts of beef and sliced ham, pottage of duck and berry compotes. Of bread there was little, as even here the harvest was long gone.

'Sire, whatever you desire is my wish,' said the Duke holding out his hands. 'I have a young daughter from my second wife who is of marriageable age. Seeing you are unmarried an alliance with my family would bring all my lands under your fiefdom, as I have no son.' Declerq's daughter was a golden-haired maid of around twenty called Louisa. She was very pretty with pale alabaster skin and pastel blue eyes. She looked at William with a kind of desperation. William apologised to the Duke, admitting though he wasn't married yet he might soon be. The news shocks shocked Paxton but William assured him later privately it was merely a ploy to discourage the old man and the young Lady's hopes.

'If I was only 10 years younger,' sighed Paxton under his breath to the King when they sat at table.

'Indeed, Paxton don't underestimate yourself,' encouraged the King. For the rest of the evening, Paxton tried to catch the lady's eye and began a few halting conversations with her. She was very shy with him and by the end of the evening it was by no means clear if he had a chance with her.

William was rather annoyed he had to wait at the estate for the other soldiers as well as to give time for Thorsbard and Klyesha to organise the food shipments. The chaos of his Capitol troubled him deeply and he was more than ready to set off the next day with the extra men the Duke would provide him. It took Paxton all his negotiating skills to dissuade the King. More men would mean a greater protection for the King he argued. He didn't want to enter the Capitol with less than 100 men and hoped there would be hundreds more to join them at the rendezvous if the estates and villages were true to the tradition of the wardstaff.

Gerard had spent long hours in consultation with Lindquist. They'd both decided it might be best to decamp to the Castle to wait out the inevitable weakening of the mob's resolve. Yet Gerard knew Strong would be hostile towards him as he'd surely been apprised of the King's reasons for pursuing him. 'What do you think would be the greatest reason for Strong to accept me?' asked the Prince.

'That undoubtedly would be the King's demise,' answered Lindquist, swiftly. A well-studied public servant of 35 or so years, Lindquist though loyal to the Prince, knew the difficulties of winning over William's army and his Courtiers many of whom worked in positions in the Castle.

'Then we stay here longer and await word of the King's whereabouts.'

As it happened, the youth whose parchment Paxton had snatched arrived at the villa the next day. 'My Lord,' said the youth whose his confidence had grown on the journey back to the Capitol, 'I have a message from Captain Paxton of the Kings Guard.'

Gerard read the letter, 'Tell me more,' he demanded. The youth described the cottage and his treatment.

'Did Paxton leave the room to write this note?' asked the Prince.

'Yes, My Lord,'

'Arh, tell me, did you stay to observe the village afterwards?'

'Yes, my Lord. The men and I observed the cottage for a day. The next morning eight Kings Guards left the cottage riding out of Hamleyvale headed west together with another group of around twenty men who followed on foot.'

'Were the soldiers all in livery?'

'Yes, my Lord.'

'And you followed them?'

'Yes, mi'Lord, we did at a distance. They travelled for two days to an Estate called 'Rosethorn'.

'Excellent. Go to the kitchen, get refreshments and wait there for further instructions.'

The young man bowed and left. Gerard turned to Lindquist, 'He was there wasn't he?'

'Perhaps, mi'Lord. As Paxton left the room, he may have gone to speak to the King.'

'Damn, we might have had him then if my men were of a greater number to attack the eight. But tell me what is he doing skulking on the border as far away from his blessed Capitol as he can be?'

'It seems strange, mi'Lord but perhaps something or someone is detaining him?'

'Lindquist I'm a fool! Strike me down for being such a dullard! Klyesha! Where is she? Importantly, wherever she is, so perhaps is he.' Gerard called to a servant to send him Ironsmith.

When Ironsmith arrived, he was relieved to see the Prince in a better mood. 'Sit down, Ironsmith. Here, have an ale.' Gerard pointed to the jug on the table where he and Lindquist sat. 'How are the men?'

'Much sore and many hurts but the servants do well by us.'

'Good, good. Do you have a few men still able-bodied ?'

'Yes, mi'Lord.'

'Then you will select five and take them to a place whose address you will be given and there you will find two young women. You will bring them to me, unharmed mind, at once.' Ironsmith nodded. 'There should be no resistance. Explain that I wish only to speak to them. Is that clear?'

Ironsmith nodded. 'Finish your ale and go.' Gerard wrote the address for him. 'Take one of my servants as they know the City better than you countrymen.'

'And the mobs, mi'Lord?'

'Just avoid them. I want no more men injured.'

Ironsmith finished his ale in one long gulp, took the address and left.

'Do you believe she'll be there?' asked Lindquist.

'No, but that is not the point, we need information.'

In Yalsbad, low stone buildings lined the docks. The City expanded out behind in a grid pattern, a mixture of half-timbered and stone buildings with some impressive official buildings such as a Chancery and the King's Palace.

'We could visit King Gunnar if you wish,' asked Thorsbard.

Lucca and 'Carl' exchanged glances. 'We have a full load of grain and supplies in two ships,' commented 'Carl'. 'Do we need to ratify an agreement or something?'

Thorsbard cleared his throat, 'In my opinion if this trade is successful, we will have a better bargaining point. If as your King has promised, I return with gold and manufactured goods, King Gunnar will be more predisposed to look on trading between our two countries favourably. Do you agree?'

'Carl' spoke up, 'As you say, you will have proof of success as opposed to just a promise. I agree. Also the sooner we reach the Capitol, the better.'

'Then we sail tomorrow. Tonight, you will partake of the delights of our Capitol,' he grinned. 'Carl' looked at 'Robert' and wondered what they might be exposed to.

Supervising the loading of cargo all day was a tiresome business, so they all retired to a local Tavern called, when translated, 'The Lonely Duck', indeed a white duck was painted on the tavern's shingle which hung outside the building.

The friends sat at old oaken trestles on benches arranged against rough stone walls amused to see many huge men cavorting with the few barmaids who were trying to negotiate the crowds with full trays of barley beer. 'Carl' couldn't for the life of her see why any woman would expose themselves to leery looks, bottom smacking or arm pinching until she saw these were accompanied by the glint of silver coins which the women kept down their corsets. After every round they had to empty the money into jars set for the purpose under the bar or else lose some as even their ample bosoms weren't big enough to store all the silver.

'Who are the pretty young men?' one of the bolder barmaids asked Thorsbard. 'Carl' and 'Robert' merely grinned when her words were translated. 'Carl' and 'Robert' then forced themselves into more manly displays of mirth. Lucca shook his head and drank from his tankard wondering when they'd finally get tired of pretending to be men.

'We have ceremonies to conduct in the morning,' warned Thorsbard, 'so don't get too drunk.'

'What ceremonies?' asked 'Robert'.

'Fresh ale has to be thrown at the ship's prows and fresh fish guts thrown into the water to calm any sea beasts lest they stir up the sea and cause our ships to sink.'

'Oh,' asked 'Carl' 'will the crossing be a rough one?'

'Not so much at this time of the year,' replied Thorsbard, 'though we have to watch out for floating icebergs.'

'What would happen if we struck one?' asked Lucca.

'We'd sink,' announced Thorsbard matter-of-factly. Lucca blanched and looked at his friends. 'Don't worry, drink up. It doesn't happen often,' offered Thorsbard.

'Pardon my saying,' coughed Duke Declerq, 'but I thought you were a redhead.'

William smiled, 'Merely a disguise, my Duke, but as you can see the colour is rinsing out every time I have a bath in the expansive bathroom you have loaned me.'

'Indeed,' replied Declerq, 'if I was more able I would have a bath more often myself.'

'Sir, the hot water would do you a great deal of good. Tight muscles and arthritis both would benefit from the heat. Your servants could lower you in and get you out.'

'You're right, Sire,' replied Declerq, 'happily the heat would just be the thing for my tired bones.'

'Permit me to say, Duke, you should close off some of your apartments with wooden dividing walls to concentrate the heat from the estate's fires. Big rooms are devastatingly drafty.'

'Do you think so?' asked Declerq, perplexed.

William preceded to draw some plans for the Duke on parchment. 'See here and here if you put a wall up with doors, the enclosed spaces will be much cosier.'

'Captain Paxton,' asked Declerq, 'is this man a King or an architect?' The Duke was astonished at the King's designs and more importantly in his interest in an old man's welfare.

'It's the least I can do, considering your hospitality to me and all the men. I shall repay you.'

'Never,' said Declerq, offended, 'For my King nothing is too much!'

William bowed to him, 'Thank you, Sir, I am very much obliged! Now, I must not keep you from your anticipated bath. Paxton and I have matters of state to discuss so if you could please excuse us?'

'Of course, Sire. Until the morning.'

William and Paxton bowed to him and left the dining room.

In the King's chambers, William looked at Paxton, 'I don't want to bring misfortune by voicing this but let's just say if the grain shipments are delayed...'

'Let us hope that they will arrive on time for Thorsbard seemed a decent enough fellow.'

'Agreed it almost seems he's a god. First my leg is cured then he has a solution for the famine.'

'Indeed, if our luck holds out, you should be back in the Palace by week's end,' commented Paxton.

'That's five days away, pondered William.

'We need time to get together the wardstaff men.' William nodded. Paxton was practical yet if they delayed any further... Truly William was deeply agitated and his desire for reaching the Capitol was growing unbearably strong. After a fortified wine, he dismissed Paxton perhaps to pursue his lovemaking towards the Duke's daughter, Louisa.

William lay on his bed but could not rest. Klyesha was in an unknown land without anyone but Lucca and Rachel for company, entrusted to a god of a man yet one he didn't really know. All he could do was hope they'd be safe and Thorsbard, true to his word, would be at the docks with fully laden ships by the weekend. Then an unknown number of subjects had to show their loyalty by heeding his call to march to the City with what weapons they owned. Again, an unknown and untested quantity. Here he had 27 men he could rely upon plus some dozen or more that Declerq promised to provide against how many? Hundreds of starving bandits in ruthless gangs in the City ready to fight to the death? The more he thought the more resolve William accumulated. Tomorrow he would act.

Ironsmith, one of Gerard's servants and five other men arrived at the locked gate which constituted the fortress of Klyesha's house.

Ironsmith did not expect such fortification and confused at first about what to do until one of his men suggested they hoist him and two or three others over the wall. This they did and their weapons thrown over as well. Next minute Ironsmith was banging on the door demanding entry.

Cook heard the commotion and trembled, 'How have they got to the door?' she whispered to Walter. She found Mrs Walter, her children and Flora, while Walter fetched James. As quietly as they could, they climbed down into the cellar and closed over the hatch. The girls were warned to stay quiet and given dolls to occupy them. They all waited with their ears peeled, listening for any further noises.

Ironsmith was angry now, 'If these people be home, we have given them plenty warning to let us in,' so he lay his shoulder against the door then backed up and ran at it. The door shuddered but held.

'Mayn't they have bolts on the inside?' ask one of them.

'Of course, stupid, they have bolts! Now you all have to push.' He counted to three and they all shoved or kicked at the door. They heard one of the hinges give way. 'Once again, men,' called Ironsmith and once again they ran and shoved or kicked the door. Sure enough, the other hinge of one of the doors gave way and Ironsmith was able to kick it open. They poured inside the house. It was a neat house with respectable furniture the like of which was never seen in the simple countryman's hut that was Ironsmith's home. He burst into the sitting room where Klyesha's elegant couches and paintings offended him deep down in his soul. He saw the clock her grandfather had made and focused his ire on it. 'Damn it,' he said and threw the clock at the wall where it smashed to pieces.

The noise brought fresh waves of terror to the people hiding in the cellar. Cook snatched up a poker, while Walter and James held spades at the ready. Anyone coming down the stairs was going to get a pummelling.

'Carl', 'Robert' and Lucca sat in the Captain's stateroom on one of the loaded ships due to sail that afternoon to the Kingdom. The timbers groaned as the ship strained at its moorings seemingly impatient to begin her journey. The friends had inspected the hold which was loaded with barrels of grain, apples and kegs of dried fish. The fish smell was overwhelming even penetrating the stateroom where they sat awaiting Thorsbard and the Captain's arrival.

'Mmm, dried fish! Can't wait to try them,' said Lucca sarcastically.

'Your problem is you've been too well fed on this journey,' returned 'Robert'. 'To a starving person, smelly fish would be ambrosia!'

'I agree with 'Robert,' said 'Carl', 'I would have to be starving to eat them.' They sat in silence observing the gentle swaying of the sea through the room's portals. Yalsbad had been a revelation for all of them. A bustling City full of people who seemed giants speaking in an unknown language. This feeling of foreignness was completely new to Lucca and 'Robert' though 'Carl' knew the feeling well from having arrived in the Kingdom from the Island of Cats and being treated as a foreigner by the Kingdom's residents. 'I know I'm impatient to get going but they do seem to have been gone a long time.'

Lucca looked at his pocket watch, 'More than two hours,' he said, standing and stretching. 'I don't know about you two but I'm taking a turn around the deck.' 'Robert' and 'Carl' followed. They were soon observing the wharves with their loading and unloading in front of well-stocked warehouses.

'We need to keep this trade going. Two shiploads won't be enough,' said Lucca. 'Hopefully the King can secure sufficient funds for further shipments until the trading of goods can begin.' As they watched, Thorsbard and the Captain, whose name was Morvik, hurried to the gangplank. They were arguing in Svart, their native language. Thorsbard held his hands up in frustration.

'Friends,' he said, 'bad news, I'm afraid. King Gunnar has found out about our cargo and the two ships have been impounded until tariffs are calculated. I don't know how long it's going to take. Believe me, I thought it wasn't necessary but I was wrong.'

Captain Morvik addressed them, 'Dock officials will be coming on board soon. I suggest you retreat to your cabins. I don't want any further problems from undeclared nationals arriving again.' The friends looked surprised. 'Again, yes. Perhaps you don't know but a week ago a ship arrived from your Kingdom with a cargo of starving people. They have been well treated but the King was not pleased to have refugees thrust into Svartlund unannounced. We don't see many foreigners here apart from the crews of trading vessels who aren't permitted to stay long in port. If you've seen, you may be seized for questioning.'

Thorsbard held his hands out an apology again, 'Go now, someone will bring you dinner. It's going to take at least all afternoon for the tariff assessment. However, I'm worried about how I'll pay.'

'I have money,' suggested 'Carl'

'Gold? Silver?' asked Thorsbard.

'Both,' replied 'Carl' taking a pouch from where it was concealed in her waistcoat and giving it to Thorsbard.

He sighed, 'I am much obliged to you, 'Carl'. I will return this money to you as soon as I can. 'Carl' nodded and they returned to the cabin they were to share on the journey.

'Do they need bribing?' asked Thorsbard when they had gone.

Morvik shook his head, 'Not these men, they're too honest surprisingly enough. Their tariffs will also be fair. I give you my word.'

Thorsbard nodded, still frustrated at the delay. They would not be able to leave now until the morning.

Splinters from the shattered cellar trapdoor fell around the frightened women and girls. Walter and James stood ready with their spades but no one came down the steps.

'Come out now!' yelled a loud, booming voice from above, 'We are not here to hurt you!'

Walter and James looked at each other. Could this man be trusted? It sounded like he'd already damaged the house. Except they didn't really have a choice. There were more men with him. If they entered the cellar, the women and children might get hurt.

'We're coming up,' said Walter. The men climbed out and were immediately grabbed and restrained by Ironsmith's men.

'Why are you holding us?' demanded James. For his boldness Ironsmith struck him across the face with the back of his hand, 'Shut yer mouth, you, young turnip. We're here to see two women.'

Walter and James struggled more but were dragged off to the kitchen.

'You must come up now,' ordered Ironsmith to the cellar's inhabitants. Cook was terrified. She didn't know what to do. Stay there or go up? Mrs Walter was worried for her husband, so she climbed up the ladder first pulling the girls behind her. Ironsmith yelled at her to stand near the wall and the girls rushed behind her, clinging to her skirts.

'Get up now or I'm coming down there,' demanded Ironsmith.

Cook wished she could dissolve into the wall. What was the world coming to that they'd had to hide for fear of their lives in the cellar? She worried most for Flora and gave her a small knife to conceal in her skirts. Reluctantly, she dropped the poker and nodding to Flora, they climbed the steps out of the cellar. Ironsmith shoved Cook aside brutally so that she fell against the wall injuring her elbow and hip. Crying in pain, Cook called out to Flora to watch out as the girl came up the steps. Flora pulled out the knife and tried to stab Ironsmith, but he swept the knife to the ground with his gloved hand and picked her up around her waist like a doll. She kicked and hit but it had no effect on him. He punched her in the face and she went limp in his arms.

'What have you done to her, you Devil?' screamed Cook while Mrs Walter whimpered against the wall protecting her children.

Ironsmith called one of his men in, 'Take her!' he said, thrusting Flora towards the man and then he grabbed Mrs Walter who screamed and screamed until he punched her in the stomach whereupon she vomited in fright and in pain. The girls were screaming and pulling at their mother.

Ironsmith yelled at them to get away, so they huddled around Cook who was almost overcome with the conflicting emotions of anger and pain, 'Leave the girl's mother alone,' she screamed.

Ironsmith laughed, 'The Prince wants her and the girl, harridan. We're going now. Anyone following us will be killed.' He said this for the benefit of Walter and James, who'd both been punched and kicked to ensure their compliance and who lay, almost senseless, on the kitchen floor.

Mrs Walter, ever the silent one, could only look in terror back at her girls and whisper, 'Now Emily look after your sisters and Cook,' before she and Flora were dragged from the house, tied up and slung across two waiting horses.

It was more than a half hour before Cook dared move and test to see if her bones were broken or not. Luckily, she'd suffered only bruising so she hurried to the front yard to secure the gate against further hooligans who might see it open and seize the opportunity to loot. The gate secured, she entered the kitchen door noting the front door of the house smashed apart. Walter and James still lay moaning on the floor, so she took cloths and water to attend to their wounds.

'Mrs Walter?' gasped Walter.

Cook shook her head, 'I'm afraid she and Flora have been abducted by those men. That horrible man said he had come from the Prince.'

'Gerard?'

Cook's eyes started to brim over. The Prince had a very poor reputation and Cook wondered if they would ever see the women again.

Chapter Fourteen

After the King left, Paxton returned to Declerq's Great Hall. Diners lingered over wine and sweetmeats. A large fireplace lit the many tapestries hanging on the Castle's stone walls chasing some chill from the room. A group of minstrels sat near the fire playing some sad little tunes. Louisa sat on a bench lost in thought. Paxton asked if he could sit with her and she nodded her head.

'How long have your family lived here?' he asked.

She looked up, 'I believe since the mid-1400s. So around 220 years.'

'A very long time!'

'Yes,' she answered.

'And do you have any siblings?'

She looked pained momentarily, 'I had a brother. However four years ago he died in a hunting accident in the forest. Now father only has me.'

'I am very sorry for your loss.' Paxton bowed his head. 'You must be very special to your father.'

'I believe so,' she murmured, 'that is why he wants me to marry well.'

'Indeed, and what kind of man do you wish to marry?'

She looked directly at him then and suddenly looked away embarrassed. Turning back, she answered simply, 'I know not much of the world of men yet a husband should be kind to his wife and babes. He should protect them from harm.'

'Will he need to be a rich man?' asked Paxton hopefully.

'Not in my case, no, for I will inherit lands enough and wealth from my father.' Paxton sighed. Perhaps, as the King believed, he might have a chance with this young woman.

In the morning however, he was dragged abruptly away from any thoughts of romance. On knocking at the King's door, he received no answer. He waited and knocked again. Still no answer. He opened the door but the room was empty and the King's clothes were gone. Not wishing to panic, Paxton searched the Castle, asked

Declerq's servants and had his men look outside. After an hour it became obvious the King had gone.

The two women were thrust brutally in front of Gerard. Both looked dishevelled and had their heads bowed while their hands were tied behind their backs.

'They put up a fight,' explained Ironsmith.

Gerard gave him a filthy look, 'Still, this was not necessary.' He walked up to the women and lifting their chins looked into their faces. 'These are not the women I wanted,' he declared.

'They were the only women in the house,' apologised Ironsmith, 'apart from an old Cook.'

'Release their arms!' Gerard ordered and a guard did so. 'What are your names?' he demanded.

'Flora,' said the dark-haired girl.

'Mrs Walter,' replied the other mouse-like creature.

'Who are you to Klyesha and Rachel?'

'Sir, I am Klyesha's Cook's niece. I was asked to stay with my aunt.'

'Why?'

'Because Mistress Klyesha and Mistress Rachel had left.'

'and you?' he pointed to Mrs Walter.

'I am the gardener's wife, Sir.'

'And since when is the garden's wife to stay at the house?'

'It's because of the riots, Sir. It wasn't safe for her and the children,' explained Flora. 'They have only a tiny hut.'

'I see and what can you tell me of the whereabouts of Klyesha and Rachel?' Gerard was now pacing the floor.

'They've been gone some three or four weeks now, Sir. They left to travel north. Cook doesn't know where. She's not heard from them.'

'She's not heard from them!' he raised his voice.

'No, Sir,' replied Flora, lowering her eyes.

'Two women just disappear on their own. Was Cook not concerned?'

'I believe they were not on their own, Sir.'

Gerard looked frustrated. 'So, who was with them?'

'They hired a carriage driver and took a male friend, Lucca the watchmaker.'

172

Gerard shook his head, 'This won't do, Flora. Was one of the men red-haired?'

'I didn't see the driver, Sir, but Mr Lucca has black hair. Raven-haired you'd call him.'

Gerard was becoming more and more irritated and tense. If this Flora was telling the truth, the women had left with two strange men. How would the King have allowed such a show of impropriety unless his plan was for them to rendezvous at some agreed point. 'Does Cook know where they went?'

Flora looked at him a little less subdued, 'I have told you already, Sir, no one knows where they went.'

'I don't like your tone Madam! I asked you a simple question and expect a civil answer.'

'You expect civility when we have been treated so shamefully today?' Flora's voice also rose.

Gerard grabbed her arm, 'You will not address me so miss-whoever-of-no-fixed-address-or-title! You are but a servant in a house little better than a brothel. I am the Prince!'

'Indeed, Sir, I recognised you. You are hurting my arm!'

Gerard yelled at Ironsmith, 'Keep that woman shackled. I will deal with this one on my own!' Gerard dragged Flora into an adjacent room and locked the door. He flung her at a couch, 'You deceitful hussy,' he berated her. 'You will tell me where Klyesha and Rachel are or face the consequences!'

Flora refused to be cowed, 'You may beat me, Sir, but if you want the truth you already have it. Do you wish me to make up some place name to satisfy you?'

'Satisfy me? I will show you what it is to satisfy me,' he slapped her hard on the face so that she nearly fainted. Stunned, she felt his face on hers and his lips mauling her neck. Violently she tried to push him away but he was too strong. Now he had his hands around her neck until she nearly passed out. Thus subdued and terrified, he preceded to lift up her skirts and pull down his breeches. Soon he was laying heavily upon her and thrusting himself inside her. She felt numb. He was hurting her but she could do nothing. He had her pinned down. His jerking came to a shuddering holt and then he released her. She pushed down her skirts as he buttoned up his breeches.

173

'I hope I shall get a bastard from you!' he threw at her. 'My barren wife is useless.'

Flora looked at him with her startled brown eyes. How could she tell anyone of this! How could a child come from such violence? She shuddered.

'Never cross me again,' he smoothed his clothes down, 'or next time you will die.'

She waited barely breathing. She found it hard to swallow and her neck felt bruised. How could anyone enjoy such an act? She had never known a man in this way before and hoped she never would again.

'Go now!' he yelled at her unlocking the door, 'Get out of my sight!' She stumbled for the door and joined Mrs Walter, avoiding looking at her face. Ironsmith was given instructions by a sheepish-looking Gerard.

In ten minutes the women found themselves flung out onto the street. It was dark and raining and somehow they had to find their way home.

Paxton was frantic. He sent some of his men to search for the King. They had been away two hours before several returned. 'We have ridden all along the roads out of here, Captain for 10 miles or more and we caught no sight of him,' said a heavily breathing Sargent.

'Webley is it?' asked Paxton.

'Yes, Captain.'

'If you want to remain Sergeant find him or at least some evidence.'

'He took a horse, our best black stallion. He's a goer that one. If he'd left early in the morning, I'd estimate he'd be 30 or more miles away by now.'

Paxton tried to slow his heart rate. 'Go and have a rest, Sergeant, but tell the men we leave in one hour's time. Understood?'

'Aye, aye, Captain,' replied Webley.

Rushing into the dining room, Paxton found Declerq. The old man was buttering his toast. 'Morning Captain. The eggs are excellent today!' he said brightly.

'Thank you, Duke but I have a more pressing matter. The King has left here, seemingly alone. My men and I must pursue him in order to secure his safety.'

'Why would he do that!' exclaimed the Duke.

'No doubt he is worried about his Capitol and couldn't wait to get intelligence as to the situation there. However, as you know, more fencible men have been gathered with instructions to come here. I beg you to feed them and then direct them to march for the Capitol and to meet us at the docks.'

'Indeed, anything to help. Is there anything else I can do?'

'Yes, if the King returns please send one of my men with word. Again the rendezvous is the docks. We'll be in one of the warehouses.'

'I can assure you I will do whatever I can but, please have breakfast. You have a long journey ahead.'

Paxton nodded and grabbed several boiled eggs and toast, 'One more thing if you could please. Give my compliments to your daughter, Louisa, and tell her,' he cleared his throat, 'tell her I will return to visit her.'

The Duke nodded somewhat surprised as the Captain was not the partner he had envisaged for his daughter.

Paxton then searched the King's bedchamber more thoroughly. There appeared to be nothing awry until he noticed a goblet of wine spilled on the floor. The King's clothes and his satchel were missing. Could he have ridden to Klyesha? Paxton hoped so. He favoured the King's chances much better in Svartlund than going alone to the City. If the King was indeed elsewhere then it fell on him to restore order in the City. This was a task he didn't savour alone. Whatever happened he would go to the City with 60 or more troops to await the supply ships and work out what to do from there. He gobbled an egg hoping the task ahead would not lead to his humiliation and death. Louisa had given him hope that he might have a future.

Flora and Mrs Walter were soaked to the skin when they finally arrived back at Klyesha's house. Afraid to call out less they attract the attention of brigands, they threw gravel at the windows on the side of the house. Cook had insisted James wait in the house in case the women returned and it was after the third or fourth handful of gravel that he awoke from his bed on the couch in the sitting room.

He jumped up and took an oil lamp out the back door and around to the front, as the front door was now barred with nailed planks. As he swung the lamp, he saw the two drenched creatures peering through the gate. Undoing the chain, he let them in and they stumbled towards him. Completely exhausted and cold, he put an arm around each woman and coaxed them to the back door.

In the kitchen he gave them blankets and linens to dry themselves and also built up the fire. Soon they had their wet shoes and stockings off, warming their feet. James fetched Cook and Walter from the cellar. They left the children sleeping and rushed to the kitchen.

'Lord look at you!' wailed Cook, deeply worried by the pale and shivering state of the women. She immediately gave them some watered brandy and hushed Walter who was demanding to know what had happened to them. 'Let them catch their breaths, man, they're soaked.' She dispatched the men from the kitchen and fetched the women dry clothes which they dressed in beside the fire.

With some warm broth inside them it was Mrs Walter who spoke first, 'They treated us like criminals, Cook,' she whispered. Cook waited for an explanation. Walter and James returned to the kitchen. 'That Prince called Gerard had us,' she added. 'They beat us. What for I don't know.' She began to cry and was comforted by her husband.

James hugged his sister, 'Are you a'right?' he asked her. She began to sob loudly and James was alarmed. What had they done to her?

Flora eventually calmed down and wiped her face. 'They wanted Klyesha and Rachel,' she got out. 'Maybe that's who that big ape of a man thought we were. I kept telling them we didn't know where the women were. That Gerard is a wicked man.' She sobbed again and Cook had a flash of real fear for her niece. Surely not, she thought as the most heinous of crimes crossed her mind. However, she knew now was not the time to ask.

'I must get them into their bed,' she said to the men, 'Not in the cellar 'tis too cold. I'll put them in Klyesha's bed and you, James, can make up a fire there. Don't ask them any more questions, just let their bodies heal and their minds be at peace tonight.'

Cook's instructions were followed and the women were soon tucked up warmly in Klyesha's luxurious bed not that they noticed its luxury in their agitated state. 'Now rest my sweets,' soothed Cook as she left them with the warm fire James had made.

Back in the kitchen the men were talking murder, 'I'll kill him,' assured James, 'if he's touched my sister.'

'I so will I,' reiterated Walter.

'You'll do nothing of the sort!' scolded Cook, 'We need you here, not hung from a gibbet on Skull Hill. We still have brigands in the City to contend with. Gerard has his answer to where Klyesha and Rachel are: we don't know! An answer can't be plucked out of thin air.'

'Well, they're well out of this place anyway,' said James bitterly.

'You hold your tongue, young man! Without them you'd have no food and would likely be dead with a brigand's pike in your back. Klyesha has provided you secure shelter.'

'Not as secure as it was,' said Walter.

'True, but Gerard's men won't be back. We've kept them bandits out so far and we will continue to do so!' Cook rose. 'Now I'm going to me bed, sick of that bloody cellar I am.' She left the kitchen. James returned to his lookout position on the couch and Walter went to sleep near his girls less they wake up in the night and call again for their mother.

Rufus knocked on Strong's door. Strong called out for him to come in. Rufus seemed upset. 'Sir, we've been cooling our heels for weeks now. Please allow me to carry sorties out in the City to establish what exactly is happening.'

Albert looked strained, 'Captain, what if something should happen to you? We'll have even less men to defend the Castle.'

'Look Chancellor, all my military training is screaming out for intelligence. We can dress as townsfolk to avoid being recognised by the King's livery. I'll take ten men and we can pretend we're looking for food but in our baskets we'll have weapons.'

Albert knew he needed information especially about the insurgents. He reluctantly agreed to Rufus' suggestions. 'Be safe' were his parting words to him.

Rufus returned to the barracks and readied his men. They even smeared some dirt on their faces and in their hair to avoid raising suspicion by being too clean. 'We're ordinary tenant farmers desperate for food. We'll go to the docks and check them out then the markets. We'll be out all day so eat well before you go as you won't find food in the City. Our rendezvous point is the East Gate because it can be approached through fields. Password is 'Rufus.' He led them to their preparations and sought out his next in command, Lieutenant Withers. He beckoned Withers into his room and shut the door. Sitting on his cot he motioned to a chair for Withers to sit. Withers was an older man of about 50 who had seen much experience as a soldier.

'As you know,' began Rufus, 'I am taking ten men to survey the City. We need to know what's happening. What I haven't told Strong but I'm telling you is that I'm going to infiltrate one of the bandit gangs. We need to isolate and capture the ringleaders if we are to have a chance of containing and eliminating the lawlessness. I might be gone days or a week. When I don't return tonight, you'll explain to the Chancellor what I'm doing. I refrained from telling him because he might have tried to prevent me going, understood?'

'Yes, Sir.'

'So, your job will be acting commander while I'm away. Continue to keep the men on watches and on high alert. If I could achieve my goal, we have a chance at returning the City to some sort of normality.'

'And if you don't return?'

'Give me a week and then report me missing in action. Do not waste manpower looking for me.'

'Aye, aye, Captain.'

'Good, I'm going to get some food.'

He was also going to see Beth, the woman who he'd rescued from bandits. Beth had settled into the barracks as an assistant cook. Her child, a baby girl, was set up in a cradle in the kitchen which was always warm. Not long after he rescued her, she told him her story.

'I thank thee, Sir, for your kindness,' she began hesitatingly, the day after arriving at the Palace.

Rufus nodded, 'How did you get to be in that situation?'

'I was looking for my husband, Ranald. He'd gone out from our small flat the day before to find food.'

'What happened to him?'

Beth bowed her head and sobbed, 'I found him dead Sir, not 10 yards from our place. The bandits had butchered him. They even tore off his clothes. I found him naked and bloody, the life ripped from him. He'd only been trying to get us food, Sir. I needed food to make milk for the baby. My milk was drying up, we were so starving.'

'I'm very sorry for your loss, mistress. How did you end up being attacked near the docks?'

'Our place is not far from there. If Ranald hadn't got food then I had to find some or die starving and alone inside. I was terrified of that, Sir. I'd rather die quick.'

Rufus agreed with the sentiment but was horrified nonetheless at the situation which preceded it. 'I'm so grateful, Sir at the food we can eat here.'

'So far we have food but one day it will run out. Can you tell me anymore? How were your neighbours faring?'

Beth swallowed, 'The old ones had already died in the flat above. Forgive me, but me and the other neighbours went through their place to see if we could find any food or anything valuable to trade. Not a scrap of food was left nor anything valuable. They'd already used it. All we could do was close the door on them.' Rufus noted the grey look of her skin and the dark patches under her eyes. Producing milk for her child was eating up her own flesh. At least he'd been able to save two souls but how many others had lost their lives?

'Thank you, Beth, you will be well looked after. Here you are safe.'

'We are forever at your service, Sir, my little daughter and I. If you need anything Sir...'

Rufus shook his head, embarrassed, 'Nothing I can assure you.' The woman was offering herself to him. Only a devil would accept such a gift from this poor creature. 'Please,' he clasped her hands in his, 'Please don't trouble yourself. You are safe here.' She nodded gratefully.

In three weeks, good food and warmth had brought colour and flesh to Beth's face and figure. She looked happy, despite a tragedy and the baby seemed to be thriving. She smiled a toothless smile at him from her cradle and he chucked her under the cheek. 'My, she's looking bonnie,' he said to Beth.

'All thanks to you, Sir,' she curtsied and smiled. Even her clothes were new to her. Some of Cook's castoffs but a bright blue and red, better than the drab homespun browns and greys she'd arrived in.

He didn't want to alarm her but he needed to explain, 'I'm going away for a few days but I'll be back soon.'

'Oh, Sir!' she said alarmed, 'not to enter the City?'

'Only for a short time. I know how to look after myself.'

Beth widened her blue eyes, 'Then god speed, Sir and a safe return.'

'Thank you. Perhaps we can talk when I return.' In the three weeks he had known her, Rufus had begun to think of her more and more.

'Yes, Sir,' Beth looked embarrassed as much as he felt.

'Anyway, I'll see you soon,' he held her hands briefly and left to eat a hearty meal in the officer's mess. It would be his last good meal for a while. A small bundle of jerky which he could easily secrete inside his jerkin would have to suffice if he was really starving.

It was time to leave. He and his men looked like a group of bandits with their dirty faces and old clothes. The guards hardly recognised them as they went out the West Gate into the unknown dangers of the City.

After the tariff collector's visit, Klyesha's ship sailed the next day. The weather was fair with a strong breeze to the South, ideal to help speed the ships to the Kingdom.

As Klyesha was returning to the Kingdom, her need to disguise was less necessary. She and 'Robert' had discussed 'coming out' in their cabin the night before and both had decided if only to be rid of the cummerbunds they would once again revert to their true selves and become women again. 'After all, woman can still shoot a musket,' explained Klyesha.

So it was, two young women appeared on deck after breakfast to take the air. Thorsbard was racking his brains as to how they'd been secreted on board. Klyesha decided to put him out of his misery immediately. 'We, 'Carl' and 'Robert' are assuming our real identities as women.' They twirled in their skirts before him.

Thorsbard sat down on a barrel completely astonished. 'Well, well, well,' he said shaking his head. 'Forgive me if I've been cursing anytime in my language,' he apologised.

Klyesha laughed, 'Even if you had, dear Thorsbard, we would forgive you. We dressed ourselves as young men in order to travel about the country safely. It seems the ruse worked!'

'Indeed, it has. I believed you were feminine young City gentleman unused to hard work or other coarse men, such were your manners. May I congratulate you on the success of your disguises.'

'Thank you, thank you, Thorsbard,' said the women giggling and curtseying.

'and Lucca and William?'

'They already knew,' replied Klyesha.

'Don't tell me you and the King are lovers?' asked Thorsbard, unbelieving.

'Yes, more than that. We are engaged.'

Thorsbard shook his head, 'Then my hospitality might be returned with a stay in the Palace.'

'Maybe, yet we don't know what will find in the City when we get there.'

'Looking forward to seeing him?'

'Indeed,' nodded Klyesha, trying not to get emotional.

Thorsbard shook his head again, 'I'm going to get a drink.'

The women laughed. When he'd left, they turned to each other and grinned. 'Well, if ever we need to become men again,' said Rachel, 'we can be assured it will work.'

'It was fun in a way looking at society from a male perspective,' replied Klyesha.

'Not fun to be nearly made love to by women,' grinned Rachel.

'So, you did notice the women looking at you when we stayed at Thorsbard's estate.'

'Yes, I did and they looked at you too.' They both shook their heads.

'Luckily no embarrassing rejections had to have been made while we were being hosted,' added Rachel.

'They were beautiful women, Rachel, but none would ever replace my William beautiful as they were.'

'Perhaps we shall take a little rum too?'

'Why not, now we know what men enjoy it's opened a whole world for us.' They walked over to the hatch which led to the Captain's cabin.

Chapter Fifteen

At the docks, Rufus and his men mingled with the crowds who lounged about in the sun hoping for ships bearing supplies to arrive. 'Any food?' asked Rufus of numerous thin-faced men.

'No get away with you! There ain't nothing here,' said one pockmarked individual. 'Go look somewhere else.'

Rufus didn't like his tone but pretended compliance. 'Anyone in charge here?' he asked pointedly.

'And what's it to you? asked the same man.

'Just wanna know,' said Rufus dropping to a vernacular. 'Me kids are starving.'

'Aren't they all?' replied the man

As they walked away a young man came up to them, 'You're looking for someone?' he asked.

'We might be.' replied Rufus signalling to his men with his eyes.

'Come with me,' he replied and headed to a dark entrance in one of the warehouses. Inside dust motes hung in sunbeams lighting the space but it still took some time for their eyes to adjust to the dimness. At the back of the warehouse space amidst barrels and sacks of wool, lay a number of men. Rufus couldn't make out their faces, but the young man beckoned him forward. 'This is looking for you,' said the young man to a huddled figure, so muffled by layers of clothes and scarves his face was almost hidden.

'Who be ye?' the man asked them.

'John Rufus,' answered Rufus, 'from Huddersfield. Me and me fellow tenants are come to the City for food.'

The man laughed a loud cackle, 'Everyone be here for that, you knuckleskull!'

'So is we are a'wasting our time then?' asked Rufus.

'Mayhaybe,' the man answered.

'And who are you?' asked Rufus.

'I be known as Slade,' said the man, 'but now you know, I'll have to kill you.'

Rufus laughed and he noticed his men tense. 'So Slade, we're wasting our time?'

'Well, what you got to trade?'

Rufus thought a minute. He did have silver coins but he also had the muskets. However, they would need them to make a hasty retreat. 'Got a bit of silver,' he replied.

'Now you be talking,' said Slade, 'Cross palms.'

Rufus took out two silver sovereigns and put them into Slade's dirty hand. He immediately bit them. 'Seems a'right,' he replied.

'So where is the food?' asked Rufus.

'It's safe but we need to steal it. Yeah, we knows where it is. That's what you just paid for.'

'So where do we go?' Slade described an area of the City Rufus was familiar with but had never visited. It was a wealthy area with rows of curbed terraces, gated parks and wide streets.'

'Won't they be armed?' asked Rufus.

'Not in the middle of the night,' replied Slade, rising from his comfortable seat amongst the wool bales. The man was tall and very thin despite his layers of clothing. 'We is going tonight. You in?'

Rufus looked at his men who nodded, 'Starvation be our guide,' answered Rufus.

Slade nodded, 'See you at midnight.'

He and his men left the docks as they still had the market to visit but at least they were in with one of the gang's leaders. Entering a home unlawfully was not something Rufus relished but to maintain their disguise, it would have to be done. Rufus hoped the King would pardon them of any prosecution. As it turned out, he need not have worried.

After surveying the markets which held only debilitated men, they wandered along streets with shops all boarded up. Few people were on the streets. They weren't approached by angry mobs as they had been when returning to the City a few weeks ago. The anger and desperate motivations of that time seemed to have abated somewhat. But they were also dressed to blend in, unlike their previous experience wearing the King's livery.

They decided to return to the wharves and sleep there until midnight, tired as they were it wasn't a difficult decision. Rufus sent some of the men back to the Castle to report to Strong on the situation in the City but he made them promise not to tell of the raid he and the rest of them were going on in the night.

After the men left the others slept. Around midnight, the young man who'd introduced them to Slade arrived and tapped Rufus on the shoulder telling him it was time to go. He led them to a small group of men who had blackened their faces with pots of greasy charcoal. Rufus and his men blackened their faces too. Truly only the whites of their eyes were visible in the light of a feeble moon.

They were shown a pile of hessian sacks and each man took one. Rufus and his men had hidden their muskets amongst the bales where they'd slept lest they prove to be suspicious as poor tenant farmers rarely owned muskets.

They moved out as a group working their way along the sides of buildings until their eyes adapted to the low light. Approaching spring, the nights were still cold and most men used the sacks around their shoulders as an extra cover against the cold. Rats scurried along the streets and one of the men almost trod accidently on a sleeping dog which growled and startled them all. Apart from the dog and the rats, the streets were quite devoid of life. Only the mad or criminals went out in the darkness and rain amongst untold dangers. Rufus was under no delusions, criminals they were or about to be.

After a long hour, the streets widened and they made out trees and parks highlighted by the sweeping and hooting of owls. The houses looked pale as the stone they were made out of was limestone. Each four or five storeys high, Rufus believed Slade was right to target them as only the wealthy could afford to live there.

'We will split up now,' said the young man at the entrance to a set of mews. Arthur here will help you break in and Henry will also help.'

'Yes,' whispered Rufus, gathering his men around him.

'Come wi' me,' said Arthur taking Rufus' arm. They entered the mews and were aware the other group had turned back to try their luck further down the street. They all stood near a small door chosen because it might be easy to crowbar open. 'Listen for dogs,' whispered Arthur. 'If there are any, we run, aye?' Rufus nodded. Henry took a crowbar out of the inner pocket of his coat and jammed it under the catch on the door. 'Usually takes a few goes.' he said. He jimmied the crowbar and pushed on the end. The wood cracked but the door held. He repeated the exercise until the door finally gave.

'Kitchen's where food is. Look for a larder,' said Arthur, 'Always is on the ground floor.'

Indeed, Rufus thought, it's the same in the Palace. They all crept in through the doorway feeling their way along the short entrance hall. They appeared to be in a corridor with a lot of doors any one of which might lead to the kitchen. 'Take a door each,' whispered Arthur. They all did so. Rufus chose a metal door hoping its solidity held something valuable inside but his foot soon found coal. It was only the coal bunker and he nearly knocked himself out with a shovel which just rested inside the door. He carefully replaced it but he had made a noise. He re-entered the hallway and followed one of his own men into another room. This was proved to be more valuable- a root cellar. It was stocked with layered beetroots, potatoes and celeriac. He and his fellow soldier, a man named Christopher, began filling their sacks.

'T'is a true harvest,' Rufus commented to him, 'but don't get too much as we have to lug it all back.' When their sacks were around 3/4 full they hefted them over their shoulders.

Suddenly, a loud sound was heard coming from what must be the kitchen. Crockery was smashing and sounds of metal clattering. Christopher was for making a dash for the exit but Rufus would not leave his men behind. They lay their sacks just inside the root cellar door and went to investigate.

An unfortunate scene was playing out before them in the kitchen which they could see as the stove cast a bright light. Three of their men and Arthur and Henry were grappling with two servants who must have been sleeping in the kitchen near the fire. Rufus knew what to do and brought the base of a heavy pot down on the head of one of them. Christopher brained the other with a rolling pin.

Unfortunately, the commotion had roused the household and they could hear men running downstairs towards them. 'Quick,' said Rufus to Christopher, 'see if there's a door you can bolt at the end of the hall.' He gathered the men and Arthur and Henry, each of whom now held some trophy of food. Christopher rushed back to tell them he'd secured the door. He and Rufus grabbed their bags of root vegetables and they high tailed it out into the mews.

Some neighbour hearing the fuss had let his dogs out and Henry was attacked by a huge mastiff who took him down. Rufus, still possessed of a saucepan, beat the dog senseless on the head until it let Henry go. Dragging Henry and kicking viciously at the other dog, the men rushed along the street and leapt over the fence into the park where they lay hidden among shrubbery to get their breaths and give any pursuers the miss. They prayed no more dogs would be let out lest they discovered their hiding place.

Perhaps the owners seeing the other dogs injured would not risk them or perhaps they were afraid to pursue brigands out onto the streets, but they waited for quite some time and no one came out of the Mews. 'I say we get back,' said Arthur. 'Can you make it, Henry?' The man nodded though his leg was bleeding and had to be patched up with someone's scarf.

They left their hiding place and was soon following lanes back to the warehouses alternately carrying the heavy root sacks and helping Henry to walk, one man on either side. Their progress was slow, worried as they were that some other group might steal their treasures but luckily it had started to rain again and ill or starving men don't relish gadding about in the wet or dark on the off chance of finding food, not in the poor areas near the docks anyway.

It was about four in the morning when they returned to the warehouse. Slade immediately insisted on seeing what they had hard won. 'My, slim pickings,' he complained, though Rufus thought they had done rather well under the circumstances. Slade soon divided up the food giving himself the lion's share. Each man got one beet, one celeriac, five or six potatoes and a wedge of cheese. Slide kept a pork pie for himself as well.

Rufus protested, 'We did all work! Why should you get so much?'

Slade was on him before he knew it with a small blade pressed against his throat. 'Protest shall thee, laddie? Care to say more?' as he pressed the knife into Rufus' throat. He held his hands out to his men who were about to rush Slade. 'This be for distribution, laddie. We have women and bairns to feed as well. Do ya git it?'

'Aye, put the blade down, aye, aye.'

Slade lowered the blade. 'Now you can see how we live here, laddie, perhaps you'd rather turn tail and head home?'

Rufus knew their escapade might have ended badly. Only closing the hall door had saved them from swords or muskets aimed at their heads. This life was a precarious one. Still, he was tired as the adrenaline started to ebb from his body. It was like being in a war zone. A war between those with food or those without. He also knew he would not have hesitated to kill any of the inhabitants of the house who tried to attack them. If that made him a criminal, then a criminal he would be, if only temporarily.

The next day they all woke late and spent the morning cooking their finds of the night before. Potato and beetroot soup with celeriac never tasted so good. All it wanted was a bit of salt and Christopher had the bright idea of getting seawater to add to the broth. Their stomachs satiated, Rufus discussed quietly with his men their next moves. They decided to question their young guide, the youth who led them to Slade whose name was Ned.

They learned that Ned had been a carpenter's apprentice working on repairing old houses. It was a very physical job yet his master had fed him well and he always had a place to sleep before the family's fire on a cold night. He earnt no money, the skills he was learning were regarded as payment but when the famine began to really bite, he was regarded as an unnecessary mouth to feed and was kicked out of the house. Being an orphan, he had no home to go to. The orphanage would not take him back. He had wandered about the City half starving until he had come across Slade at the docks. Rough as he was, Slade had given him an alternative to starvation- stealing. This was how they'd survived the last month.

Rufus did not blame them, indeed in the same circumstances he himself would have taken a similar turn. What would the City gain if men like Slade were hung? Still, lawlessness would see the entire fabric of society broken down. The situation could not continue. 'Do you know of any other gangs?' asked Rufus.

Ned readjusted himself on the bail to be more comfortable. 'Every district has gangs,' he replied. 'Sometimes we've had to fight them when they've tried to muscle in here and occupy our space. Slade can be pretty ruthless and his men. Many a bandit we've thrown into the harbour who's tried to take us on.'

Rufus blanched. They were a group he'd have to stay on the right side of.

'Our raid last night, only one man injured sometimes it's a lot worse,' continued Ned. 'Sometimes we've lost half our gang, murdered by angry men protecting their houses and food. We just get more men from the markets to replace them.' Ned spoke proudly of their endeavours but to Rufus it was a hopeless situation. Eventually, even the rich would run out of food. What would they all do then? He hoped fervently the King was working on solution and one which would begin soon before everyone in the City was on their knees.

Indeed, the supply ships carrying Klyesha, Rachel, Lucca and Thorsbard were on their way back to the Kingdom. Men from all over the Kingdom who remained loyal to the King and who weren't needed at home were making their way to the Capitol. Carrying their own supplies, homemade weapons or sharp farming tools, these men marched slowly to the south where the Capitol lay. For the first time in 100 years, their King needed them to act as police and bring the Capitol back within the protection of the law.

Paxton with his own men, men from Rosethorn Estate and men from dozens of other estates and villages were marching along the lanes and highways towards their rendezvous at the docks. Some were on horseback but most were on foot. At each road junction, more men joined their army of civilians. Tall, short, young and old, men determined and men afraid, men skilled and men untutored, farmers, tenants, blacksmiths and carpenters, builders, stone masons, bakers, cooks and stable workers all had heeded the call and all were marching. Within days they would reach the Capitol and Paxton wondered how he would feed them all. If the ships didn't arrive, they would literally be sunk and all he would have succeeded in doing was to increase the number of hungry and angry men in the City. Was he leading a solution to the Revolution into the City or was he merely increasing the chances of the whole of society sinking into a lawless chaos? And in all this configuration of men with their simple arms on the roads and in the vastness of the City, where was the King who was supposed to be leading them? Had he turned coward and simply run away from a problem whose scale no one could really fathom? Could Paxton blame him? Or was William just trying to save his own life? For if angry men saw him, wouldn't they want to hang him? The man who they thought had brought disaster on them all?

Before Paxton reached the City one of his problems was about to be solved. Around dusk that day, Thorsbard's two supply ships entered the Capitol's harbour. The captains had been warned not to dock until a friendly army could be seen on the wharves. Until then, they would lay to a mile or so from the docks and set sailors to scout out any vessels which approached them and be prepared to fire. They could not risk being approached by vagabonds who'd stolen skiffs.

So that night, they all sighed with relief to be inside of the harbour and have safely covered their journey, yet they were also aware that coordination of ground troops was necessary to allow them to dock and that they could not move from their positions until it was safe to do so. Nobody knew how long that would take.

Chapter Sixteen

Gerard's brilliant scheme was soon to come to fruition. Unable to bribe men to his cause with baskets of food, he decided to use a more underhand tactic which would in one stroke give him the Kingdom. He would make use of the printing presses. To this end, he and Lindquist had stolen out the night before to the only newspaper office in the City. Printing was a very new invention in the Kingdom. Paper was expensive and the technology slow, but a City newspaper was printed once a week called 'The Proclamation'. It advertised goods for sale, lost dogs or children, jobs and pieces of low-grade sensational news about the few criminals the City possessed. Since the famine and the general disorder in society, the presses were silent. No one wanted to sell the paper on the streets and there was no one to buy it anyway. The newspaper had closed and the printers all but returned home. Only one man remained to keep an eye on things. This man was called Edward Moore.

He was roused from sleep by a loud knocking on the newspaper office's door. He demanded to know who was disturbing his sleep and was surprised to see it was the Prince whose face he recognised lit by a lantern the Prince carried.

'Let us in, man,' demanded Gerard.

Edward hesitated but thought he'd better open the door as the Prince was sure to have reinforcements.

The men stepped in out of the rain-soaked night. 'Do you recognise me?' asked Gerard.

'Yes Sir, you are the Prince. My name is Edward Moore.'

'Good. Now, we are sorry to disturb your repose, Edward, but we want your help. As it seems no one else is here, are you able to run the presses by yourself?'

'That depends on how many pages you were thinking of printing,' he replied.

'Only a one page circular but we'd need about 1,000 copies. Is it possible?'

'Anything is possible, Sir. Do you have a copy of what you want printed?'

Gerard handed him a roll of parchment. Moore unrolled it and bringing it near a candlestick began to read. 'This very inflammatory, Sir. I'm not sure it's legal.'

'Oh, it will be but I will take full responsibility for it. No consequences will come to you as the printer, I can assure you. There is no need to sign who printed it or where.'

'However, that would be easily deduced Sir.'

'Be that as it may, you have my word no repercussions will come back to you. When can you have it done?'

'A week.'

'Mr Moore, I can't wait a week. You have tomorrow to get it set up and printed. I'll be back here at midnight tomorrow to pick up the circulars.'

Moore went to protest but the look on Gerard's face gave him pause. Gerard was an influential and wealthy man, not one he wished to get on the bad side of. 'I will do my best, Sir. The cost will be ten gold sovereigns.' It was a large amount but it was also risky and Moore wanted to be properly compensated.

Gerard opened his purse and handed over five gold sovereigns, 'Five now and five when we pick them up, agreed?'

Moore nodded his head and shook the Prince's hand. Now he knew what it felt like to be Judas in the biblical story who would betray Christ for 30 pieces of silver.

It was the waiting that was worst. Klyesha spent hours looking pointlessly at the docks for signs of William and his army. Her skin, never pale as Rachel's, assumed again the nut brown tone she sported when rescued from the Island of Cats. To pass the time, she used a line and sinker and fished for their supper. Plenty of dried fish was available but no wanted to eat it when succulent fresh fish was available. She taught Rachel how to cast a line and at what stage to pull the line in. Lucca didn't join in. The Captain had collected clocks and pocket watches from all over the ship for him to repair. As Lucca always had his watchmakers' tools with him, he was too busy repairing timepieces to join them. In fact, he was in his element. It was weeks since he'd had his hands in any delicate time-keeping mechanism and he'd actually missed it.

Thorsbard was not so easily entertained. Totally bored at first, he eventually found some sailors with chess sets and encouraged a shipboard competition which he inevitably won. He taught Klyesha the game and for a time she became quite expert but the sight of the black or white King and Queen pieces always gave her a pang. With a heavy heart, she returned to fishing.

It was around noon on their third day in the harbour that a sailor in the crows' nest reported a large contingent of men on the docks. Thorsbard demanded a telescope and scanned the docks back and forth until he had a sense of who was there. 'I believe they are our men,' he finally announced as the others waited impatiently for his verdict. He handed the glass to Captain Morvik, who described what he saw. 'There are many men carrying weapons, all orderly, no screaming idiots can I see.'

Thorsbard took back the glass and looked again for the man who would confirm who they were but he couldn't see him. He was of course looking for the King and there were tall redheaded men there but no one who looked like him. Paxton was harder to make out, being dark and of average height. 'I can't see Captain Paxton,' he announced to the waiting viewers.

'Shall we go in anyway?' asked Klyesha agitated.

Thorsbard looked at Captain Morvik who nodded. 'We should go in slowly and leave ourselves room to retreat if need be,' he announced.

The men were instructed to heave up the anchor and set the sails on course for the docks. The sister ship from Svartlund would of cause follow their lead. There was just enough wind to make their slow way towards the docks and as they did so, the larger numbers of men encamped there became clearer. They indeed looked like a hastily put together army with clothes of all colours and the men themselves of every variety. The ship held to some 50 yards off the docks and dropped anchors once again. Thorsbard would not advance until Paxton himself or the King presented themselves to him. It did not take long.

Out from all of the men, a dark-haired man stepped forward and waved one of the King's flags from a hastily made flagpole. 'Thorsbard,' yelled Paxton from the docks, 'Welcome to the Kingdom!'

Thorsbard waved back and in his large booming voice hoped to soon have an ale. Paxton laughed and asked for permission to come aboard. The Captain called for a skiff to be lowered down to ferry Paxton aboard and soon he was climbing down a ladder from the Wharf into the small boat.

Klyesha did not know why but she was quite overcome to see the reliable Captain Paxton now in the King's livery climbing over the gunwale onto their ship. Paxton was surprised to see her and Rachel amongst his friends and it took a while to work out who they were

'My, my, Mistress Klyesha and Mistress Rachel, you two took me for a fool!'

She laughed, 'That was not our intention, Sir, believe me.'

Paxton bowed to them and shook Thorsbard's, the Captain's and Lucca's hands, 'Believe me sirs, I have never been quite so pleased to see anyone in my life. Was your journey successful?'

'Aye, Captain, your Kingdomers will have tears in their eyes when they behold the contents of the hold of ours and the other ship,' he pointed behind him.

'Two ships!' laughed Paxton, 'That is most impressive. The King will be very pleased.'

'And where is the King?' asked Klyesha.

Paxton adjusted his face, 'Why back in the City,' he lied. He could not bear to bring bad news at such a happy time. Klyesha had to be content though a nagging worry still occupied a part of her.

'Will you partake of some rum?' asked Captain Morvik, leading the way to his stateroom. There they all spent the next hour planning how to unload their precious cargo, where it would be stored and how it would be guarded.

When pressed to explain why the King was not with him, Paxton was uncharacteristically vague. Klyesha decided it best not to interrogate him though Rachel urged her to try. 'Not everything the King does am I Privy to,' whispered Klyesha. Indeed, Paxton may have made use of this excuse himself had he thought of it.

As the evening was rapidly approaching, Paxton was rowed back ashore and the plan was to begin unloading the cargo at dawn. The fencible men would make human chains to transport the crates of fish to storage in the warehouses. The barrels could be rolled to separate warehouses each for grains, fish or cheeses which would make distribution simpler. Paxton would arrange for clerks amongst the men to record everything stored because it still needed to be paid for.

'Distribute them everywhere,' ordered Gerard, 'We want as big a crowd as possible.' Lewis and Ironsmith nodded. They'd both read the circulars and shook their heads. It was Gerard's boldest move yet and it was so extreme it just might work.

The men and their helpers set out at dawn. The Capitol held more readers than any other part of the Kingdom. Indeed, Stirling University founded in 1556 by a relative of the King's had produced many fine scholars who in turn taught schools. Education was still the privilege of the rich, as few poor people could afford the fees, but many middleclass children of merchants, artisans and craftsman attended schools, both boys and girls. This meant a reasonable proportion of the City's inhabitants could read, while those who couldn't read could listen to circulars read out to them.

So, it was by noon of the same day, the son of a bootmaker came upon one of the Prince's circulars and began reading it to a growing crowd of his father's customers. Others who passed by also stopped to listen.

The circular read:

'People of the Capitol are you sick of being hungry? Are you afraid of the lawless gangs who have taken over our fair City? Are you tired of hiding in your homes night and day afraid to venture out even for fresh air?

Your time of hunger, fear and lockdown will soon be at an end. The man who is responsible for your hunger, your pain and your isolation will this day meet his well-deserved fate.

Who is responsible for your Hunger? Who has brought desperate hordes to our City to steal, pillage, rape and murder? Who has deserted you all in your time of need while hiding in luxurious estates in the country? Who has stuffed himself with rich provender while you have watched your children grow grey with hunger day by day? Who has turned his back on his responsibilities as a sovereign and ignored you all in your greatest hour of need? That man is William Stirling. He is the one who calls himself King but has been no King to you. If anyone deserves punishment for his incompetence, it is King William.

195

I invite you all today to Skull Hill at 3 o'clock to watch the villain dangle from the highest gibbet we can build. When William hangs, you citizens of the Kingdom will be free to choose a King who will not forsake you. A King who will feed you and restore the Capitol to its former glory. Join me today friends, to say farewell to the tyrant William.

Your faithful and humble servant,
Prince Gerard.'

Paxton had found Rufus the day before almost unrecognisable beneath dirt and ragged clothing. Captain Rufus had shouted. Paxton turned to see a beggar running towards him and drew his sword.

'Captain, it's me,' shouted Rufus, who stood rooted to the spot when he saw the sword.

'Rufus?' asked Paxton incredulous. Soon the pair embraced and all the negative scenarios each had envisaged the other might face suddenly dissipated.

'You got here!' they both said simultaneously and laughed. 'Indeed,' said Rufus, 'and you recruited all these men!'

'Yes. Men loyal to the King still exist. They were compelled by honour and fealty to win back our Capitol. There are hundreds!'

Rufus was impressed, 'and hundreds more it seems,' he said, indicating the rows of men who at that moment were marching into the docklands.

Beaming, Paxton commented, 'To tell you the truth we never knew how many would heed the call. But this is most impressive.' He organised some of his soldiers to settle the new troops and give them a corner of the warehouse in which to rest.

Klyesha, Lucca, Thorsbard and Rachel stood on the docks as crate after crate, barrel after barrel and cheese after cheese were passed along the rows of men to be stored in the warehouses. Rufus saw them and nodded.

'I trust you can explain your appearance,' said Thorsbard.

Rufus laughed and held out his hand to Thorsbard, 'I've been spying on the rebels and had to join them. Do I not look the part?'

'Indeed, you do, Captain Rufus,' said Klyesha amused.

'Mistress Klyesha, I'm impressed to see you a'right. How has it been in the City?'

196

Puzzled, Klyesha realised Rufus did not see the connection between her and 'Carl'. 'Oh, it has been unimaginable,' she answered, winking at Rachel. Rachel giggled.

'I am pleased to see you so well,' commented Lucca, shaking Rufus' hand. 'We came on Thorsbard's ships from Svartlund where we sourced all of these supplies.'

Rufus raised his hands in amazement, 'I have had first-hand experience of privation and this ...glorious...food will lift the spirits of City as nothing else will.' They all stared then at the hive of industry, the unloading of supplies from gang planks of the two ships now secured to the docks with men shifting crates like ants.

'There is more to come should your people ever need it,' said Thorsbard proudly.

'A magnificent effort, Sir,' commented Rufus, somewhat overwhelmed.

'Have you seen the King?' said Paxton to him quietly taking him away from the others.

'No, Captain, I have not, though these last four days some soldiers and I have been surveying the City gathering intelligence about the gangs. Could he be back in the Palace?'

'I have no idea. He just disappeared from Rosethorn Estate without saying anything to anyone,' confided Paxton.

Rufus raised his eyebrows, 'Would the King have willingly left in such a way?'

Paxton shook his head, 'Truly, I do not know. I was hoping he'd meet me at these docks. This was the rendezvous point but so far no one has seen him.'

Rufus drew him further away from the others, 'Could he have been abducted? What should we do?'

Paxton fiddled with his sword hilt, 'We have a massive logistic exercise before us to distribute this food fairly and calm any rebellious elements in the City. We may yet have pitched battles to fight. I am needed here. I cannot leave all of this,' he spread his arms wide, 'to look for the King.'

They were surprised by Mistress Klyesha who had walked up behind them. 'Captain,' she said sternly, 'you cannot discuss the King without me. You must tell me where he is.' Her face was quite pale as she steeled herself for their words.

Paxton held her gently by the arm, 'Mistress, I do not wish to distress you, but we have not seen the King for several days. I was hoping he was with you.'

'In Svartlund?'

'Perhaps he might have followed you?'

'I sincerely hope not. Not with his injured leg. The snow is quite severe in Svartlund. Also, he did not know the way to Thorsbard's estate.'

'True,' said Paxton, 'he also knew you would be soon at the docks here. Such a journey would seem foolish.'

'Then what else might he have done?' she asked plaintively.

Rufus looked away, hiding his face. Klyesha grabbed him by one of his dirty sleeves, 'Why do you look away, Captain? What is it you are thinking?'

'Do you trust him?'

'What does that mean?' Klyesha demanded.

'Well, he is no fool. He has either chosen to remain hidden or someone has taken him.'

A grey colour stole the red from Klyesha's sun-kissed cheeks, 'So you think if he set off alone, he has been attacked again or abducted?'

'It's possible,' said Rufus.

'Yet, Rufus, we don't know for sure,' counselled Paxton. 'We should not upset Mistress Klyesha for no reason.'

She tried to calm her heavy breathing for to lose her wits at such a time was to betray William in a way. Rufus was right, she had to trust William and believe he had not deliberately put himself in harm's way again.

'Please Mistress, return to the ship. Wait in comfort. There are too many ugly and dirty men here. We will bring word of the King as soon as we find out anything new.'

Klyesha grimaced and turned away. She and Rachel walked back onto the ship taking care to avoid any barrels being rolled out. By the time they reached the cabin, Klyesha was in tears. Rachel reasoned with her but all Klyesha saw stretching out before her was more and more waiting until William's arms were around her again.

Into the back of an open dray, Gerard's men thrust the tall redheaded man. His face was swollen from a beating, one of his eyes almost shut. He knelt on the dirty straw, his hands securely shackled behind his back. One of the servants took pity on him and poured water on his face some of which dripped into his mouth, which he drank. He was very thirsty.

'Well brother, it has come to this,' said Gerard. 'All your missteps and foolish decisions have led you here. Today you will pay for your mismanagement and the last sounds you will hear will be the boos and jeers of your subjects denouncing you as a tyrant.'

The prisoner looked directly at Gerard but said nothing. Indeed, his mouth was so dry, despite the little water he just drunk, he could not speak. Humiliated and degraded by nights in the dungeon of Gerard's villa, he had given up hope of being rescued. In the whole City, he was friendless. No one would care if he died and they will spit on his broken body before it was thrown into a pauper's grave. Gerard had made no secret of the destination of today's journey. He knew it would end at Skull Hill and the gibbet.

It was already early afternoon when Gerard and his ragtag army arranged in lines around the dray set off for the execution. People must have read Gerard's circular, or had it read to them, for many now rushed to line the streets when word spread the dray was approaching with the King. No rotten fruit or vegetables were thrown at him for all were long ago eaten, instead sticks and small stones were thrown. He gasped each time a stone hit his face or head and small rivulets of blood ran into his eyes and down his cheek, so he appeared to be crying blood. Soon his appearance was likened to Christ as he approached his execution and some pitied him then and said his kingship had had some good qualities, that in the Assemblies he'd been fair. Those supporters were soon howled down by his opponents who reminded them all, 'We are starving!' and 'The King is to blame!' So, any sympathies were soon put down like tiny spot fires in a baker's shop.

The crowds increased as the procession neared Skull Hill, which was a small rise just outside the Capitol where many a criminal had met their end. Here in better times, the City's inhabitants had crowded with toffee apples, roasted corn cobs and newspaper packets of nuts to snack upon as they watched the executions. They all fed on the condemned man or woman's final words, for if any wisdom was to be enunciated surely it would be in the criminal's last speech on earth.

Edward Moore, the printer, was there with quill and parchment at hand to record the scene. This was an historic event. Never in the history of the Kingdom had a King been hung, never had a crowd so desired his death and never had a man more deserved such an end as this one whose mismanagement had brought starvation and civil unrest upon them all.

It was around 2:30 in the afternoon that a copy of Gerard's circular was thrust into Paxton's hands by one of his men. So busy had they all been at the docks and so formidable in numbers that Gerard's men had not distributed any circulars there. The soldier had found this one outside the docks blown on some fortuitous wind perhaps.

Paxton literally yelled when he read it and screamed for Rufus to assemble a band of armed men to make for the place of execution. Klyesha looking at the docks from her place on the deck saw the commotion and ran towards Paxton to see what had happened.

'You can't come!' he ordered her, thrusting the circular into her hands. She read the paper quickly and pushing all emotion away sprinted back to the ship, threw off her skirts and pulled on her breeches, screaming at her friends to bring their muskets. She grabbed hers and ran back down the gangplank. Soon she was joined by Thorsbard, Lucca and Rachel and each read the circular as they hurried to join Paxton's soldiers who'd rushed out of the docks. Breathless, they caught the tail of his men and joined them as they jogged towards Skull Hill.

'It cannot be,' shouted Rufus to his friend.

'Gerard is capable of anything,' yelled back Paxton.

Soon their group had joined the swelling numbers of the City's inhabitants moving towards Skull Hill. Alleys began to fill up and jam and their pace slowed. Paxton cursed that he didn't have a horse. William would die for a lack of a horse. He pressed forward through the crowds and at one point fired his musket over them, whereupon many flung themselves at neighbouring houses creating a gap Paxton, his men and Klyesha and her friends rushed into.

Still their progress was agonisingly slow. Lucca looked at his pocket watch. It was 10 minutes to 3 o'clock with miles to go to get to the site of the gibbet. Klyesha stumbled on in despair then but Lucca and Thorsbard held her up.

'Come, Mistress, we must press on,' argued Lucca.

Rachel could not stop the tears streaming down her cheeks. Unable to get into her breeches in time, she tied her skirts up under her belt. Her white bloomers showed underneath, but she had no care. They must get to the King in time.

The dray was now at the bottom of the rise which held the gibbet. The hangman, his face masked in black, waited for his charge on the platform which held the gallows. Gerard's men had to crowd around the prisoner to prevent him being assaulted by the crowd. Gerard had thoughtfully brought a whip which he cracked around at anyone who got too close from his position on his horse. The crowd saw the King dragged from the dray by several of Gerard's men who held him up as his legs were weak. There were twenty or more steps set into Skull Hill to bring the condemned man to his fate. Gerard's men held him up as they slowly climbed these steps. As they climbed, the jeers of the crowd rose up and chanting began. 'Kill the King. Hang him dead. Kill the King. Hang him dead.'

Still stuck among crowds, Paxton and his group heard the chilling chanting coming from Skull Hill. Pushing forward, they could just see in the distance the outline of the gibbet on the hill. The crowd was packed around them now and it was almost impossible to move forward. Klyesha was screaming in frustration as she saw the King being supported up the steps- so near and yet so far. She fired her musket then and some people moved away in fear but the crowd was so packed there was nowhere to move.

Paxton scanned his surroundings. There was a row of houses closer to the hill. If they could climb up on their roofs, their muskets might be within pistol shot of the executioner or even of Gerard. It would be a desperate action for muskets at such a range were notoriously inaccurate. Still, they must try.

Paxton grabbed Rufus and another soldier and they pushed their way to the houses. They would have to climb up on the outside and follow the sloping roofs. Timbered houses have many footholds so they climbed up one angled timber at a time until with a tremendous effort they could get onto the roof. The shingles of slate was slippery and some covered holes. One of Paxton's first steps went straight through the roof and he had to be pulled out by Rufus and the soldier. They stepped more carefully then until they could squat on the nearest house to the gibbet.

Klyesha and her friends watched their progress, unsure of what they were doing but hoping fervently they had a successful plan in mind. They kept moving forward as best they could to assist Paxton's efforts on the ground.

Klyesha vowed she would shoot Gerard herself while he sat with his wicked whip smirking for all the world to see, apparently at finally being able to overcome his enemy, his brother the King.

By now the crowd saw the King and his helpers had reached the gallow's platform which stood high above them all giving a clear vantage of the scene to enfold. The executioner spoke something to the King who nodded. He placed the rope around the King's neck and he staggered, almost fainting. The men held him up.

As he stood there, a quiet hush came over all the excited crowd as the long-awaited last words of the King were about to be spoken. They waited so quietly, many could hear their own hearts beating.

Paxton, Rufus and the soldier on the roof waited too, trying to gauge the best and safest moment to shoot the executioner.

The prisoner looked out at the crowd, his last view of anything on earth. He saw the hatred and loathing on the people's faces hungry for his death. Crows gathered in the sky, landing on nearby trees as they waited for their supper which would be his own flesh.

He opened his mouth and tried to speak but no words came out. The crowd became restless and one called out cruelly, 'Speak tyrant!' Yet the prisoner could not utter any reply. The executioner became impatient. Paxton waited for the moment. The executioner moved to the lever which would release the trapdoor causing the prisoner to fall and the noose to tighten around his neck.

'Kill the King' became the dominant crowd chant once again, 'Kill the King! Hang him dead! 'Down with the tyrant!'. Their chants rose and rose until even the crows left the trees disturbed by the noise.

Paxton readied his musket, but the executioner remained standing directly beside the prisoner. If Paxton's shot went wide he would kill the King. 'Should I take the shot?' he asked Rufus urgently.

'You must,' replied Rufus, 'there is no other way.'

Paxton took the shot. The executioner fell but his body pushed the lever forward anyway. The hatch under the prisoner gave way.

His legs dangled underneath him and the noose began its choking work.

The crowd was stunned by the shot which killed the executioner but they cheered as the prisoner hung anyway, convulsing before them. A cheer rose up and loudest of all to cheer was Gerard himself.

Klyesha fainted and Thorsbard picked her up and slung her over his broad shoulders.

From the countryside close by, screams rang out in the crowd. A group of horses came thundering in from the fields. The men were dressed in the King's livery and they fired muskets as their horses cantered in. The crowd frantically spread out in all directions for fear of being crushed by the horses. They fled back into the fields anywhere where there was space. Some were crushed under the hooves of the horses but they came on. In front of them was a tall, red-haired man dressed in the King's livery.

'Make way for the King,' he shouted to the fickle crowd, 'Make way.'

At the base of the hill, he lept from his horse and carrying his sword ran up the steps to the gibbet. Here, he grabbed the hanging man and with his other hand hacked at the rope. Soon he was cut lose and the King dragged the rope from around his neck. His soldiers had followed him and they attended to the man, one beating life back into his chest.

To everyone's astonishment, William stood raising his sword and addressed the rabble. 'I am your King, William. This man is my cousin, Henry, who Prince Gerard fooled you into believing was me.'

'Down with the King!' yelled people in the crowd.

'You will be fed,' he yelled over them. 'Today at the Docks we have unloaded food from our neighbour, Svartlund. Go in an orderly fashion and you will be fed. Anyone who uses violence will get none. Bring your baskets and boxes. Now go!'

The crowd unable at first to comprehend the turn of events began to disperse. Those of Gerard's men who could, mingled into the crowd and disappeared. As soon as William had arrived with his troops, Gerard had started cracking his whip to create a space in which to ride away. The crowd who had until then been on his side, surged forward. One man, who was wearing gloves, grabbed the tip of the whip and pulled. Gerard had to let go to remain seated on his horse. He scanned the area seeking a space in which to escape but there was none. As William's troops forced their way towards him, Albert Strong leapt from his horse and kept hold of Gerard's reigns. He was dragged up to the gibbet to face his brother.

Henry, almost lifeless, had begun to breathe again and he was given water.

'You are a devil of the worst sort,' William addressed Gerard. 'You chose to kill an innocent man, our cousin, to dupe the citizens into believing it was me. No doubt you would have had me killed as soon as I showed my face.'

Paxton and Rufus, at first horrified Paxton's shot had hung the King, now cheered from the house rooftop at the sight of William and his troops. They climbed back down and were making their way to the gibbet as did Lucca and Rachel. Thorsbard was attending Klyesha who was still in a faint.

Surrounded by his troops and now his friend, William grinned from ear to ear. 'Sire, said Paxton falling to his knees, 'if ever we needed you, it is now.'

'Paxton, most loyal of all my men, give me your sword,' said the King. Paxton did so, unsure what the King would do with it for it was his ill-timed shot which had hung Henry.

'Stay on your knees.' William raised the sword and brought it down gently on Paxton's shoulders. 'Today you will be Sir Paxton, Knight of the Realm. Arise Sir Paxton.'

Paxton stood up truly humbled. 'Well deserved,' commented Rufus slapping him on the back. 'Where is Thorsbard and Klyesha?' asked the King scanning the circle of his friends.

'She fainted, Sire,' said Rachel and Thorsbard stayed with her.

'Take me to them.' William followed Lucca. Klyesha lay in the back of the same dray in which the false King made his way to his fate. Thorsbard was wiping her face with a damp cloth. William was dismayed to see the colour drained out of her face. 'Is she still alive, Thorsbard?' He nodded. William climbed into the dray gathered her onto his lap. She began to stir when he softly called her name and began stroking her cheek. She opened her eyes and could not believe she was seeing her beloved William before her. He said, 'It was not me on the gibbet, my love, but my cousin Henry who does resemble me. I have been in the Palace readying the troops.'

Klyesha nodded and William called for water. The run to Skull Hill and the heightened emotion there had exhausted her and him both. After drinking, she sat up. Her friends surrounded the dray and William was beside her. It was as if she had woken from a bad dream.

'Go and fetch Henry,' said William to Paxton and Rufus, 'we must take them both quickly now to the Palace.'

'What should be done with Gerard?' asked Lieutenant Withers.

'Bring him on horseback to the Palace. If he tries to escape use that whip on him.'

Everyone was somewhat overwhelmed by the turn of events. Lucca looked at Rachel as she too was exhausted, and he made her get in the dray with the others. William returned to his horse to accompany his soldiers back to the Palace.

Most of the square was empty now after William had promised food at the docks. Paxton and Rufus borrowed some of the soldier's horses to ride back to the docks and oversee the distribution of the food. They would turn no one away today without food even if it took all night.

There were those who resented the appearance of the King such as Slade and his men. They had come to see the execution too but had crept away when the King and his men appeared. Slade had seen Rufus greeting the King and realised he was a spy. He ground his teeth at Rufus' deception and vowed revenge. He took his men to the markets where they would hold up for the day vowing tomorrow to send some of his men, unknown to Rufus, to get food in the morning.

The King's 200 or so soldiers, half of them mounted but all armed with muskets, accompanied William and the dray back to the Palace. The mobs for the moment did not attempt to attack them but this was no reason to believe that danger was over.

When they reached the Palace, William directed his men back to the wharves to help Rufus and Paxton with an orderly distribution. If riots broke out, all their good work would be in vain.

Soon they were inside the Castle and William led them to his rooms and ordered food. Even the Palace was running low on supplies, but the kitchens managed a bowl of hearty beef broth with vegetables for everyone. William left them to eat excusing himself.

He went to his bedchamber where Henry had been brought to be attended by his own physic and several apothecaries. 'How is he?' William asked the physic. Henry was in a bad way. His throat was really swollen and he was finding it difficult to breathe.

'He's lucky the noose didn't break his neck,' said the physic, who was applying cold cloths to Henry's neck. Henry was propped up with cushions to aid his breathing.

'I'll give him tincture of poppy,' said one of the apothecaries.

'I'm giving him menthol to ease his airways,' said the other.

William was very angry and the more he looked at Henry the angrier he got. He praised the healers and turned and strode from the room to the dungeons. 'Where is he?' he demanded of one of the guards who pointed to a cell where Gerard sat slumped down in one corner.

'Brother,' he spat as William approached.

'Never call me that again, heathen!' cursed William.

'See how I duped them until you came along. Where have you been?"

'None of your business but thank God I arrived when I did otherwise Henry would be dead and me too soon as I appeared here.'

'I hope he dies!' swore Gerard.

'You should hope he lives otherwise I will determine your fate and if I decide you hang in the morning from the same gibbet you set up for Henry.'

Gerard scoffed but some of the venom was drawn from his responses. 'What will you do with Sophia?'

'Sophia, I imagine, would have enjoyed seeing me dead but only under your influence. I will make provision for her but she won't come to the Palace again. She should share some of your ignominy.'

'You still have to win over the people,' scorned Gerard.

'I will explain to them that the grain destruction and the subsequent food riots were all orchestrated by you to put me in a bad light. Let them judge me then. I have been away organising food for them while you have merely been trying to take the throne.'

'And I almost succeeded.'

'Yes, except for some exceptional men and the others who helped me, I might not be here.'

'More's the pity.'

'Let me leave you to your rancour, traitor, your own bitterness will blight your life if you get to live longer than tomorrow. I suggest you pray Henry lives.'

Gerard just looked at him with black and beady eyes. William left him without a backward glance and returned to his guests.

They all wanted to know what had happened to him since they left for Svartlund. He took a goblet of wine and asked for some hot broth. Sipping the wine he began, 'First of all, I thank you all for the success of the supply ships. The Kingdom owes you an incalculable debt. Without them the food riots would have continued until anarchy took over. Soon we would have been ruled by ruthless gangs and ordinary citizens terrorised.'

Thorsbard responded, 'It was my pleasure, your Majesty. Anything my country can do now or in the future you need just ask.'

'Thank you again, Thorsbard, as much for your help as your doctoring. My leg is almost healed.' Thorsbard nodded his head.

'We owe you so much, dear Thorsbard,' said Klyesha whose meal had restored her colour.

'I hope you shall visit me again,' the King included, 'We should not be strangers.'

William was eating his soup. He wiped his mouth with a napkin and took another sip of wine. Leaning back in his chair and putting his feet up on a foot stool, he began, 'Captain Paxton and I, as you know were gathering troops from estates and villages to bolster my troops here at the Palace. We left Hamleyvale soon after a messenger came from, he said, the Palace to find me. I was immediately suspicious and believed Gerard was behind those inquiries, so we left that day for Rosethorn Estate, two days ride north-east. We stayed there for several days making it another collection point for the troops. The estate owner, Duke Declerq made us very welcome and I believe Paxton has formed an attachment to his daughter.'

Klyesha laughed, 'The old bachelor!'

William grinned, 'He's only in his 40s. Anyway, back to my story. I became increasingly suspicious of Gerard's motives. Either he wanted to capture me or kill me or he had some other plan in mind to seize the crown. His latest exploit, pretending our cousin Henry was me and staging his execution shows how diabolical is his mindset. He would sacrifice anyone to get to the throne. I knew you were safe, Klyesha, and I thanked the Lord I'd sent you with Thorsbard where Gerard or his spies could not find you.'

'However, I could not rest knowing he planned somehow to take the Palace and win over my troops, so I left Rosethorn Estate early last week without telling anyone. Paxton would have stopped me or sent a guard with me thus alerting anyone in the City to my presence, so I went alone knowing some simple country clothing would disguise me.'

'It was risky,' commented Lucca.

'Yes it was, but lingering in the countryside not knowing what was happening here was a bigger risk I felt, so I entered the City leading my horse as if I was taking it to my master. It was cold and raining. This was enough to discourage banditry on the streets, so I was able to get to the Palace. If I encountered anyone, I asked him if there was food anywhere, they all shook their heads. I was just another country beggar seeking food though more than one suggested I ate the horse.'

'Anyway, I went to the Palace and convinced the guards to let me in. Some of Rufus' returning soldiers brought news from the docks of the situation in the City which had somewhat calmed. I still do not know what Gerard was planning. I might have had him arrested in his City villa for it soon became apparent that he was there but we had no real evidence of rebellion against him. We were at the ready to act when after lunch today one of his circulars was brought to the Palace. Now we could act. We set out with 200 troops to Skull Hill but unfortunately, we soon encountered massive crowds in the streets and could not move forward so we had to retrace our steps and ride around the Palace to get to the Skull Hill from the countryside. That's why we were delayed and thank God we did not arrive too late to save Henry.'

'How is he?' asked Thorsbard, 'Does he need my help?'

'You may see him, my friend, but my best physic and two apothecaries are attending him. He's a strong young man but the noose did terrible damage to his neck, we just hope he will survive.'

Klyesha shook her head, 'How could Gerard be so cruel and how did he plan to take the throne seeing you weren't dead?'

'The thing is,' replied William, 'everyone would have been convinced I was dead. As soon as I appeared, he was going to have me murdered and he could simply say he'd had my cousin Henry killed because maybe he'd attacked him. No one would have questioned it seeing they assumed the King was already dead. Then Gerard would have had himself crowned because I have no heir.' Klyesha looked at him and he returned her gaze.

'I also believe he orchestrated the grain destruction by neglect to ferment food riots and discredit me.'

Lucca shook his head, 'Such a scale of widespread misery and death just to get your crown!'

'Indeed,' answered William, 'It beggars belief that one person is capable of such evil.'

'Will you hang him?' ask Thorsbard.

'I would, yes, after a short trial but I've decided to let Henry decide his fate when he can speak and think about it.'

'Some small amount of justice then,' commented Rachel.

'Yes, a small amount in the face of massive social upheaval. What he didn't seem to think through was how to feed everyone once he was King.'

'Perhaps he'd stockpiled food,' said Lucca.

'It's possible,' said William, 'We will have to find out. It might have been part of his plan.'

'He seems to have had a lot of help,' suggested Thorsbard, shifting himself in his seat.

'Yes, that's my next task to find out who helped him and interrogate them. We don't know where he'd been hiding before he returned to his City Villa but we shall soon know.'

Chapter Seventeen

The inhabitants of the City Villa were being escorted under guard to the Palace. They included Ironsmith and Lewis and some of their men who'd left Skull Hill immediately after King William arrived. Ironsmith and Lewis had returned to loot what they could from Gerard's Villa knowing he wouldn't be back. They lingered too long and it was their undoing. William's guards had surprised and captured them in the very act of stealing food and jewels. William organised for the Villa to be guarded against looting so no one else could enter it for spoils. He had a plan for the future of the Villa and this involved preserving it.

Ironsmith and Lewis were brought before William after his guests had retired to their bed chambers for the night. They were thrust before him their hands tied behind their backs. William sat in a high-backed chair. 'Just to make things clear from the start,' warned William, 'you'll both be tortured if you fail to tell me what I want to know. Which by the way, is everything from the moment you joined forces with the Prince.'

They'd given the guards some attitude so both were sporting bruised faces and sore limbs. This apparently was torture enough because they were soon telling William everything they knew about Gerard.

'I want to know who else was helping him apart from the men you brought from the countryside?' asked William after listening to their narrative for several minutes.

Ironsmith looked at Lewis and they had a quick discussion then Ironsmith said, 'There were a number of people who came from the Palace, most of whom we never met however there was one older man the Prince often seemed in talks with. He be known as Lindquist.'

'Arrh!' exclaimed William. Lindquist was the chancellor's right-hand man and privy to much that went on in the Palace. His information would have been invaluable to Gerard. William looked at the two men trying to decide their fate. 'Why did you agree to serve Gerard?' he asked.

'He promised us food,' replied Lewis.

'Yes, we were all hungry,' agreed Ironsmith.

'So this was enough to betray your King and assist him in executing me?' The men had no answer. Not only were they traitors but, as they believed, they were willingly involved in having the King hung.

'How do you feel when I tell you it was my cousin, Henry who you helped hang? An innocent man.'

The men shifted nervously. They'd be hung as traitors themselves whether it was the real William or not who they helped hang. 'Guards take them to the dungeons. The Assembly will decide their fate.'

William turned wearily to his wine but desisted at the last moment. He needed to join Klyesha and wine was not what he wanted.

In the morning, William took a company of guards and rode to the wharves. Thorsbard rode with him as he was anxious to see how the supplies would last. The wharves were heavily guarded with Paxton's and Rufus' companies as well as the 300 or so fencible men who had come to the Capitol at the King's request. They were dressed in all manner of costume both rustic and fine. They all sported yellow arm bands to denote allegiance to the King in the absence of proper livery.

In between the rows of guards wound a long line of citizens carrying baskets and sacks. William was shocked to see how drawn and haggard most of them looked as if they were tired beyond caring. He dismounted and left his horse with a guard and together with Thorsbard they entered the first warehouse. Here they were assaulted by a strong smell of dried fish. Men had kegs of the fish open and were distributing handfuls to the people who paraded past them. Fish was not a favourite amongst people of the Kingdom and many of them had not eaten fish previously. Often during the morning, William heard the men questioned about how to prepare them, 'make a stew' being the most common answer. 'What else is there to eat?' was another oft repeated question and the answer was apples and cheese in the next warehouse and 'In a day or two you'll be able to buy bread from the bakers.'

William found Paxton who looked both tired and triumphant. 'Everything is going well, Sir. There are enough guards to prevent problems. We've had a few people who weren't happy with the fish. They were told in language easily understood it was 'fish or no other meat.' Most seem to change their attitude then.

'What's happening to the grain?' asked Thorsbard.

'We've sent the grain carts under guard to the several millers who operate in the City,' said Paxton. 'They'll distribute the subsequent flour to the City's bakers who will ration it out to the local people. They are taking down people's names and they'll get one loaf of bread a day until we run out.'

'Any idea when that might happen?' asked William.

'No idea,' replied Paxton, 'but we'll keep in touch with the bakers to let us know when supplies are getting low.'

'I can easily organise more shipments,' offered Thorsbard.

'We will need them, dear Thorsbard,' said William as they left Paxton to continue his work. 'It's spring so we'll be able to plant some of our own crops too but as you know these things take time. I'm sending out my men into the countryside to assess the situation. Their excess produce will have to be sent here as well as any animals they can spare. But we may need to rely on Svartlund for food for several months yet.'

'May I also suggest you organise your own fishing fleets to step up fishing. What's the situation there?'

'Not great. Our fishing fleets are almost non-existent. We are not a fishing nation but we'll soon have to be.'

'I can get my kralls to show your citizens how to fish. Even from the wharves it's possible.'

'Wonderful. How are your people liking the Villa by the way?' William had installed Thorsbard's people in Gerard's Villa where his servants were looking after them.

'It's quite luxurious for them. Hot and cold water by the faucet. They aren't used to such luxuries.'

'They deserve some special treatment. Can you organise instructors to come to the Palace tomorrow?'

'Indeed, they seem quite bored by luxury and want to help.'

'My people need to get a taste for fish. Somehow I think they'll enjoy fresh fish more.'

Thorsbard grinned, 'I know dried herring is an acquired taste, however it's very nutritious.'

'Don't get me wrong, my people are happy to have their bellies filled. For that, you have our eternal gratitude, my friend!'

When they returned to the Palace, Thorsbard left to join his people at the Villa. Klyesha came immediately to him, 'Sire, I need to see Cook and my house. They have had no word of us for months now.'

'You want me to come?' he asked.

'No, Lucca will go with us.'

'He's not enough. Lieutenant Withers and five of his men will go with you. We still don't know exactly how dangerous the City still is.'

Nodding her head, Klyesha looked to him shyly and whispered, 'Do you want me to return tonight?'

William pulled her into his arm, 'Not one more night are we going to be apart,' he whispered in her ear, 'Now go, so that you are back soon!'

Klyesha smiled and went to her bedchamber where she collected a coat and changed into more robust shoes. Rachel came in and they left to get Lucca and find Lieutenant Withers.'

'Pity our carriage is still in Hamleyvale,' said Klyesha.

'Oh, well perhaps one day we can journey to collect it?'

'Not soon hopefully. I was so keen to travel but I just want the comforts of home now.'

'Isn't that why we travel,' asked Rachel, 'to appreciate home more?'

Klyesha laughed and they went to find Lucca.

When they reached Klyesha's house they were all dismayed at the state of it. All the windows were smashed as well as one door. The doors were boarded up and a strong chain and bolt kept the front gates shut. The front garden generally, was littered with debris and loose cobblestones.

'What has happened here?' cried Klyesha. 'I hope Cook and her niece are a'right!' As they couldn't get in, some of the guards helped several to climb the wall whereupon they disappeared around the side of the house.

After a few moments Walter the gardener appeared with him. 'Mistress!' he exclaimed, 'We are honoured you have returned.' He unbolted the gate and let everyone in

'What has transpired here, Walter?' asked Klyesha.

'The rioters, Mistress. In the first few weeks after you left, they came trying to get food and when they couldn't get in, they smashed the front of the house with cobbles.'

'Is everyone alright?' asked Klyesha, as they hurried around to the back door.

'You can see for yourself, Mistress,' answered Walter quietly.

They were soon in the kitchen where Cook was busy at the stove. When she turned to see her mistress home, Klyesha was shocked at how thin she had become. They embraced and Cook began to cry. 'We are so pleased to see you,' she sobbed. Klyesha cried with her.

'I am so sorry we left you with all this to suffer,' offered Klyesha.

'We did our best,' said Cook, wiping her eyes. 'I am sorry for your house.'

'It is no matter. It can be repaired,' soothed Klyesha. 'Now, how is Flora?'

Cook looked strange and her mistress immediately knew something was wrong.

'Rachel make us all some hot broth please?' asked Klyesha leading Cook into her sitting room 'Now sit down and tell me everything.' Klyesha held her hand while Cook related the trials of the first few weeks. How they had retreated to the cellar, the lack of food and how Walter's family had joined them.

'And how are they?' asked Klyesha.

'Mistress Walter was a quiet one to begin with but after Gerard's men took them, she's been really depressed.'

'Gerard's men!'

'Aye, they took Flora and Mrs Walter. I think they believed they were you and Rachel.'

'And?'

'Oh, Mistress!' said Cook, breaking down again.

'Tell me when you're able.' Klyesha waited for a few moments during which she noted the absence of her grandfather's clock.

'They... he...assaulted Flora.' Cook finally got out the words. 'She wouldn't tell us for weeks.'

'Who assaulted her?' Klyesha sat very still. Henry, the tom cat , rubbed up against her but she ignored him.

'The Prince. He's an evil man,' spat Cook.

Klyesha stood trembling with anger, 'Where is she?'

'She's a lying down on account of her sickness…'

'She's not?'

'Yes, with child, Mistress, I believe.'

Unable to speak, Klyesha left Cook and looked for Flora who she found in her bedroom.

'Mistress!' cried Flora sitting up, 'I'm so sorry this is your room.' Flora looked much paler since Klyesha had seen her months before.'

'Please, don't get up! I am very sorry you were caught up with Gerard's evil because they thought you were me.'

'Aye, Mistress. They who broke in to find you, did not know who you and Rachel were. I regret one of them, a big brute of a man, also broke your grandfather's clock!'

'The clock is not important, you are. We will do everything we can for you. Please don't worry.'

'But Mistress, how am I to bring up a child alone? A child of such a man!'

'Do not worry. The King and I will help you. We will give you every assistance if you choose to keep the child.'

Flora shook her head and began to cry, 'I wish I was dead!' she sobbed.

'Nay, nay,' said Klyesha, rocking her in her arms, 'We are back and you aren't alone. Don't forget that!'

She left Flora and returned to the kitchen. Cook was sitting eating a thin broth. The general mood was sombre. 'Lieutenant, I don't want to leave my servants here alone any longer. Please organise a dray and horse to take them to the Palace.'

'Yes, Mistress Culaine, anything else?'

'I'll need the front door repaired. Can you leave some men here to guard the house and supervise the work?'

'Aye, Mistress, consider it done.'

Lucca suggested he stay as well but Klyesha refused as he had his own household to attend to.

'While my household goes to the Palace, we will visit your house, Lucca. The Lieutenant will come with us.'

Rachel was more content because she had already heard from her family, the Bakers. They were happy and safe and so she could stop worrying about them.

Klyesha then made a more complete examination of the house and garden. It would take weeks to remedy the damage, but it was the human cost of her journey which weighed most heavily upon her. Her servants were her friends and their welfare came first.

So, it was some hours later with Cook, Flora, Mrs Walter and the girls established in the Palace, they took Walter, James, Lieutenant Withers and a soldier to Lucca's house. Klyesha had brought her musket just in case. They walked past whole terraces which had been burnt and looted, their contents strewn about the streets. Lucca's house was not far from the street of watchmakers in a row of pretty gabled two storey houses once painted in bright colours. It was clear that most of the houses had been damaged in the riots. All ground and first floor level windows were boarded up. Anything that could be torn from facades had been: shutters, oil lamps and decorative timbers. It was as if the rioters were taking revenge on the houses themselves for being fortresses and not letting them in. Each terrace also had a very high walled garden which also must have frustrated the rioters. Here in alleyways, they'd seen graffitied obscenities in chalk or paint showing anger at the rich people who they believed suppressed them and they supposed lived within.

Lucca knocked on his black enamelled door, its doorknocker crowbarred off and its paint chipped and scratched. They waited a long time before a voice demanded to know who they were. Soon the doors opened to Lucca and he was embraced by Susanna, the dark-haired daughter of his elderly housekeeper, Margaret. They entered the hall while Susanna locked and bolted the door.

'Are you well Susanna?' asked Lucca, ushering them all into his sitting room. Walter, James and the soldier stood politely against the wall. He introduced her to their party.

'Aye, Mistress Klyesha, I have heard a lot about you,' said Susanna.

'And you, Madam. I hope you and your mother are well.'

Susanna shook her head, 'It's been terrible, the fear alone and hearing rioters on the streets. They burnt down a whole row of terrace houses.'

'We saw it. Thank God yours remained safe.'

'Indeed. Where would we have gone, I cannot tell as my mother is quite elderly and unwell.'

'How is Margaret?' asked Lucca.

'She is well, better than many. The food you brought Master Lucca before you left kept us well but it has nearly gone. We would have been starving in a few days.'

'There is a lot to tell you, Susanna, but you should know the King has returned. We ourselves have been to Svartlund and brought back by ship many food supplies. The City will be fed again.'

'Well, that is uplifting news, Sir. From Svartlund? My! I thought no one went there!'

'Not anymore,' reassured Klyesha, 'Now they are our trading partners.'

'Such a relief', commented Susanna, who began to cry.

Lieutenant Withers added, 'Madam, the City will soon be under control again. The King has brought many new troops to help put down the rioters.'

'They are wicked men, Sir,' answered Susanna, 'They didn't care who they attacked or harmed.'

'Certainly they are desperate men. Hungry and angry. However, the new food supplies will quell much of that anger.'

Lucca explained he would stay and see his elderly housekeeper and put things in order. James volunteered to stay with him to help resupply the household. Walter would return with the others to oversee the repairs to Klyesha's house.

'I will stay too,' said Rachel surprising her friend, 'I can help with the housework as Susanna has carried the burden for too long.'

Lucca was both surprised and pleased, 'You are welcome, Mistress Rachel.' He bowed.

'As you wish,' said Klyesha quietly for she would miss her friend. 'Bakers will soon have bread you will be pleased to know,' she said to the tear-streaked Susanna bringing a small smile to her face.

Klyesha, Walter, Lieutenant Withers and the soldier left to return to the Palace. Klyesha expressed her gratitude for their company as both she and her friends had been worried about their homes.

'As we have seen up close those worries were justified,' said Withers.

'Indeed,' agreed Klyesha.

They travelled for several blocks through the Potters' District onto the Cloth Merchants' District. As they turned the corner from the Cloth Merchants' Street to go past another burnt out street, Lieutenant Withers tensed and stopped.

'Martin,' he said to his soldier, 'There on the left!' Along the street partially concealed by a broken brick wall, were a large group of men camping out in the ruins.

'Let's go back,' whispered the soldier, 'and travel down a different street.' So, they turned and retreated to go down the parallel street. It was relatively quiet, some of the buildings were smoke damaged but otherwise intact.

They were passing the entrance to a short lane when members of the encampment rushed at them yelling with weapons held aloft. Lieutenant Withers and the soldier drew their swords and began sweeping swings at the men. Withers yelled at Klyesha and Walter to run. As there was no time to fill and cock her musket, Klyesha took his advice and ran. Walter was close behind her as they ran for their lives along the street. Fortunately, there were no more alleys to open out before them to allow more of the men to trap them in the street. Still, they knew they could not run forever. Klyesha was surveying possible escape routes or places of safety as they ran.

Towards the end of the street, a woman opened her door and called them, 'Get in here! It's safe!' Quickly they lept through the doorway into a narrow dark hall. The woman closed the door behind them.

'Thank you, Mistress,' said Klyesha, breathless. 'The rioters attacked us.'

'They just began staying in those ruins,' she explained leading them to her kitchen.

'Everyone's been afraid to go out. Come warm yourselves by the fire.' They entered the tiny kitchen and stood in front of the range warming their backs.

'Could we trouble you for some water?' gasped Klyesha. Soon they were sipping from brimming goblets.

'Can you tell us about those men, Mistress?' asked Walter.

'They be devils they is. I think they'd even eat children if they could get hold of any. We're all on alert all the time less they try to break in and steal food, not that we have any much.'

Klyesha introduced herself and Walter. The woman's name was Marissa. She lived alone.

'What can you tell me about what's happening out there?' asked Marissa.

'There is good news,' said Klyesha. 'Two ships from Svartlund have brought food to the docks. It's being distributed from there.'

'Not much use to me, Mistress. How am I to get there safely?'

'Yes, I can see it would be a problem, but the bakers will soon have bread. If you can go safely to a baker's shop.'

'Oh, aye, that is good news but the only shop is past that burned out street where they are encamped.'

'Perhaps if you townsfolk banded together?'

'It's a thought. If we could arrange it. Is the bread being given away?'

'Yes, I believe so. One loaf per person per day.'

'Well then it might be arranged. I'll go to my backyard and call my neighbours. When should we go?'

'The grain needs to be milled. It might be best to wait a few days.'

'Oh aye, and what will you do Mistress?'

Klyesha looked at Walter. It was a difficult situation and being too dangerous to go out onto the streets again perhaps they're only chance was to stay awhile.

'Do you mind if we stay here awhile, Marissa?'

'You are welcome to what little I have. The company will be a nice change for me.'

'You be married, Mistress?'

'Oh no, Walter is my gardener,' said Klyesha immediately wishing she'd said something else.

'Are you a wealthy woman then, Mistress?' asked Marissa.

'I own a house not much bigger than yours,' answered Klyesha cautiously, 'Not far from here in the Watchmaker's Street.' For indeed to return to Lucca's might be their safest option for Klyesha was beginning to feel uneasy about Marissa and her welcome.

When the woman left her to talk to her neighbours over the fence, Klyesha voiced her concerns, 'Can we trust her?'

'She looks harmless enough, Mistress,' said Walter.

'But her friends might not be. They could trap us here and use us as hostages.'

Walter creased his brow, 'Do you really think she might?'

'We could just leave and hope the rioters don't see us and make our way back to Lucca. At least we feel safe there,' argued Klyesha.

'I say we go,' said Walter.

Their minds made up, they left the kitchen and made their way to the front door to find it was locked.

'We'll have to ask her to unlock the door,' said Klyesha.

'And if she won't?'

'Well, we are two against one.'

However, that was soon to change.

Chapter Eighteen

Dinner was served in the King's apartments without Klyesha. William had sent out a detachment of soldiers with lanterns to Lucca's house but they had still not returned. The waiting was excruciating and William blamed himself for not taking more care with Klyesha's adventures. He was very much caught up with the food distribution. The hostility of his people in the crowd at his supposed execution was not something he could soon forget. They hated him with their very souls. All their hardships, privations, grief and losses were laid on his shoulders at Skull Hill. Perhaps the execution might have been cathartic for them certainly the circular made Gerard out to be a humble but suitable replacement for him. How simply people had been duped. It was as if they swallowed the lies more easily because they were so extreme. But what he needed to examine deeply was whether the accusations held any truths?

The worst aspect was the famine and food riots might have been prevented if he'd understood the situation more clearly. He could never afford to have unreliable people in charge of important things like food. He'd been so proud of his re-introduction of cats but they were a solution too little too late. The damage had already been done.

However, he remembered Albert Strong's words to him yesterday. 'People have come from all over the country to support you. They have left their families and homes to fight for you, don't forget that.' These thoughts buoyed him up and the fact food was being distributed again.

Finally, a soldier knocked on his dining room door and gave his report: 'Sire, Mistress Klyesha, Walter, Lieutenant Withers and Private Martin left Lucca Culaine's house at around 3:00 pm. They have not been seen since.'

'Did you retrace their steps?'

'Impossible to know exactly where they went to return to the Palace. We searched around the streets but apart from debris and burn out buildings we found nothing.'

'Burnout buildings?'

'Yes, Sire, one whole terrace of buildings near the Cloth Merchants has been burnt to the ground.'

'I see, thank you soldier. Tell the men to return to their barracks but please return to me in the morning for further instructions.'

'As you wish, Sire,' said the soldier saluting.

William was fuming. How could he have let her slip through his fingers? He drank down a whole goblet of wine. It was going to be a long sleepless night.

Lying on his back with a pike in his chest, Lieutenant Withers knew he was going to die. It was foolhardy to traverse the City was so few men. He regretted not being able to report to the King and was ashamed two citizens in his care were missing. Private Martin had fought the mob until the last drop of his blood, much of which surrounded him as he lay dead in the alleyway close by. The rioters were gone. Perhaps they feared more soldiers would come and hunt them down. Withers was sure they would anyway. His death would be revenged. It was with this thought he closed his eyes.

Walter and Klyesha stood on the wrong side of the locked front door. They were whispering about what to do next while Klyesha primed the musket. Walter went to the kitchen and returned with an iron poker. It wasn't much of a weapon but it was heavy with an iron ball soldered to one end. He held the other end ready to use it.

Was she being paranoid? Something had flickered in Marissa's eyes when she said Walter was her gardener. She knew that look. It was a mixture of desperation and opportunity. A look she'd seen on many faces in the crowd at Skull Hill.

As the musket was ready to fire, Mistress Marissa came creeping down the hallway from the outside entrance. Behind her were at least five men. They looked remarkably similar to the rioters they'd seen camped in the nearby burnt-out buildings. The arch just inside the front door held an alcove and cast a shadow over Klyesha and Walter so Marissa didn't see them. She and the group marched into the kitchen. Klyesha lept like she'd never lept before and rushed to close the door on them. She held the door tight while Walter bolted it. Immediately those inside started hammering on the door.

'Out the back,' whispered Klyesha and they ran for the back door taking the key which they used to lock it from the outside. They found themselves in a small walled garden full of debris and long grass. Now fully dark, they crept about stumbling over rubbish until they found a gate in the back wall. It was already open where their 'saviour' had led in her co-conspirators. They listened at the gate and hearing nothing, slipped out into the alley.

They could hear men laughing in the distance and saw them in the light cast by smouldering fires much further down the alley. It was too dark for the men to see them.

'Quick' said, Klyesha, still holding the musket ready, 'down the alley.'

This alley joined the one where Lieutenant Withers and Private Martin had taken on the rioters. They had fought down one and along the other until, knowing the fight was hopeless, they'd attempted to run. Private Martin was already mortally wounded and did not get far. Klyesha and Walter passed by his body unknowing he was there however, they heard a moan ahead of them in the alley. Someone was lying injured. Klyesha hoped it was one of the rioters then realised they would have moved one of their own not left him behind injured. She peered down at the body in front of her and recognised the King's livery. 'Lieutenant Withers,' she whispered to Walter.

They bent to look at their protector horrified to see the pike in his chest.

'It looks bad,' said Walter.

'Break the shaft of the pike but keep the point in,' whispered Klyesha.

Walter was strong as gardeners tend to be and he quickly snapped the shaft of the pike. 'Now, help him up. We'll have to get his arms around our shoulders and drag him.' Withers was a dead weight and couldn't help them because he was unconscious. They did their best but they couldn't move him far.

'We'll have to drag him into another backyard. Come on,' said Klyesha. They dragged him a few yards. Walter tried the gates of backyards until he found one he could open. Together they dragged him into the yard and propped him up against a wall. 'I'll stay with him,' said Klyesha, 'You'll have to go and get help. The Palace is best. We need soldiers to fight the rioters. Here take my musket!'

'No, Mistress, I've never fired one. You need it. I'll go. I may not run fast but I can run a long way.'

'Godspeed, Walter. Bring us back help!'

Walter was gone in the next second, carefully closing the gate which Klyesha latched behind him. She looked at the darkened windows of the house in whose yard they hid and hoped and prayed there was no one at home.

Slade and his cronies managed to break through Marissa's kitchen door. They were furious when they realised their prey had fled.

'They can't have gotten far,' suggested Marissa to try and soothe Slade's temper. She'd let two wealthy people slip through their hands. They would have been good under threats to take them to their own house for more pickings. The troop numbers at the wharves precluded them getting supplies for themselves and there'd soon be troops patrolling the streets looking for them. It was important to get the supplies and use the wealthy person's home as a hideout. The gibbet still stood at Skull Hill and no doubt soon rioters would be hanging from it. They needed to disappear from the City streetscape as soon as possible. Marissa's house wasn't big enough for all of them; they needed to find a replacement soon.

Despite staunching the blood flow from Wither's chest, he was barely breathing. Klyesha could hear gurgling sounds of blood coming from his lungs. He needed urgent attention from a physic, pain killers and a safe and quiet place to rest. This dirty and cold garden would see him dead in hours.

She remembered the Island of Cats, how the surging sea and the repetition of day and night helped her in the terrible, lonely aftermath of her mother's death. Her cats kept her warm at night, their purring soothed her troubled mind and anxious temperament and their silken fur when petted gave her a feeling of comfort and closeness. She had learnt patience in those months after her mother died. She learnt not to pine for things which she didn't have. Only in the Kingdom had she become hungry for new experiences, for friendship and human closeness. Only here had she learnt to be impatient to see William and to be with him forever.

What if Walter failed to return? How would anyone find them here? Now she started to feel around the garden for more weapons. The musket was basically only good for one shot. If more than one man came at them, she'd need something else for defence. At the moment, Withers was passed out but if he awoke and began screaming? If they were caught in the garden, there was not much hope. She would fight them until she was overcome but Withers would die. Was there another way?

Walter was a man of the City. He had been gardener in many wealthy people's homes. As he ran past one of them, a thought occurred to him perhaps he could get help to Klyesha and Lieutenant Withers sooner? Risking a little time, he ran up to a familiar front door. The family were wealthy cloth merchants and he'd styled their garden until a year ago when the apprentice he taught took over from him so Walter could get employment closer to home.

He rapped urgently on the door, hoping someone would answer and recognise him. A servant called to him through the door so he answered her and she recognised his voice. He asked to speak to the master of the house. The servant explained they were at dinner. He said he urgently needed the Master's help.

It took a few precious minutes, but the Master came, a tall man called Mr Longhouse. Walter explained Klyesha's predicament and gave directions to the garden in which she and Withers were hiding. He explained he would get troops from the Castle but feared they'd come too late. He added that Klyesha was betrothed to the King and Longhouse's efforts would be amply rewarded. Longhouse listened to him carefully. He was reluctant to leave his house in the night as the City was so dangerous but he promised he would gather some men with weapons and attempt either a rescue or defence of the woman and the wounded soldier until help came.

Walter expressed his eternal gratitude and continued his journey to the Castle. Longhouse assembled his male servants, his two sons and going next door, gathered five more men from his neighbour's. Thus, a party of a dozen armed men left 20 minutes later following the directions Walter had given them.

Beating his open fist against his bedchamber door, William could wait no longer. Pulling on a cloak and grabbing his sword, he made for barracks. He would take 20 men and search the whole district where Klyesha and the two soldiers had disappeared until he found them. He vowed to cut down any rioters he saw. They had been through too much together to lose hope in their future now.

Assembling a small pile of rocks, Klyesha turned to her next objective: the back door of the terraced house in whose garden they were hiding. She had found a rusty metal bar with one end flat and this she intended to use as a crowbar to prise open the door. All the windows were completely dark. It was dinnertime as her rumbling stomach told her, so if people were in the house some noise or light from dinner or the kitchen should be apparent. She listened intently at the door and as there were no noises, she started to push the bar between the door and its door frame.

It was then she heard the swearing and shouting of rioters in the alleyway, their tone and anger conveyed they were after her and Walter. They were banging on the stone fences and gates of the back yards in the street in the hope of raising the residents and perhaps questioning them. It was a fool hardy approach as Klyesha was sure any self-respecting citizen would be more inclined to redouble their defences at such provocation but perhaps they had more friends in the street than just Mistress Marissa?

Klyesha pushed at the door frame desperately hoping it would crack but not alert the men to her presence. Twice she had to duck down as they went past in the alley way lest their rushlights caught sight of her in the shadow of the door.

Again and again, she levered the crowbar into the door frame and pulled. Finally, she heard it crack. The wood was breaking free from the latch. She shoved her shoulder against the door and desperately pushed. Being small but also strong from her physical life on the island, the door eventually gave way. It seemed however, to only go so far. She realised there must be something pushed up against the door inside. Perhaps a further protection against intruders? She could just get one arm through. It did feel like a heavy chest. How could she move it? Just then Lieutenant Withers started to moan.

Angling herself so she could push on the door with her feet, Klyesha shoved as hard as she could. The chest gave way. Perhaps there was enough room to slip through? She shoved again with all her strength, what was left of it, as space was needed to drag Lieutenant Withers through the door. Now the door was half opened but the effort had caused her to somersault backwards down the steps. She landed feeling shaken on her haunches but luckily, she was only bruised. She rose carefully, dusting herself off. What lay ahead was an even more difficult task, that of dragging Withers by herself up the steps and through the doorway.

Walter was almost at the Castle when the gates swung down and he saw the King mounted on his horse, his face lit by a Lantern.

'Sire,' yelled Walter.

William halted his men and drawing his horse aside dismounted next to Walter. 'Who are you?' he asked, for he'd never met Walter before.

'I am Mistress Klyesha's gardener, Sire. I have come from her. I don't know the name of the street but I can take you there.'

William didn't waste words. He indicated for Walter to mount the horse behind him and with Walter giving directions, they cantered into the City.

Mr Longhouse and his band of family and neighbours were almost at the entrance to the alleyway which indicated by Walter was Klyesha's hiding place. As they entered the alleyway they heard a group of 20 or more men approaching them.

'Make way or suffer the consequences!' challenged Longhouse, his tall figure looking imposing as he drew his sword. His men were arranged around him holding rushlights up to see their foes.

Slade swore at them, explaining the fate they faced if they came any closer. Klyesha heard them threatening someone. The someone they threatened must be friends to her. She gently lay Withers down close to the steps where she'd managed to drag him. Perhaps she could help her new unknown friends? She started by dragging two apple crates to the back wall of the garden. She set one up on the other and next she filled her pockets with broken cobbles. If rioters could throw cobbles and almost destroy her house, she could return the favour. She climbed up onto the apple crates but unable to see more than dark shapes backlit by the friendly group's lights she nevertheless had targets. She aimed for their backs as a wider target than their heads. Raising the first rock in her hand, she hefted it with all her might. Many a time on the Island of Cats this was her favourite game from childhood to teenage times. She could even kill a seabird with a well-aimed rock.

When seabird is your only alternative meat to fish, she'd never hesitated. She didn't hesitate now.

The first rock caused a scream and one of the tardier members of Slade's group crumbled to the ground. Several of those in the back were confused by the felling of their friend but believed the blow came from their enemies ahead. It made them angry and they surged at Longhouse and his men.

Klyesha threw more of her rocks now, some fell clattering onto the stone alleyway itself but several more struck home, disabling more of Slade's cronies. As the groups were now a tangled mass of fighters, she desisted from throwing her missiles fearing she'd injure some of her friends. However, one person had observed her figure poking over the back of the terrace's garden wall. This person came at her with a raised stick and as she been looking the other way managed to strike Klyesha a hefty blow to the side of her head, whereupon she dropped like a lead weight from her position on the apple crates.

That person was Marissa. 'Throw rocks at my friends, you devil! I hope you never get up again!' Thus, ranting and screaming at Klyesha, Marissa was found by William and his men as they cantered into the alleyway behind the fighters.

'Seize her!' commanded William to his closest soldiers. The man dismounted and grabbed her while William and his men, still mounted, rode up to the fighting groups and demanded they put down their weapons or be crushed by the horses in the narrow alley. Longhouse stepped forward and introduced himself to the King.

'We came to rescue the Mistress Klyesha, Sire, and encountered this rabble,' he shouted.

Walter quickly identified him as friendly. Longhouse and his men prevented Slade and his rioters running away. They surrendered on threat of being murdered by the soldiers behind them. Slade told his men to drop their weapons and swore and spat on the ground. William's soldiers quickly moved among them tying their hands behind their backs and tying them one to each other so they could be dragged back to the Palace.

William found Longhouse. 'I thank you heartily, Mr Longhouse. With no challenge I hate to think what this group might have done.' he turned to Walter, 'Where is Klyesha?' Walter indicated the yard where Klyesha and Withers were hidden. The gate was locked but they soon had it down. Holding his light aloft, William saw Withers first and rushed to check on him. His wound was terrible but by some miracle he was still alive. It was Walter who found Klyesha knocked out cold and slumped by the wall. He cried out to the King.

William ran to him and picked Klyesha up. She flopped like a broken ragdoll. 'Oh, my darling!' he cried, 'Are we too late?' He felt her neck for a pulse and cried with relief to find her still alive.

'I thought she were dead, Sire!'

'Thank God she is not. But something or someone has felled her. We must get her to the Palace.' He tied a scarf gently around her neck to support it and together they lifted her from the base of the wall. Others had picked up Lieutenant Withers and using some improvised planks were already carrying him towards the Palace. His injury was too severe to risk him being taken there by horse.

William mounted his horse and giving directions to his men as regards to the prisoners, he cradled Klyesha on his breast and set off for the Palace at a steady pace, all the while cursing he had allowed her to go to her house so poorly protected in this City where danger still lurked in any alleyway. He was also proud of her volunteering to remain alone behind to protect and nurse Lieutenant Withers who may yet owe his life to her. He only hoped whatever had reduced her to this unconscious state was not fatal. He did not dwell on this unpleasant thought long. He could not bear it if she didn't pull through and smile at him with his beloved Klyesha's smile again.

Thorsbard greeted them as both Withers and Klyesha were brought into the King's apartments for treatment. Klyesha was laid on a couch and Withers was taken to a kitchen where the table could be used for operating. Thorsbard examined Klyesha's head feeling a huge lump the size of an egg on her skull slightly to the back above her left ear. He felt around the lump and despite bleeding, her skull didn't appear to be cracked. He ordered cold compresses for her head while he shone a light into her eyes. Luckily the pupils were reactive as he feared the pressure and swelling might yet impinge on her brain. He gave an apothecary instruction on medications and went to see Withers, leaving William to nurse his fiancé.

Withers was in a bad way. Thorsbard took his doctor's bag and ordered his instruments boiled while he examined the wound. The spear had been thrust into his right lung. The lung needed to be drained of blood and the damaged tissues sewn up. Quite familiar with such wounds from his doctoring in Svartlund, Thorsbard knew what to do, however, he also knew such a wound had a poor rate of recovery. He would do what he could for Withers and leave the rest to the gods.

The operation was assisted by four guards who held the patient down lest he struggle. Another man administered him tincture of poppy and held his head in a vice-like grip so he couldn't shift and move his chest.

Withers fortunately remained unconscious throughout the long procedure. The men tired though and had to be replaced several times. Thorsbard cleaned the wound with alcohol and arranged for Withers to sit up in bed to help him breathe. A drain had been inserted into his lung with a cap to keep the air in or allow the lung to be reinflated when the blood drained out.

Thorsbard was exhausted. He kicked off his shoes, put up his feet and ordered a large goblet of ale. It was indicative of his status regarding William that such relaxed behaviour was not commented on nor condemned.

William left Klyesha's side to give Thorsbard a report. 'She's breathing evenly but we've been unable to get her to drink. The cold compresses are being changed every 20 minutes and the lump on her head seems to have reduced.'

'Good, good,' murmured Thorsbard his eyes shut. 'We will leave her to rest tonight and try to rouse her the morning. Time is a great healer.'

'I hope so as I feel extremely guilty for allowing her to go into the City with such inadequate protection. Thank God, Walter made his way to the Palace for we might never have found her.' Walter had excused himself to join his wife and children so they no longer worried over his return.

'Will you hang them?' asked Thorsbard who'd heard about the about the attacks of Slade and his men.

'Probably,' replied William, his eyes closed from weariness. 'The Assembly can decide their fate. Thank you from the bottom of my heart, dear Thorsbard for the work you have done here tonight. Do you think Withers will live?'

Shrugging his shoulders, Thorsbard explained the chance of complications and the low survival rate of men with such wounds. Svartlunders used pikes and spears often in hunting, so such wounds were commonplace he explained to William.

The King was emotionally exhausted but he refused to leave Klyesha's side. 'I will nap here,' he told Thorsbard, 'but you must go to bed.' He rang a bell and a servant led Thorsbard away to a nearby bedchamber so he could rise and check on his patients later in the night.

Despite his weariness, William's heightened emotional state kept him from sleeping. He'd drank too much wine so he called for hot chocolate. He sent all the servants to bed asking only for ice to chill Klyesha's compresses.

She lay in her auburn dress, its fine fabric smutty and ripped from her exertions. Her shoes too were battered and rubbed as they lay discarded on the floor. How was it all his hopes for the future lay covered by a tartan rug on his couch? She looked so small and vulnerable yet indeed he'd seen her pile of rocks in the terrace yard and the loose cobbles in the alleyway and guessed she'd attacked the rioters in the only way she could. She'd not used her musket and he understood why as muskets were best fired by three rows of infantrymen, reloaded as the other row fired. As a one-off weapon it was almost entirely useless. In her situation rocks had been a wiser choice. To think she dragged Withers almost inside that house showed she was much stronger than she looked. He hoped that strength and resilience would help her pull through. Now his lids were so heavy he could do nothing but sleep.

They were all awoken by shrill screams in the night. Withers had regained consciousness and also an overbearing awareness of the pain of his injuries. Thorsbard rushed to his side, soothed him and administered more opium. He sat patting his hand until the old soldier fell again into a narcotic induced sleep.

Klyesha felt like she was drowning. One moment she was looking out to sea and the next moment she'd been catapulted into the surging ocean fighting to keep her head above the crashing waves. Her dress was very heavy and she reached down to rip the skirts away and remove her shoes. Always she kept her mouth shut as, time and time again, huge waves crashed on her head throwing her body around like driftwood. One tremendous wave lifted her up

231

and threw her at a rock shelf where the overhang hit her on the back of the head. She floated like a dead thing until pushed and pulled by the surge. The cold black was pulling at her skull and her mouth, going down her throat into her lungs.

Her hand reached out as she fought against losing consciousness. If the black took over she would soon drown. Reaching with all her might, she pushed herself up under the rock shelf, her bare feet scrambling for a foothold. Still her hand reached out grasping long ropes of seaweed while spiky and squishy things rubbed and scratched her legs.

She pulled and pulled on the seaweed until she got herself as far up the rock overhang as she could. At last, she was out of the surge of the waves and she coughed and gasped for air.

Only then did she hear her mother calling her desperately. All hope seeming stripped from her screeching tones. 'Klyesha! Klyesha!'

Finally, she managed to call out and her mother heard her. Such relief sounded in her voice as if nothing else mattered in the world.

She shifted violently in her sleep and the movement caused a terribly sharp pain to knife into her brain. She tried to call out, but her tongue was glued to the top of her mouth. When the pain finally subsided, she slept again.

This time she was in a meadow of brilliant white flowers set against the deep green of the grass which flashed like diamonds before her. Everywhere was a buzzing of bees dipping into the centre of each flower, thick balls of pollen trailing from their legs. A huge flock of birds emerged from the horizon. Blackbirds all in a long pointed 'v' formation rushing past her head screeching. They began to dive and peck her with their sharp beaks.

She ran and pulling her straw hat down to protect her neck. Still, they came dive bombing, ripping the dress from her back and breaking the skin until her back was spotted all over with blood.

She saw a deep forest with thick vines reaching down along the ground. Under these fallen vines she threw herself crawling on all fours. Dirt and rocks scratched her knees and bare feet. Yards and yards she crawled until at last she could hear no more the shrill and menacing cries of birds. In the dark warmth of the vines she curled up and soon fell asleep.

She was awoken by the purring of a cat and the licking of her face. It rubbed itself along her bare arms. She opened her eyes. It was her little black cat long escaped from her house but returned now to comfort her mistress.

The light was very bright and she squinted as it set off her headache again.

'Now, my love,' soothed William stroking her face, 'You can keep your eyes shut if the light hurts them but you must talk to me. You've been asleep for two days. Thorsbard was beginning to think you dropped into a coma.'

'Where's my cat?' asked Klyesha acknowledging William's presence but hoping her dream was real.

'Here she is,' said William, lifting the small cat and putting her on Klyesha's chest where she started to purr. Klyesha, her eyes tight shut however knew by the cat's purring and her shape that it was her own cat, Roxy, back.

'But how?' she asked.

'Cats have nine lives they say, don't they?' observed William, trying to repress the surging joy he felt filling his chest. 'In all this famine, she may have been eaten but she kept away from danger. A farmer came to the Palace apparently a week ago, before I got here, and brought your cat who'd been eating mice in his barn. Reluctant to catch her and stop her destroying the rodents, he gradually tamed her with dishes of milk and when he could finally catch her, he found the collar I'd given you. The collar is, as you know, somewhat luxurious and thinking he might get a reward for the cat, he brought her to the Palace. As you know I instituted severe penalties to anyone who mistreated a cat so he was quite keen to show he'd looked after her.'

'One of the servant girls who'd waited upon you when you first came here, recognised her as your cat and has been looking after her ever since. Of course, on hearing the tale I rewarded the farmer handsomely. Wanting you to wake but not to pull you abruptly from your healing sleep, I thought your cat might do it for me.'

'My healing sleep! It was nothing but nightmares, yet somehow at the end I dreamed of my Roxy and she is here, really here!'

'Well, that's enough talk. I will fetch Thorsbard and organise refreshments for you.'

'I am very hungry,' said Klyesha.

'No doubt. I won't be long,'

Her cat kept purring on her chest and the beautiful rhythm felt healing and soothing. Here was one good thing to come out of all this horrible violence and suffering. She slowly stroked her cat and the pain in her head started to slip back like the tide from the shore.

William returned with Thorsbard who examined Klyesha. She needed the collar on for a while, he advised. Klyesha's neck was protected by a padded collar of the type worn to protect the neck from armour.

'Any blow to the head can also damage the neck. It's not too cumbersome,' he explained. 'Try to walk when you can, even if you lean on William.'

Very willing to help, William offered his services. She wanted the garderobe. After relieving herself, William ordered her a bath and fresh clothes. He helped her into the bath himself and washed her. 'It seems our roles are reversed,' he laughed reminding her of his bath in Hamleyvale when his injured leg was still septic.

She luxuriated in the warmth and feeling clean again however, William was dismayed to see a dark purple bruise which had spread to her cheek and neck from the back of her head. He bathed her head carefully using towels to avoid the neck padding from getting wet.

'How is Withers?' she asked.

William looked pained. 'Despite Thorsbard's best efforts unfortunately Withers died.'

'He died trying to protect me!' she said.

'I know, so did the young soldier who accompanied him, Private Martin. They will pay those rioters!'

Then Klyesha remembered her visit to Cook and her household. 'We cannot accuse Gerard of killing my cat but there is another terrible crime he has committed.' Klyesha explained how Flora and Mrs Walter had been abducted, the villains believing they were herself and Rachel. Then she told him about the rape.

Williams knuckles went white and he stood unable to contain his emotions but unwilling to get angry before his love. 'I will deal with this,' he said through gritted teeth.

A wave of sadness washed over Klyesha. How must it feel to have a brother who was both an attempted murderer and a rapist?

William came back to her with sweet smelling oils for the bath and dropped them in one drop at a time. He brushed the dirt out of her hair and fashioned it into a rather inexpert topknot. As she was feeling weak again, he lifted her out of the bath and dried her gently, helping her dress in a sleeping shift and gown for it was already late at night. He carried her to her bedchamber and brought her food and drink on a tray.

'Henry?' she asked, after a few moments of silence.

William turned back to her, 'Surprisingly well. His voice is less hoarse. He sports bruises on his neck as spectacular as yours and he too is still in a neck brace. We've had a conversation.' He didn't elaborate. The conversation had not been easy.

William had visited Henry earlier in the day as he sat on a balcony taking in some fresh crisp air. 'Are you not cold out here?' he asked.

'No, I'm used to the outdoors. I am not a good patient. I chafe at confinement,' explained Henry.

'However, you are a patient and your neck may still be very delicate.'

Henry looked at him strangely then. 'I felt the absolute hatred coming at me from your people William, they all wanted me, you, dead.'

'Yes, I understand what a harrowing experience it was for you.'

'I don't think so, William you could come near to feeling the depth of it. My life flashed before my eyes.'

William didn't know what to say. Henry had very nearly died in his stead. He probably wanted to know what William had done to be so hated, 'Please forgive me,' he began.

'You didn't try to hang me, Gerard did. But tell me this, why do they hate you so much?'

William hung his head in shame. Henry was so like him they looked like twins but he did not deserve to take the blame for William's inadequacies. 'They were starving and I let them down. I should have seen this coming. I wasn't aware of how desperate things had become.'

'Could you have prevented the food riots?'

'Don't you think I've asked myself that again and again?' replied William, looking Henry in the eye. 'I will never again trust that matters of such import are left neglected I can assure you.'

'Do you think the people will just forget?'

'I don't know, I hope so.'

'Maybe you should abdicate!' Henry said, the anger at his treatment resurging.

Astonished William stood up, 'I don't intend to relinquish anything, not yet, not now when the situation is still volatile. Perhaps later when all is calm and peaceful again.' He surprised even himself to say one day he might leave the throne to someone else.

He walked towards the balcony door, 'Anything, anything else you need, anything at all, you just have to ask.'

Henry snorted as if to say what can you give me to make up for what happened to me. William closed the door and went back inside.

Chapter Nineteen

For a week, the food supplies kept being distributed overseen by the meticulous Paxton and the enthusiastic Rufus. People seemed most overjoyed to taste bread again as it was a staple everyone missed sorely. Already the two supply ships had departed for Svartlund to be reprovisioned with more grain, cheese, dried fish also ale. William got reports from all the City's bakers every day, as well as from the warehouses on the docks. His harassed clerks had to keep careful records. The men of his treasury were not happy to be handing over so much gold to Svartlunders, but William persuaded them the food would soon be paid for in goods. He had listened to many merchants and the town's burgers and bankers and they agreed to set up a trading exchange. The people could pay for their food and soon they would with cloth, manufactured goods, gold and silver. The traders would sell the imported food in shops and bakers. Soon the economy would not have to be propped up by the Royal Treasury.

Also, all Gerard's portable assets had been seized and they were considerable, both from his City Villa and his elusive country estate. These bolstered William's own personal wealth and would tide things over until the trading exchange and the City's burgers took over.

The small pockets of rioters who remained in the City were another matter. Every day William's troops were out on the streets keeping order. They were usually mounted to give them more protection from attack. Already the Palace dungeons were crowded with known dissenters and hardened criminals as well as those denounced by their neighbours for looting, rape and rapine. The troops William and his men had gathered from all over the country to put down the rioters, needed at first when things were desperate, had largely been sent home with the grateful regards of their sovereign. Ample food had removed the main complaint from those disaffected. It was only those men who had become used to the spoils of crime whom the troops still had to guard against. A nightly curfew at dusk reduced the potential of trouble erupting, for anyone found on the streets after curfew was arrested.

The next major issue for William to address was justice both on a large scale and a small one. Daily Assemblies weighed evidence against rioters, men like Slade and his lieutenants who were hung. Marissa who had betrayed Klyesha was also hung for abetting the rioters, giving them succour and for her vicious attack on Klyesha. Slade was hung as a murderer, the deaths of Withers and the young soldier laid on him as commander of the rioters. Innocent householders had also been killed by his men in the course of their stealing expeditions. Evidence had been gathered and weighed up. Everyone got a fair trial, was allowed a defence and a voice. Only the most deserving received the ultimate sentence. Lindquist had been found trying to escape on a ship. He too was hung. The hunger of the gibbet was assuaged on a daily basis. At least three prisoners were hung every day for a week. These spectacles served as a deterrent to any recalcitrant rioters continuing to exhibit antisocial behaviour.

So, it came to Gerard's trial.

Despite his arrogance and confidence at the start of his campaign against the King, Gerard was now a dishevelled, unkempt common-looking prisoner. Gaol had stripped away his sense of entitlement, his cunning and his ambitions but not his attitude. He knew he deserved to hang, but his mind fought to adjust to the idea.

He was brought before the Assembly in the morning. The day was bright and the chamber well-lit. It was very crowded with officials, courtiers and prominent citizens decked out in their finest jerkins, coats and breeches. The women wore hats and lustrous dresses which crackled when they moved. The Herald stamped his mace as the King entered dressed in his finest royal blue brocade. His mood was sombre to say the least: Klyesha's brush with death, the conversation with Henry and the enormous weight of rebuilding the Kingdom was taking its toll. Today his own brother would be condemned one way or another. Henry came in, still in a neck brace, and sat on a chair to the King's right. He sat awkwardly, nervous to be once again surrounded by a crowd, however this time he had nothing to fear from them.

Gerard was brought in shackles and sat before the King. The Herald stepped forward and read the charges:

'Gerard Stirling, formerly 'Prince of the Realm', you are charged with sedition against the King by knowingly writing and circulating a handbill preaching rebellion and treason. You took an innocent man, Henry Stirling, and because he resembled the King tried to convince the population of the City when you hung him that you were in fact hanging the King.'

'You assembled a traitorous army to take over the Kingdom made up of rioters and bandits who sought to harm the King and you used them to help hang Henry Stirling.'

'You raped an innocent member of Klyesha Culaine's household who had been unlawfully abducted along with another woman of that household Mrs Walter whom you detained and mistreated.'

'You stole 50,000 sovereigns from the King's Treasury and kept them as your own.'

'You deliberately and wilfully neglected the preservation of the Royal Granaries in order to ferment food riots that would help you disgrace the King and turn the people against him.'

Considerable murmuring and discussion of the last charge arose in the crowd, for this was the first time the King had tried to defend himself against the accusation which precipitated the food riots and as a result caused so much hatred towards him.

'What say you do these charges?' asked William in a stern voice.

Rattling his manacles Gerard laughed, 'Even if I were innocent, you would find me guilty, brother, for it is in your interest to do so. This Court, so called, is biased against me. You cannot give me justice!'

'I can and I will,' said William soberly. 'Call the first witness.'

'I call Edward Moore, Printer' said the Herald. Edward Moore was ushered into the chamber from a side room.

'State your name,' said the Herald.

Moore stood as steady as he could, but the truth was he feared for his own involvement in the seditious circular. 'I am Edward Moore, Printer and Editor of 'The Proclamation' the City's newspaper.'

'Tell us what happened several weeks ago when you were approached by Gerard Sterling?' asked the King.

'He came late one night together with another official. They demanded I print a circular they brought. I told them I thought it inflammatory and probably illegal. The Prince, whom I recognised, assured me there would be no repercussions on me. I felt I could not refuse.'

'He is the same man who is there?' The Herald pointed to Gerard.

'Yes, Sire.'

'So, you were paid?'

'Yes, Sire,' Moore said hesitatingly, '10 gold sovereigns. He demanded it to be ready the next day.'

'How many copies did you print?'

'1000, Sire. Men from the Prince picked them up the following afternoon.'

'Do you regret printing the circular?'

'Yes, absolutely, especially as I was there to witness the hanging of the man on your right.'

'You saw Gerard organise and hang my cousin Henry Sterling?'

'Yes, Sire. I wrote an article about it for 'The Proclamation'.'

'And how many copies of that issue were circulated?'

'About 5,000, Sire.'

'So, you have done a little to overturn your involvement in a seditious act. Would you become involved again in such a plot?'

'No, Sire, on my life, I would refuse,' added Moore.

'I am satisfied this man, Moore, is telling the truth. Gerard Stirling had the circular printed and he carried out its threat to hang me but in reality we know Henry was his unsuspecting victim. The first charge is proved.'

'Bring in the next witnesses,' called the Herald.

Ironsmith and Lewis was shuffled into the room in their leg irons. 'State your names,' said the Herald. They stated their names.

'Is this the man before you who recruited you to train disaffected farmers and villagers to create an army for him?' asked William

The men looked at Gerard and as he could no longer take revenge upon them, they readily agreed.

'And what was the stated purpose of that army?'

Ironsmith answered, 'We was to support the Prince to become King after the King was hung.'

'Did you willingly follow Gerard or were you coerced?'

'I don't know what the word 'coerced' means Sire, beg pardon,' said Ironsmith.

'It means did Gerard force you to follow him?'

'No, Sire hunger did. We was promised food,' said Lewis. Ironsmith nodded.

'Were you promised gold?'

'Yes,' said Ironsmith shamefaced, 'and a position at the Castle.'

'So, you didn't follow him just for food?'

'No, Sire, I guess not,' said Ironsmith panicking.

'How many soldiers were recruited?'

'Around 150 I believe.'

'Would that have been enough to storm and take the Castle?'

'No, I believe not.'

'So, Gerard came up with this plan to get rid of me and by right of succession thereby take the throne which he couldn't do so merely by force?'

'I believe so,' said Ironsmith. Lewis nodded.

William shifted in his seat and spoke under his breath to Henry.

'Men, did you believe he was actually hanging me at Skull Hill?'

'Yes, we did.'

'You have freely admitted here to Court that you helped Gerard Stirling train an army to support him as King, indeed to help him become King by hanging me, the rightful King. You admitted you would take gold to act traitorously towards your King. That makes you mercenaries and traitors to your King. You have acted treasonously therefore, I sentence you both to be hung until death.'

The men were near collapse when dragged from the Court. Gerard's already pale face blanched even more.

'The second charge of assembling a traitorous army to murder me as King is proven. Call the next witnesses.'

Gerard shifted uncomfortably in his chair. The next charge would reveal his base nature more than any other.

Flora and Mrs Walter were brought in front of the Court. Both women were extremely nervous. They stated their names.

'I know this is very difficult for you,' William addressed the women. 'I am very grateful you both have been brave enough to come here today. State what happened after you were both abducted from Mistress Culaine's household.'

Flora spoke up, 'We were taken before the Prince,'

'And what happened then?' asked William.

'He wanted to know where Mistress Klyesha and Mistress Rachel were, Sire.'

'And did you tell him?'

'We said again and again, we did not know. They had gone on a trip some six weeks before. We were minding Mistress Klyesha's house but we hadn't heard from them.'

'Were you mistreated?'

Mrs Walter raised her hand, 'Yes, we was. Our hands was tied behind us. Those men who were here before, the big one. He beat us.'

'Anything else?'

'Flora was taken into another room by the Prince. After a while, she came out very upset.'

'Mistress Flora, what happened to you in that room?'

Flora almost fell. She dreaded what she'd have to admit here in front of everyone. 'Sire...'

'I know this is difficult, Mistress Flora, but we need to know.'

'He accosted me, Sire,' said Flora pointing to Gerard.

'You mean, he raped you?' asked the King.

'Yes, Sire,' said Flora.

Gerard raged against his shackles. 'You believe this common tart?' he screamed. 'Anyone could have bedded her. Prove it!'

'Are you with child, Mistress Flora?'

Flora broke down and sobbed. Mrs Walter had to speak, 'Yes, she is Sire.'

Gerard was astonished. He had got a bastard on her. He didn't know whether to be pleased or not but it was a child he'd never see.

'Might I add, said the King, 'these are respectable women. They are not the common women of the streets. Time will corroborate their story in the likeness of the child, however as it remains one person's word against the other, the charge of rape cannot be proven at the moment. We shall set that charge aside for the time being.'

A small victory thought Gerard.

'Has the prisoner anything to add?' Gerard shook his head and the women were led from the Court.

'Next witness,' called the Herald.

A tall thin man stood in the centre of the Assembly Hall. 'I am Thomas Knox.' said the man, 'I am Treasurer to His Majesty, King William.'

'What information do you have?' the King asked.

'We have done an audit, Sire, of the former Prince's finances and his estates. He has accumulated far in excess of his annual allowance. The true income from his allowance as Prince and his estates, we have estimated to be at around 30,000 sovereigns, however by assessing his present wealth, we find an amount in excess of 50,000 sovereigns whose origin is unknown.'

'Do you have any idea where that money came from?' asked the King.

'Yes, Sire. The former Prince has been seen accessing the Treasury Vault, Sire. Our accountants have found discrepancies between bills paid, allowances given, and the principal sum of monies in the vault. We believe one explanation is that the 50,000 sovereigns were stolen over time by the former Prince.'

'Thank you, Master Knox.'

'What is the prisoner's response?'

Turning in his seat, he faced the Assembly, 'So what if I availed myself of funds? I was responsible for various sectors of the management of the Kingdom and required the funds for them.'

'Can you please indicate to the Court your areas of responsibility in the Kingdom?' asked William.

'I was responsible for roads and the storage of grain.'

'I myself inspected the granaries in the last three months,' explained the King. 'Every one was in a shocking state of disrepair. Vermin over ran the grain piles, roofs were rotting and the guards complacent. No money, that is not recently, had been spent on them. What is your response?'

'I cannot be held accountable for the corruption of minor officials. The money was given. They must have pocketed it themselves,' he sneered.

'How often did you inspect the granaries?'

'Every month,' said Gerard.

'That is a lie! Bring in the next witnesses!'

Ten men dressed in rural clothing came into the Court.

'State your names and what you do,' called the Herald. They did. They were all grain guards or workmen.

'Has this man before you visited your granary in the last month?' asked the King. All the men said no. 'Has he visited your granaries in the last year? All the men again said no. 'So, neither did you visit nor were you aware of the state of the granaries which is your responsibility. It's also your responsibility to check any corruption of local officials but the money never went anywhere near the granaries, did it?'

'Prove it!' yelled Gerard.

'We just have, together with the very full unspoilt silos of grain on your own estates, we may assume meant you knew of upcoming food shortages and sought to stockpile your own. Perhaps this grain was to be used as leverage or to feed your mercenaries? It is plain to see it was you I trusted to oversee the proper care of the granaries and you completely neglected them so that the people would lay the blame for food shortages on me. So desperate were they for food, they wanted to see me hung. I fully take responsibility for not checking on you or the granaries myself, however all your actions from the food riots onward were to put yourself in a better light to steal the throne once you had fermented the anger and distrust of my people towards me. You have pilfered from the Treasury for years in a deliberately conceived plot to make yourself King. You provisioned a secret estate and set about a chain of events which led to the hanging of an innocent man, our Cousin Henry Stirling, who sits at my side here. What have you to say?'

Rising from his chair, Gerard looked at the sea of faces around him, 'I deny all the charges this pathetic individual seated on the throne there has thrust upon me. He was so concerned with you all, that he absented himself from the Capitol at the start of the food shortages to pursue a woman, a woman who was found destitute clothed only in cat skins on a remote island. A woman barely literate, totally unschooled in the manners of society. This is your King, people, and you so deserve him.'

William didn't flinch, 'I declare all the charges proven except for the rape which we set aside until such time as a child is born. I will not debase myself to answer the slander just thrown at me but I will acknowledge Thorsbard Strum, whom you see there in the audience. It was he who negotiated the food trade which is currently feeding all those in the City. I met him while I was away. Not only did he save my life, he saved the lives of everyone in this

City. I grant him all former estates of Gerard Stirling now confiscated by the Crown in reparation for the money stolen from the Treasury apart from the City Villa which I grant to Henry Stirling in reparation for almost losing his life in Gerard's twisted plot to get rid of me.'

'As to Gerard's punishment I grant the ability to choose what shall happen to him to his victim, Henry Stirling. He will decide Gerard's fate. Are you ready Henry?'

Henry stood. He still wore the neck brace but his clothes were finer to denote a Cousin of the King. He was handed a loudhailer by the Herald to amplify his damaged voice. He began by bowing to the King. 'King William,' he began, 'Members of the Court. By some miracle I was saved who should have died. The man who tried to hang me you see before you, Gerard Stirling. I was beaten and mistreated by his men to the point I could not even speak at Skull Hill to reveal my true identity. I was hung voiceless with no one to defend me. It is a miracle that I can see justice before me today. Gerard, you deserve to hang for your crimes, treason, theft, plotting against the throne and attempted murder, however that death is too quick for you. You deserve to suffer. I condemn you to banishment on an unknown and remote island, where you shall live out your days until death with no one to speak to nor to hear your poison.'

Henry sat down and there was much murmuring in the crowd. No one expected banishment, everyone thought he would hang. Gerard was dragged from the Assembly kicking and shouting obscenities about the King. Gradually, the crowd dispersed back to their homes with many tales to tell. No doubt *The Proclamation* would describe the trial in detail in its next edition.

William left the dais with Henry. Gerard's actions would forever stain his family's honour yet the trial had helped to leach the poison from a suppurating wound. Perhaps now their society might begin to heal. Only William knew Gerard would be sent to the Island of Cats with only two cats for company and the same provisions provided to Diana Culaine when she was banished for merely trying to protect her beloved cats.

Henry and William sat in his sitting room, goblets of wine and platters of food beside them. The speech had sorely tried Henry's vocal capacity and he sat with his hand cradling his throat. William too was emotionally exhausted. His brother had reached such a low

245

point in criminal activities and had such a hatred of himself, he was glad in a way he would not hang. Henry was right, Gerard needed time to reflect on his behaviour and to suffer. For suffer he would, trying to survive on the island which once had been Klyesha's home. A place remote, windswept, isolated and harsh but an environment where she thrived and her character was forged. William had little doubt Gerard would not last long there, however he vowed he would go and see for himself in a month or two and establish if he was still alive, if privations had softened his attitude and sucked the venom from his soul.

William had thought long and hard before he breached the subject to Klyesha. She had returned home to supervise renovations. Her dark purple bruise had faded to green and then yellow and by now had almost disappeared. He found her bucket in hand, scrubbing the sitting room carpet as it hung on the washing line.

He cleared his throat so as not to frighten her, but she started anyway. He was soon covering her neck with kisses. 'How is this preparation to be my Queen?' he teased.

She laughed in his arms. 'I shall become so bored I might have to take up embroidery!'

'Is that such a bad thing?' He held her tight.

'Know yet, I've never picked up needle or sewn flowers in my whole life. I'd rather repair clocks.'

'Or make maps?'

'That too.' He released her and taking the bucket poured out the muddy water. 'Hey,' she protested.

He advanced to the well and drew her fresh water. 'Let it be known I helped clean your carpet and every fishmonger and baker in this City will want my job,' he warned.

She loved his ginger beard, his blue sparkling eyes and long, curly, dark red hair. What would their children look like, she thought? She continued the carpet cleaning while he watched her, perched on a tree stump, 'Is the work done?'

'On the House? Yes, did you see our new blue door?'

'Yes, the handsome forget-me-not blue.'

Like the blue of your eyes, she wanted to say. He was so happy today though, she didn't need to add to his vanity.

'We've replaced all the windows and shutters too.'

'You could put bars on the windows.'

'We could and perhaps we will, however heavy shutters will do for now. Is the curfew finished?'

'Yes,' he said, chewing on a fresh stalk of grass. 'Paxton and I believed it was time. The troops have swept the discontented from the streets.'

Klyesha smiled, 'Your citizens will be relieved at that news.'

'Can you sit for a moment?' he asked.

She found an edge to the stump and attempted to sit on it but he pulled her onto his lap. 'I miss you,' he whispered into her dark hair.

'I miss you too,' she murmured.

'Come back with me!'

She turned her face to him, 'Shouldn't we...'

'Be wed?'

'Our lovemaking could result in a child,' she warned.

'Has it?' he inquired.

'Not yet, but one never knows.'

'They come if they're wont to, and on that subject I have a proposition.'

'Oh?'

'Flora's child, it will be my nephew.'

'Or niece.'

'Yes, or niece. I want to adopt it. I think we should adopt it, Klyesha.'

She was surprised, 'And what might Flora think?'

'Well, she'd have to agree, but the child could be next in line to the throne.'

'If we have none of our own.'

'Obviously we will try but if God does not grant us, Flora's child needs to be prepared.'

Thinking for a while, Klyesha got off his lap.

'Are you angry?' he asked.

She looked at him seriously, 'No, I'm not. I just never thought...'

'That I would acknowledge it?'

'Yes.'

'My brother hated me. He was as far from a brother's nature as could be but his child is innocent.'

'You don't want him or her to be a problem in the future?'

247

'Yes, someone else raising him could cause trouble.'
'You also don't want him raised a servant?'
'No.'

William swung her around by waist, 'So, beauty, I think we better be married soon.'

Chapter Twenty

So it was that two weeks later the City had reason to celebrate. All the streets were covered in blue and yellow bunting and the Cathedral in the City's Central Square was filled with flowers. Guards in the King's livery lined the entrance to the Cathedral. As the bells rang out twelve, the royal carriage left the Castle and made its way past cheering crowds. The horses were all black and glossy, their horse brasses shining in the sun. Captain Paxton was mounted and in armour as he led the King's carriage. Klyesha's carriage was escorted by Captain Rufus in his armour, similarly mounted.

The people were curious as to who this woman really was. Rumours circulated that she'd been washed up on an island as a baby and raised by merpeople or selkies. Some said she made noises like a sea creature when she spoke. Others said under her dress she had fins.

Rachel wore a dark red velvet dress with a gold sash. She was already a maid of honour as she and Lucca had married the month before. He also accompanied them in their silver carriage. As Klyesha's closest living relative, her cousin Lucca would walk her down the aisle.

By the time the bride's carriage reached the doors of the Cathedral, William was already waiting at the altar dressed in military uniform as a general and carrying a three-cornered hat. Henry stood beside him wearing a navy brocade suit as his groomsmen.

However, it was to the bride all turned as the King's choir sang out a traditional wedding song. She was dressed in cream with a silver and blue sash. Her hair was pinned with small white roses and her train was ermine. There was nothing of the plain or savage about her now. In sophisticated City finery, she was as beautiful and elegant as any City maiden on her wedding day. But this was no ordinary wedding, or ordinary day. The sovereign's wedding was an event to be spoken of by those present for generations to come. It was a once in a lifetime event for the bride and groom and also for the people.

Lucca in a pale grey suit of brocade led the bride down the aisle. Walter's young girls were dressed in pink as flower girls and they scattered rose petals in the wake of the bride.

Trumpets triumphantly heralded her nearing the front of the Cathedral where William stood trying to look solemn but failing. He could not contain the huge smile on his face.

Klyesha's heart was beating hard. The situation was completely overwhelming. Never had she seen William as King until this day. He'd always been her William, her rescuer. Now she realised the gravity of becoming Queen and the realisation was unsettling her inner core.

Still, she breathed deeply as Lucca's strong hand briefly grasped hers, 'Courage little cousin,' he whispered. Then all the power of the sea, the surging waves, the crashing thunder and lightning lifted her soul as they had done on wild and stormy days on her island. If she could weather those storms alone, how better would she weather them with William's strong and comforting presence at her side?

They made their vows these two seemingly mismatched bride and groom. Savage and King. Yet they were also just a man and a woman made for each other if melded in different crucibles but molten now and soon to be poured together into the same mould. This strength, their weaknesses, all shared. Their past and their futures now woven together like plaited trees. This would sustain them. Klyesha would bring a humble common sense and strength to their shared sovereignty and William would bring his experience and the greatest lesson he had ever learned: how to value that which was almost lost to him.

The wedding bells rang out in the great Cathedral bell tower, a monument built by William's grandfather in honour of his wife whose grave now rested near William's own parents' graves which lined the walls behind the altar. William had visited them earlier and laid garlands, sad his family could not share his joy this day.

Now married, the couple walked along the aisle to their carriage, many guests throwing flowers and small boys shook rose water over them. Into the carriage they climbed. There lay sacks of coin set ready which they both distributed to the jubilant people on the long journey back to the Castle.

There they feasted on the best food Thorsbard could procure together with liqueurs and cheeses from other lands. They danced and they laughed and for a few hours at least they could all forget the privations, lawlessness and violence of the last few months.

The next day William surprised his new wife for their honeymoon by telling her to pack warm clothes and waterproof outer clothing. She did so without asking where they were going. Soon after midday, they made their way to the docks where one of Thorsbard's ships awaited them. 'We're going to Svartlund,' she cried.

'Yes, we are and other countries beyond. It's high time I went on a diplomatic mission.'

'So, we will be working?'

'My darling beloved,' said William, 'now you are Queen you will never stop working but perhaps for a few weeks we can just relax.'

'Is it not too soon to leave the City?' she counselled.

'No, now's the time. I have neglected our neighbours for too long. I have left Henry in charge together with Albert Strong, Paxton and Rufus. They are more than capable.'

They stowed their packets in the largest stateroom on the vessel. 'It wasn't such a long time ago that I stood here, pining for you,' said Klyesha a smile around her eyes.

'Never again pining, I have outlawed pining. We will do everything together.' They clung together on the deck as the ship parted from the docks, well wishes cheered them with ribbons and confetti.

'How fickle they are,' remarked William, 'just a month ago they all wanted to stretch my neck.'

'Please do not speak ill of my subjects,' said Klyesha.

'Oh, *your* subjects, Queen, I forgot. However, I don't really trust them.' He lay back on the calico bunk, his hands crossed under his head.

'Be that as it may, we must lead them,' said Klyesha.

William threw a cushion at her and laughed out loud, 'You sound to the throne born more than I!'

Klyesha threw the cushion back at him.

The next two days they sailed on a route familiar to William, lesser so to Klyesha for they had one unpleasant task to fulfil before Svartlund.

It was around midday on the third day when they anchored near a small island. As it was Spring, flowers on the island blossomed yellow and pink against the dark foliage of the native succulent pig face. Together with the deep purple of heath flowers, the island looked almost a paradise until you saw the treacherous and sharp rocks which lined most of the periphery. Only in one small bay with a tiny spit of sand were they able to land the skiff rowed by four of Thorsbard's sailors. Thorsbard himself, his tall pale blond-headed figure was soon stepping out onto the sand. He turned to help Klyesha, but she'd already lept nimbly from the vessel and with skirts hitched up was sprinting across the sand. They left the sailors to guard the skiff. William soon followed but the men held back to allow Klyesha her joy unbridled.

Oh, the smells. She missed the deep rich smell of the sea, the burnt herbal smell of the heath and the wafting waves of earthy smells from the sea bird hatchery. It was there she was headed through well-worn tracks within the heath. As she ran rabbits scattered, and small, brown mammals, the native rats. No cats ran beside her this time or mewed from their cosiness in the heather. Long gone, her cats were now fat and in service in granaries or were fed royally from China plates by their devoted masters and mistresses. Rachel was minding her own beloved Roxy and Henry the Tom while they ventured on their honeymoon.

Soon she was climbing lichen-covered, smooth granite rocks which mounded like pincushions to the west of the tiny island. Here in crevices, the seabirds bred. The chittering and clacking rose in waves of 'chip, chip' sounds. The smell from the guano was overpowering. If only she and her mother had possessed vegetable seeds, they would have harvested a paradise here.

William scanned the island for any sign of his brother, Gerard. He could see nothing, they would make a better investigation later, so they followed Klyesha.

Little balls of grey fluff, the seabird chicks, flattened down at her approach. Most of the parents were either out to sea fishing or delivering their partly digested catch directly into the red mouths of their young. They ignored her as if she were part of the island's wildlife, as naturally there as any of them. It was only when Thorsbard and William approached that they began stamping their feet and arching their necks sensing danger.

252

'You must have had some feasts here,' remarked Thorsbard, 'Fat young chicks, adult birds and eggs. It was no wonder you thrived.'

'Physically perhaps,' agreed Klyesha, 'however it was lonely. Strangely, I didn't actually know what alone or lonely meant until I was in society.'

Fascinated by the multitude of life, William was quiet. He pictured Klyesha when he first met her as she raised a bow and arrow ready to fire. This island had been her crucible. No wonder she faced so bravely the dangers in his Kingdom. They watched fascinated as parent after parent disgorged their gullets into the mouths of their greedy young.

'How do they know their own young?' asked Thorsbard totally mesmerised, their attention focused on the birds.

No one turned until it was too late.

William placed his foot on a rock which was unsteady and feeling his ankle go from under him, he lurched sideways. The fall saved his life. The huge rock coming through the air meant for him instead knocked Thorsbard to the ground. As he fell 20 or more birds lifted off from the rocks in fright. Thorsbard did not move. William cried out a warning to Klyesha and she turned to dodge another rock just in time.

Gerard was rushing at them with murderous intent.

William struggled to get up as a sharp pain coursed through his ankle. He desperately looked for a weapon and then realised the dagger he always carried was in his boot. He soon extricated it but wasn't able to move. He saw Gerard racing towards Klyesha. She turned to face him but then deftly skipped between rocks to put distance between him and herself. He pitched another rock at her, but she ducked in time. Lunging for a rock, she sent it flying towards him where it collided with his jaw. He fell backwards but soon spun around and was on his feet. William too searched for rocks but they were all too big to move near him. All he could do was coax Gerard close enough to him to use the dagger. In the seconds in which Gerard spun around, Klyesha found two more rocks. She knew she would have to make them count. William was disabled and Thorsbard knocked out.

'Oh, the little Cat woman is encumbered by her skirts,' taunted Gerard. 'Did you think you could come here and live, you she devil.

Do you think your filthy seed will sit on the throne of the Kingdom? Never!' he screamed. Running at her, the first rock hit him on the nose. She heard it crack and saw the blood spurt. Disorientated Gerard lashed out with his foot and kicked her in the stomach. She fell sickeningly between two rocks, wedged like a beached dolphin in an alien terrain.

Winded and in pain, she screamed as his hands found her throat. Gasping for breath, she struggled to free his hands but in their grip was the iron of madness and desperation. His fury made his face a contorted monster mask. Crazed by loneliness on the island, he blamed her for all his misfortune, for all his carefully constructed plans turning to dust.

Just when Klyesha's breath had almost left her body, Gerard's grip slackened, his eyes opened wide, showing the whites, and blood began to pour from his mouth. William threw him aside and pulled Klyesha clear from the fissure in the rocks. This time there were no words for the foolishness of him allowing his brother a second chance on the island when all reason said he should have been hung.

Klyesha was coughing and hurting all over, as she bent on all fours in the sand gasping for breath. He looked at her face and she nodded, so he limped back over to where Thorsbard lay. Gerard's body remained prone on a rock with William's dagger sticking out of his back. Thorsbard was groaning as he tried to sit up holding his shoulder. He could barely speak for the pain. 'I think he's shattered my shoulder!' William helped him up and fashioned a sling for his arm out of his scarf.

'Sit down,' said William while I get Klyesha. She was now soaked from the incoming waves. He helped her to her feet and together they hobbled back to where the rocks were surrounded by dry sand and Thorsbard sat panting. They were a sorry group for the next half hour, trying to overcome pain, to get up and continue back to the boat.

When they had not returned, the sailors given the task of minding the boat heaved it up on the sand further from the waves and went to look for them. It didn't take long as the island was quite small. The sailors ran when they spied the three. 'It's my ankle,' said William, 'either broken or strained. I'll wait here with Thorsbard, please take Klyesha back to the ship.

'No,' croaked Klyesha, her voice husky, 'I can walk. I'm only bruised.'

'What happened to you?' asked one of the sailors, astonished.

William pointed to the inert body of his brother, 'He happened, my brother.'

The sailors looked at each other in dismay. 'Lean on me,' said one. Another two got Thorsbard up and walking. The fourth helped Klyesha. They made their slow way back to the ship. 'What about the body?' asked one of the sailors.

'He can rot there where the seabirds can pick his bones,' said William bitterly.

They were soon back on the ship. Thorsbard was in great pain, but the ship's doctor declared his shoulder dislocated by his fall, not shattered. So, with the shoulder put back in, Thorsbard's pain and anguish had lessened considerably. Klyesha was found to have some badly bruised ribs and neck. She was put to bed despite protests and drugged into asleep. William's ankle was sprained rather than broken or dislocated, otherwise he wouldn't have been able to rescue Klyesha in time. The doctor strapped it for him.

When they were recovering in their cabin there was time to reflect. Klyesha was angry Gerard's body would stay on her own Island of Cats, forever tainting its memory.

'What were we thinking? That he'd just been sitting next to a fire when we arrived?' she said.

William really despised himself. So why was he not better prepared? It was because all this time he *had* prepared himself to see Gerard's body decaying somewhere on the island. City bred, spoilt at Court, he could not conceive Gerard would survive. Yet he had surprised him before and now surprised him again but this time his attack was very nearly fatal. William felt so ashamed.

'You killed your brother to save me and Thorsbard, William, you have to remember that,' counselled Klyesha, seeing him in torment.

'I know. However, it should have never come to that. I wasn't precautious enough. Do I feel guilt for killing my brother? No, I do not. Only that I thoughtlessly put you in danger once again.'

'And I forgot the first thing I learnt on my island.'

'What was that?'

'To always be observant. To never turn your back to danger. I almost drowned several times when I turned my back on the sea.' William grabbed her and hugged her, horrified.

'There's a lot I haven't told you about my island,' she observed.

'We have all our lives ahead of us for you to tell me, my love'

'Yes, we do.'

As for the Island of Cats, no one remembered the two cats, one ginger male and one black female left there with Gerard until the ship was half a day's sail away. Klyesha woke the next day thinking of them, but it was too late to go back.

'Will they survive?' asked William.

'I know they will,' replied Klyesha wincing as she turned in the bed. 'If Gerard did not harm him there is a lot of food for them there.'

'That is something,' commented William, rubbing his ankle as his leg rested on a stool. 'We will visit again in a year's time and take off excess cats for the Kingdom's purposes. They are very important to our economy.'

'So is fishing,' said Thorsbard knocking on the door of the cabin, a smile spreading across his face, 'Have I told you about the 45 different types of fish that can be dried?

'No, you haven't,' answered William groaning, 'but I'm sure you will.'

Acknowledgments

Sometime in March of 2022, I was listening again to a CD of Dido's I'd had for a long time. The song *'Hunter'* has the lines 'If you were a King up there on a throne, would you be wise enough to let me go, I want to be a hunter again...' I thought the situation could make a good short story, so I decided to write it. However, it would not be contained by a short story format instead it evolved into the novel you perhaps have just read. Klyesha does have a certain wanderlust and, at times, William is not a very wise King. However, they prove to be more compatible than the characters in the song.

I've always said to students of mine in High School, if you have a good idea the story writes itself. The book took only about three months to write and it is the easiest book I have ever written. It just flowed. The other influence was Shakespeare. Miranda in *'The Tempest'* is similarly awestruck and overwhelmed by the men who arrive on her island on which she has grown up with only Prospero, her father and Caliban, a creature, as company. Also Shakespeare uses the device of a woman posing as a man in several of his comedies-*'A Merchant of Venice'*, *'As you Like It'* and *'Twelfth Night'* as a ruse for the character to test the man she loves. This device is used in the novel and perhaps requires the same 'suspension of disbelief' used when Shakespeare employs it. However, I have noticed generally, that men and women can be quite easily transformed with the right haircut or style and the right clothes into a convincing member of the opposite sex. That Klyesha hangs onto the device a little too long and is caught out is one of its downfalls.

The setting of the novel is fantasy though its historical period roughly equates to the late 1600s. The characters refer to their land as 'The Kingdom', their Capitol as the 'Capitol' or the 'City' and the Palace is known simply as the 'Palace' or the 'Castle'. This emphasises the insular aspects of this society and its parochial shunning of trade or influences from neighbouring countries. The famine in the Kingdom forces them reluctantly to widen up to a bigger world.

William realises at the end of the book he can no longer shut his society off from the world, indeed, this insularity is part of the reason for the famine leading to riots and insubordination which had such devastating effects.

Many thanks to my readers, Una Berglund and Judith Flood and to my son, Anthony Lee, and my family for support during the writing and editing of this manuscript.

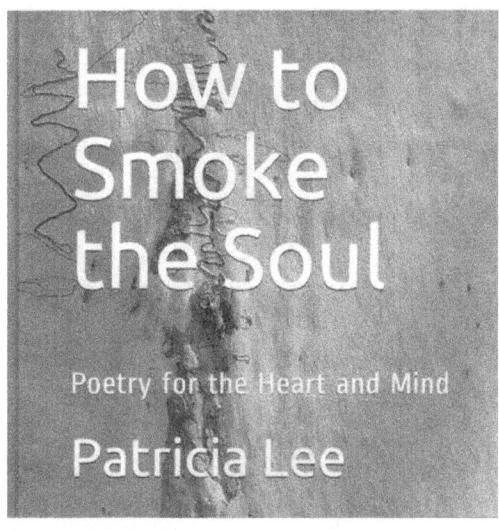

Collected over a twenty year period, Patricia Lee's carefully constructed, passionate poems showcase a contemplative philosophy grounded in nature yet also reveal the complexity of human experience- wonder, love, injustice, family. Poems about art and history explore how humans have struggled with the limitations of their own worlds. Finally, two humorous dialogues set in railway stations lighten the spirit.

Intended to help heal hearts and stimulate minds, the poems are juxtaposed by the poets own detailed and eclectic artworks which are a journey in themselves through the Australian landscape and imagery. Notes at the end of the book are useful in explaining Australian idioms and references.

Overall, a calming, yet at times, deeply personal and arresting foray into late 20th Century and early 21st Century free verse and prose poetry.

Recommended for students in Years 9-12 and for the general reader.

'I found myself so deep in thought throughout, and also ashamed that I don't stop and see what you see. We can all take a lesson from this. The poems were moving, deep, so

full of life, hurt, pleasure, observations, earth, wealth of beauty, society's shallowness, calmness and acceptance.' Judith Flood, reader.

A fascinating and rare glimpse into post-World War Two family life in Australia.

'If only the walls could speak'. It is 1947 and recently demobilised young Royal Navy sailor Dusty Miller has returned to Australia to set up house with his wartime sweetheart and wife, Wendy. The walls really do speak in this heartfelt narrative as five houses narrate the poignant struggles of Dusty and Wendy when they begin their married life in post -WWII Australia from their first home reluctantly shared by a disgruntled and obnoxious tenant to juggling a new baby and Dusty's resentful family 'fresh off the boat.' With houses difficult to find, furniture very expensive to buy and returned servicemen vying for jobs, they often turn to self-sufficiency to survive such as when Wendy, on a tiny budget, sews the whole family new outfits for the Queen's Royal Visit in 1953.

Largely autobiographical, the book is a sequel to *'Ripples of War'* by the same author.

The Life and Times of
Charles Frank Field
1850-1950

Patricia Lee

This is the story of a remarkable Australian and his 100 years of life. Charles' story draws in many threads: the cruelty of the convict system, the elegance of Adelaide City's foundations, the copper boom in South Australia, the goldfields of Tibooburra and the wheatfields of Ungarie, the long working hours of shop assistants and the uncertainty of business enterprises, the isolation and humour of country living, the tragedy of two World Wars and its impact on ordinary Australians. Charles' own writings show a mind always seeking improvements, a lively sense of humour with an ability to revel in politics and open discussion and the sheer *joie de vivre* characterising his long life.

One hundred years of Australian history is a broad sweep of the canvas. However, the story begins even earlier in the troubled agricultural fields of England with the bankruptcy of Charles' grandfather, Daniel Field and the emigration of his parents, William and Martha, to a better life in Adelaide in 1839. Wherever possible, first-hand accounts, rare documents and vivid images recreate the times Charles lived in as his story progresses from South Australia to New South Wales and finally to Victoria where he died in his 100th year.

This is a unique view of Australian history appealing to the historian and the general reader alike.